Also availabl...
and C...

Act Like It
Pretty Face
Making Up
The Austen Playbook

HEADLINERS

Lucy Parker

carina
press

carina
press®

Recycling programs
for this product may
not exist in your area.

ISBN-13: 978-1-335-21599-4

Headliners

This edition published by arrangement with Harlequin Books S.A.

For questions and comments about the quality of this book,
please contact us at CustomerService@Harlequin.com.

Carina Press
22 Adelaide St. West, 40th Floor
Toronto, Ontario M5H 4E3, Canada
www.CarinaPress.com

Printed in U.S.A.

For Madeline

Author's Note

Headliners is a stand-alone romance, but it
does contain spoilers for the previous book in the
London Celebrities series, *The Austen Playbook*.

HEADLINERS

Chapter One

October. A dark day in October.

There were scenes in life so gut-punchingly beautiful, they were impossible to do justice with words.

Like the final rays of the falling sun, glittering across the Thames as the river turned dark and impenetrable, a silken blanket of shadows.

The infinite wonder of the night sky, a stretch of potentially endless stars, the scope beyond human comprehension.

Or the video footage of the biggest wanker on British television single-handedly cannonballing his career in less than three minutes.

Life: just when you seemed to be heading down a path of total bullshit, the light would return, birds would sing, and your greatest professional rival would walk the social-media plank for the viewing pleasure of—Sabrina Carlton leaned forward to check the stats—over one million people.

It was the number-two trending video in London. Joy upon joy.

On the laptop screen, even the grainy resolution of the phone recording couldn't disguise the sculpted angles of Nick Davenport's face. The man had a jawline that could slice a diamond. Scores of people across the country regularly voted him into the Most Eligible lists, because they'd never met him in person, and an elderly woman had once tossed a pair of knickers at him, like he was the lost fucking Beatle. The camera loved him, and he had the regular paparazzi snaps to prove it. He probably painstakingly pasted them onto his main fan site every evening. She would not be swayed in her opinion that he'd created Nick's Chicks himself.

However, she doubted that he'd be saving this video to his hard drive.

"The man has the charisma of a boiled egg." Nick's voice was hard-edged with scorn as the words came clearly through the computer speaker, dropping one by one into the heavy silence in the room. "And he inherited most of his fortune from family members who didn't make decisions with their dick."

Crossing her legs, Sabrina propped her chin on her knuckles and slid her glance sideways to where present, in-the-flesh Nick sat in the chair farthest from her own. His spine was a rigid straight line, and his usual plastic charm had iced over into a mask of imperturbability. The only sign of life on his face was the muscle moving in his jaw. If the footage of this spectacular error of judgment went on for much longer, he was going to grind his teeth into shiny white dust.

Without moving anything but his dark eyes, his gaze suddenly locked on hers.

His jaw started to tic to a faster beat.

On the laptop, the camera angle did a hasty swoop as the eavesdropping staffer holding the phone was forced to step farther back from the door of Nick's dressing room in *The Davenport Report* studios. Sabrina's stomach copied the flip-flopping motion. The sudden rolling blurriness was making her feel seasick, which really distracted from the epic vindication of this moment.

Unfortunately for Nick, the audio remained crystal clear.

"He's a short-sighted, selfish ballsack masquerading as a human being," past Nick continued curtly, and current Nick shifted slightly in his chair. His long fingers curled into a fist against the fine grey wool of his trousers.

"At the rate he's going, he'll strip the network to a bare-bones framework, devoid of either originality or quality. The morning show is already a ratings wasteland; now he wants to screw up the evening programming, as well. I'd have more faith in the bloody goldfish at reception to head up the organisation proper—"

Hania Aronofsky, the executive head of programming, reached out and tapped the control pad, finally muting Nick mid-sentence. Something Sabrina would frequently like to do herself.

For long, fraught seconds, nobody said a word. Then, moving her hand to her mouth, Sabrina coughed. "Slow clap, Davenport." With studious care, she smoothed down her leather pencil skirt. "Verbally eviscerating the big boss while on company premises, and without bothering to even close the door first. If you felt it was time for a career change, it might have been more politic to just type a letter of resignation."

For the first time since they'd all been summoned into Hania's office, Nick produced an actual expression. Which lowered the temperature of the already chilly room by another few degrees.

As it happened, she agreed with every scathing word he'd uttered about Lionel Grimes. The billionaire had thrown both their careers into stressful upheaval this year, after he'd acquired and merged their respective networks. Shortly thereafter, he'd confirmed his intention to streamline the two evening news-commentary shows into one, and do at least one of them out of a job. Their CEO was bumptious, rude, and intolerant, and he had a track record of using his media outlets to promote whoever was currently hanging off his arm.

However, regardless of the brutal truth in Nick's commentary, there was a place to express that opinion in such colourful terms. In one's head.

At every turn, Nick was determined to prove himself an arse.

Likely for the first time in his life, he had now become as silent as his frozen image on the screen. There wasn't much he could say; the phrase "didn't have a leg to stand on" had been invented specifically for this situation.

Hania was turning a pen in circles between her fingers. On each rotation, she tapped the end of it against the desk, and the rhythmic sound was like a clock ticking down. Possibly on Nick's continued employment. "Not the wisest move in your career, Nick."

When he spoke at last, his words were a stiff staccato, not the usual velvety voice that was one of his greatest assets. When he wielded it like a weapon, it could bite deep and dark; if he wanted something, it glided along nerve endings like a cascade of warm honey. "I've already apologised to Grimes."

That must have been an uncomfortable conversation. Grimes was rabidly conscious of his public image.

Sabrina suspected he put a lot of money in influential pockets to control his media profile, since even the press he didn't own tended to near canonise him in print.

"It was unprofessional to speak like that on the clock, in this building." Nick made a faint, derisive noise in the back of his throat and again shifted his weight. With jerky movements, he pushed up his shirt-sleeves. A painful-looking scar on his right forearm wound across smooth brown skin and compact muscle in a jagged line. "And I will admit that not closing the door when the hallway was crawling with interns was...ill-judged."

If that was how he'd phrased his official grovel, she was surprised his job had survived this long.

Hania arched strong black brows at him. "Just a *touch* unfortunate." She suddenly smacked her pen down. "Within twenty minutes of that video going live, he was on the phone to legal, requesting a copy of your contract."

Several of the management team in the room moved abruptly, with a rustle of clothing and the squeak of leather cushions. Nick didn't flinch, and Sabrina had to reluctantly admire his calm as he said, evenly, "Which expires very shortly anyway."

Her contract was also up for renewal. She'd been hoping it would be replaced with a thicker one, for the new show, but that was looking increasingly doubtful. She'd thought it would be a tight race to the headline contract, until Nick had pulled a stunt a few months ago that still made her want to pick up the stapler on Hania's desk and go to town on his treacherous bastard face. However, Grimes didn't like bad press for his staff any more than he accepted it for himself, and her reputation had taken a battering.

If Grimes weren't such a dickhead, they could co-found a support group for all the people roasted online because of Loose Lips over there.

Once more, Nick's eyes briefly met hers, but she couldn't read his expression. "I assume that the Friday episode of *The Davenport Report* will be the last."

Sabrina was conscious of a surprisingly mixed emotion in her gut. A ribbon of anger wound tighter around her insides every time she thought about him. If he ended up on the front of the *Media Times*, advertising the new show, she suspected that her temper—which tended to be explosive when it came to the boil—would just about send her fizzing around the room like a rogue Roman candle. But within that, buried very, very deep, and very, very weak, was a tinge of empathy.

She couldn't stand Nick Davenport. They'd been trading barbs for a long time; as far as she could remember, the inciting incident had been Nick's arrogant behaviour at her first TV Awards. The jabs and jibes at each other on their current respective shows had started off relatively lighthearted, encouraged by both their teams, since the public had been immediately on board with the rivalry. They were the subject of dozens of memes on social media, and people tweeted her with Nick's subtle insults on an almost daily basis. She assumed they did the same to him. As time had gone on, however, things between them had taken on a sharper edge, and what had begun as contemptuous amusement had soured into actual antipathy, coming to a head with his vile actions last summer.

If someone gave her a voodoo doll of Nick, she

would happily insert a very large pin into a very sensitive place.

But.

She had worked like a busy little demon to get where she was. It had taken years to earn a lead presenter contract. Television was a brutal, competitive industry, with a lot of people jostling for a small number of places. Nick, for all his smarm and insincerity and back-stabbing, would have put in hard yards and overcome a lot of obstacles to have secured his own show in his thirties.

They'd devoted hundreds of evenings to their work, sacrificed a certain amount of social life, and invested heavily in many of the guests they interviewed and the stories they told.

The fact that all of that could be taken away in seconds, on the decision of one person, bloody sucked.

Hell.

She was having a moment of one-sided, near mateyness with *Nick*.

Fortunately, Hania's next words sent any budding charitable feelings veering back into the more familiar territory of "Eh, just fire the prick."

"Lionel has made it clear that he doesn't want two evening shows splitting the ratings and would rather focus on launching one strong competitor for the market. With a senior presenter who can pull in a majority audience share. In every research poll until recently, the two of you topped the popularity vote." Hania's tone turned desert-dry as she eyed each of them in turn. "Commonly used descriptors included *sexy, charming, likeable. Honest. Trustworthy.*"

A dark flush started to heat Sabrina's cheeks. No

prizes guessing where this was going. She turned away from Nick, not wanting to give him the satisfaction of seeing her expression.

Everyone else had been sitting in such a funereal silence that she was getting a very ominous feeling about the outcome of this meeting, but Hania's second-in-command offered up a wry "I don't think anybody can accuse Nick of lacking honesty, at least."

But as for the *trustworthy* label—

As her younger sister, Freddy, had once put it: "Fit as fuck, but slipperier than a wet bar of soap."

"No," she said now, and was surprised that her own voice was so level. "It's my forehead that's received the big red *Liar* stamp."

And Freddy's. The sudden memory of her sister's face on that summer night, as they'd stood together holding an iPad, watching their family scandals being splashed across blog after blog, tightened Sabrina's hands into fists.

It had been Nick's choice—his deliberate, personal choice—to break the news on his show, in the most damaging way possible, that her famous playwright grandmother had actually been one of the most blatant plagiarisers of the past century. Sabrina's family had profited for decades on Henrietta Carlton's massive literary fraud, entirely unknowingly by Freddy and herself, wilfully in the case of their father.

Nick had jumped on the opportunity to whack her out of the running for the plum job, like a scheming mouse strutting around with a choice bit of cheese. He'd thrown all of them to the tabloid wolves, and many people, hungry to believe the worst, had vocally turned against them. Deceit and shame were always more interesting than simple ignorance.

Bad enough, the blow to her own career, but when it came to Freddy getting shit in the press—Sabrina had no desire for an actual baby at any time ever, but she was prepared to go full-on Mama Bear where her sister was concerned.

Nick had gone taut about the mouth now, his usual expression when the plagiarism fiasco raised its ugly head.

"The situation with your grandmother is also unfortunate." Hania was the queen of understatement today. She pushed back from the desk a little and steepled her fingers in front of her chest. She was a full-figured and strikingly beautiful black woman in her fifties, with very snazzy taste in suits and long-lashed eyes that missed nothing. "There's nothing quite like misbegotten wealth to rile up the British public."

Sabrina's father had controlled the finances from Henrietta's estate since her death, and Sabrina hadn't taken a single pound from him since she'd turned eighteen.

When it came to PR, mud spattered easily and stuck indelibly, but it was still a bloody joke that her own career was taking the hit for a piss-poor decision her grandma had made decades ago.

"Our polls indicate a statistically significant decline in your popularity with the public," another member of the team chipped in, sounding apologetic. "You've lost some viewers in the past months."

Judging by the tone of comments on her Instagram, Sabrina suspected "some" was putting it kindly.

"Nor did it help matters when you decided to punch

an A-list actor in the face in front of the press," Hania said more severely, although there was definite empathy as well as censure in her expression. "Whatever the provocation."

Sabrina winced.

To add another understatement to the pile, that had not been a good night. The discovery about her grandmother, closely followed by the revelation on a live TV broadcast that Joe Ferren—her long-time, on-and-off, film-star boyfriend—had graduated from charmingly unreliable to unfaithful dicksack.

However, despite his despicable behaviour— "I apologised, sincerely, to Ferren, and issued a public statement." The flush was rising in her cheeks again. "I shouldn't have hit him. I've always spoken out against violence on the show, and I stand by that. It's never okay, and I strongly regret it."

She was lucky he hadn't pressed charges, and suspected he'd exercised his influence to make sure the matter went no further.

She was relieved.

She still never wanted to see him again.

Fortunately, he'd at last stopped with the guilt flowers. Swallowing hard, Sabrina gritted her teeth for a moment to keep her expression cool.

"To sum up, then," Nick said, and the timbre of his voice still sounded…wrong. Mister Smooth a bit off his game. "Grimes wants a crowd-puller in the hot seat but is probably emailing my headshot to an assassin, and a number of sad sacks with TV licences think Sabrina is the most corrupt personality to grace their screens since Palpatine." Had she just been compared in a work conversation to the *Star Wars* Dark Lord?

"Job prospects at the network aren't looking too flash for either of us."

He was still unnaturally calm, but if they were both out on their backsides here, there was no way he'd take it that easily. She'd already had a front-row seat to the lengths Nick would go for his career prospects.

And while *she* might not sacrifice all fair play and human decency to score a contract, she wasn't prepared to just sit back and let her work be yanked away from her, either, and she'd come to this meeting prepared to fight.

Almost unconsciously, she folded her arms, and Hania looked thoughtfully between their faces. There was a curious speculative quality in that look. Sabrina would go so far as to call it calculating.

"You're both on shaky ground." Like Nick, Hania's composed response seemed to resonate with meaningful undercurrents. "But fortunately, the key word is 'crowd-puller.' The bottom line is the ratings, and where there's bad publicity, there are also people tuning in."

"Hoping for an even bigger crash and burn," Sabrina muttered.

Hania looked over her shoulder and nodded, and a staffer by the door went out quietly.

As Sabrina watched him go, suspiciously, her gaze collided with Nick's again, and again she pointedly turned away.

"Well?" A shade of exasperation was creeping into Nick's demeanour as Hania dragged out the suspense.

Their boss started turning her pen in circles again. "You are correct in that you've both knocked yourselves out of contention for the evening show. That position will be offered elsewhere."

Sabrina released a long breath, and Nick closed his eyes momentarily.

"So that's it?" she said, with a slight feeling of un-reality. Despite the setbacks since the summer, apparently she hadn't really expected this to happen. "We're both out?"

"Of the evening programming, yes. Your nights are going to be considerably more open." Hania looked past Sabrina again, as the office door opened. "But if you agree to my suggestion, you're also going to have to start getting up a lot earlier."

Nick turned his head first, and his entire body went still.

She swung around and was greeted with her own smiling face on a full-length poster board. Her printed image had been placed back-to-back with Nick's, and someone had done some excessive editing, because she'd never leaned on him in her life.

Her gaze travelled from their glossy heads to the sarcastic advertising copy scrawled across the card-board: *'tis the season for peace and goodwill. And miracles.* Wake Me Up London *with Sabrina Carlton and Nick Davenport, weekdays at seven throughout December.*

They broke the silence with an unusually united sentiment.

"Oh, I don't think so." Sabrina physically retreated from the horrifying prospect.

"I hope that's a bad joke." Palpable outrage from Nick. His fingertips were digging hard enough into the arm of his chair that she could see his knuckles flexing. "I don't mind the odd piece of human-interest filler—nobody wants doom and gloom 24/7 and there are people who deserve recognition—but the morning show has been egregious rubbish for years. If you seriously think I'm going to sit there and smile inanely while people with too much time on their hands argue about—what was one of their scintillating topics, the ethics of putting tutus on puppies?—you can think again. And why am I second billing on the poster?"

"Alphabetical and moral seniority," Sabrina said breezily. He was so annoyed that she'd recovered a bit of composure in response. She inclined her head towards their chummy-looking cardboard selves. "And it pains me to state the obvious, but you're literally the poster boy for inane smiles, Troy McClure. Bit late to change your brand now."

Nick's jaw had stopped twitching, but his eye picked up the slack.

From her seat close to the offending poster, a member of the social media team cleared her throat. "Er… is the plan to boost *WMUL*'s embarrassingly shit ratings by turning the set into a *Hamlet*-style bloodbath? Because it'll be job well done in any scenario that puts them on the same couch."

"I've worked for the network since I was twenty-one," Nick said, slipping back into his shield of drawling amiability. It tended to net more wins. *One may smile, and smile, and be a villain.* "I've headlined alone for almost four years, and I've made a damn good job of it."

"Yes, you have," Hania agreed. "You're excellent at your job. Witty, tenacious, attractive—the public accolades are spot-on." Before Nick's head could expand too far, she continued, "You also humiliated your boss in a public forum. If you wanted to keep your name on the evening billing, you should have exercised some discretion. You're on such thin ice here that one false step is going to drop you right in it. I hope I'm making myself clear."

She walked around her desk to sweep a glance up and down the poster board, before she leaned a companionable elbow on it. "Happily for us all, the public is fascinated with your obvious feud. You surmise correctly that *Wake Me Up London* is in a losing battle where the ratings are concerned. I have a feeling that the two of you could salvage that situation."

Nick opened his mouth again, and Hania finished, "And you've got from the beginning of December until Christmas Eve to prove me right."

Sabrina's stomach did a sharp flip at the note in the other woman's voice.

"On Christmas Eve, after a run of successful shows and a drastic reversal of *WMUL*'s ratings, you will appear to represent the show at Carols by Candlelight at the Royal St. Michael. After which, we will discuss the renewal of your contracts. However, if by then you prove my brilliant idea an abject failure, *WMUL* will be offered to Peter King."

Nick made a slight, very speaking noise, and Sabrina just managed to keep her feelings from her face. King, a long-time presenter currently hosting *The Arts Review*, was an obnoxious prat.

There appeared to be no shortage of them around here.

"You can't do that." Her father's stubborn gene came

out and she couldn't stop the last-ditch protest, but the implacability in Hania's expression was clear.

"For all his *other* qualities," Hania said, with a meaningful look at Nick, "Lionel is a shrewd business-man, and he won't slaughter a cash cow." Charming. "But he's also difficult to shift when he forms a judg-ment, and he's currently not impressed with either of you. I've convinced him to give you one more chance. Do not let me down." She relented a little as she stud-ied their equally grim faces. "I have every faith that you can do this. You both have X-factor in spades, and a spark of professional genius, and I don't use a com-mendation like that lightly." Carefully flicking a piece of fluff from the jacket of her hot-pink suit, she added, "Who knows, you might even enjoy the challenge. Try not to actually kill each other in the process."

Sabrina turned to look at Nick.

For long moments, they surveyed each other, Sa-brina rapidly considering and discarding any alter-native route here. A frown tugged at Nick's brows as he, too, seemed to quick-fire debate the best course of action.

Then it was as if silent communication passed be-tween them, so palpable that the words might have been carved into the frosty air.

"I'm not racking up my first all-encompassing pro-fessional failure because of you, you manipulative, selfish, back-stabbing dick."

"I'll walk any path necessary to get my career back on track, and I'll drag you along kicking and scream-ing if I have to."

Nick's dark eyes glinted.

Sabrina sat up a little straighter.

Challenge accepted.

This wasn't going to be pretty.

Chapter Two

December
23 Days until Christmas Eve

Sabrina was smiling, but anger and dislike glimmered in the depths of her dark green eyes.

He was so used to that expression that his brain was now superimposing it over a magazine image. Nick tossed the copy of the *Media Times* aside, and their two-dimensional promotional selves slid along the red linen tablecloth and came to rest against the pepper grinder. A waiter delivered plates of food to the next table, where a woman casually picked up her phone and turned it in his direction. When he glanced over, she blushed and hastily put it down on her lap.

Iain shot him a penetrating look before he reached out a finger and lazily flicked the magazine around so he could see the cover. "The new breakfast TV pinup boy," his brother drawled. Stepbrother, technically, but that was a waste of a prefix. It made zero emotional difference.

Head tilted, Iain studied the result of the most uncomfortable photo shoot of Nick's career to date. The photographer had consistently tried to get Sabrina to drape herself over him. *"Could you put your arms around his neck, love? And get a bit closer, like."* The man clearly hankered after a gig shooting models for romantic novels.

After a dozen increasingly patronising "loves," several "darlings," and one very ill-advised "girlie," Sabrina had been visibly simmering, trying to keep her temper. She'd obviously have liked to string them both up by the balls and throw them off Waterloo Bridge. Nick had suggested that the other man call her by her name. She had not been noticeably appeased.

"You look so enthusiastic about the prospect in print," Iain commented. Picking up the magazine, he held it mockingly close to Nick's face. "It's like a living demonstration of the comedy and tragedy masks. Why the hell did you agree to this trial? *Wake Me Up London* has been scraping the bottom of the ratings barrel for years, and you're dead set on prime time. I know you're a smooth bastard, but do you see yourself chatting up reality show rejects at the crack of dawn? And do these people know what you look like first thing in the morning?"

"Oh, cheers for that." Nick sat back and moved his arm from the table as another waiter put down a sharing platter of jerk chicken and coconut rice. The smoky smell of spice and garlic was usually a comforting sensory warmth, a reminder of the settled, secure part of his childhood, but with only a handful of hours remaining until his reluctant *WMUL* debut, his appetite was shot. "Thank you," he added, with more sincerity, to the server.

Murmuring his own thanks, Iain picked up a large silver spoon and ladled some of the food onto Nick's plate. "This gig doesn't sound like a natural step in that ten-year plan of yours." Iain, forever the no-nonsense member of their family, didn't waste time with hedging. Bluntly, he added, "I'm not sure Markus would have been breaking out the congratulatory champagne."

Nick had just picked up his knife and fork; the skin of his hand grew taut as his knuckles flexed. Keeping his voice very even, he said, "Dad's been gone for years." In some ways, that was still surreal. In others, it felt like another lifetime had passed since his mother's second marriage to Iain's father, her long-time best mate. "It would be a little pointless to seek his approval on this, wouldn't it?"

"So you'd think." Iain was equally toneless; however, his gaze was shrewd. Correctly surmising that Nick had no desire to discuss his late parent, he diverted the conversation back to its original lane. "It's going to take serious graft and a minor miracle to overtake *Rise Britain* in the breakfast ratings before Christmas. If you can pull off the bloody unlikely—do you actually want the permanent morning contract?"

"In the long-term," Nick said with grim deliberation, after swallowing a mouthful of beautifully spiced chicken, "hell no. But I well and truly shot myself in the foot with the Grimes incident, and the first step towards career rehabilitation is dragging *WMUL* to the top of the charts and putting in a stint there."

He'd made some fucking abysmal choices this year. He was reaping the consequences, and he was prepared to pay his dues. And after the YouTube cockup, he was currently lucky to still have a network pay cheque at all.

Laying down his fork, he slipped his hand around
the back of his neck, digging his fingers into the knotted muscles. His body felt like it was on taut strings.
He couldn't remember the last time he'd been able to
properly relax—or hell, to really push the boat out and
laugh. Genuinely couldn't remember. Even a bit of time
out tonight before the endurance challenge began in
the morning wasn't doing much for the constant tension in his gut.

Iain cut a decisive line through a chicken thigh.
"And you've got a co-presenter who'll take the first
opportunity to castrate you with a rusty teaspoon. You
don't make life easy for yourself."

A mess of emotions caught Nick, again, in a hard
punch.

Even without his brother pushing her front and centre, it was futile trying to get Sabrina out of his head.
She was there constantly.

So was the regret. And the frustration.

He'd fucked up, she had not, and essentially, she
was in the dock right now for other people's crimes.
He was well aware of his culpability.

Sabrina made an art form out of sarcastic one-
upmanship, and a career out of pissing him off, but the
only thing she'd done to warrant public censure was
flatten Joe Ferren's nose.

Personally, Nick considered that incident the only
bright spot in the whole nightmare.

His hand was clenching again; he forcefully released
his muscles.

Iain was still watching him with far too much perception. "You're going to give this your all as a means
to an end. And—take some credit—you're a bloody

hard worker. You half-arse nothing. How does *she* feel about Operation Breakfast Chatter?"

"Conversation on that point has been short and hostile," Nick said, with a humourless twist of his lips. "She'd rather stick pins in her eyes than spend hours every day with me, but I think she'll happily embrace the brief itself. Verbally, Sabrina can slice you in half at fifty paces, but fundamentally, she's…strong. Adaptable. She can find the best in a situation and she doesn't just settle, she'll truly enjoy it. Throw herself in and make it her own." He became aware that Iain's scrutiny had subtly altered, taken on a tinge of amusement. "What?"

"I'd be interested to observe Sabrina Carlton in person sometime," his brother murmured obliquely. He picked up his wineglass, holding the stem loosely between two fingers. "So, when she's not cutting people down to size, she walks around strewing rainbows and unicorns, does she?"

By his tone, he was all for the former quality, but the latter was not an appealing prospect.

Drily, Nick said, "No, that would be her sister." He liked Freddy Carlton, Sabrina's irrepressible sister. He suspected most people did—the theatre actress was a sweetheart—but he also found her goddamn exhausting. She'd hooked up with one of his closest friends, and it was a trick getting his mind around the idea of Freddy the eternal optimist and Griff the natural-born pessimist.

One of his *formerly* closest friends. The knots in his neck shot a spike of pain into his temple. His long friendship with Griff was another casualty of the choices he'd made during the plagiarism fiasco. Every attempt to reach out afterwards had been met with an iron wall—justifiably. However unlikely Nick found it, Griff was apparently heart-deep in it with Freddy, and her polished reputation on the West End had taken some dents.

For that reason alone, Sabrina would happily brandish that rusty teaspoon.

"Sabrina's more of a closed book than Freddy," he said, curtly, and cut into another piece of chicken.

Although she'd been broadcasting her opinions loud and clear lately.

She unequivocally despised him.

Over the years, there were times when he'd been unreservedly furious with her in return, times when it was impossible to resist riling her flammable temper, and times when he'd wanted as far away from her as possible for his own peace of mind.

He also felt every bloody cell in his body become alert when she came into a room, as if something inside him woke up and went into a state of intense high frequency. It was that sharp pull and equally hard push.

Obviously, physically, she was beautiful, but that wasn't what zapped into him and itched beneath his skin when he was around her.

By profession, he was trained to dig and dive in search of truth. Yet he'd found it safer, for a long time, to keep a certain distance from Sabrina.

In terms of literal proximity, that wall was about to come smashing down. He had no idea what was going to unfold—and he'd never liked surprises.

Across the table, with an ironic twist of his wrist, Iain tilted his half-full glass. "Cheers, then. To your career getting back on track as quickly as possible."

He lifted his brows. "And to you *and* your bollocks surviving the storm that's about to break."

22 Days until Christmas Eve

Sabrina considered herself a morning person. However, she also considered that mornings began at 10:00 a.m.

When she hobbled into the *WMUL* studio at 5:00 a.m., not certain that she was actually alive, she immediately put her arm across her bleary eyes. Oh, Jesus. She'd forgotten how the breakfast set was dressed. Bright, chirpy shades of neon buttercup everywhere. It was like someone had exploded the yellow Teletubby, and the contrast between the walls inside and the pitch-black sky outside was physically painful. Maybe the withered ratings couldn't entirely be blamed on a succession of unpopular presenters. Viewers were probably trying to preserve their corneas.

"Hideous, isn't it? My influence around here would fit on a Tic Tac," a voice said cheerfully, "but I'm making it my personal mission to see how many times a day I can bring the benefits of off-white paint and neutral furnishings into conversation."

Sabrina turned as a freckle-faced young woman advanced on her, holding a reusable coffee mug and a paper bag.

"I could try to bribe one of the guests in the baking segment today if you like. If they'll make a few diva demands about not wanting to be interviewed inside a giant sherbet lemon, I'll turn up the temperature on their competition's oven. Coffee?" She held out the mug, and Sabrina pounced.

"Salvation." She pulled the lid off and just about

shoved her entire face in it, breathing in the scent of espresso. "Thank you so much." Peering into the bag the girl had extended, she pulled out a large muffin with a crusty brown-sugar topping. Her body clock was still set to her daily routine for *Sunset Britain*, her defunct evening show—ruthlessly she quashed a pang; she was having no regrets and no longing for the past, in any form. Between post-show meetings, industry events, and mostly shit-awful dates, she'd usually gone to sleep around two in the morning. She couldn't remember if she'd ever been up for the day at this hour, and she'd expected she wouldn't feel like eating anything until after the show.

She took a large bite of the cinnamon-spiced muffin. Not so.

Swallowing, she smiled at the friendly bearer of carbs. "I'm Sabrina Carlton. I don't think we've met."

"No, I'm a new hire. Emily Warren." Emily glanced around the relatively quiet set. Most of the team would be in the corridors beyond, the behind-the-scenes prep already in full-motion. "I've been assigned to personally assist you and Mr. Davenport." She cleared her throat. "Um, when I mentioned my role to security downstairs, she laughed and said 'good luck.' I'm not quite sure how to put this, but—you seem fine, so is it him I need to worry about?"

"I suspect it was the fact you've been assigned to us both in proximity." Sabrina sipped her coffee. "And I sincerely apologise in advance. But I wouldn't worry on a personal level. I can't imagine Nick's an ogre to work for. On average, he manages one successful jibe a week and he generally uses it up on me. And he has legions of little old lady fans around the country who'd testify that he's such a nice boy, ever so charming."

Emily was obviously suppressing laughter. She also looked as if she was mentally weighing her salary against her potential role as intermediary, and rethinking her recent life choices. "Well, I don't think he's here yet, but Sonia has a couple of outfit choices for you in The Closet and she wants you to sign off on one before the editorial meeting."

The visit to The Closet, the network stylists' messy little treasure chest of a room, perked Sabrina up enough that by the time she'd gathered Outfit Option A to her chest, she'd stopped yawning through every fifth word.

She unabashedly enjoyed this bonus of the job: new clothes every day, and if she fancied keeping any of them, she was allowed to buy them for a bargain-rate price. She'd picked up some of her favourite shirts for a fiver apiece. Holding the silk of the Grace Kelly dream dress against her body, she twisted in front of the mirror and turned for Sonia's inspection.

The head stylist considered her from face to feet. "It's definitely your colour," Sonia said. "And since Nick usually opts for a blue shirt, you'll complement each other well." Sabrina couldn't help a slight movement, and Sonia rubbed the tips of her fingers against her lips. "This is going to be an interesting month."

Sabrina realised that her fingers were digging into the silk, creasing the delicate fabric. "I would never let personal differences with a colleague override professionalism."

The word *colleague* had a sour taste on her tongue and legitimately caused a burning sensation at the backs of her eyeballs, like she'd slammed a tequila shot and bitten into a lemon slice. Nick Davenport: as of today, her partner in crime. Her—as the security guard at reception had put it with a twinkle in her eye—*work hubby*.

It was probably too early in the morning to break out the non-metaphorical tequila.

"Quite," Sonia agreed, with no sign of sarcasm. Then she pursed her lips. She didn't say any more, and she didn't need to. She'd been Sabrina's stylist for *Sunset Britain*; they'd worked together for years. Front-row witness here to every jab traded between the evening shows, and she was fully aware of the Henrietta debacle. "Just keep reminding yourself that you *are* a professional." Sonia took the dress from her, gave it a gentle shake, and hung it on the current-day rail, under the label with Sabrina's name scribbled on it. "And that more jobs than yours are on the line, if the baton passes to Peter King."

"Thanks for that, Son. Really easing the pressure there." Sabrina glanced at her watch and made a bolt for the door. Showing up late on day one wouldn't be a good look, especially when Nick was probably already sitting in the conference room. She bet he was wide awake, shaved, ironed, and colour-coordinated.

Deep breaths.

According to the briefing she'd received last night, one of the guests they were interviewing today had been involved in a plane crash, then stranded on a small island with her husband and both of his mistresses, none of whom had known about each other. If all four of those people had managed to return to London relatively unscathed, Sabrina could sit on a couch next to Nick for a few hours.

Every weekday.

If they did it really well and Nick kept talking his way out of other jobs, potentially until they were old and grey.

She could do a professional exterior. Any internal sobbing was her own business.

"Do me a favour," Sonia said as Sabrina reached the door. "Wait until at least eight before you blow a fuse, would you? I bet a tenner on you, and I can't afford to lose the pool. My kid's school trip is to fucking Disneyland Paris next year." She gave her characteristic bark-cough of a laugh as Sabrina raised a succinct hand gesture in response. "Get it all out now, babe. This is the breakfast slot. Strictly PG zone. Anything stronger than a 'gosh darn it, Nicholas' on the broadcast and you're out on your ear."

As she walked rapidly through the now buzzing corridors, the sound of Sabrina's heels tip-tapping on the linoleum seemed to echo the rapid thumps of her heart. She felt a bit sick.

She really was *dreading* this, and it made her angry that she had to. The change to the breakfast show was a monumental shift, and the clock was ticking until their deadline, but she'd always enjoyed a challenge. And, frankly, she'd welcome any chance to rehabilitate her image and dial back the number of nasty comments on social media.

But working closely with Nick…

The reaction online to the new line-up had come fast and furious. At least initially, the show was likely to receive a boost in viewership. There was a car-crash fascination about the whole concept; on Hania's part, it was marketing genius. Whether they could sustain that interest, though, was open to doubt. Presenters on opposing shows trading the odd barb was good for a snicker and a bit of gossip, but an interaction charged with very real dislike quickly became unpleasant and toxic to watch. In a multiple-presenter format, chemistry was key, and Sabrina had serious qualms about how her chemistry with Nick was going to manifest on-screen.

And on a personal level—she looked at him and every sickening, dismal, mortifying moment of that night last summer came crashing back. Her grandmother's dishonesty. Her father's complicity. Ferren's betrayal. The smirking triumph of Sadie Foster, Freddy's horrible West End co-star who'd gleefully fed Nick his intel. And Nick's ruthlessness in going public with that information. She could struggle along with her father, and do her best to move on from the others, but Nick—everywhere she looked, everywhere she went, every curveball fate threw at her, there was Nick.

Quite literally, there was Nick, as she pushed open the door to the meeting room and several people looked up from around the wide wooden table. A large, open box of doughnuts sat askew in the centre, and most people were talking at once around mouthfuls. As she returned their greetings and slid into her chair, Sabrina tried and failed not to stare at him. She'd come in with her hackles already half raised, prepared to counter his usual arsehattery and smooth exterior perfection. She'd had him pegged as the sort of human irritant who kept busy evening hours but still managed to perkily hit the gym at 6:00 a.m.

He looked bloody awful.

He hadn't acknowledged her entrance, but she wasn't certain he'd even *seen* her entrance. One thick-lashed eye was struggling to open, the other hadn't bothered. The tag was sticking out the neck of his cosy navy jumper, and this was the first time she'd ever seen him unshaven.

In general, Sabrina was in favour of facial hair. There were few things sexier in the morning than rolling over, breathing deep of a man's scent, and nuzzling into a stubbly cheek. Beards had magical transformative powers, especially for gentlemen of kind heart but minimal chin.

Nick, however, had been blessed with bone structure that would have made even Rodin say "Too unrealistic" and chisel a few cracks and crevasses into it. The emerging beard just made him look blurred and scruffy.

"Good morning," she said tightly to the horrible painting of Mephistopheles over his shoulder, prepared to make *some* effort for the sake of the job and their colleagues' comfort, but not enough to look him in his one squinty eye while she did it.

He made a noise that began as a mumble and ended in a sort of moan, and sounded like a yawning golden retriever.

Fenella Price, their new producer, looked between them with raised eyebrows. "Jeepers. I'm glad I erred on the generous side when I allocated your hair and makeup time in the schedule. It's a walking case of Instagram versus reality."

At that remark, Conceited Ken straightened his back and opened his other eye.

Fenella smiled at him sunnily. She'd streaked her short hair with festive red and green since Sabrina had last seen her, and was wearing one of her endless collection of band tees. "Welcome to the world of the living. Drink your coffee, have a doughnut, and get to bed earlier tonight. Now, we're all very excited about the new direction for the show—"

The briefing went on, and Sabrina felt her brain start to properly engage as she scanned through the notes, reacquainting herself with the material she'd read last night, the prompts and background info on each guest.

"As you're aware," Fenella said to the assembled team, "we're working loosely to an advent calendar theme throughout the month. We'll run stories as prompted by current events and hot topics on social media, as they arise, but every day Nick and Sabrina will partake of a pre-scheduled task or challenge."

In other words, they'd liven up the morning toast and Weetabix around the country by regularly making absolute arses of themselves.

"Daytime TV," Nick murmured as he stirred a spoonful of sugar into a second coffee. "Where the only thing lower than the comedy bar is the pay grade."

His voice was a low rumble, still husky with sleep. His eyes met hers briefly, and for a split second, she thought she saw a flare, a flash of something. His irises were the colour of bitter tea.

"The highlight of today's show will obviously be the competitive bake," Fenella went on, shuffling her notes. The rustle of paper broke Sabrina out of a strange, surreal sensation that had momentarily gripped her mind and body. She shook her head slightly, and moved her shoulder so she was facing the producer. "The *Ultimate*

Cakemaster final airs next week, so the finalists will get to show off their skills on-set today and amp up excitement for the finale, a win-win for the network. And obviously we thought it would be more interesting to see them working in tandem for once, before they're pitted against each other for the title. Team Johnson/Meyer versus Team Carlton/Davenport."

Nick swallowed his coffee too hastily, and Sabrina's pen stopped on the margin note she was scribbling. "I thought we were just going to, you know, arbitrate and encourage."

And eat a load of cake.

She'd been looking on the baking segment as the incentive for the day. The carrot to the proverbial stick that was Nick.

"Nah, you definitely need to do it." A crew member who'd been transferred from her *Sunset Britain* team spoke up, displaying quite a lot of semi-chewed doughnut. "You're a goddamn baking queen. I only ever showed up to all those staff birthdays for your brownies. You might have to throw the competition; it's probably not a good look if the baking maestros lose out to the interviewers."

"Hmm." Fenella suddenly looked pensive. She narrowed her eyes at Nick. "And you're our resident biscuit prince. We may have to do a little salt and sugar switcheroo at their station," she said to Jess Kapur, her assistant, and Sabrina had no idea if she was kidding or not.

"I'm sorry," she said. "'Biscuit prince'? Another of your self-proclaimed titles, Fit Nick?"

The skin over Nick's cheekbones went taut. "I did not *self-proclaim—*"

It was probably fortunate for the progression of the briefing that Fenella interrupted. "He's a Davenport, Sabrina."

"Yes. I am aware of his name. In all its incarnations."

"As in Davenport's Double Delights."

At the age of eight, Sabrina had overheard her parents arguing because her father had taken a role in an Edinburgh panto after promising not to work that holiday period; "It's Freddy's first Christmas, and you love being Father Christmas for Sabs. You've always at least done the stockings." Thus had reality crashed in and the magic died.

She felt similarly disillusioned now.

Double Delights, only the best biscuit in the UK—one half spiced coconut-y goodness, the other half loads of thick dark chocolate—*weren't* the brainchild of Not-So-Saintly Nicholas over there?

The man was even in her biscuit drawer now.

"You own the Davenport's factory?"

Jess giggled. "You sound like Dorothy discovering the truth about the wizard."

Setting down his mug, Nick looked at Jess with lazy ruefulness. "Behind the magic, just a blustering middle-aged man? Ease up, Kapur. I'm thirty-four." He glanced briefly at Sabrina again. "My mother owns and runs Davenport's. She started selling biscuits from my grandparents' kitchen, completed two business degrees that she funded herself, was the first black British woman to win the top commercial innovation award in her field, and now employs over a thousand people."

The weary—and over the past few years, increasingly hard—lines of his face softened dramatically as he spoke. Nick when talking about someone he obviously adored was almost unrecognisable.

Sabrina swung her crossed leg as she studied him speculatively.

"You'll become more acquainted with the woman behind the biscuits mid-month," Fenella said. "We're broadcasting from the factory in Bermondsey on the launch day for their new product line for the Shining Lights charity." She tapped her nails on the tabletop. "To return to today's schedule—you're both baking, viewers will love it, try to make a few mistakes."

As she finished speaking, she scrawled a note on the pad in front of her and pushed it towards Jess, who read it and nodded.

With growing suspicion, Sabrina watched the corners of Jess's mouth twitch.

Chapter Three

Blindfolded biscuit decorating.

Sabrina was rapidly becoming a lot less fond of Fenella Price.

Phil Meyer, one of the finalists for *Ultimate Cake-master*, the current Sunday evening obsession around the country, was just about bent double so that Layla Johnson, his petite fellow contestant, could secure the length of black silk over his eyes. The pair of them had been chuckling and jostling one another, and obviously having a grand old time as they effortlessly produced a stack of perfectly browned, crisply shaped ginger-bread people at their station.

They also looked far too unsurprised by this exciting turn of events; evidently, they'd been given a heads-up in the green room that things were going to take a farcical turn.

Sabrina winced as she glanced back at the pile of biscuits on the Carlton/Davenport station. Their lines of figures looked flat-out tragic. Several were missing limbs after she'd accidentally dropped a tray while trying to avoid bodily contact with Nick, and at least half of them were burnt, after the biscuit prince had forgotten to take them out of the oven. He claimed the temperature had been set too high.

And unlike the piping bottles at the opposite station, their royal icing had an interestingly crunchy texture, because Nick Davenport, usually a veritable Renaissance Man, had no idea how to crack an egg. He'd bounced the shell off the side of the bowl like he was slam-dunking a basketball.

"I thought you knew how to bake," she muttered under her breath as she slipped the blindfold around Nick's head. She was tall even without her heels, so they didn't need to resort to Phil and Layla's acrobatics. He made a quiet sound of protest when she pulled the tie too tight, and she slipped her fingers under it to loosen it. "Sorry."

He'd managed to transform in the hour before they went live, and now looked as alert and dapper as ever in his crisp suit. She could smell him, this unusually close. His skin had a warm scent of oud from his cologne and, faintly, vanilla from the bottle of extract he'd spilt all over his hands. Sabrina could almost taste it in the back of her throat.

She smoothed the silken fabric into place over his short black curls. "What happened to the scion of the baking dynasty?"

For the first few minutes of the segment, she'd thought he was just embracing the direction to fudge things a bit, make sure their guests looked suitably expert. After she'd watched him poke curiously at the butter with the handle of a wooden spoon, and the acrid bitterness of burning sugar had reached her nostrils, she'd realised he wasn't acting, he was just shite.

"My mother knows how to bake." Nick put up a

hand to touch the blindfold. "Fenella chose to believe that gene passed on to me, and I chose not to correct her."

"Your mother launched one of the most popular biscuits in the UK, and you don't know how to cream butter and sugar. Didn't she ever have you in the kitchen with her?"

"She shared your attitude about my egg-cracking abilities." Nick's tone was dry. His head turned slightly towards hers. "After one attempt to teach me how to make a cake, she politely suggested I go to the park instead.

"I can cook," he added, with a tinge of defensiveness. "My grandparents had a food business for years, specialising in Guyanese and Caribbean dishes, and my grandad would have kicked up hell having a grandchild who couldn't feed himself. I just don't bake."

His grandparents had emigrated from Guyana, she remembered that from an interview he'd done with Valentina Moreno, a Colombian glass artist.

Valentina had once collaborated with Sabrina's friend Elise on a piece for which they'd won a prestigious award. It was an incredible sculpture; from one angle, light radiated across the angles of an angelic face, glittering as if it had been scattered with crushed crystals. When the viewer shifted position and the light moved, the entire mood of the piece changed. The face became mocking. Maddening. During a night out, after two glasses of wine, Elise had asked Sabrina to suggest a title for it.

Unfortunately, Sabrina had been on her third glass by then, and particularly exasperated with Nick that day, and *The Nicholas* now had pride of place in the lobby of a major London bank.

It hadn't improved inter-show relations when Valentina had revealed that snippet of information to Nick on *The Davenport Report*.

She nudged his hand away as he continued to pluck at the blindfold, and found a smile for the viewers. She couldn't get over how self-conscious she felt. She'd lost her camera-shyness years ago, and she'd always felt more of a good adrenaline buzz than actual nerves before each episode of *Sunset Britain*. Somehow, knowing that thousands of eyes were scrutinising their every move right now and fingers were busy typing commentary into social media, she felt like ants were crawling over her skin. She'd actually felt herself blush more than once.

"Let's face it," she said, raising her voice and injecting a cheerful, bantering note. "Blindfolds or no, we're about to be thrashed." She cast an amused glance in Phil and Layla's direction. Phil was gesturing playfully with an icing bottle, while Layla squeaked and pushed the dripping nozzle away from her clothes.

Sabrina had been following *Ultimate Cakemaster*. It had become a Sunday night tradition for her friends Akiko and Elise to get a babysitter for their daughter and come over with something chocolatey. Freddy occasionally joined them to watch, but she'd been so busy with rehearsals and now the opening weeks of her new West End musical, that she tended to spend her one day off attached to her boyfriend at the lips. She was still participating in their betting pool, though, and had her money on Layla, a tattooed librarian from Sheffield, to win. Sabrina had backed Phil from the first episode. He was a plumber from Liverpool with a bald head, twinkling eyes, and a deft hand with fairy cakes.

He also had an uncanny sense of direction. Sabrina stood next to Layla on the sidelines of the set, as they hollered out directions and the men wove back and forwards between the tables of icing bottles and the workstations, squirting one colour after another onto the gingerbread shapes.

"Turn a bit to the right," Layla called. "And three more steps."

Phil stopped with unerring accuracy and reached out to grope for a biscuit, then started piping blue icing in an amazingly neat line. With his left hand, he felt for the bowls of sweets and placed a Smartie, with great care, on the biscuit's abdomen.

"Bit higher, mate," Layla called out. She was giggling helplessly. "It's a button, not a testicle."

"Stop!" Sabrina shot out a useless hand as if she could physically yank Nick back from the standing light he was about to accost. She'd been watching the other two and enjoying the slight alleviation of tension their antics had brought, and hadn't noticed Nick was weaving off-set like a drunken doe. He came to an abrupt halt, one arm going out before him, and closed his fingers around the metal pole beneath the light.

"Congratulations, Sparks." He'd started calling her that two years ago, when he'd discovered at an event that her middle name was Parkes, her mother's maiden name. It had annoyed her then, and it annoyed her now. "What a crack-shot navigator." On which sarcastic comment, tossed in her vague direction, Nick turned and took a tentative step forward. "Should I keep going or will I end up falling off the South Bank under your direction?"

Sabrina made a face he couldn't see. "Ten steps forward, then left." Out of the corner of her eye, she saw Phil successfully reach the supplies table again and pick up a bottle of yellow icing. "Left. *Left!*" Tossing her hands up, she found herself ridiculously shouting, "Northwest! No! North*west!*" like a really aggressive compass app, and Nick yanked his head around, firing an exasperated expression away from her, towards the studio doors.

"Are you fu—kidding me?" He censored himself just in time. "What do you mean, *northwest?*" Turning in another circle, he felt out in front of him. "I barely know where the bloody *ground* is right now!"

The crew were already laughing, Layla was in hysterics as she watched Phil finally succumb to the disorientation and totter over to the wrong station to draw a wobbly heart on one of Sabrina and Nick's legless casualty biscuits, and it was infectious. Sabrina started to giggle as Nick threw his own hands up, then planted them on his lean hips. He shook his head, but she saw a small smile tug at his mouth.

It turned into a fully fledged grin when he finally made it to the table, bending down to bang his forehead against it in despair when she told him to grab the red icing.

"*Red!* The red one!"

"Sparks. Which part of the blindfold concept are you not getting?"

They lost the challenge, but the biscuits were surprisingly tasty, Sabrina discovered after she braced herself to sample one, ignoring Fenella's instructions

in her earpiece to put her finger in the icing and make
sexy "yum" sounds. Somebody had been watching
too much Nigella.

Nick did make a deep sound of appreciation in the
back of his throat, obviously enthralling Layla, who'd
been staring at him with lustful eyes, and Sabrina
wasn't sure if that had been an equal-opportunity di-
rective to sex it up for the camera, or if he was just really into his desserts.

He lifted an eyebrow when he caught her sidelong
glance, and licked a crumb from his thumb.

Layla audibly sighed.

Their final guest of the morning, the plane crash
survivor with the amorous weed of a husband, was
less impressed with Nick's legendary charm. Understandably, after being trapped with her spouse and his
illicit girlfriends on an island smaller than the average
London borough, she already had something of a down
on men, and Nick didn't improve her opinion when he
got her name wrong during the interview.

"It's Karen," she said in an arctic tone. The expression on her face was one Sabrina usually reserved for
the discovery of rogue spiders in her bedroom. "Angela is my husband's PA. Mistress B, if that makes it
easier to keep the personalities straight."

Sabrina cleared her throat and managed to sympathetically steer the conversation back to the woman's
ordeal, but turned to look at Nick with the same disbelief that stiffened Karen's spine when he interjected
a question and again called her by Mistress B's name.

He recovered with a sincere apology and his usual
aptitude, but every few seconds thereafter, he tapped
his cue card against his thigh, a fidgeting gesture so

out of character that it completely threw Sabrina off and she ended the interview with a warm "Well, thank you so much for coming in to talk to us today, Angela."

Quite obviously, Karen could have happily shot them both.

"My dudes." That was Jess in their earpieces this time. "What the fuck."

Exactly.

Sabrina apologised, again, to Karen after they went off-air, but the other woman was terse in her response, and Sabrina didn't blame her.

"What the hell was that?" She kept her voice low as she walked off the set at Nick's side, tugging her earpiece out and unhooking her microphone to hand it off to Emily, with a word of thanks. "Well done. We're both going to come off horrendously. The poor woman."

Nick removed his own mic with a sharp tug that pulled his lapel askew. "It was on the cue card."

"What was?" Frowning, Sabrina took the card he handed her. Printed with the *WMUL* logo, it contained a few reminder prompts for the interview. They used the teleprompter for the lead-ins, but when they were chatting to a guest, they received prepared questions and then moved with the flow of the answers.

He was right; his cue card clearly stated that Karen's name was Angela.

"Well, that's an unfortunate cock-up." And would have been just about unheard of with her former team. "I suppose everyone's still finding their feet with the new format."

Nick moved his broad shoulders, shrugging the fine grey fabric of his suit jacket back into place. He shot

her a look. "I wasn't planning to demand a full-scale
internal investigation and the typist's head."

"I implied nothing."

"And I'll personally apologise again to Angela."

"Karen."

"Jesus. What the fuck is wrong with me?"

"A question for the ages."

In the green room, the support staff had laid on a
spread of brunch foods. Apparently there were perks
to the morning slot. On *Sunset Britain*, the most they'd
got was a cup of tea and the odd digestive biscuit before the broadcast. Sabrina studied the platters and
picked up a slice of French bread topped with cream
cheese and salmon. Biting in, she ducked out of the
way as the sound engineers came in and swarmed on
the table like hungry ants. The place was a tip—there
were empty coffee cups everywhere, and a few lipstick-
stained tissues, and magazines had been left strewn
about on chairs. Feeling sorry for whoever had to clean
up the aftermath each day, she swallowed her last bite
of salmon and tossed the tissues in the bin.

When she reached down to pick up and straighten
the magazines, she froze, bent forward with her hand
touching a glossy cover. Her fingertips were resting
on Ferren's cheek.

Slowly, she straightened, holding the tabloid and
looking down at her ex-boyfriend's face. She recognised the setting behind him immediately and glanced
at the publication date. Recent. This week's edition.
He'd been photographed outside The Funnel Club, once
one of their favourite spots for a date night.

The headline splashed across the page was a bad
pun about Ferren and his latest co-star, who was leav-

ing the club a few steps behind him, looking slightly worse for wear. As far as Sabrina knew, the woman had been married for at least a decade, but that didn't preclude anything in the film industry, and Ferren's own beliefs on infidelity seemed to have become rather lax.

She studied the photograph, brutally testing her own reactions to it.

Their relationship had always been tumultuous. She'd met him as a twenty-two-year-old journalism graduate, when he'd been a jobbing actor, paying his rent by tending bar at her local pub. He'd given her a beer on the house, made a joke about the gingers in the room sticking together, and looked at her with eyes that spoke of smoky rooms and pressing body heat. In the nine years since, they'd clawed their way to career success and boomeranged back to one another in a blur of arguments and wall-banging sex, on and off more often than a faulty traffic light. They'd both dated casually in their off periods; however, when they were on, they were *on*. They'd had an agreement from the beginning about fidelity. Sabrina didn't cheat and didn't do cheaters. If she was in a relationship, she committed, she trusted, and she expected the same in return.

In her twenties, she'd seen Ferren as the romantically erratic love of her life, the person she would eventually come back to for good and all.

In her thirties, she saw him as a hard-learned lesson.

No more men who tried to tear her down to pad their own ego.

As she carefully set the magazine down on the bench lining the back wall, she heard jocular greetings behind her and felt the tense zap of Nick's presence before he appeared at her shoulder.

Speak of one of the devils.

He lowered the cup of tea he was holding. "I apologised again to Karen. She'd still push me in front of a moving bus without a second thought, but she probably won't register a formal complaint."

"In less good news," Jess said pointedly, tossing back long waves of glossy dark hair as she bustled past, "if you value your egos, I'd avoid looking at the show hashtag on social. We were doing quite well for a while—people were all over the bants and biscuits— but the majority thought you were taking the mickey on purpose and sympathy was with the wronged wife. Ratings are moving up, but it'll be a landslide crash if you keep coming across like a pair of snide schoolkids. Serious ground to make up tomorrow, my loves."

Sabrina had only heard half of that, as Nick's gaze landed on the magazine cover.

There was a fractional pause, that for some reason grounded her attention back in the here and now.

"That's bullshit," he said, jerking his jaw towards the headline. "I've known Mika and her husband for years, and she still sits on his lap in public. They're so into each other it's embarrassing to be around them. Actors might have a divorce rate through the roof, but there's no way she's fucking around on him with Ferren." Coolly, he added, "For one thing, she has better taste."

It was like icy starch wicking its way down her spine; being around him was at least fantastic for her posture. She refused to rise to the bait. "For your friends' sakes, I hope it's standard tabloid trash. Other than that, it's none of my concern."

Which was true, but in her renewed annoyance with

Nick, came out petulant. He said nothing in response, but the twitch of his left eyebrow spoke sceptical volumes.

If this interaction continued any longer, it was going to devolve into the sort of unprofessional behaviour she was trying to avoid. At their worst, the two of them could do a cracker impression of circling warplanes. She came in as the Spitfire, all weapons blazing; Nick was the Avro Lancaster, biding his time and then suddenly dropping the high-damage bombs.

She shoved the rest of the scattered magazines into a semi-neat pile, and an older one with a tatty cover, the sheen worn off the paper, ended up on top.

Now she was looking at her own distraught face, as well as old photographs of her grandmother, and of Violet Ford, the playwright who'd actually written *The Velvet Room*, the play Henrietta had shamelessly stolen in decades past, and inset images of Freddy snogging Griff, Violet's great-nephew.

Until Nick had broadcast the plagiarism exposé in the grounds of Griff's country estate, the two men had been downright chummy, although she couldn't imagine what on earth they had in common. Now, as far as she knew, Griff hadn't had a word to say to Nick in months. For an emotionally retentive iceball, he'd gone very protective over Freddy.

Sabrina approved.

Putting one finger on the offending cover, she pulled the magazine towards her. The rasp of the paper against the wood was suddenly very loud. The room had, for the moment, emptied.

Although the crackling vibes emanating from Nick were occupying a lot of space.

"Don't read that shite again," he said abruptly, edgily, as she did herself a masochistic turn and flipped open the cover. She remembered this particular article. *London Celebrity* could always be trusted to go straight in from the first sentence.

> *Henrietta Carlton's elder granddaughter is, of course,* Sunset Britain *presenter Sabrina Carlton, as infamous for falling out of prestigious London clubs with her now dramatically ex-boyfriend Joe Ferren as she is for discussing the nightly headlines. With Ferren seen departing Heathrow with a flattened nose, and the source of the Carlton family wealth cast into a very shady light, Sabrina, who owns a multimillion-pound flat in Notting Hill and is a vocal critic of both street violence and financial corruption, should perhaps clean her own ill-gained house before she points an accusing finger at others. A source close to the Carlton family, which includes West End star Frederica Carlton and writer Rupert Carlton, says he isn't surprised by the shocking revelations. "Typical bunch of hypocritical luvvies—"*

She actually rented her flat, for an extortionate monthly sum that drained most of her salary, but was worth it just for the built-in bookshelves. As if she could afford to buy a flat like that in Notting Hill. She was a broadcaster with shaky job security, not a hedge fund manager.

Facts, guys. Facts. Try them sometime.

At least there was one certainty in life. Even if she

found herself down at the Jobcentre come Christmas Day, she'd rather take a position scraping dried-up chewing gum off the desks at the local school than work for *London Celebrity*.

"That story is months old." Nick had ditched his empty teacup and curled his fingers into his belt, and when she slid her eyes sideways in a speaking look, he was very tight about the mouth. "And I imagine you've already memorised it word for word."

It *was* a little difficult to erase the phrase *fox-faced fraudster* from her brain, yes.

You happened to be born with red hair and a slightly pointy nose, and people made you sound like an unpleasant Beatrix Potter character.

"It's old news for you," Sabrina said, and heard the bite in her words. The horrible, draining anger coiled up inside her abdomen again. She despised how it felt, what it did to her. "Just one of the many occasions you threw all moral standards out the window to advance your career, was it? Just a distant memory now, superseded by every other questionable thing you've done since? Newsflash: for those of us still copping the flak from the fallout, it's not 'months old.' It's current, living reality. And if you've seriously justified your behaviour that night on the grounds that it was just business, a story the public deserved to know—when you not only hurt my family but hung out your own friend's private business for the world to rip apart—then we're wasting our time even trying to make this contract work."

She pushed the print copy of *London Celebrity* against his chest, the collection of lies and bullying rhetoric sandwiched between his heart and her palm, and as he automatically reached up to catch it before it could fall, she turned and left the room.

She'd had well and truly enough of him for one day.

And for some horrific reason, she was just about in tears, and hell no was she ever going to cry in front of Nick Davenport.

Chapter Four

Day one of the *WMUL* advent calendar, blindfolded biscuit-decorating. Day two, taken over by the announcement of a royal engagement. Day three, and Fenella had decided to give up on the ratings race and just murder them with hypothermia.

With an effort, since his hand had just about frozen to it, Nick managed to keep his microphone steady. It was currently extended towards the grinning teenage boy closest to him. Despite the constant splattering of icy water over the side of their creaking boat, the kid was dressed for a day at the beach and seemed to be having the time of his life.

It was, objectively, a beautiful winter's day. The sky was a pale blue, the air was crisp, and they currently had a perfect view of the White Tower, flanked by the ancient stone walls and a scattering of skeletally bare trees. Glimpses of London at its best. He'd just prefer to be admiring it from a warm room, not a rickety wooden boat on the grey, churning Thames.

As the motorboat carrying the bulk of the camera crew trolled alongside them, however, he tried to look as if he lived for subzero-temperature boat racing. It was for a good cause. The Oxford and Cambridge rowing teams were doing a five-kilometre length of the river in a pair of replica historic longboats, to celebrate the opening of a maritime exhibition at the British Museum and raise money for a youth programme. The race had been hyped up for sponsorship for months; Nick just hadn't expected to be on-board for it.

He and Sabrina were extra weight for the Oxford team, with two of the *WMUL* relief presenters providing additional commentary in the quieter, less windblown surroundings back in the studio. The Cambridge side had been joined by Xander Grimshaw and Rachel Mays, the extremely popular presenters of *Rise Britain*.

He leaned forward to speak to another of the students, and grinned at the teasing response.

At his side, Sabrina shivered violently again, and pressed—probably involuntarily—against Nick's shoulder. She'd gone very quiet the past few minutes; she usually talked happily with guests on the show.

As the student finished abusing the opposition and reconcentrated his efforts on his oars, Nick glanced at Sabrina again. Her teeth had been chattering since they'd left the dock. The wind was picking up, and he moved, angling his body to try to shield her from the worst of its bite.

The boat juddered as the coxswain, a lanky teenager with messy brown hair and spots, called out encouragement to the crew and they shot forward. Sabrina put a hand down to grip the edge of her seat.

The active camera view switched back to a panning shot from the motorboat, and Nick saw her swallow hard. He suddenly realised how pale she was beneath her makeup.

"You all right?" He pitched his voice low, although with their mics lowered, he doubted they'd be heard over the lap of oars and creaking of wood and the constant shouts and cheers from the banks.

Her lips parted, then clamped together once more. More sharply, he said, "Sabrina."

"Motion sickness," she got out between her clenched teeth. "I don't do well in boats. Or the backseats of cars. Only okay in trains and planes." She took a few shallow breaths. "Which is lucky when 'Planes, Trains, and Automobiles' is the unofficial theme for this month."

This weekend, they were both flying to France for a night, for the wedding of a network colleague at a resort in the Alps. And at some point during this advent calendar joy, they were doing the Murder Train, which had switched up its usual dinner-theatre format for a special Christmas-themed whodunit and was running a one-off daytime excursion for charity.

"For charity" was the other unofficial theme of the month, which was both fantastic, for the causes receiving aid, and ensured that neither of them could balk at any activity without looking like a selfish dickhead. The more cynical atoms of Nick's brain couldn't help thinking Hania and Fenella had taken that into account.

In this case, however— "Why didn't you say something when we got word about this?"

The boat crested, and she made an awkward movement on the wooden seat. He switched his mic to his right hand and reached out to grab her leg, steadying her.

"Good cause," she managed. She was staring at his

fingers on her knee; he immediately removed his hand. "And I took a tablet. It just isn't working."

The water moved them in a rocking movement that made even him feel a bit nauseous; Sabrina put her hand over her mouth. She looked miserable—and understandably horrified, considering where they were if she did get sick.

"Can I try something on your arm?" he asked abruptly, and she frowned.

"What?"

"I interviewed an acupuncturist once. She said you can naturally ward off motion sickness if you apply pressure to a certain point on the wrist. It could be bullshit."

Sabrina made a sceptical sound, but they had another close-up and more commentary coming any minute.

She flicked a look into his face, and moved her arm fractionally in his direction.

Keeping the movement subtle, his attention seemingly fixed on the finish line in the distance, Nick pressed his thumb under the heel of her palm, and rubbed a slow circle over her pulse.

Reflexively, her hand gave a tiny jolt against his leg.

"Is it helping?"

"Um. Maybe. A bit. Thanks." She sounded strained.

One side of the rowers suddenly got completely out of sync with the other and the boat took a sharp turn. This wasn't the serious business of the annual Boat Race. The kids were hamming it up for the cameras. Caught off guard, Sabrina jostled into him, and her hand slipped down, sliding against his. On pure instinct, their fingers linked.

Two seconds later, with the coxswain ordering everyone back into formation, they were back on a straight route, gliding across the water, and he and Sabrina were holding hands. For a frozen moment, Sabrina stared at their entwined fingers, before she lifted her gaze to his face.

They both simultaneously remembered that they were sitting in front of a live camera, just as the wind caught at a student's lightweight novelty hat. Sabrina was already in the process of jolting away from Nick when the cardboard Viking horns smacked right into her cheek, almost getting her in the eye. She stumbled back and up, promptly caught her shoe on something, and tripped sideways towards the edge of the boat.

Nick lunged forward to grab her arm.

And, with quite a lot of momentum behind them, they both fell into the Thames.

It was complete, mind-numbing shock. Sabrina had half a second of stomach-flipping *"Oh no"* and then not even time enough to squeak before she hit the surface with a painful splash. A heavy weight pushed her down, icy water surged over her head, and all sound disappeared except for the rushing noise of water in her ears. Choking, she flailed, and her body hit against something, which grabbed hold of her.

She did irrationally think *Eel!*—an eel with hands, apparently—in that panicked moment, but when her head broke the surface, it was just Nick.

Sound returned, and so did her ability to make noise, which came out indeterminate and much deeper than her usual tone before she found words. "Oh my God." Her teeth were chattering so hard, from adrenaline as well as cold, she could hardly form syllables. She pushed her wet hair out of her eyes and blinked, trying to see clearly. A strong current was pulling at her legs. Thank God for life jackets.

"*Fuck*." Nick's arm was tightly around her, holding her to his body. Even through several layers of sodden clothing, she could feel him shaking. "J-Jesus Christ, that's cold. Think the seasickness is t-telling you something, Sparks. Either st-stay off boats or stay *on* boats. You're a menace."

The river reached up to slap her in the face again, and he hauled her higher against him. Sabrina's arm felt like a dead weight, foreign object when she lifted it free of the water and wrapped it around his neck. The cold had sent her brain cells into an instant coma, and she was incapable of mustering a retort. The most she could manage was a whimper and a stuttering, "S-s-sorry. F-f-f-fuck."

So close to Nick that she could see the water drops on the ends of his eyelashes, she felt his breath on her cheek as she all but climbed his body. From awkward hand-clutching thirty seconds ago to her only available source of warmth.

Other voices finally registered when a life buoy hit the water beside them, and she looked up to see that their flanking motorboat had cut its engine and was hovering a short distance away. It was filled with openly gaping members of the crew. Sabrina's attention fixed on Fenella, who was bundled up like she was setting off on an Antarctic expedition and looked toasty warm. The producer was shaking her head, one arm crossed over her middle, the other hand cupping her cheek, her whole attitude radiating disbelief.

As they were towed efficiently towards the boat and hands seized hold of Sabrina's arms and the back of her life jacket, the sound of clicking cameras was so rapid-fire on the banks and surrounding boats that it carried across the water loud and clear.

She had a feeling that very shortly, when she'd defrosted, a world of embarrassment was waiting.

On the bright side, the nausea was gone.

"We've gone back to Harper and Meg at the studio and this footage is inset right now, without audio," Jess informed them in a hurried undertone as Sabrina sat down, dripping, on a padded seat at the side of the boat, and Nick lowered to sit beside her. "If you could manage some smiles and try to look like you have a sense of humour about this. Is anyone injured?"

The engine revved up, speeding back towards the start-line dock a lot quicker than they'd been travelling in the longboat. Emily, a woollen hat pulled low on her forehead, put thermal blankets around them. Their usually chatty new assistant appeared to be speechless.

"You're both going straight to the hospital, regardless." Fenella had one hand on her earpiece. She spoke a few words into the attached mic, then cut into their mutual protest. "Don't argue. Better safe than sorry. And it's a required measure for our insurance. How are you feeling?"

"Cold." Sabrina huddled deeper into her blanket. "Otherwise intact. Are you okay, Nick?" She turned her head and accidentally brushed against him as he moved.

Clutching her cold hands together beneath the insulated wool, she clenched her fingers hard.

Nick's expression appeared very…curated as he addressed Fenella. "Bloody freezing, these shoes are a write-off, and I'm even more grateful that the river is no longer a parasitic, polluted mess; otherwise fine. What happened with the race? Did we nobble it for Oxford?"

Hell. She'd completely forgotten about the reason they'd been out on the river in the first place. Sabrina rose a little, craning her head to see the university boats, but they'd already reached the finish line in the distance.

"Against the odds and despite the disadvantage of having a *Monty Python* act on board," Fenella said very drily, "Oxford crossed the line first. The kids were going to stop and try to fish you out, bless them, but we waved them on."

"Ha!" Jess suddenly made a crowing sound, where she stood holding her phone. "Called it. Requests are already coming in for a statement about how long they've been seeing each other."

Nick looked up sharply. "What?"

The expressions around them ranged from speculative to borderline flabbergasted.

"If the two of you are involved in a romantic relationship," Fenella said as the boat slowed down, nearing the bank, "then we need a *whole* other discussion about the plan going forward, and I think we'd all have appreciated a prior heads-up."

Her tone reminded Sabrina exactly of the head teacher she'd once had, whose disciplinary stare could wither a cactus from fifty paces.

"Pretty weird relationship," someone muttered, not all that quietly. "Hate-fucking, maybe."

"Just because I shouldn't be allowed anywhere near a boat and I took Nick down with me? Come on." God, even breathe wrong and some people would diagnose secret shagging.

Jess grinned at her. "Not so much the pratfall, babe, as the hand-holding and snuggling beforehand."

Two spots of warmth returned to Sabrina's aching body as her cheeks flamed. "We weren't—" She looked from Fenella's lifted brow to Nick's poker face, and the last scraps of her energy departed in a rush of exasperation and mortification.

Back on shore, they took off their sodden life jackets and walked right into the hell-pits of a paparazzi station. People were taking her photo for the national tabloids while she looked like a drowned mole rat, but at least they had the endless badgering questions to lessen the tension.

"Are you together? Was the fall staged? How long have you been seeing each other? Did Joe Ferren know? Were you in on the plagiarism story?"

She was wet, she was cold, and the inside of her mind was a jumbled, chaotic mess. Her defences were low, and she was so not in the mood for this.

Without responding, she ducked her head and tried to push past, but one of the more aggressive paps reached out and grabbed her arm.

The atmosphere changed immediately, drawing in and becoming watchful. Sabrina hadn't realised Nick was so close behind her, but he was suddenly there at her shoulder, and she could feel the tenseness of his body, like a coiled spring.

She didn't wait for him to speak or act. Without

looking away from the photographer, she said, very evenly, "Take your hand off my arm. Now."

A heart-thumping beat passed, before the pap let go of her and stepped back, hands raised, a gross, greasy smile pulling at his mouth. "Hey, hey," he said, soothingly. "No offence intended. Just doing our job."

"Get a new one." She headed for the company cars without looking back, and with as much dignity as she could muster with squeaking shoes.

"Snobby bitch." The voice carried clearly behind her on the breeze. "Built her career on her dodgy family, and thinks she's better than us because she's on the telly."

She bit down on the inside of her cheek, but didn't stop walking. Nick, however, who'd given her an unreadable glance before continuing to walk at her side, suddenly turned back.

Fenella came up between them and herded them forward like a sheepdog rounding up errant ewes. "Don't feed the trolls," she said calmly. "You both know better than that. Or do I need to send you to PR for a refresher course?"

"It's— Oh, *hell*." Nick had pulled off his wet jacket, and his shirt and jumper were plastered to his torso. In the few areas of exposed skin, Sabrina could see goose bumps. He sounded completely fed up, looked like he was grinding his teeth, and for a moment he seemed to be debating saying something else. With another muffled curse, he spun on his heel and stalked off towards the cars.

Sabrina watched him go, unable to piece out any single emotion from the multitudes that seemed to be tying her insides in knots.

Fenella cleared her throat, turning one of her hoop earrings meditatively. "I think we can safely say that things could be going better."

Chapter Five

The chocolate cake gleamed under the studio lights, six layers tall, covered in thick, cascading ganache. It looked as if it had been lifted straight out of a patisserie window.

And it tasted like a sponge soaked in household cleaner.

There was absolutely no way Nick could bluff out the latest disaster. Horrific manners or not, if something so astringent that it tasted like the popular conception of cyanide entered your mouth, instinct kicked in.

Lunging for a paper towel, he ducked behind the counter and spat out his forkful of cake. Sabrina's legs were next to him as she leaned over the sink.

"What on *earth*—" Fenella snapped in his earpiece.

Silently uttering words that wouldn't pass the censor, Nick stood up. He turned to meet the rapier stare of Chef Marco, the network's most temperamental celebrity cook, who was standing with pursed lips, tapping a utensil against the palm of his hand. The man was an unrelenting pain in the arse. He could kick up hell over a dropped fork, and he'd already had a tantrum over Sabrina handing him the wrong bowl. He'd snapped at her, Nick had snapped at him, and the segment had gone south from the start.

Now, with a soggy ball of poison cake soaking through the paper towel in Nick's hand, Marco appeared to be contemplating homicide.

Her nose still wrinkled—the aftertaste was horrific—Sabrina looked at the cake on the counter, and Nick saw her eyes narrow.

By some miracle, they weren't decapitated with a spatula by an enraged chef, but he was still ready to knock back the cappuccino Emily handed him after the show, as the crew gathered around for the Friday treat lunch. Sabrina took her own cup and twirled it to read the name scrawled across the side in purple ink, and Nick noticed what was written on his.

He had "Hardy"; she had "Laurel."

The theme of their first week, neatly encapsulated in festive Starbucks cups.

Fenella's summary of their progress so far was laden with all the expletives Nick had managed to suppress. She kept them in meetings all afternoon, and they still had the network ball tonight.

Briefly, he made it home to change, before he had to pick up Alan, his Yorkshire terrier, from the dog-minder and drive him over to his ex-wife's flat. They'd adopted Alan during their short-lived marriage six years ago, and it was Tia's turn for custody.

He got stuck in a dozen different traffic jams on the way, and if he didn't have a date to pick up shortly, he'd have happily skipped the ball, gone back to his flat, and spent the rest of the night on the couch.

He was not in the mood for another unsolicited performance review, even from one of his favourite people.

"What a clusterfuck," Tia said cheerfully. Widening her eyes at the mirror she'd propped against her espresso machine, she poked at her lower eyelashes with a mascara brush. She was doing her makeup at her kitchen bench in case there were any extra salacious details to be had out of Nick. "Everyone at work is taking bets on what's going to go wrong next."

Tia worked in their PR department, and for someone whose job hinged on everyone else's career running smoothly, she currently looked way too amused.

Nick grimaced, pushing back the jacket of his tuxedo and tucking one hand into his trouser pocket. "Good to know we're providing light entertainment." Even if not in the way prescribed.

It was getting beyond a joke. Every show this week had started off to plan, then within an hour—chaos.

From headline broadcaster to the host of a failing breakfast show and one half of the unintentional Carlton-Davenport comedy team. He supposed, in a worst-case scenario, they could always take their act on the road. Add in some juggling routines, maybe. Do a few magic tricks. It couldn't get much more ridiculous than it was already.

"So, what happened with the cooking segment today?" Tia leaned forward on her stool and adjusted the skirt of her red silk gown. "Because I had a very unhappy colleague who had to spend a good hour pacifying an ego-bruised chef."

"God knows." Nick rubbed at his neck, trying to salvage his mood before it completely tanked. He wasn't particularly looking forward to the ball, but he didn't ask someone out and then show up as a walking thundercloud. "Somehow we ended up with white vinegar subbed in for water." There had been vinegar on the set, for use in the cinder toffee bubbling away on the stovetop and drowning out most other scents, but clearly a bucketload shouldn't have been dumped into the "We prepared this one earlier" chocolate cake. "We still haven't worked out how the mix-up happened."

But suspicion was stirring. The dunking in the Thames on Wednesday couldn't be blamed on anything but a rogue hat and Sabrina's total lack of sea legs, but the other small incidents were mounting up. And from the look on Sabrina's face today, they were on the same wavelength. For once.

Somebody on the crew was either impressively careless, or messing with them on purpose. He wasn't sure whether it was intended to help their cause where the ratings were concerned—tune in to see how next the seasoned broadcasters could screw up a straightforward lifestyle show—or the reverse. If the latter, their possible saboteur was chalking up a series of wins. The viewers were already getting annoyed at what looked like a scripted farce. According to Jess, who closely monitored the social media response, people were also buzzing with rumours as to whether his on-screen tension with Sabrina stemmed from a private habit of going home and rolling each other around a mattress. With cynicism warring with gossip, their ratings share had stalled, and could now go either way.

He'd issued a denial through his press rep yesterday that there was any personal involvement with Sabrina—he hadn't bothered with the standard "we're just good friends" line; anyone who'd seen their evening shows would laugh that one out of court—but naturally people believed what they wanted to believe.

Nick thought it was pretty clear that in the event of Sabrina nailing him into a wall, it would literally involve metal spikes and a sledgehammer. However, he couldn't blame people for the raised eyebrows, after they'd sat with entwined fingers during the boat race.

Tia finished outlining her lips with a red pencil and studied the result critically. "I think someone on your crew is taking the piss," she said frankly, coming to the same conclusion. "How many enemies have you got in the studio?" With the tip of her little finger, she removed a tiny smudge of red, and sent him a mischievous look between fluttering lashes. "I would usually say there's not much mystery about who's pinning your face to a dartboard, but in this instance, I don't see Sabrina as the culprit unless she has a masochistic streak. It's her career on the line as well, and thanks in part to you, she's already created enough work for my department lately."

Nick sat down on the edge of the couch in the open-plan living area and pushed his fingers into his hair. "I don't need the reminder."

With her lipstick in her hand, Tia swung on her stool and turned to look at him. The teasing twinkle faded. "I still can't believe you did that." There was more concern than censure in her voice. "Even when we were together and I thought you were driving yourself too hard and getting a bit single-minded, I didn't think you'd— I mean, Nick, come on. I know it was all about getting the scoop when you were growing up, scoring the deals, but...there's good journalism, and there's throwing people under a bus. You're not—not *ruthless.* Ambitious. Stubborn. Overly fond of your own reflection. But not ruthless."

"And on that note, I need to be on my way." Flicking back his shirtsleeve, Nick checked his watch. "Doesn't time fly when your ego is being shredded?"

"Nice try. You've still got almost an hour before you have to pick up Whispering Willow."

Lifting his head, Nick raised an eyebrow. "Tia."

"What? The woman's a walking ASMR video." Unrepentantly, Tia mirrored his gesture. "And the two of you have nothing in common, although I suppose you might not realise that immediately if you can only hear one word in thirty when she speaks. Your first date was a dud; why are you wasting time going out with her again?"

"How do you know about our first date?"

"Please. She works in the building. You have to widen your hook-up pool by at least a city block if you want to stay out of the rumour mill."

Nick was extremely fond of Tia. Their marriage hadn't worked, but their friendship was rock solid, and although he knew that other friends still found it strange, she'd essentially become a sister to him. He considered both her and her second husband family.

But there were times when she was fucking annoying.

"We're not 'hooking up.'"

Tia giggled suddenly, and at his look, laughed harder. "Sorry. I keep thinking about you and Sabrina in the boat race. Count my vote for that as the best performance so far. I was having an absolutely shit morning on Wednesday and it really improved my day."

"Thrilled we could oblige. Appreciate the support."

"Hey, I was genuinely worried there for a good twenty seconds. Until it became clear you weren't actually going to drown. At which point, it became freaking hilarious. I mean, Sabrina Carlton, the network glamour girl, and you, Mr. Haute Couture, bobbing about—"

"The visual is pretty well fixed in my mind, thanks."

"Do you think she was trying to push you under when she started using your shoulders as a ladder?"

"I wouldn't be surprised."

The front door opened, and Alan lost his mind. They'd both been usurped in the dog's affections by Tia's husband. Rugby hooker Geoffrey Mackintosh, a man the size of a double-decker bus in both stature and good nature, picked up Alan and grinned around.

"Honeys, I'm home. How's the fam? Christ, you look gorgeous, Tee." Easily holding the wriggling dog out of the way of Tia's dress, Tosh bent and kissed her enthusiastically on the mouth, then turned. Nick caught the glint in his eye but didn't dodge in time before he, too, was the recipient of a burly one-armed hug and a smacking kiss on his cheek. "You don't look half bad, either, bro. Scrubs up all right for such an ugly bastard, doesn't he?"

With a final knuckle rub on the dog's head, which just about sent Alan into a blissed-out coma, Tosh put him down. "Glad to have you back, little dude. Although you're looking a bit stout there. I see your father's been overdoing the treats again." He laid his cheek on the top of Tia's head.

"You're messing up my hair," she said with no heat, her eyes soft. "And you're running late."

"Shower, shave, tux on. Fifteen minutes." Tosh kissed her temple and straightened. "When the canvas is this good, the prep is minimal."

"Such shrinking violets I marry," Tia said wryly, and he yelped when she pinched his rear. "Go and get ready, Gilderoy. Nick's about to tell me that he's finally getting his goddamn act together and mending fences with Sabrina."

Tosh was poking around the half-eaten plate of crackers and cheese on the bench. He put a wedge of Camembert in his mouth and chewed thoughtfully. Swallowing, he said, "Dunno. He trashed her whole family tree on live TV. Hard to come back from that."

"But she was holding his hand the other day," Tia pointed out, and Tosh made an acknowledging sound.

"True, true. And if she was going to enact an elaborate Shakespearean revenge plot, she'd probably have done it already. There *may* be hope he can salvage the situation."

"Unless he fucks it up again."

"Strong possibility."

"Sorry," Nick said, "would you like me to leave so you can continue this discussion?"

"No, no," Tosh assured him. "You're not a third wheel, mate. This conversation is definitely directed at you." With the toe of his boot, he carefully nudged Alan away from a dropped cracker and bent to pick it up. "Why don't you try apologising? You know, 'Sorry I forgot that I don't work for the gutter press—'"

"'And that I listened to a vile little cow like Sadie Foster,'" Tia cut in. Having started her career in theatrical PR, she had intimate knowledge of the more trying personalities on the West End. She'd recently informed Nick in no uncertain terms that Sadie was on a level of her own, and he was a total wanker for cooperating with her schemes.

He'd interviewed Sadie several times in the past, and he'd never warmed to her. There was always a strong disconnect between the motions of her mouth and the expressions in her eyes. Some actors could produce a seamless public mask, a projected persona that went unquestioned. Sadie was not up to that standard. It was like a CGI effect that was ever so slightly off; it drew attention to the falsity, and every so often you saw glimpses of the reality beneath. He'd always put her in the difficult guest category, sweet as honey the moment they went live, but likely to be a demanding little pill beforehand. Until the night of the plagiarism scandal, however, he hadn't seen the full extent of the vindictiveness behind the innocent smiles.

She'd played her part that day with glee, first in the hesitant performance she'd put on, disclosing the facts about Henrietta Carlton's plagiarism—"Oh my goodness, isn't it going to be a big scoop for *Sunset Britain*"—to both himself and his producer, who'd just about salivated at the mouth. Her vicious enjoyment had been even more apparent when she'd attempted to break Sabrina with the revelation of Ferren's infidelity. And then there was what she'd done later, probably, Nick still thought, because of Sabrina's stiff-shouldered refusal to crumble under her spite.

Sadie had set the ball rolling; Nick's producer had picked it up with avid enthusiasm and made his own position clear, and the pressure he'd applied had flirted with the edges of blackmail.

None of that was much of a sop for Nick's conscience.

When it came down to it, he'd played his own part. He'd made a choice. And there was no undoing it now.

That cold fist in his midsection tightened its grip again.

"I have apologised," he said, very levelly, as he got to his feet. "Of course I've apologised. She doesn't want to hear it."

He propped his hands on his waist, curling his fingers into his belt. "If I could go back and undo it, I would." Sabrina's face that night, both when she'd been sliced into by her dickhead ex, and when she'd confronted Nick later—

She was strong and proud and whatever challenges she faced, she fought her corner like a fucking lioness, but when the anger cracked, her hurt and pain was palpable. And it went in like a knife.

"I hate that I hurt her." The words were wrenched deeply out of him. A surge of something else sparked hotly in his gut, and he deliberately closed himself off to it, his voice coming out harshly as he threw up a defensive wall. "Although I'm not convinced that she wouldn't have done the same thing if the roles were reversed."

Tosh drew in his breath with an exaggerated hiss through his teeth. "Oh, oh. *Mate.* I hope you didn't include that factoid in your 'apology.'"

Tia was still looking knowingly at Nick. "No. I don't think so. If you genuinely believed that, you wouldn't like her so much."

He was silent for a few breaths. "There are a lot of

words I'd use about Sabrina Carlton. *Liking* is not one of them."

Obstinate. That worked. *Snarky*. *Questionable taste*—she blasted shit music through their dressing room walls, she'd named some horrifying and very public sculpture after him, and for years, she'd been hung up on a guy that anyone could see was an absolute prick.

Despite their history, she was still a stranger in a lot of ways. There were a million things he didn't know about her, couldn't answer about her.

But he was also certain that if someone gave him a piece of paper and a pen, he'd be able to draw her profile accurately down to the last eyelash.

He'd been dead right that this job, seeing her every day, was going to force some things into the open. He'd never felt so complicatedly about anyone or anything in his life, and he didn't enjoy being ripped apart on a daily basis.

Releasing another sharp breath, Nick bent down and gave Alan a last rub on his stomach, which actually did look a bit more bulbous than when Tia had dropped him off a fortnight ago. "I'm heading out. I'll see you two later at the venue."

"So smoothly he ignores the subject." Tia shook her head at him.

"There is no subject. There's blind insinuation and gossip, and a job to do."

"Nick." At Tia's suddenly serious tone, Nick turned back at the doorway. "Right now, the focus is forming a solid partnership with Sabrina and kicking *WMUL* into gear. But if you saw an opportunity to get your old job back, would you take it?"

He didn't reply, but she was studying his expression carefully.

"Yeah," she said. "That's what I thought."

Tosh looked up from where he was crouched next to Alan, and they shared a glance.

That, this time, contained zero amusement.

Chapter Six

Until the woman whisked Sabrina's date away right under her nose, she'd thought that the pretty brunette Nick had brought to the ball was shy.

Aware that eyes everywhere were observing her over glasses of champagne, she stood at the side of the dancefloor and watched Davod, the rugby player her friends had set her up with, dance with the other woman for the third song in a row. He'd cast the odd, half-embarrassed glance back at her, but his eyes would immediately return to Willow's face. Sabrina had never seen anything like it, two people so instantly enamoured of one another. It was like watching Pepé Le Pew and Penelope Pussycat doing cartoon heart-eyes and a decent salsa.

Tonight was not improving her already poor opinion of setups. The dreaded realm of "Have you met my friend Mike? He's very well informed about car engines and thinks that women can't read their own menu." Unfortunately, Akiko, who was currently eight months pregnant with her and Elise's second daughter, had turned into a raging matchmaker in her third trimester. She'd decided that Sabrina had now had time to get over Ferren, and deserved some good sex, and had triumphantly produced Davod Ingram. Professional rugby winger. Part-time history student. Extremely muscular thighs. Apparently.

"He fancies you," Akiko had said, "and he preferred your show to Nick's."

On the basis of that sound good sense, Sabrina had invited Davod to the ball tonight.

And within half an hour, she'd somehow ended up side-by-side with Nick.

Thoughtfully, she took a sip of wine. "Why does she keep whispering like that?"

Nick had introduced Willow, a researcher for a popular reality show, but Sabrina still had no idea what that short conversation had been about, because she hadn't heard a word the other woman said. The music was loud even when people weren't speaking at the approximate decibel of rustling silk.

Nick swirled the ice in his whisky glass. "I tried to bring the conversation around to that point in the car."

"And?" Sabrina glanced at him, her eyes skating over his tall form in the designer tux, then resolutely returned her gaze to the safer territory of the briefest date she'd ever had.

"Legit didn't hear the answer."

"It is sort of soothing to listen to."

"Dangerously." Nick lifted the whisky to his lips. "I almost fell asleep at the wheel twice before we'd even made it out of Paddington." After a moment of silence, in which they watched Davod spin Willow through a complicated series of steps—if the rugby star went on *Strictly Come Dancing*, he was a lock for the final— she sensed him looking at her. "How long have you known Ingram?"

Sabrina looked at her watch. "About ninety minutes." And it looked like that would be the sum total
of their acquaintance. Lucky, really, that she hadn't
opened the door and been knocked flat with sexual
sparks.

At this point, she might as well call it a day soon,
and get some decent sleep before her flight to France
in the morning. It would be another late night at the
wedding reception tomorrow.

Nick turned to consider the contents of a waiter's
proffered tray, and his shoulder brushed her. As Sabrina played restively with the bangle around her wrist,
Hania appeared before them.

Their boss was dressed for the festive occasion in
a tailored gold lamé suit. Her cheekbones glimmered
with co-ordinating gold-toned highlights. She looked
fantastic. She also had her warning look on. "Good,
you're here," she began, then stopped and frowned at
them. "Are you here together?"

"No," Nick said, turning back with a small mince
pie in his hand before Sabrina could issue her own denial. "We brought Juliet and Romeo to the party, and
have now been jointly cast as background extras while
the epic love story unfolds."

"I see," Hania said, and clearly didn't. Briskly, she
continued, "This is your heads-up to be on your best
behaviour in front of the invited press tonight, which
means play nice, keep it professional, don't shoot your
mouths off in public, and ideally, don't punch anyone
in the face. Such fun, isn't it, that I have to have this
conversation with two of our leading broadcasters?"
She raised her glass and gave someone a toothy party
smile, then smoothly angled her body to bring the three

of them into a confidential huddle. "You can at least breathe easy about a face-to-face with Lionel just yet. He's scrapping his usual token appearance this year. Another commitment."

Lifting her hand, she waved at another newcomer, then glanced between them again, her attention fixing on Sabrina. An odd expression crossed her face and she seemed to consider further speech, but decided to grab another glass of champagne from a passing tray and leave them to it.

"Did she seem jumpier than usual to you?" Sabrina spun her own glass between her fingers and realised she was now standing once again in solo conversation with Nick. Standing very *close* to Nick. Their sides were touching, and when she spoke, his head inclined towards hers.

They might as well just start vertically spooning. Could they *make* less effort not to look like a couple on a date.

It was like being in a car and continually losing concentration and drifting towards the centre line. Time to get off the M3 before a crash occurred.

"I'm going to get another drink." She zipped away, almost spilling her still half-full glass.

Davod caught up to her at the bar, which was located as far as was geographically possible from Nick while still remaining within the same four walls. A flush set deep into his blunt-edged cheekbones. "Sabrina—look, I'm really sorry. I mean, shit, this is your work do—"

Her earlier amusement spiked anew. He was about eight feet tall, had biceps the size of watermelons and more facial hair than Father Christmas, and he looked like a little kid who'd just been told off for pinching sweets. "Davod, honestly it's fine. It was a first date. And this obviously doesn't happen every day for you."

"No. No, it definitely doesn't." His face was still tense with anxiety, but he was staring fatuously through the crowd at Willow again, where she stood presumably having a similar conversation with Nick. Hordes of gorgeously dressed, expensively scented people kept parting like the Red Sea every time Sabrina's eyes wandered back in that direction. So obliging.

With an obvious effort that warmed the cockles of her cynical little heart, even as it didn't exactly bolster her ego, Davod dragged his attention back to her. "Would you like to dance?"

She shook her head, but she was laughing. "No, thank you. Go and enjoy your first date with Willow."

His grin was sheepish, but with that light in his eyes she could see a glimmer of what Akiko and Elise had been talking up.

Ah, missed opportunities.

Over the bowl of peanuts that the cute bartender handed to her, she got stuck chatting with the former weatherman from *Sunset Britain*, who had a habit of using climate-related phrases in everyday small talk. She'd never known if he was pulling people's legs or if his occupation had infiltrated even the language neurons in his brain.

"...he left under quite a cloud," the man confided in a hushed tone, so that Sabrina had to lean in to hear him. They should have made enunciation the theme of the ball this year. Her fellow gossiper fiddled with his bow tie. Despite his verbal tics, she'd always found him endearing because of his resemblance to Professor Porter in the Disney *Tarzan*, a film she'd seen about eight

hundred times with Akiko and Elise's daughter, Lizzy.
"I can't quite recall the particulars now. My mind's getting a bit foggy these days." He suddenly brightened.
"Oh, I met your sister at the theatre the other day. What a charming young woman. Such a lovely sunny smile, and she so obviously enjoys her work."

"Yes, she's on cloud nine with the new show—"
Blimey. It was contagious.

Another group of people joined them then, rescuing her before she found herself spouting atmospheric terminology for the rest of the night. Her companion got pulled away to meet someone, and Sabrina turned to greet the two people who'd obviously engineered the save.

"Sorry to butt in and rain on Willard's parade," Tia Mackintosh said, grinning. "We didn't want to steal anyone's thunder." The PR manager was looking like a curvy goddess in her sparkling red gown, her dark hair wound into a complicated plait. Sabrina had worked with her multiple times during her contract on *Sunset Britain*, and Tia had helped pad some of her fall after the confrontation with Ferren. Sabrina had always liked her, although they'd been colleagues and budding friends for quite a while before she'd realised that Tia, among the many hats she wore, was Nick's ex-wife.

What surprisingly good taste in partners on the one side, and abysmal on the other.

"But we got wind of the idea you might be in need of an intervention." Geoffrey Mackintosh's hazel eyes were twinkling. She'd met Tosh at several events in the past, and interviewed him more than once. He'd been her favourite athlete to have on the show, because he knew full well that her knowledge of team sport would fit on the head of a pin, and he forced her to continually counter his good-humoured attempts to trip her up. He was a merciless teaser and a lot of fun.

"Stop. I'm begging you. My dress was not designed for laughter and you'll increase your own workload if I have a wardrobe malfunction. Poor Willard."

Tosh reached around Sabrina to scoop up a handful of nuts from the snack bowl. "What's happened to Davod?"

Sabrina gestured at the dancefloor, where Davod and Willow were pressed close together, now barely swaying while the beat of the fast-paced song thumped around them. "Love at first sight."

"What?" Tia's expression caused a renewed bubble of laughter to rise in Sabrina's throat. The evening was at least proving to be the break in stress she needed, albeit unexpectedly. "Are you serious? Whispering Willow pinched your date?" She looked so flabbergasted that Sabrina stopped trying to keep a straight face.

"Wait—Davod's just *left* you here and gone off with another chick?" Easy-going Tosh looked genuinely annoyed. He started to turn. "What the fuck, man. I'll have a word."

"No!" Sabrina shot up a hand. "Thanks, but honestly—as first dates go, it would have fizzled anyway."

"No connection?" Tosh's frown smoothed out, and was replaced with something slightly enigmatic. "Really. Interesting."

"And Willow's ditched Nick? Where *is* Nick?" Twisting, Tia peered into the crowd.

"Over there." Tosh nodded in the direction of the archway that led out to the hotel foyer. "He obviously wasn't into his date, either, so why the face?"

Nick was pacing by the archway. With one hand cupped around the back of his neck, he was talking into his phone, and his frown was visible even from a distance.

"Probably lost a source for his next exclusive scoop," Sabrina said, then grimaced. She'd shot for sarcasm and landed squarely on bitterness there.

Tia and Tosh exchanged glances, and Tia hesitated, biting her lower lip. "Look," she said after an awkward pause, "I know Nick behaved atrociously over the issue with your grandmother, and his priorities are fucked, but he's not a total bastard."

"I hope you don't write promotional copy for Nick, gorgeous," Tosh remarked. "Because I reckon the word for that endorsement is *underwhelming*."

Tia ignored her husband's interjection. "I admit we're biased." Her expression was earnest, and the lights overhead glittered off the beading on her bodice as she shifted closer to Sabrina to be heard over the swelling hubbub of voices. "We love Nick. He's family." Sabrina started to speak, but Tia rushed on. "He's extremely not-perfect, and he's made some absolutely clanging mistakes. But if we were in trouble, Nick is the person we'd go to."

"That'd be risky." Sabrina couldn't help it; the words slipped out. "You'd probably find your troubles splashed across every blog in the country within twenty-four hours."

"I don't think—"

"Tia." It was Sabrina's turn to cut in, politely but firmly. As much as she liked these two, she was not in the mood for a talking-up-of-Nick conversation. Actions spoke louder than words; especially words coming from a third party. If there were apologies to be made—expressions of actual, genuine regret, and not just to her—it wasn't Nick's family who needed to voice them. "I respect that your relationship with Nick is not my relationship with Nick, and he's someone you care about."

She looked at the ground for a moment, watching the beams of coloured light sweep patterns across the wooden parquet. She held herself with one arm across her ribs, her fingers curling against the boning in her gown, before she met Tia's watchful gaze. "But I—"

"Would rather leave him in the Thames next time?" Tia asked ruefully, and Sabrina accepted another glass of champagne from a waiter.

"It'd be tempting."

Nick had been unexpectedly amused when Willow took one look at Sabrina's mountainous rugby player and all but bolted for Gretna Green. That emotion was now dissipating into a wave of renewed contempt for Lionel Grimes. Switching the phone to his other ear, he stepped out of the way of a couple of dancers moving towards the archway. They were probably looking for some fresh air in the foyer. There were so many bodies in the ballroom that the smell of five hundred different perfumes and colognes was rising with the heat.

"I met with the director of Shining Lights UK and your friend Lainie Graham today, to finalise plans for the Peppermint Pixies launch," his mother was saying. "We've decided to extend the on-sale period until Easter. A limited-edition line, with a hundred percent of the profits on each packet sold to be donated to Shining Lights." Maria's voice took on a crisp edge of disapproval. "Which will hopefully compensate for some of the funds they were expecting from Lionel Grimes."

Nick shook his head.

He'd put Lainie in contact with Grimes last summer, as a potential patron for the children's cancer charity she'd founded in memory of her teenage sister. Grimes had initially pledged ongoing support—and then in October, Sadie Foster, his current girlfriend, had caught wind of the agreement.

Sadie had a grudge against both Lainie and her husband, the actor Richard Troy, and her personal spite had taken precedence over the well-being of the children supported by the charity. Under her influence, Grimes had ghosted on Shining Lights, several other so-called philanthropists had followed in his wake, and Nick was disgusted with all of them.

On Sadie's part, it would have to rack up as an all-time low.

He supposed the woman must have at least one redeeming feature, but she was hiding it well.

"I can see why you've been so unimpressed with the head honcho," his mother said. "But perhaps it would be best to express your opinion of him in a less public forum next time. Or, if you must be secretly filmed and plastered across the internet, at least elaborate on *why* you're drawing such unflattering comparisons, so censure falls where it ought."

Inarguable point.

"You're a bloody marvel," he said, "picking up the baton like this. Above and beyond."

"The business is doing very well and I've been looking for another fundraising partnership. This is a wonderful cause, and I was very impressed with Lainie.

No airs and graces at all. With all the awards she's won recently, she must be a household name now, but she's much less impressed with herself than most people with celebrity status in this country. You, for example."

"The unconditional love and support, Mam. It's really a warm glow."

Through the busy crush of bodies in the ballroom, Nick could see a familiar flash of red. Sabrina was talking to Tosh and Tia. Light flashed and sparkled off the scattering of crystals that curved down from the neckline of her black gown to where the fabric stretched tautly over her hip. As he watched, she tilted her head and her long hair moved in ripples down her back.

"By the way, you're still all right to have Pippi for 'Go to Work with Family' Day on Tuesday?" Maria asked. "She's excited about going to a TV studio with her famous Uncle Nick."

Turning his back on the scene in the ballroom again, Nick refocused his mind. "I've already cleared it, and our assistant's offered to keep Pippi with her in the studio while we're filming."

No need to check that Pippi was aware he'd be working most of the time she was there. For a kid who wasn't even nine yet, his niece was well-informed in general. Nick had once watched her breeze through an old '90s game of *Carmen Sandiego*, and she'd barely needed to look up a single fact. He had dim memories of playing the same game in the pre-Google days and annoying his parents every five minutes for help with clues.

"Oh, good." A sly note entered Maria's tone. "And you *are* rather good with her, you know. You're quite sure you don't want to swell the ranks of my grandchildren? All these misguided women who post your photo everywhere—there must be one who'll put up with you in person."

"I'd take a bullet for Pippi, and I'm happy that kids exist in the wider world, but I don't want them to exist 24/7 in my flat. It's enough work having a part-time Alan."

"Are you at a party? What's that music?"

"It's the network holiday ball tonight."

"Oh my goodness." His mother sounded appalled. "Why didn't you let the call go to voicemail? Do you have a date just sitting there?"

"My date was last spotted heading off into the sunset with an athlete built like a battle tank."

There was a brief, speaking pause.

"Good grief, Nick. You're even worse than Iain. At some point, do you both have to wonder if it's you?"

On which supportive note, he returned his phone to his pocket and re-entered the fray. He actually enjoyed most industry events. If he didn't like talking to people, he'd have fucked up his choice of career, but this did tend to be a fair-weather business, and when you'd recently taken a fall from grace, people were far too pleased about it.

Naturally, because he seemed to have an internal GPS where she was concerned, he ended up back next to Sabrina within minutes of returning to the ballroom. She stepped left to avoid him, he went right, and they collided.

"Sorry," they muttered simultaneously, and Nick drew his head back when a large amount of her impossibly thick hair tried to get into his mouth and nose. It was like the curling tendrils of some horror-film plant;

it made his fingers twitch with the urge to touch, but appeared to have a life of its own.

Automatically, he put his hand on the bare skin of her upper arm and steadied her. This close, he could see the freckles on her nose, just visible beneath her makeup. Her eyes were very green, and tonight, the colour of the waters of the Valle Verzasca in Switzerland.

In terms of the look contained within, an Antarctic comparison would be equally accurate.

Her frosty gaze suddenly switched sideways, over his shoulder, and her breath touched his cheek as she groaned softly. "Oh, that's all the night needs."

"What?"

"Presenter-in-waiting incoming." Her face lifted into what Nick thought of as her poster smile, the expression she wore in the promotional images for the show. From zero to charming in one second flat, like turning on a lightbulb. She could easily have followed in her family's footsteps and taken to the stage. Most people couldn't move faux pleasure farther than their lips; Sabrina could even brighten her eyes on cue.

Frowning, he turned, and silently echoed her groan when he saw Peter King advancing on them. It was difficult to miss him in the crowd. The host of *The Arts Review* was dressed as a traffic light. Nick assumed he'd been going for a holiday theme with the red blazer, green trousers, and migraine-inducing amber waistcoat. He had the right face for whimsical attire. Every one of his features ended in a point, which gave him the vibe of a middle-aged Puck—aided by the perpetual expression of brewing mischief.

King pushed past a few chatting crew members and stopped in front of Nick and Sabrina. His attitude suggested a veteran actor stepping onto a stage, flinging wide his arms, and waiting for applause. After a short, deliberately uncomfortable pause, he spoke in his characteristic drawl. "The new dream team. I see our prime-time prince and princess have tarnished their crowns and slipped down into the lowly realms of the early-morning wake-up call."

Another beat as he looked back and forth between them, his eyes shrewd and assessing, and then a glint appeared. "Little dismaying to court a job for months and then realise you risk being pipped at the post. By two people who see your dream job as a banishment to the naughty step. But breathe easy. Any stomping great scenes will have to wait for another evening. Outrage would ruin the line of my suit."

"I don't," Sabrina said, "see the breakfast show as a 'lower realm' than the evening show."

The left side of King's mouth compressed as he observed her. "*You* might not." He let his eyes drift sideways to Nick's face.

Sabrina also glanced at Nick. "Hmm" was her inscrutable response, and Nick moved one shoulder in an irritable shrug.

King watched them above the rim of his champagne glass. "Do keep stretching your physical comedy muscles each morning, won't you? Nobody can say you're not innovative. Who'd have thought of turning the lifestyle show into a sitcom?"

Sabrina's tone was as deathly sweet as her smile. "I believe you've recently started writing a theatre column, Peter?"

King flicked an invisible speck from his tie. "Yes, I was snapped up by the *Express*. An opposing voice

to your friend at the *Westminster Post*, Ford-Griffin.
Or rather, your sister's *intimate* friend?"

Sabrina returned him a bland stare.

"I thought Ford-Griffin's review of the *Anathorn*
musical was very restrained, for a man who generally
drips acid in such a pleasing way. Sheer coincidence
that his girlfriend has a leading role in it?"

"*Anathorn* has deservedly received glowing reviews
across the board, because it's a fantastic production,"
Sabrina said. "And for someone who's worked alongside Griff, you can't have been paying much attention if you think he'd allow bias to interfere with his
judgment."

"True," King mused, rubbing the pad of his thumb
in small circles against his chin. His gaze moved back
to Nick's face. "He is generally a straight shooter. No
tolerance for double-dealing. He's a close friend of
yours, too, isn't he, Davenport? Or has there been a
little hiccup there?"

A renewed and painful jab, and sure as fuck not
something he was going to discuss with King. Nick
kept his face completely blank of expression.

King smiled again, a knowing quirk of those sharp
pixie-like features. He took a sip of his wine and said to
Sabrina, in a suspiciously conversational tone, "Given
your close connection to the source material, you'll
have heard about the big casting shake-up with *The
Velvet Room*, of course? The revival doesn't open until
the new year, and apparently it's already racked up as
many 'oops' incidents as your takeover of *WMUL*." He
hummed under his breath. "Davenport exposing your
grandmother's plagiarism seems to have set all *sorts*
of things in motion."

The mention of *The Velvet Room* had a vivid effect on Sabrina. Despite the stuffiness of the ballroom, the temperature in the immediate vicinity dropped dramatically.

Why did Nick think that a hundred years from now, he was going to be standing in the afterlife with Sabrina glaring daggers at him while, for the five-thousandth time, some helpful third party brought up the plagiarism exposé?

With a small movement, she turned her shoulder to him and addressed King as if Nick had faded out of existence. "I can't say I've been keeping tabs on the new production of *The Velvet Room*."

"No. Well, I suppose it would be a waste of energy. You've been struck off the register for royalties, haven't you?" King murmured, but couldn't get a rise out of Sabrina beyond a stiffening of her shoulders. Nick suspected she'd had that dig so many times now it had lost most of its impact. A nerve twitched in his cheek. "I'm surprised you haven't had the news from your sister, though. The theatre circles are all abuzz with it today. Mitzi Housken has been forced to leave the stage for personal reasons. Read: rehab. And the director's reportedly dissatisfied with her understudy, so they've brought in a new eleventh-hour leading lady. I'm not sure if you know her," he said with studied innocence. "Sadie Foster."

In the silence that followed, he watched their faces and the curve of his lips deepened. "But, of course you know her." He checked his watch with a flourish. "Must dash. I'm in the studio tomorrow, doing the voice-over for a botanical documentary. Stealth plants, you know, that creep into a garden unexpectedly and force out all other growth." His look of cheerful bonhomie was unblinking. "Enjoy the rest of your evening—and best of luck for the rest of the month."

As he disappeared back into the crowd, the circling coloured lights overhead flashed a progressive pattern of pink, purple, and blue across Sabrina's unreadable face. After a moment, she tilted her head to speak to Nick without actually looking at him. "Aren't we interviewing the core cast of *The Velvet Room* revival soon?"

Nick pushed his hands into his pockets and lifted his gaze to briefly study the lighting setup on the ceiling. "Yes."

"The puzzle of why Hania keeps darting away from me like a cat on hot embers: sorted. Fuck me." Sabrina scrunched her nose and looked expectantly over at where the band were organising themselves for the next song. "I wonder what it'll be."

"What?"

"The next song in the soundtrack of the evening. My life has become a series of cinematic irony, so I have high expectations."

The guitarist on the dais strummed a few notes, and Nick felt his eyebrow lift as the lead singer crooned out the first line.

Of "It's the Most Wonderful Time of the Year."

With a graceful twist of her wrist, Sabrina touched a finger to her temple in a salute. "Flawless, universe. Well played."

Chapter Seven

17 Days until Christmas Eve

Paris in the spring might be iconic, but the French Alps in winter were breathtaking. Literally. Sabrina felt the cold bite of the air like a dozen icy shards in her nose and lungs, but after the almost muggy heat of the reception room inside, it was deliciously head-clearing. Standing on the terrace with her back to the closed glass doors, the music and voices and laughter within were a muted hum. Outside, it was almost magically still and quiet. The winter sky was a cascading stretch of stars that would be hidden by cloud and pollution in London, the valley of chalets and hotels a tapestry of flickering lights. Snow-capped mountains towered into the night, an eerily silent wall of shadows, but somehow, despite the vastness of the landscape and the sparkly veneer of wealth and determined gaiety pasted around it, it seemed sheltering and intimate when she stood here alone. Just—life, stripped right down to this one moment.

Sabrina breathed in again, closing her eyes, and caught the faintest smell of baking rising from the basement kitchens, even this late at night. The restaurant here was famous for its pastry. She'd been here once before, almost five years ago, and that one scent was so evocative that she suddenly saw the scene before her as it had been then.

The intimate serenity and endless possibilities of night replaced by a summer sky. Wisps of cloud, one circling into the shape of a bicycle. An old-fashioned penny-farthing.

A scoffing laugh—*What d'you mean, a bike, it looks like a lion, see, there's the mane.*

That's the front wheel, you wanker.

Need to put your glasses on, babe.

The snow melted away to reveal rolling planes of green and gold. Bare arms and legs. The buttery tang of fresh croissants. A hand, coming around her to hold the iron railing. Tanned skin dusted with red-gold hair and freckles.

It was like remembering the fragments of a dream. A faded page from someone else's story.

In the coolness of the night, Sabrina looked down at the railing and her own hand closed over it. Everything in the resort was shiny and polished, but there was a faint roughness under her palm, a scattering of rust beneath the glossy paint.

The burring sound as her phone vibrated in her bag made her jump. Cuddling her wool coat closer around her shoulders, she pulled it out and checked the screen, and a jolt of alarm clutched her stomach.

"Griff?" she said hurriedly as she took the call, glancing at the time. It was after midnight. "Is Freddy all right?"

She might have come to appreciate her sister's boyfriend, despite his personality drawbacks, but they didn't go in for late-night deep and meaningfuls. Even during more civilised daylight hours she didn't pick him as one for a cosy gossip. Her mind had gone straight to a crisis.

"Yes. I mean, sorry, no, it's me." At the chirpy sound of Freddy's voice, the tension locking Sabrina's shoulders released. "My phone's gone on the blink, so I stole Griff's. *Bonsoir, ma grande soeur.* How's France? Do you like her dress? Is there cake?"

Laughter bubbled up like the champagne circulating the reception hall. All night her sister had been singing and dancing on the West End, and her energy was still sparking through the line. "France is freezing but stunning, and I wish I were here for more than twenty-four hours. The bride is an elegant vision, and there are three tiers of lemon drizzle cake covered with yellow and gold-sprayed roses."

"Lemon drizzle," Freddy said thoughtfully, with a barely suppressed tremor of something lifting the words. "Maybe I'll have that for our cake, too."

Sabrina had been shifting her weight from one stiletto heel to the other, suddenly very aware of just how cold it was outside, but she went still at that. With a rush of warmth from within, she hit the button requesting a switch to a video call.

"*Ma petite soeur,*" she said, when Freddy's face appeared on the screen. Her sister had propped her chin on her raised hand and her fingers were visibly trembling—and there was an impressive princess-cut addition to one of them. Sabrina looked into sparkling brown eyes that were more familiar to her than her own, and saw absolute, pure happiness. Her own smile grew. "Am I officially getting a grumpy bastard of a brother?"

A flush of pink appeared in Freddy's cheeks. She was so beautiful, and she looked so much like their mother at that moment. It was as if both people Sabrina had always loved most were here with her under the quiet, starry sky.

"We're getting married." Despite the excitement that was making her fidget and shake, Freddy spoke very steadily. Once more, it was brought home that, at some point as time slipped past, her madcap baby sister had turned into this capable, confident woman. "He had a speech planned, but I jumped the gun a bit and it got jumbled. He went all scowly and sexy. It was great."

Sabrina shook her head, grinning. "Both of you perfectly encapsulated in a few sentences."

"I'm so happy, Sabs." Said so simply, and it made Sabrina's eyes sting.

"I'm thrilled for you, Freddy. And congratulate Griff. He doesn't waste time. I remain surprised but impressed that he's so self-aware about the best thing that's ever happened to him."

"We're planning a celebratory drink with the family, on Tuesday evening before the show. Can you come?" Freddy's expression was both hopeful and apprehensive.

"By 'the family,'" Sabrina said, trying to sound enthused, "I assume you mean—"

"You, me, Griff and his family…and Dad." Freddy hesitated only briefly, but caught Sabrina's involuntary grimace. "I know things aren't great with you two, but—"

"But I can deal for an hour or two, to toast your fu-

ture husband's good fortune." Sabrina's resolute tone
was as much for herself as Freddy. Every conversation
with her father recently had devolved into an argument,
and the prospect of sitting down at a table with him
right now made her stomach feel cold and hard, but—
it was just a drink. It was for her sister, and her future
brother-in-law. She was a grown woman; she could
manage one fucking drink with civility for their sake.

"It'll be fine," Freddy assured her. "And Dad's been
in a good mood. I think things are picking up for him
again workwise."

Their father had taken a massive career hit after his
part in the plagiarism scandal had been exposed. He'd
had to step down from his role as a theatrical manager,
much to Freddy's relief, Sabrina imagined, after her
years of dancing to his tune. He'd primarily been working with Griff's parents lately, brokering deals for their
bespoke dollhouse business. Whatever their history, he
was her father, her surviving parent; she didn't want
him to struggle financially. However—

Why did that blithe comment from Freddy make
her skin prickle with foreboding?

She wasn't sure she wanted specifics just now. This
was meant to be a treat night away, a breather from her
own professional—and personal—stress.

Bending her head, she peered through the glass
panel in the door. Admittedly, optimistic to think she
could leave all her troubles in London, when half the
network staff had also traipsed across the Channel and
were currently shrieking and swaying in a conga line.

She didn't see the primary cause of her raised blood
pressure in the chaos. Conga dancing would probably wrinkle Nick's designer suit. He seemed to have

an endless supply of them. He'd gone less formal for their colleague's wedding than last night's tux, but still looked like he'd walked off a model shoot.

Like her, he'd come without a plus-one today. She wouldn't invite a casual date to someone's wedding even if the ceremony had been down the road in Notting Hill, but they'd missed an opportunity to see if history repeated itself with their respective partners. They could set themselves up as unintentional matchmakers in every country on the continent.

"Brave of the bride to invite you *and* Nick," Freddy said, reading her mind. "I'm surprised neither of you has ended up *in* the lemon drizzle cake. Or are you keeping a tactful distance?"

That had been the plan. Following the trend of this month, it had gone awry from the beginning. She'd ended up seated directly behind him and had spent too much of the ceremony studying the contours of his head and the way his hair curled against his neck. They'd been put at the same table for dinner, directly opposite one another, and every time she looked up from her chicken, enigmatic dark eyes had turned away from his chatty neighbour and fixed on her face.

Quite a *lot* of people had turned away from their neighbours when he'd loathsomely winked at her and she'd fumbled her wineglass, spilling rosé across the white linen tablecloth.

It was like she was undergoing some sort of cosmic test.

"At this precise moment, the stars *and* the spirits seem to be shining on me," Sabrina said drily. "He's temporarily disappeared. I'll let you get back to celebrating with the groom-to-be. Spare me any salacious details. *Mes* ears can't take it."

"Says the delicate flower who once no-showed on her own category at the TV Awards because she was shagging her boyfriend in the loo." Freddy's expressive face morphed into lines of "Oh, shit."

Sabrina sighed. "I'm not going to fall apart because you obliquely refer to Ferren. And it was a snog in a maintenance cupboard. I didn't win that award, anyway. That was back in the days when Nick was still taking it every bloody year."

Freddy was studying her intently through the camera, with discomforting perception. "It's okay to still feel sad about it, as long as you don't take him back."

"That ship has not so much sailed as cannonballed to the bottom of the sea." The atmosphere under the canopy of the night sky encouraged brutal honesty and reflection, and she said, slowly, "What happened last summer… I don't think it was even the emphatic end of everything with Ferren that hurt so much. It was the forced clarity. I wish I'd been honest with myself a lot earlier. Recognised that things had become pretty fucked up before it got to the point it did. I can't regret all of it, but I do regret that."

"I just want you to be happy," Freddy said quietly. "The difference when he isn't around—it's like swapping between a full-colour photograph and its negative. If you're going to be with someone, they shouldn't… *fade* you. You shouldn't have to make yourself less so that they can be more. I think—the people you love—when everything else goes to shit, they should be a safe place…" She bit her lip. "I'm probably not saying this right."

"No." Sabrina had to clear her throat, hard. "You said it exactly right. You usually do. But maybe we should leave it there, for tonight." With her free hand, she held the sides of her coat together at her throat. "I'm over the moon for you both. I'm also cold, and cake and a very comfy bed await."

Freddy was still frowning, but Sabrina heard a door open and her sister's attention was dragged sideways. Griff spoke in a low voice. Freddy rolled her eyes at him, but a reluctant giggle escaped.

Sabrina found herself smiling again. Affection was a warm balm inside her. "You glow," she said, and Freddy instinctively touched a hand to her hair and leaned forward to see herself in the smaller box on her screen. "Not literally, egghead, but since you've met Griff, you're just lit up." She felt her smile twist, lifting at one corner. It was a mannerism she'd inherited from her father; she was reminded of him even as she did it. "Note taken. Avoid the light-faders. If they don't make you glow, let it go."

"Hear, hear. That sounds like a mantra from a wanky yoga class, but I'm in favour."

Making a face, Sabrina tucked back a loose curl she could see sticking out from her head in the corner of the screen. "It did, didn't it? Christ."

"Mmm. You're very Notting Hill sometimes."

"Excuse me. Who also lives in Notting Hill? Could it possibly be the future Lady of the Manor?"

"Be fair," Freddy said. "Griff's manor house is practically falling down. His father sneezed the other day and one of the chimneys fell off. It's more like Fawlty Towers than Downton Abbey. I don't think anyone's expecting me to pull out the tweeds and corgis once we tie the knot."

"I suppose if you'd fancied playing a society princess, you'd have auditioned for *The Velvet Room*." Sabrina cleared her throat. "Speaking of which—"

"They've cast the She-Devil of Soho. I heard." Freddy grimaced. "Half the people on the West End must be gluttons for punishment. Sadie Foster front of house is very different to Sadie backstage, so I *sort of* get why she has a fan following, but if you've actually worked with her for more than two minutes—who the hell would contract her again? Is she still shacked up with Lionel Grimes?"

"Snuggling and cooing all over London town, apparently." Sabrina groaned. "Tune in later this month for *WMUL*, the reunion episode: me, Nick, and Sadie, together again on one couch."

Her sister said something that would have every society princess in earshot clutching at her pearls. Freddy chewed on her lower lip. "Drop them and interview my *Anathorn* crowd instead?"

"If I were in charge of booking, I'd have you in a heartbeat."

"Jesus." Freddy sounded just like Griff, then. "Not exactly smooth sailing, is it, salvaging *Wake Me Up London*? Good thing you enjoy a challenge."

Sabrina did, however, have her limits; and apparently the universe was going to test them every step of the way. After blowing Freddy a kiss and ending the call, she stepped back into the reception hall and was immediately met with a query about Nick. A week-long professional partnership, and they seemed to have become permanently linked in people's minds. All night, she'd been asked casually about his food preferences, whether he drank, which way he leaned politically, if he knew such-and-such person, even what his holiday plans were, as if she were a walking Nick Davenport almanac.

"No," she said politely to the frowning groomsman, drawing on every gene she'd inherited from centuries of actor ancestors. "I'm afraid I don't know where he is. I haven't seen him for a while."

"He was giving me a hand, looking for the champagne jeroboam for the send-off. If you find him, tell him one of the bridesmaids tracked it down, would you mind?"

It was easiest to just agree, and she received a cheerful hair-ruffle for her trouble that made her feel simultaneously six years old and like his maiden aunt.

Most of the wedding party and the majority of the guests were in their twenties, and by this point in the night, absolutely trolleyed. Sabrina ducked neatly under an out-flung arm as an enthusiastic dancer lost his balance and spun himself into a heap of laughter.

Tragically, approximately one day after her thirtieth birthday, she'd lost the ability to party for multiple nights in a row with no aftereffects. She was still feeling the wines she'd had last night at the ball, and she'd switched to sparkling water after the one spilled glass of rosé.

And was now fairly desperate to find the loo. Returning the deliriously happy bride's hug as she squeezed past, she escaped into the quiet coolness of the atrium outside. The resort was built like a rabbit's warren, corridors winding off in all directions.

Even the bathrooms were like something out of Ver-

sailles, and she reapplied her lipstick in an ornate mirror that could have hung in the V&A. Despite the lure
of lemon drizzle cake, she felt strangely restless and
reluctant to return to the hall straight away. Her fingertips trailing along the carved walls, she walked idly
around the ground floor. It had been such a rush flying
in and getting to the resort on time that she hadn't seen
much beyond the event rooms, and when she'd been
here five years ago, she'd spent most of that weekend
in a suite.

Her attention caught by twinkling lights through a
window, Sabrina cupped her hand against the frosty
glass and peered out, then exclaimed softly with pleasure. At the end of a snow-dusted path was a little
wooden door that could have come straight out of her
favourite childhood storybook, Christmas lights draped
over it in a festive arch.

Without thinking, she found the nearest exit and followed the path through the crisp night, her heels loud
on the slippery bricks.

Call it journalistic instincts, not sheer nosiness.

She admired the stonework on the outside of the
little building and reached for the lion's head knob on
the pixie door. Expecting it to be locked, she twisted
it and pulled hard, and lost her balance when the door
swung open with ease. Trying to regain her footing,
she stumbled forward a few steps.

"Don't shut the—!"

The heavy door hit her on its return swing, pushing
her the remaining step into the room beyond. It thun-
ked back into place with an ominous clicking sound.

Inside the surprisingly well-lit space, Nick caught

himself in his lunge towards her. His bossy command ended in abrupt silence.

They stood staring at one another, before Sabrina turned and put her hand on the door. The lovely antique door, which had no handle on the inside.

The only knob in the room was standing behind her, scowling.

With her shoulder, and not much hope, she shoved against the wood, and yielded the expected result of nothing. Not even a creak.

"Unless you think I've been sitting in here for over an hour for fun," Nick said, "infer correctly that the door locks and doesn't open from this side."

Her grandmother's melodramatic gene tended to out itself during moments of crisis. Flattening both hands on the door panels, Sabrina leaned forward with one cathartic thump of her forehead and a silent rail at whichever higher being was gleefully fucking with her.

"What's the point in the lock working this way round?" she asked the universe, and it responded very wryly in Nick's voice.

"Trapping unsuspecting, would-be thieves? Used to be a cell? Or, on current form, simply because it's us? Could you hear me calling from outside?"

"No."

"Right. It is soundproof, then. Excellent."

Steeling herself, she turned. "Since the latest instalment in the *Laurel and Hardy* show won't affect ratings, I suppose we can't blame this one on our friendly local saboteur."

Nick pulled his dress jacket tighter across his wide chest and sat down on the edge of an upturned wooden barrel. He was shivering. They'd individually managed to lock themselves into a wine cellar, and it was, as her grandpa would have said, colder than a witch's tit in here.

"You do think so, too, then," he said thoughtfully, his eyes narrowing on her face.

"That somebody in the studio is having a laugh at our expense? My belief in coincidences is down to a fine thread after the vinegar fiasco." Sabrina looked around, taking stock of their surroundings. Stone walls, with wooden shelves holding dozens of wine bottles. And a cabinet for spirits. No windows and just the one door. Electric lights all over the ceiling, but no sign of a phone or an intercom. And—she pulled her phone from her bag and looked at the screen—no service.

Brilliant.

She looked at a rickety bench set against one wall, then closed her eyes briefly, put down her bag, and drew off her coat. Arranging the skirt of her dress, she sat down on the barrel next to Nick, and spread the coat over both their shoulders. If he'd been in here for over an hour already, in just that thin jacket and shirt, he was probably hurtling his way into hypothermia. She had no desire to be trapped with a corpse.

He jerked in surprise and tried to push the coat back towards her. "I'm not taking your coat." He sounded genuinely offended. "Put it back on before you freeze."

"I've got my jacket, too, and the coat's still keeping me warm—"-*ish* "—like this. Your teeth are chattering. It'll be a waste of money if your veneers fall out. Take your half and hope none of your bits fall off from frostbite."

There was another loaded beat of silence, before he exhaled audibly and pulled about 30 percent of the coat around his neck. With an efficient movement, he tucked the rest tighter about her. "Thank you." Like the air circulating around her feet, his tone was cool. "And I don't have veneers."

She crossed her legs and energetically wiggled one cold foot. Her woolly slippers wouldn't have been the best look with her dress, but right now she'd cry for comfort over style. On a breath that puffed into a visible cloud, she muttered, "You *would* just be born with teeth like that."

Nick shifted on the barrel, the side of his body pressing into hers as he swivelled his butt about. Under the knot of curls at the base of her neck, Sabrina could feel tiny baby hairs standing up; she ran her fingers lightly over the skin there, and shivered.

"You have a pretty perfect smile yourself, Sparks."

That had cost thousands of pounds and years of uncomfortable orthodontia.

Before she could blink over his unexpected, unemotional response, he went on, murmuring in that silken voice, "Once in a blue moon, when I see the real deal and not the Miss Congeniality mask."

Sabrina stopped bobbing her foot. "Oh, keep going," she said, after she'd just about bitten through her tongue. "I might get out of here yet. The gods like to punish blatant hypocrisy. A few good lightning bolts coming this way could blast me a new exit."

"Don't misunderstand me. That wasn't criticism. It was admiration. This is a tough, fickle industry, and nobody will survive without decent armour. And PR-friendly cladding over any…defects of temperament."

She took back another 5 percent of the coat.

They sat listening to the sound of each other's camera-ready, clattering teeth. The temperature was dropping further, and seemingly instinctively, they pushed their shoulders closer together.

"This is a celeb hot-spot and there's a major function on," Sabrina said at last. "Surely they'll be coming back and forth from the wine cellar."

"Unless it's secondary storage." Nick spoke with a shade of grimness. "Or intended for aesthetics rather than function."

"But you came out here looking for the champagne jeroboam, didn't you? Did someone not direct you?"

"No. We were asking the kitchen staff if they knew what happened to the jeroboam." Nick shifted again. "I came out here because—"

Was that a trace of embarrassment in his voice?

He cleared his throat. "I saw the fairy lights through the window. And the whole setup reminded me of a book I liked when I was a kid."

For no reason, her attention had fixed on his eyelashes. They were short but very thick. His words registered. "*The Brambletons*? By Margaret Haskell?"

He was looking at her, too. A faint, non-mocking smile touched his mouth. "Yeah. It looked just like—"

"Mr. Mackleby's house." Sabrina pulled her gaze away and focused on the rack of wine bottles directly in front of her. The different-coloured glass made an interesting pattern under the lights. "That was my favourite book when I was little. My mum used to read it to me." She swallowed. Then from habit, she tried to toss her currently pinned-up hair, in a gesture of strange defiance against her own thoughts. "I read it to my goddaughter now."

Nick was still watching her. She could feel it against her skin. "I read it to my niece."

The ceiling lights were starkly bright, presumably so people could see the labels on the bottles and not accidentally serve up a priceless vintage to someone who'd paid for five-pound plonk—or whatever this resort considered a cheap bottle, which was probably about fifty quid. Despite the quaintness of the interior, there was nothing intimate about the setting. And yet, when she would usually desire to know as few personal details about Nick's life as possible, she found herself asking, "How many brothers and sisters do you have?"

With a movement that looked distracted and almost automatic, he caught the edge of the coat that had just slipped off her knee and pulled it back across to cover her. "I have a stepbrother. Although I think of him as a brother, plain and simple." When she glanced at him, he'd also moved his gaze to the wine bottles. "Iain. He's eight years older than I am, was a Michelin-starred chef in a former existence, now bakes some of the most expensive cakes in the country, and is the grumpiest bastard you'll ever meet."

Despite the less than flattering summary, there was nothing but fondness in the words.

"Grumpier than Griff?" Sabrina asked deliberately, and felt Nick's body stiffen on his next breath.

"Iain occasionally makes Griff seem garrulous by comparison." From beneath the coat, she heard a jangling noise, as if his hand had closed down on something in his pocket, keys or coins. A frown flickered over his expression, and he added with a total lack of enthusiasm, "He'd like half of you."

"*Half* of me?" Sabrina repeated, and looked down at herself. "What, is he a leg man or something?"

"Metaphorically speaking." Nick also glanced down at what was visible of her legs. "He'd appreciate your temper. He'd have less time for the flirt side."

He seemed to find that last observation cheering; a small smile appeared.

Sabrina debated whether to respond to that, but she was too cold to muster indignation over a basically accurate description. She did have a quick-burning temper, and she was a flirt.

At least no one could say she was in denial.

About that.

"And he has a daughter?"

"Pippi. She's eight." It was like when Nick had spoken of his mother; his entire demeanour transformed as his mind went to his niece. Genuine warmth broke through, and Sabrina found that she couldn't look away. "And smart as a whip. Iain used to have her two days a week, but her mother died last year, so she lives with him full-time now. If he's away working an event, she stays with my mother and stepfather. She's coming to the studio on Tuesday morning for a school thing."

"Her mother died? I'm sorry. The poor girl."

She hadn't meant to let anything personal into her tone, but Nick's expression changed. "She seems to be doing all right, but they were close." He appeared to weigh his words. "I know your mother died when you were young, as well. You can't have been much older than Pippi?"

"I was ten." Sabrina stared blindly at the bottles. The light was playing off a blue one, creating a shimmering effect that reminded her of water glinting in a puddle. "Almost ten. It was a week before my birthday."

"An accident?"

She could hear the rhythmic sound of Nick's breathing in the stillness. It was...*too* comforting.

"Yes." More curt than she'd intended. Her tone effectively distanced them, whacking a few bricks back into place in the wall between them.

She felt jumpy, as if the slightest movement, the merest rustle of fabric or a single drop of water falling from the pipe that ran around the ceiling, would result in something changing.

Then Sabrina shivered, hard, compulsively; and something in Nick did seem to snap. He stood up in a movement that was nothing like his usual fluid grace. "This is ridiculous. We can't just sit here all night and slowly frost over. Plan A."

He was at the door in a few strides. After contemplating it from corner to corner, he took three steps back, then slammed his foot into it.

The result was an extremely loud noise. From Nick.

Sabrina looked from him to the door. "Very Jason Bourne," she said, with polite admiration.

"Thank you."

"How badly did you hurt yourself?"

Nick was inspecting his foot in its shiny leather dress shoe. "I may have one or two bones still intact."

She pulled the coat higher around her neck. "Not that I don't appreciate the effort, but if we've established that the door can't be toppled with sheer masculinity, what's plan B?"

He lifted his head and inclined it towards the cabinet of spirits. "A medicinal drink. What do you fancy?"

"I'm not sure alcohol actually wards off a chill—" Oh, to hell with it. She stood up and joined Nick at a rack. "We can't just steal the resort's spirits."

"I'll reimburse them." Nick pulled out two bottles and studied the labels. "And by universal law, the moment you do anything you shouldn't, somebody walks in. I give it ten minutes of cracking a bottle before we're back indoors. Vodka or whisky?"

"Vodka," Sabrina said, and he handed her one of the bottles.

Resuming his seat beside her on the barrel, he unscrewed the whisky and looked at her.

"To the happy couple," he said drily, and with a resigned sigh, she clinked her bottle against his and took a cautious sip.

"It was a beautiful wedding." With her thumb over the top to prevent spillage, she twirled the bottle back and forth against her knee. "I'm glad it all came off well for them. With the minor exception of guests locking themselves in an outbuilding and committing grand theft liquor."

Nick leaned his head back against the stone wall and closed his eyes. "They picked a good location. I'd like to see more of the resort. Ideally, the heated parts. Assuming that we will make our return flights tomorrow, and the staff don't eventually open the door in a couple of decades to discover a roomful of empty bottles and a pair of middle-aged alcoholics, maybe I'll come back sometime."

"I've been here before," Sabrina said, to her immediate regret.

"Skiing holiday?"

"Of sorts." She couldn't stop her nose from wrinkling, and took refuge in another mouthful of vodka. "I came a few years ago with Ferren."

She had time to uncross and recross her legs, and painstakingly peel off a corner of the label on her bottle, before Nick's lengthy response of "Ah."

For a solid twenty minutes, they sat in a wordless atmosphere that made Sabrina's toes curl in her shoes, and stared expectantly at the door. They broke the monotony halfway in by trading liquor bottles. The night had already taken a swift downward turn; she might as well mix spirits.

When Nick's promised staff member failed to burst in and bust them, Sabrina couldn't sit still any longer. She *was* feeling less cold. She was also starting to feel detached from her own legs. Even her nose felt a bit like putty, when she put up a questing hand. If she kept downing whisky to avoid looking at, talking to, or thinking about the man brooding next to her, things were going to go from muzzy-headed to completely rat-arsed.

Hooking her handbag closer with the pointed tip of her shoe, she opened it and dug inside. Thankfully, she'd been running so late before the ceremony she hadn't had time to unpack everything from the flight, so she had both her main sources of stress relief to hand.

Nick had been sitting with one knee propped up, the vodka bottle idly dangling from his long fingers, but he set it down she pulled out a half-knitted hat and a half-eaten block of chocolate.

Calmly, Sabrina broke off a square of chocolate and put it in her mouth, then passed him the remainder of the bar and picked up her knitting. The familiar click-clack of the needles was an instant soother, although she'd dropped a stitch on the plane. She held the hat up to the light.

Nick, who'd automatically taken the chocolate from her hand, looked down at it, then with slow deliberation, his gaze moved back to her knitting. The look on his face was the most fun she'd had since the Mr. Mackleby door had hit her on the arse and trapped her here.

He opened his mouth, closed it, shook his head, and snapped off a piece of chocolate.

"Do you usually take knitting to a wedding?" he asked after a time, sitting up and looking around.

"No. I always take knitting on a plane. I didn't have time to switch my stuff over to my evening bag." Sabrina didn't raise her eyes from her needles. "What are you looking for?"

"A rag. I don't want to get chocolate everywhere." Nick held one hand away from his clothing and her coat.

Tucking her tongue between her teeth, Sabrina carefully unpicked a stitch. "Use your pocket square."

She might as well have suggested he strip naked and use the rest of the chocolate as body paint. He couldn't have looked much more appalled.

Rolling her eyes, she rummaged one hand back into her bag and held a tissue in his direction.

Nick wiped his fingers clean and raised his eyebrows. "You're making Mary Poppins look like a light packer. You don't happen to have a chainsaw or a battering ram in there, I suppose?"

"I have a bottle of diet Coke and about six rolls of Polo mints." She made a little humming sound in her

throat. "You once did a show about makeshift survival manoeuvres. I recall a really fit soldier rigging
an explosive device with sweets and a can of lemonade. If you want to have a shot at blowing the door off
its hinges, knock yourself out."

"Why do I think you mean that literally?" He looked
torn between bemusement and reluctant amusement as
he studied her from head to busy hands. "This would
be a turn-up for the gossip pages. Sabrina Carlton, permanent resident of the London party scene, knitting
scarves like a little old lady."

"As usual," Sabrina said, "Nick Davenport, fellow
frequenter of the clubs, talking utter shite. I've been
knitting since I was seven, and if you'd like to expand
your mind a little, you'll find that loads of people of
all ages enjoy it. Including a lot of men. And if you'd
like to use your *eyes*, it's quite obviously a hat. You
pretentious fuckhead." That last, in the nicest tone she
could muster.

"A *lot* of men?" The scepticism was clear.

"Thousands of them. You ought to try it yourself.
It's an excellent stress outlet, and would leave you with
less time for treacherous wanker acts. A win-win. I've
got spare needles and wool in my bag." She laced her
next words with blatant provocation. "But it does take
some skill, and we all know you don't react well to
failure."

"I may be competitive, Sparks, but I grew out of
dares twenty years ago." Said the man who'd been successfully goaded into his current job in approximately
three minutes. Nick got up and did a few restless turns
of the room. Rubbing his hands together, he blew on
his palms.

Sabrina could feel his attention still on her. It was probably a combination of the booze and boredom, but he seemed, despite himself, quite fascinated with her emerging hat.

Leaning against the wall, he pushed his hands into his pockets. "Is it difficult for you?" he asked suddenly, watching the movements of her fingers. "Being back here…after the way things went with Ferren." There was a fractional hitch in the rhythm of that sentence, before he said Ferren's name. She had a strong feeling he'd been going to call her ex something else, unlikely to be flattering.

"Not especially." Sabrina kept knitting. "You've never liked Ferren, have you?"

It was so quiet that the scrape of his shoe sole on the stones was unnaturally loud.

"I can't say I'd queue up to see his films." All very aloof. "And he wasn't high on my list of favourite interviews, but he has his…decent points."

"In other words, you think he's a prick."

"Oh, I think he's an absolute twat." The glimmer of a smile put an indentation in his lean cheek, but it retreated into seriousness as their eyes met. "Are you—" Immediately, he cut himself off. A muscle pulsed near his mouth.

She knew, with absolute certainty, what he'd been going to ask. The broadcaster gene coming out, the instinct to pry for intel. It was none of his business, but she found herself answering. Slowly, her hands stilling, she said, "A few years ago, an old friend of mine was killed in a plane crash. We'd been close since school days and saw a lot of each other in London. The night that it happened, her brother rang to tell me. It had been a long, awful day already, and it was such a... knock-out blow, out of nowhere, I didn't know what to do. I needed someone... I needed help. And without even thinking about it, I left my flat and went to my best friends'." She bit down on the inside of her cheek. "That whole, long night, it didn't even occur to me to ring Ferren. I *bone-deep* needed comfort, and I didn't go to him."

Setting down her knitting, Sabrina pulled her knees up. "After everything ended between us for good, I kept thinking about that." She traced the label of the whisky bottle with her thumbnail. "And I think...it says quite a lot."

She listened to her breaths, and his.

"I think it says it all." Nick was very still, his head resting back against the wall, but something in his voice made her stomach do a curious flip. He hesitated, then continued in a slightly rough tone, "About eight months after Tia and I married, her father died suddenly. He'd raised her as a single parent. She was devastated. Three weeks before it happened, she'd unexpectedly run into Tosh again. They'd gone out together in their teens and split over some misunderstanding at uni. When Bill died—it was Tosh that Tia wanted."

Sabrina couldn't decipher a single emotion in his face. They might have been doing a *WMUL* debrief, talking about the lives of strangers rather than his own past.

"Did you love her?" She asked the question he'd skirted around with her. She hadn't intended to, but it came out baldly.

Nick was equally blunt in his answer. "I love her

to bits. If you mean was I *in* love with her—I thought I was, once. But I didn't know what that could really mean until I saw Tia's face when she was tearing herself apart wanting to go to Tosh and feeling that she couldn't. What we'd had, even at our best point, was a weak shadow of what they'd lost and could obviously have again. We both grieved. For Bill, and for the end of one route our lives could have taken. But in the separation—it never felt like I was losing something. It always felt like we were putting things right." He shot her an ironic glance. "She didn't break my heart, you'll no doubt be disappointed to know."

A handful of sentences that had come from deep within them both, leaving Sabrina, at least, feeling exposed, and the previously stark, cold atmosphere of the room now very definitely intimate.

Perhaps Nick echoed her growing discomfort, because he bent and caught the neck of the vodka bottle between two fingers. As he unscrewed the lid, he said, "I think, before Tia and Tosh: The Sequel happened, she would have said the third party in our marriage was my job." He took a swig of vodka, grimacing as he swallowed. "My...ambition."

"What a shocker," Sabrina muttered.

Ambition: like the booze they'd consumed, it was all good in moderation and the road to ruin in excess.

With some misgiving, she eyed the whisky she'd just sipped. She had a feeling they could blame these two bottles for this entire heart-to-heart.

She had another mouthful, anyway.

"Oh, hell." Nick dropped the vodka back to the ground. "Give us the spare needles, then."

The startled laugh that broke from her throat sounded distinctly tipsy even to her own ears. "What?"

"My flight home is in—" Nick checked his watch. "Twelve hours. I can't just stand here knocking back neat spirits all night. Let's have some of this hyped-up stress relief. Bring on the knitting lesson."

"You're serious?" She definitely hadn't been. He sat down and held out his hand, snapping his fingers, and she met the glint in his eyes. "All right. We know you can't bake. Let's see if you can do *something* with your hands."

His mouth lifted, but he let the obvious opportunity and several possible punchlines go.

Sabrina fished out her spare needles and a ball of grey wool, made a slip knot, and cast on the first few stitches before she passed them over. Hands over his, with a lack of hesitation that was totally fuelled by the alcohol, she guided his fingers as she explained basic garter stitch.

His warm breath touched her cold cheek when he leaned in to see better. She was clumsier than usual, and she resolutely refused to look at him after one piercing glance that tried to catch and keep hold of her, but she managed to get him going.

In more ways than one, I think, taunted a terrible little voice in her head—or less cerebral regions—when her thumb slid along Nick's wrist as she drew her hand back, and a jolt went through his body.

His jaw was taut enough to crack walnuts, and that reaction hadn't been due to the chilled temperature of the room.

Sabrina tried to lose herself in her own knitting, reaching over occasionally to correct his technique—

careful not to touch his skin again—but her mind felt misty at the edges and her body felt conversely on edge.

In a flustered attempt to break the tension, she blurted out the first thing that came to mind. "Freddy and Griff are engaged."

She immediately kicked herself. She didn't know if that was meant for public knowledge yet, and she'd just casually informed the town crier. "She just told me tonight and I don't know if they've announced it. I realise it'll go against the grain, but could you keep that to yourself, please?" She'd spoken without any particular emphasis, but Nick's shoulders tensed. "And there's no point having a defensive strop. You have form."

His needles were clacking very aggressively.

He spoke, however, very evenly. "No one will hear about it from me. I'm happy for them. Still a bit surprised—if you'd asked me at the beginning of the year, I'd have given higher odds to Colonel Sanders and Ronald McDonald tying the knot than those two, but I've seen them together, and I barely recognised Griff. His eyes smile."

Such a simple way of putting it, and yet a perfect description. Sabrina slipped a look sideways through lowered lashes.

Nick's eyes definitely weren't smiling, and his mouth was grim as he concentrated on his uneven rows of stitches. "Are relations still frosty between Griff and your father?"

Since that was all tied up in the Henrietta situation, she was surprised he'd voluntarily tiptoe anywhere near the subject. Cautiously, laced with suspicion, she said, "After months of Dad trying to put the boot into Griff's film about my grandmother, and then how badly his actions have backfired on Freddy—I don't think Griff will be calling him 'Papa' any time soon, no."

Nick swore and held up his knitting. He poked at it with one finger, like a scientist inspecting a mystery specimen. "This doesn't look right."

"You've dropped stitches. Stop prodding it like that. You'll make the hole bigger." Sabrina took it from him and started correcting where he'd gone wrong.

Which was a lot easier to do with knitting than in other areas of life.

"Awkward for Freddy?" Nick asked, a bit gruffly, as he watched what she was doing. "That Griff and Rupert don't get along?"

"Utterly loathe each other would be more accurate. But she'll cope." Sabrina kept her head down. A loose curl slipped from her now messy updo and fell forward over her cheek. At her side, Nick's elbow bumped her as he moved and then sat back again just as abruptly. "Freddy makes the best out of any situation. She'll focus on all the things that make her happy and be grateful for them, and everything else will seem minor by comparison."

"Not a bad quality to have," Nick said quietly.

"No. Pretty great quality to have." Sabrina passed him back his needles. "And Griff will no doubt be as civil as he can temperamentally manage, because he's fathoms-deep infatuated with Freddy. And my father—" Had bloody well better keep his complaints to himself.

"Your father?"

"Is apparently preoccupied with work right now, so hopefully he'll congratulate Freddy sincerely and then leave it alone." Again, Sabrina regretted every word of that the moment it left her mouth. Which part of "This is Nick Davenport, novice knitter and professional tattler" was not sticking in her brain? That worm of disquiet over her father's new business interests was wiggling again, and the absolute last thing she wanted was Nick's inner Sherlock raising his head and his magnifying glass.

She glared at the whisky.

"That probably wasn't fair," she said, after a period of experimenting whether it was possible to will yourself into stone-cold sobriety. "Dad does care about Freddy's happiness. They've always had a bond that goes beyond the theatre thing. Even when he was driving her up the wall, trying to push her career the way he wanted it to go, she was a Daddy's girl."

Nick had taken back the knitting, but just held it in one hand as he studied her. "And you?"

If there had ever been a connection between her and her father like the invisible thread between Freddy and Rupert, it had long ago dwindled to a wisp.

"Not as close," she said briefly, and flicked him another glance. "How about you?" Belatedly, her brain engaged and a flush spread through her cheeks. "That was stupid. I'm sorry."

She didn't know anything about his father as a person, but she was aware that he'd been a political correspondent. He'd broken the Halston-Fischer scandal, the affair that had almost brought Parliament to a standstill when Sabrina had been at school. Even her own father, who was totally uninterested in politics, had followed that story with avid interest, and the journalist at the head of it had scooped multiple awards and accolades.

She also remembered that Markus Davenport had passed away some years ago.

Nick shook his head. His face was expressionless. "It's all right." He'd knocked a few grey loops off his needle.

Without thinking, Sabrina reached out to smooth them back on. His hand twitched under her touch. "You're following in his footsteps."

It was like watching a new wall come down, literally as if a shade were closing in his eyes.

He didn't reply, but his mouth twisted.

After a while, he held up the knitting again, surveying it with the serious resolve of a climber standing at the foot of Everest. Sabrina tried to resume her own, but as time passed and whisky softened the edges of her thoughts, her eyes grew heavy. She listened to the familiar clicking sounds, exhaustion creeping up her spine and washing through her body. Her own needles hung precariously from her loose grip, and her head started to droop to the side.

Her mind was a drifting cloud.

Eyes half closed, she jerked upright for the sixth time in as many minutes, away from the firm pillow beneath her cheek, which shifted and breathed.

"Go to sleep, Sparks." A deep voice, winding around her like warm, satiny ribbons. "Everything's okay."

Two fingertips pressed oh-so-lightly against her cheekbone, and she swayed, so easily he might have yanked rather than nudged. Her cheek came back to rest against a broad shoulder. It wasn't much softer than the stone. She rubbed against it, eyes trying and failing to flutter back open. Warmer than stone. And it smelled good. Sabrina breathed in deeply, and was asleep before she could exhale.

She half-woke several times, shivering and trying to get closer to the warmth beside her. Then against her, under her. Her nose pressed into a cosy curve. Prickly skin. Arms around her. Hug. Nice.

Consciousness returned with gentle languor. Sabrina opened her eyes slowly, blindly, then closed them again. Winding her arms tighter, she inhaled the scents of sleepy man and crisp morning. So good. When she moved, stubble rubbed against her brow.

Dreamily, she let her fingers wander. He was wearing a lot of clothes. Her fingertips traced down the sculpted lines of his throat as he stirred, feeling as he swallowed. His hand moved on her back, stroking down her hip to the curve of her thigh.

As she mindlessly pressed her lips to his neck, he pushed his fingers into her hair and nuzzled her head with a murmuring sound, a low rumble in his chest. Arching, a sinuous, satisfying stretch against him, like a cat waking up from a nap, Sabrina trailed kisses along his jaw, and he brought her hand to his lips. A gentle, sensual nip at her fingers, before he lowered his head.

Her eyes were still closed when their mouths brushed. One of them kissed, the other kissed back, she barely knew who was who right now. It was all so natural, so instinctive, but drowsy affection flared into lust, so rapidly it made her breath catch, a shaken noise against his mouth as he coaxed hers open with teasing darts of his tongue. Sabrina's stiff, chilled body was dissolving into tingling heat. Gripping his neck, she pulled herself closer, her tongue meeting his. He was so…silky. And demanding. Arousal was a dark, heavy thrum, beating in time with her pulse, sliding through her limbs.

They were both making noises now, little urgent hitches. He lifted her to straddle him, and she pushed her pelvis into his, rolling her hips to grind against his erection. His hands slipped down her back, his fingers compulsively gripping the flesh of her bottom.

Her teeth closed over his bottom lip.

"Er...*bonjour.*"

Faint and mortified, the voice came from behind her, and Sabrina lifted her head and turned to meet the astonished stare of a woman dressed in the stylish uniform of the resort staff.

For three breaths, she just stared, dazedly, her hands still holding on to muscular shoulders, and then—ice-cold awareness. It was like an electric current shocking through her body, and below her, Nick—*oh my God, Nick*—was absolutely rigid.

Very, very rigid.

Sabrina's neck muscles pulled painfully as she looked back down at him. In his eyes, she saw a mirrored return of consciousness and sobriety, and a dawning, mutual, "*Holy fuck.*"

His hands detached from her arse as if he'd been zapped with a cattle prod.

He snapped upward and managed to get to his feet in one swift movement; however, with Sabrina ensconced, frozen, on his lap, he ended up holding her with one arm around her waist, the other looped beneath her left thigh. And his brain was obviously still struggling back into full gear, because he just stood there, clutching her as if they were demonstrating a really ungainly tango.

"Down." Her attempt at speech was a strangled squeak, and he jolted.

"Right." He set her back on her feet, and caught her waist as her heels wobbled. "Are you—"

"I'm fine," she said tautly, her eyes on the hotel staffer, who was holding a clipboard and a phone, and looked as if shock would shortly become laughter. "Um...*bonjour.*"

As the meaning behind that registered, she looked through the open door behind the woman and saw weak winter sunlight. Which meant it was probably after eight o'clock in the morning.

She'd slept for hours...on Nick Davenport's lap. And then—

It was even colder with the breeze coming through the doorway, but her cheeks were searing hot. She couldn't look at the man at her side.

"Have you been in here all night?" The other woman had controlled her impulse to giggle, and now looked concerned as she spoke in fluent English, taking in their shivering, dishevelled appearance. "This wretched door. The inside catch is almost impossible to find if you don't know the trick."

The inside catch.

From the corner of her eye, Sabrina saw the violent clench of Nick's jaw. She fully agreed with the sentiment.

"Quickly, come back inside." The attendant ushered them outside into the morning air. The ground glinted with ice, and frost hung in the trees like lacy cobwebs. It was shockingly beautiful.

It was shocking, full stop.

The moment they stepped into the incredible

warmth of the hotel hallway, it was like a portal closing, everything that had just happened in the pixie
room taking on an even more surreal quality. They
might have returned from fucking Narnia.

Firmly assuring their hovering rescuer that they
didn't need to see a doctor, they just needed hot show-
ers and two enormous pots of tea, Sabrina walked jerkily to the lifts. The hairs on her skin were prickling, as
if his fingers were still stroking her.

They stepped into the lift, and Sabrina stared
straight ahead as the doors slid closed.

"Sabrina." His voice was rough. He pressed the button for the third floor.

"Don't." One tight word. She hit the button for level
four, swallowed, and shut her eyes. The impulse to
touch her lips was twitching at her hand. "Please."

The lift came to a smooth stop. Nick walked out
onto his floor, his face set into concrete lines. In the
tiny gap before the doors met and took her away, their
eyes locked.

That look burned through her.

Her hands were still shaking as she found her key
card in her bag and fumbled to unlock her door. Sensation—pain—was returning as she defrosted, and she
was very aware of the ache in her joints and the blis-
ters on her feet. She sat on the edge of the amazing bed
she'd never slept in and kicked off her shoes. Then she
leaned forward and put her head in her hands.

She stayed hunched over, thinking about nothing,
thinking about everything, until a knock at the door
made her jump, and she rose on unsteady legs.

It was a different attendant, with a tray of complimentary tea and pastries. She took them with grateful

thanks and a large tip, and silently blessed the poor woman who'd had to start the day with a front-row view of Sabrina basically giving Nick a lap dance. She was very thoughtful.

Unfortunately, she was also very financially savvy, and she'd been holding a smartphone.

By the time Sabrina boarded her flight that afternoon, her "raunchy hotel romp" with Nick was the headline story in *London Celebrity*.

Chapter Eight

15 Days until Christmas Eve

The drumming of Fenella's long nails on the conference table was like the ominous rhythm of the *Jaws* theme.

Tap-tap, tap-tap, tap-tap-tap-tap-tap.

"Official statements issued via respective publicists just last week. 'Personally involved? Us? The absurdity!'" their producer drawled, her eyes moving to Nick. She'd look at him for precisely five seconds before switching the judgment back to Sabrina; and repeat. For some reason, the unblinking, inscrutable stare was reminding him of a lizard. "End scene. Cut to shot of grinding and groping in a liquor store."

Nick crossed his legs at the ankles. "It was a private wine cellar." He kept his voice mild, but could feel a betraying nerve flickering at the corner of his mouth.

"Hardly private, I think. In the middle of a hotel that frequently features on the pages of *Society*." Fenella raised her eyebrows. "I don't need to ask if you're aware what's happened on social media since those photos went up yesterday. I think *explosion* is a good word."

Yes. He was well aware. He'd woken up to paparazzi outside his building, and been hit with another barrage of flashes on his way into the studio. And a load of questions that had made his teeth grit, many of them about Joe Ferren.

The prevailing theme of the coverage seemed to be "I knew it." Half the stuff his publicist had shown him told a fairy tale of a long-time secret affair, most likely conducted under Ferren's nose. Since Sabrina's ex had ego enough to fill the Atlantic, he'd probably kick off at being depicted as the short, thick end of their isosceles love triangle. On the other hand, it diverted the blame from his own, factual infidelity. The tabloid press had been quick to seize on that angle.

People were pulling out old footage from *The Davenport Report* and *Sunset Britain* as if they were hunting Easter eggs, posting clips of him or Sabrina mentioning each other—usually unflatteringly—as evidence of their hidden relationship, trying to put a timeline on it.

"As previously discussed," Fenella said, "I would have preferred the courtesy of honesty on this subject. Your private lives may be your own, but in this case, they make a walloping great impact on my show."

"We were honest." Sabrina spoke for the first time in a while.

Nick had kept his eyes away from her, with some difficulty, after an initial searching glance. Looking at her now, he could see the signs of strain on her face. Her own publicist would also have been called in to work yesterday on a Sunday, and Sabrina's instinct would have been to refute everything.

It was going to be a little difficult to pass this off

with a blank denial, given that the entirety of Britain could, with a few clicks, see them writhing on a wine barrel in high definition.

"We are not and never have been dating." Sabrina's eyes caught his, before she shoved her hands through her hair in a ruffled gesture that was unlike her. Usually, she would toss her curls and stick her already up-tilted nose higher in the air. She was such a fucking princess sometimes.

For the first time in over twenty-four hours, a smile flashed through him.

"This was just—" Once more, Sabrina—never at a loss for a snarky comment for him, or a flirtatious smile for almost anyone else—seemed flustered.

"A shit-ton of alcohol, by the look of it," Fenella supplied helpfully. Her eyes were narrowed, and knowing the way her brain worked, Nick wasn't sure he liked that assessing quality. "Or a safety measure, was it? Sharing body heat to ward off hypothermia? A bit of mouth-to-mouth resuscitation when someone succumbed?"

Without makeup, the little pinpoints of Sabrina's freckles stood out against her pale skin. A pink flush now swept over them.

Even after the broadcast exposing Ferren's "peccadilloes," as one outlet had called it—a bullshit, soft-serve term for his fucked-up behaviour—and all the fallout from her grandmother's scandal, she'd kept her head high and her attitude at level ten. If she'd broken down behind closed doors, she'd never given the press the satisfaction of showing vulnerability in public.

But right now…there was something in her eyes. A flicker of bewilderment?

Whatever it was, it reacted on Nick as if a voice inside her had called out and something rose up in him to answer. For a moment that gripped his muscles with tension, it was almost overpowering, the instinct to get up and go to her, to pull her back into his lap and his arms until that air of uncertainty became her usual provoking smile.

He was obviously too old to drink two nights in a row. The hangover had shrivelled his brain. Fenella already thought they were dragging one another into handy storage cupboards the moment they left the studio, and Sabrina would rather kneecap him than cuddle him.

"We need to decide what tack to take," Fenella said thoughtfully, reaching for her coffee. They were currently alone in the editorial room. The rest of the team were waiting outside for the telling-off from teacher to end so they could start with the planning meeting for today's show. "In terms of a statement."

"The 'tack' we'll take," Sabrina broke in emphatically, "is the truth."

Bouncing her crossed leg, Fenella sipped from her mug. "'Weddings make us drunk and horny'? That's the official public line you want to run?" She went on before Sabrina could retort. "I want to see how things gel, first. You aren't children, and you've both been around the block a time or a dozen. And you've both dated famous. You know how these things work. Some people would have had you shagging on no more evidence than a shared look. The hand-holding during the Thames fiasco got the rumour mill cranking. Dry humping on a beer keg? They'll be waiting for a summer wedding."

Ignoring their expressions, Fenella put down her coffee and inserted the end of a stylus pen between her lips. She sucked it while she plotted. "You'll look disingenuous if you deny anything right now. Half the viewers already think you're putting on an act—on which note, if you could stop falling off things, into things, out of things, and trying to poison the guests, that would be terrific. Thanks."

Sabrina glanced at Nick, her eyes meeting his squarely for the first time since they'd left France. There was a question in their guarded green depths, and very slightly, he shook his head. Until they had actual proof that someone was spreading seeds of chaos on-set, they couldn't cry poltergeist to Fenella.

"No," the producer said, decisively. "For now, maintain a dignified silence and we'll see which way the pendulum swings. Leaving people guessing, a bit of 'are they or aren't they' is always good for the ratings, and heaven knows we could use the boost."

As she left the room to summon the rest of the troops, she shot over her shoulder, "But do my blood pressure a favour and sort your shit. Either come out as a couple or stop crawling all over each other. There are more cameras than people nowadays. Privacy is obsolete. And if you do go Instagram-official, for the love of God, don't break up and make things awkward in the studio. I want this to work. As annoying as you two are, I have no desire to work with Peter King."

Sabrina sat forward and put her hand on the table. "Nick—" she said in a low voice, but the door opened again and Jess bustled inside, closely followed by a gawping Emily, who was holding their folders of notes for today's show and had obviously been reading things online, and the rest of the team.

Whatever Sabrina had been going to say, it was lost in the burst of voices, laughter, and teasing glances. She hesitated, looking at him, then shook her head, took a folder from Emily and adjusted her glasses as she started to read.

Exhaling, he opened his folder and pulled off his own glasses to rub tiredly at his eyes. Like her, he generally wore contacts, but since his day now started in the middle of the night, it was a couple of hours before he could open his eyes wide enough to put them in. It was becoming a morning ritual in the makeup room, leaning close to one mirror while Sabrina took another, alternating the days in which one of them dropped a lens on the floor.

The editorial meeting was necessarily brief, as they'd lost time due to Barrel-Gate, as Jess chirpily dubbed it. There were no excursions outside the studio today. They were interviewing the women at the centre of a school controversy, and the coup of the morning was Dexter Lester, the semi-reclusive millionaire who'd invented a stream of popular toys, including the number-one sell-out toy for this Christmas.

In the hallway afterwards, Nick lightly touched Sabrina's elbow before she could disappear into the makeup room. He waited until the crew members behind them had continued on. Several people were obviously lingering as long as possible to listen. "We need to talk," he said bluntly.

He half expected a denial, but she pulled her lower lip between her teeth and nodded, albeit reluctantly. "After the show? Where?"

"Leave before me, go out the back way, and I'll meet you round the block at The Diner. Late lunch and/or just a bucket of black coffee. My shout."

A ghost of a smile, gone in a blink. "I'm still hungover. I intend to eat a cheeseburger the size of my head and every greasy chip on the premises. You've been duly warned."

Nick stood in the hallway for a moment after she'd gone. Then he shook his head and got on with it.

After discarding a shirt that emphasized the redness of his bloodshot eyes, he came out of wardrobe semi-human, but the bright lights of the studio were uniquely calculated to punish heavy drinking. He was sleep-deprived, on edge, and he'd developed a slamming headache. Emily brought him a glass of water and a couple of paracetamol tablets without being asked. She was a huge upgrade on his last assistant, who'd sold stories about him to a women's magazine and systematically stolen his pens.

"Thanks a lot, Emily." Nick tossed back the tablets and drained the glass. "Good weekend?"

Emily pushed back a strand of dark hair that had escaped her ponytail. "Awesome." She was bobbing about like a helium balloon on a string. Jesus. Youth. It wasn't yet dawn, but he had a feeling she'd already been to the gym, returned all her emails, and probably got a head start on her taxes. She shot him a mischievous look. "Maybe not as interesting as yours."

Raising his eyebrows at her, he said mildly, "I'm sure you're well aware that there are multiple sides to every story, and it's often the least truthful one that generates the most clicks."

She returned him a respectful smile, but before she

skipped over to the doorway to greet Sabrina, he heard a distinct mutter of "Whatever, dude, I've got eyes."

Nick watched Sabrina adjusting her mic and her earpiece. As she reached around to tuck her silk blouse into the back of her skirt, her eyes met his.

Something flipped over deep in his gut.

The universe at least cut them a break professionally. For the first hour, the show went off without a hitch as they covered breaking news topics and current events, and assisted in baking a French Toast casserole. Chef Marco refused to crack a smile and kept griping under his breath, but they'd triple-checked the ingredients this time, Sabrina was keeping an eye on the oven temperature, and they'd both gingerly sneaked an early taste of the sample dish. Nothing but sugar, butter, and cinnamon. The way things had gone so far, Nick had expected anything from baking soda to petrol.

The production team ushered in Dexter Lester at a time when kids were likely to see the TV before they left on the school run. Nick could already predict a dozen complaints from parents on Twitter about promoting expensive toys that would inevitably appear in letters to Father Christmas. Although from the briefing, he gathered that half the kids in the country were already shouting like Veruca Salt for their very own— he checked the teleprompter as Lester took his seat on the couch—Wibblet.

Nick had several thoughts about the Wibblet, none of which he could express on live television in front of its inventor. However, if he couldn't quite muster raptures over a toy that looked like a furry aubergine with feet, Lester had no problem compensating. The toy magnate had an explosion of red curls and could easily share a gene pool with Sabrina, which made it even more inappropriate that he flirted with her incessantly as he banged on, justifying the extortionate price of the Wibblet. If that was how much one toy cost these days, the pitter-patter of any tiny feet in Nick's house were definitely going to be clawed and furry. Alan could be entertained for days on end with a plastic ball stuffed with peanut butter. Kids, apparently, preferred a mouldy-looking, possessed vegetable that said inane things in a deadpan voice, and leapt at them without warning.

Sadly for Casanova and his money-spinner, the thing clearly creeped the fuck out of Sabrina. It undermined Lester's attempts to chat her up.

"You have beautiful hair," smarmed the man with basically the same hair, randomly in the middle of a discussion on app development.

Over the past few years, Nick had seen Sabrina deal adeptly with flirtation, lechery, and outright harassment while cameras rolled and clicked.

"Thank you," she said calmly. "Obviously demand for the Wibblet is currently huge, and it's been sold out since last week. I believe you're expecting the next shipment to disappear from shelves almost imme—"

They'd been told that the voice-activated robot could jump a short distance, but that was quite different to seeing it in action. Whether it was her tone or a key phrase, the demonstration Wibblet chose that moment to show off its ability. It launched itself at Sabrina, smacked into her chest, and bleated, "Hug me."

She did not hug it.

Nick's earpiece was remotely connected to Sabrina's mic and he just about lost his hearing thanks to the noise she made. Over the past few days, he had also seen her deal with pests of the non-human variety— a spider had dropped on her arm from the ceiling in the green room on Friday, and everything she'd been holding at the time had taken an immediate header into the wall.

On which basis, he could have predicted the fate awaiting the Wibblet.

As her shriek hit decibels that a car alarm would envy, she grabbed the weird little fuzzball by the leg and flung it across the studio. For a person who hated sports, she had an arm on her like a pro cricketer. The Wibblet sailed into the kitchen set, knocked a glass off the bench, and finally hit the floor, where it lay amidst broken glass like the most violent crime scene in Toy Town.

Total could-hear-a-pin-drop silence.

Sabrina lifted her hands to her cheeks like the kid in *Home Alone*. Lester stared at the fallen Wibblet and stretched out a wavering arm, like an extra on *Titanic* farewelling a loved one at the dock. If he'd had a handkerchief to hand, he'd have dabbed his eyes and then waved it.

Nick lost it. Over a decade of on-screen self-possession out the window.

"I'm *so* sorry," Sabrina said to Lester, who no longer looked at all enamoured. "Oh my God, shut up, it's not funny." That last to Nick, who was laughing so hard he had to lean forward and rest a hand on the low table between the couches. Despite the automatic reprimand, a quiver shook the words, and her green eyes were alight. He'd hold up his hands with respect and concede every TV Award for the next twenty years for the way she leashed it down. She hurried to take the hopefully deceased Wibblet from Jess, who'd extracted it from the puddle of glass, and came back to apologise again. "I hope it's not broken."

If it was, the network would likely pay without a murmur, just for the mileage for the monthly blooper reel.

Lester almost snatched the toy from her. "They're designed to be very hardy," he said stiffly. "Although not intended to be catapulted across the room. It was trying to make friends."

(A) It was a ball of plastic.

(B) It had obviously been programmed with the social skills of its CEO.

Lester set the Wibblet down on the table and said, with total confidence, "Can you dance?"

The thing went nuts.

Nick had no idea what the expected response was, whether the toy usually started doing pliés or broke into a dramatic Argentine Tango, but if it was *meant* to shriek at the top of its mechanical lungs and spin in circles like a bloody Catherine wheel, he questioned the sanity of any parents who'd put one of these under the tree.

Alan occasionally lost his head and ran in mad circles around the flat; this was similar, only louder, considerably more irritating, and potentially hazardous.

Sabrina yelped in surprise when the Wibblet careened into her legs. She bent down to rub at her shin. It went for Nick next, and he was the one who had to pull out some swift footwork, dancing backwards to avoid it.

During Lester's rundown, he'd showed them how

the toy could be trained to repeat new phrases and engage in simple conversation. There were now some audible words emerging from the high-pitched bleeping, and they were not breakfast-slot friendly. This one had picked up its vocab at either a backstreet bar or an Arsenal/Chelsea match.

Three different voices were snapping commands into Nick's earpiece, nudging at his dulled headache. It was the final straw when the foul-mouthed menace hit Sabrina hard enough to make her squeak with actual pain.

Nick booted it away from her. The last the viewers at home saw of it was a purple blur flying past the cameras, and if it hadn't been broken beyond repair before, there was a good chance it was now.

A break in the cacophony in his ear, before Jess's voice— "Aaand the pair of you just murdered a Wibblet live on TV during the kiddie hour. Happy holidays, children. The therapy's on us."

The Diner was exactly what it said on the tin—a retro, American-style diner that did great pancakes and even better burgers. Sabrina picked up her tall frosted glass to drown her sorrows in a strawberry milkshake. On the bright side, having to do ridiculous stealth manoeuvres to get here unseen, like a pair of pretentious prats in a bad film, seemed to have paid off. After years of creating headlines with Ferren, she had a finely tuned paparazzi radar, and she'd put money on the place being clear for now.

Less gratifyingly, her career was devolving into an utter joke.

Across from her in the secluded booth, Nick reached for his coffee.

And she got prickles up her leg every time his foot brushed hers under the table.

The traumatised kids of Britain weren't the only ones who needed that therapy.

She set down her glass. "So, what would you like to discuss first? *WMUL* the sitcom, and what we're going to do about it? Or the photos, and the extremely upsetting fact that you've been a self-serving toad, yet I don't find you physically repulsive."

Nick had just swallowed a mouthful of coffee; he coughed several times, putting his cup down so quickly that several drops splashed across the plastic tabletop. "Wow." He reached for a napkin.

Sabrina dragged a steaming-hot chip through a puddle of tomato sauce and nibbled at the end of it. They were already on their second basket while they waited for their burgers.

"And you're still single with chat-up lines like that, Sparks? Incredible."

"I've asked you not to call me that." Smoothing back her hair, Sabrina finished her chip and went for another.

"You quite like when I call you that," Nick said in that sleek voice of his. He reached for the chip basket as well, and his fingers collided with hers.

They stilled. Then deliberately, featherlight, Sabrina grazed her nails up the length of his fingers. Beneath the fine wool of the jumper that stretched over his chest, a tiny shudder fired tension into his body. Mutual, nonsensical attraction. This was the worst year ever.

"When I call you Sparks, you tilt your head and tuck

your hair behind your ear. You do that when you're pleased about something." He'd withdrawn his hand, abandoning the chips, and there was a strained note in his voice now.

Sabrina stared at him, her heart beating a bit too fast.

"I could also point out," he added in a more normal tone, "that you have at least six nicknames for me, none of them suitable for polite conversation."

Her phone buzzing in her handbag saved her a reply. With an automatic "Excuse me," Sabrina checked it, wincing when she saw Elise's name on the screen. She already had unanswered texts from her friends, and she'd sent four calls from Freddy to voicemail, delaying the inevitable.

As Nick sat back in his seat and stretched, his movements lithe and graceful despite his broad frame, and his eyes very alert, Sabrina cleared her throat and hit Accept. "Hi."

"Hello." In one banal word, there was already a giveaway lilt to Elise's tone. "Bad time?"

Sabrina didn't pull her gaze from Nick's as he reached for his coffee again. "I'm just grabbing a bite to eat. Actually, it's good timing. There's a guy here who keeps talking to me. You know the type. Fancies himself something rotten and won't take the hint."

Nick lowered his cup long enough to pull a gruesome face at her, then quick-as-a-flash, smiled charmingly at the waitress who set a large cheeseburger in front of him.

Despite herself, Sabrina snorted.

"I see," Elise said. "I would ask you to say hello to Nick for me." Sharp as ever. "But I don't like him and

I don't feel like it. I'm guessing this is not a good time to explain what *on earth* is going on? Freddy says she spoke to you on Saturday and you barely said a word about Nick, beyond the usual 'he's here, he's a prick, hate, hate, moving swiftly on.' After which, apparently you hung up and shagged him on a wine barrel. Did you hit your head when you belly-flopped into the Thames?"

"I did not sh—" Recollecting where she was, Sabrina curtailed herself just in time. "I did not. It just… looked bad."

"It looked like soft porn. How hammered *were* you?" Elise hesitated before asking, with obvious doubt but also a thread of danger for Nick, "He didn't…take advantage or anything?"

"No," Sabrina answered with absolute finality on that point. "He wouldn't do that." Nick's moral compass wasn't exactly pointing true north in the professional field, but…sexually—and oh good God, how had this even become a thing—she didn't have so much as a flicker of a bad feeling. On the scale of Men in the TV Industry Being Sleazy Bastards—he was one of the good ones.

"No, well, it did *look* like fairly enthusiastic participation on your part, when you were hanging off his bottom lip. Forget the horseshit about the long-time secret affair, but are you going out now? Have I interrupted some cosy lunch date?"

Sabrina felt like she'd done nothing for the past twenty-four hours but answer "no" to a variation of the dating question. She added another to the stack now. "Absolutely not. We're sorting out a work issue. End of."

Chapter Nine

Increase in the ratings within forty-eight hours of Barrel-Gate: 38 percent.

Chances that Sabrina would murder Fenella before the day was out: 95 percent.

She looked down, again, at Nick's hands lightly holding hers. He was entirely respecting boundaries here; it was a very impersonal hold. But—*come on.*

"Indeed. The lost art of the compliment," the silver-haired author of the latest bestselling networking book continued enthusiastically. "Powerful in both professional and romantic connections. If you keep maintaining eye contact—"

Their producer claimed this last-minute addition to the morning line-up was down to an opening in Hendrick Betz's tour schedule. Clearly it was not at all intended to incite further social media frenzy.

"I generally bring together strangers to demonstrate the steps, but you can deepen a bond even with a colleague or friend whom you already know and like," said the man who'd obviously never watched their shows before. "Why don't you start, Mr. Davenport?

Nick lifted a brow at her in such a silky way that she picked up her fork, flicked the top bun off his burger, and ate his gherkin. He was unnaturally fond of gherkins, actually kept a jar of them in his work fridge.

Mission achieved. Visible outrage. She extracted her own gherkin and ate that, too, before he could rally.

"Upload 'O rly?' GIF here," Elise said, and, unable to flip her friend off over the phone, Sabrina subbed in a pointed noise.

"With all due respect and much love, could I maybe call you back? You know, sometime next year." She reached for her milkshake. "I've had a very stressful morning and I'm trying to self-soothe with crap."

"Food or men?" Elise made a throaty sound of her own, this one amused. "Yes, I saw part of your morning during my tea break. RIP Wibblet. I'm fucking gutted, by the way, because I was hoping to use your connections to score one. Lizzy's *obsessed*, and I can't find one anywhere. Even online, scalpers are charging more than I spent on my car. There was supposed to be a new shipment before Christmas, but there's a manufacturing delay, and the shops have waiting lists."

"Why would you even consider buying her one? They're *demonic*."

"They're irritating," Elise agreed. "But the one you beat to death was an unfortunate dud. All the posh kids at Lizzy's school have one—hence it being the only thing she's ever wanted and all she'll ever need, Mummy—and I've never seen one behave quite like that. They certainly don't usually swear like an Irish sailor."

Sabrina absently pushed her glass away again, her mind working rapidly. "Really."

When she'd ended the call, ignoring another pointed remark, she said to Nick, "Apparently the Wibblets aren't meant to act like that one did."

"They're not." Nick had eaten his whole burger already. He pushed his plate away and sat back. "I looked them up on YouTube. They do jump and they do walk around and pick up basic speech, but they don't careen about like dodgems. Lester brought in a rogue one."

"What an unfortunate coincidence," Sabrina said. "When we're trying to look like less of a put-on comedy act."

"Isn't it."

Rhythmically, she turned her fork in circles. "Are we actually thinking someone—what, tampered with the Wibblet? Or swapped out Lester's toy for one they'd programmed to go bonkers? That's next-level sabotage. And if we've picked up an archenemy with genius tech skills, I'm daunted. I'd be gone in the first scene of a superhero film." She rubbed her thumb along the fork. "If someone's messing with us this hard, it's a lot of effort to go to. Have either of us really pissed someone off enough that they'd—" She stopped. "Hmm."

Nick's full attention focused on her. It was almost palpable, when he did that. He had the knack of making whoever he spoke to feel like the only person in the room.

"Never mind," she said. "I temporarily forgot who I was talking to. That would be a definite yes."

"Most popular broadcaster five years running," Nick murmured, tauntingly. "Most people think I'm charming."

It was always a sad moment to be reminded of the world's enormous population of idiots.

"'*But it is certain I am loved of all ladies, only you excepted,*' quote I sarcastically." Sabrina held the handle of the fork between thumb and finger and swung it like a pendulum. "And I'm not sure the gentlemen are that sold on you, either. I doubt *charming* would be high on Lionel Grimes's list of adjectives."

Nick's lips compressed. Still a sore point.

"That was a one-off error of judgment."

"Hardly one-off. I'd say you're racking up a score of '*errors of judgment.*'" A bitter note cut through her instinctive response. She took a steadying breath. She'd flung a milk bottle during her final bust-up with Ferren—not at his head; she was temperamental, not homicidal—and if she got too worked up with Nick right now and tossed the remains of her milkshake, she'd probably be barred from future burgers. "What prompted that, by the way?" She asked more as a distraction than anything else, a deliberate swerve in the conversation, but curiosity suddenly stirred.

Grimes was a dick, but Nick *was* usually career-savvy to extreme levels.

He sat back. "Difference of opinion."

"How very vague and bullshit. Right up there with 'we're just friends' and 'we still care about each other very much.' In other words, 'we're shagging like rabbits,' 'we hate each other's guts and will never speak again,' and you've got dirt on Grimes."

"A friend of mine—Lainie Graham, the actress—is the founder of the Shining Lights UK children's cancer charity. I connected her with Grimes for a sponsorship and he promised ongoing support, then backed out because Sadie Foster whispered poison in his ear."

Sabrina stared at him. "You are joking." He lifted

his eyebrows. "Jesus." She actually had to take a second to process that. "He bailed on a kids' cancer charity because his girlfriend threw a sulk for…reasons. What exactly *does* the bubonic plague of the West End have against unwell children?"

"I doubt if she thought any farther than firing a shot at Lainie. Cycle of retaliation: Sadie dripped her usual bile at Lainie, it got back to Lainie's husband, who had Sadie dropped from consideration for a major production, and Sadie stonewalled the contract for the charity."

"And took a role in *The Velvet Room* instead. Interesting machinations of fate," Sabrina muttered.

She bit into her burger, wiped grease and most of her lipstick off her mouth with her napkin, and glanced down at her phone when it buzzed with a text.

It was a message from Charlie, Griff's brother, asking if she wanted a lift to the engagement drinks tomorrow evening, because he had a meeting near her building.

"Problem?"

She continued looking at the screen after Nick's coolly voiced question; then she tapped out a yes and thanks to Charlie, and lifted her head. "Charlie. Kindly offering me a lift to the family celebration tomorrow night for the engagement."

"You're pleased about the engagement," Nick said, watching her, "so why don't you want to go? Your father?"

His producer on *The Davenport Report* must have loved his habit of perpetually hitting bullseyes. Sabrina did not. Yet she found herself answering. "It's working out the way it should for Freddy, with Dad. I think

they'll end up close again, now that he doesn't play a professional role in her life. I sincerely hope they do. In my case…"

She stared at the burger on her plate, her appetite gone. "Things haven't been good between us for a long time. For about five seconds, after the truth came out about Henrietta, I thought it might be the beginning of—" She shook her head, fiddling with her fork. "But it seems to have got worse. There's just simmering resentment, on both sides, and I don't want it to affect Freddy. Especially now, when this is such a happy time for her."

She hadn't been looking at Nick, had just been very aware of his tense stillness as soon as she mentioned her grandmother, but she raised her head now. "You know, I'm surprised, in a way, that you resorted to those tactics with the plagiarism scandal. I'd have said you backed yourself strongly where your career is concerned. Even before that underhanded fuck-up, you were confident you'd come out on top with the new evening contract."

An Elvis song was playing on the jukebox in the corner, and people around them were laughing, but in their booth the air was oppressive. "A Little Less Conversation" might prove to be wise advice, but if they were going to pull themselves out of the mud where *WMUL* was concerned, they had to get to a point where they could at least talk to each other without someone risking strangulation with a mic cord.

Nick was scrutinising her with the exact same degree of calculation and a similar air of treading carefully. "If I set a goal, I achieve it. Usually. But I would say the same thing about you. And I wasn't taking it

for granted that I would get that contract." His eyes kept her in a firm grip. "Put it this way—I rate myself high enough to recognise a fairly deadly opponent."

"So, it was coming down to the wire, the race was a little too close for comfort, and then along sashays Sadie with her cup of poison. And it drops right into your lap. A chance to publicly discredit me and sweep me out of your way."

"No." There was no hesitation before he spoke now. "I saw a massive story that was about to break, and I swiped it out from under you. Everything happened extremely quickly that day and I didn't stop to consider all the possible consequences. It was made clear to me by my producer that with Sadie bubbling over with gossip, it was coming out anyway, and it was a choice of run with the lead or drop the ball. I made a choice that I regretted the moment I did it, but can you honestly say that had the situation been reversed, you wouldn't have been tempted to follow the same course?"

They were locked in a weird, prickly bubble. If someone so much as breathed loudly near them right now, Sabrina would probably jump out of her skin.

"Yes," she said. "Tempted, yes. I wouldn't have done it, though. Not in those circumstances. Not when it closely involved one of my friends. Not on his property. Not to the woman he was obviously falling for. There has to be a line."

Nick made a little jerking gesture with his head and mouth. "I'm not arguing."

A knife-sharp edge sliced through her difficult composure. "And I sure as hell wouldn't have stood in front of a camera and—with no evidence whatsoever, because it was total *bullshit*—told the whole country

that you'd willingly participated in the deception and knowingly spent dirty money. And that your sister was likewise complicit. You're lucky I didn't sue you for fucking libel."

His eyes flashed, and he'd sat forward before she'd finished speaking. "And *now* I'm arguing. I didn't so much as mention your name that night, nor did I point a finger at Freddy."

Words of disbelief rose to Sabrina's tongue, but his look was so steady that she remained silent, watching him narrowly.

"I didn't," Nick said pointedly, "even chuck your father's name into the mix, although in his case, the mud clearly splattered at an accurate target." She clenched her jaw, and he wisely didn't pursue that path. "It was Sadie Foster who used my report as a springboard and whispered in tabloid ears. Did you actually watch back the broadcast?"

"I saw plenty of clips, in the multitude of stories that picked up the report and ran with it straight into the realms of criminal fraud. That was enough." And those clips had made her furious, absolutely; but they'd also made her feel sick. She hadn't wanted to examine the breadth of feeling that had twisted her gut into knots that night, and she balked at any lurking implications now.

Nick was forging on with his customary ruthlessness. "I reported the facts as far as we'd been able to verify them, the suggestion that it wasn't Henrietta Carlton's hand that penned *The Velvet Room*. Which was like igniting a firestorm of rumour and innuendo; it enabled Sadie to turn the knife and point a finger at you—probably because you didn't give her the satis-

faction she wanted when she threw Ferren's infidelity in your face—and I have admitted and do admit that I'm culpable for that." They were both breathing too quickly. "And I'm truly, genuinely sorry for that."

Loud noise still coming in bursts and waves around the diner; sudden silence in their small corner.

Sabrina ran her hand over her forehead and across her eyes. She needed a second alone, away from his steady regard.

Dropping both hands into her lap, she nodded, just fractionally.

"I'm not playing Fenella's game and dancing around the press reports about us," she said to the salt shaker on the table. "We're not together. We say we're not together. I'm raising a glass tomorrow night to Freddy and Griff and everything that's between them. It's real and it's genuine, and it's not something to…parody, even for the sake of the ratings."

Something flashed in the depths of his eyes, sharp and somehow a stab in her own chest, before he tipped his head. "Consider a second denial issued. Although it would be naïve to think we can wave a magic wand and vanquish all speculation." His lips twisted. "However false."

That was proved true within five minutes, when Sabrina pushed open the door of The Diner and stepped out into a freezing-cold street and the clicking of long-barrelled cameras. Someone had tipped off the paparazzi. The questions started immediately, the teasing comments, the crueller provocation, every tool they had in their arsenal to get a better headline.

Already feeling raw and exposed, she was slow, too slow, to put on the right face, the appropriate ex-

You're looking into Ms. Carlton's eyes, that silent signal of 'I see you, I'm interested in you,' establishing a rapport..."

Retribution, Fenella. Swift and bloody.

Nick's eyes were signalling something, all right, and it was not creating a rapport.

She curled two fingers, digging her nails into his palm, and the sudden lurking laughter in his face deepened.

"And express the first genuine compliment that occurs."

Nick's lashes lowered as he, too, glanced at their linked hands.

Raising their clasped palms as if he were about to declare his love in a cheesy old film—he was such a cock—he said, with great kindness, "You have very nicely shaped nails."

Another of her nicely shaped nails pinched into the base of his thumb.

"Well," Hendrick said, blinking but determinedly positive, "that's a good start. Ms. Carlton?"

"Please, call me Sabrina," she said for the third time, without looking away from Nick. She tilted her head at her obnoxiously amused rumoured lover. "You've got such a strong work ethic."

His fingers flexed on hers.

Hendrick beamed encouragingly. "And—" He turned towards Nick, who'd already opened his mouth.

"You have very spectacular hair." Suspiciously bland. "It somehow seems to fit with your personality."

She was currently experiencing a bad hair day of truly epic proportions. Every so often, she emerged from the shower and her curls decided to explode into a ball of frizz. The show's stylist had given up this morning and tried to just plait it, but Sabrina kept catching a glimpse of herself on the monitors and random corkscrews were leaping for freedom in all directions. It looked an absolute mess, and she expected multiple people to point that out on social media.

And again, *total* cock.

"I really admire your self-belief and your tenacity." She stopped short of batting her eyelashes at him like one of the fawning fangirls who flocked around him at events. Her stomach became queasy very easily at this hour of the morning. "Even in the face of overwhelming evidence otherwise, you persist in seeing the best."

He laughed aloud. Sabrina wasn't expecting it, somehow; nor was she expecting the reciprocal bubble of amusement that suddenly fizzed in her chest. His real smile came out when he laughed, throwing creases into his cheeks and warmth into his eyes.

He was still smiling a little when he looked at her again, but something else came into his expression then, something that made her instinctively curl her fingers around his. "You're...a catalyst."

She wrinkled her nose. She could just imagine where this was going.

"People come into your orbit and you bring out the best in them." There was an odd note in Nick's voice, as if he were speaking almost against his will. "You make people feel good about themselves." Little upward-tilted lines appeared at the corners of his eyes. "Present company excepted." Slowly, he added, "You make people want to be...better. Happier. You strike a match. Ignite positive change." His smile now was faint and fleeting. "Sparks."

Only semi-conscious of what she was doing, Sabrina released his hand and moved hers to her throat, covering the pulse point that felt as if it was visibly racing.

If this were radio, they'd be having serious dead air. Her mouth felt too weird and woolly to speak. As it was, people in thousands of living rooms around the nation could watch Nick slide into inscrutability after a handful of words that had turned her body into a kaleidoscope of butterflies, while she sat blinking at him.

"Sorry to interrupt," Fenella said into her earpiece, "but are the British viewing public getting in the way of your private moment right now?"

"For reals, though, kids." Jess now. "Just elope already."

That snapped Sabrina back into professional mode and sanity. She turned with a smile and a targeted question for Hendrick, but as she slipped them back into the interview, she was overly conscious of her movements and her speech. Flustered around the edges.

She didn't look directly at Nick again for the rest of the morning.

"How cute was that?" Emily was irrepressibly enthusiastic as she brought Sabrina a bottle of water and took the unclipped mic. "What Nick said about you during the Betz interview. I couldn't borrow the book Betz left, could I? Once I graduate next year, I could really use some subliminal positive coercion on the job market." She handed Sabrina the updated brief for the next morning. "You two are obviously growing on each other. That's good. I was sure I'd have to help someone hide a body before Christmas. And speaking of cute—his niece is a doll."

"You can keep the book," Sabrina said absently, her

fingers tightening on the sheaf of papers. Nick was walking over to the young girl who'd been shadowing Emily all morning and watching the goings-on in the studio. Sabrina had met Pippi for a few minutes before the show, and been greeted with a polite handshake and a query as to whether Sabrina knew that having red hair probably meant she'd genetically require more anaesthesia than most people during surgery. Quite small for her age, she had a wan, pointed little face. Her light brown hair was very straight and knitted into an intricate French plait.

Nick flung Pippi up into his arms, while she shook her head at him with the air of a disapproving little old lady, then revealed a few missing teeth with a slow smile. She returned his hug before he put her down and pointed out a piece of equipment to her, putting his hand on her head and gently turning it in the right direction.

Sabrina wrenched her gaze away, and turned back to Emily. "If you ever fancy any of the freebies that come in, just shout." She found a smile. "Acknowledged perk. And you're doing an amazing job. We both really appreciate it." Emily, always so bright and bubbly, flushed and looked a bit awkward. "Especially when you must have a lot on your plate. I heard you're studying, as well?"

"Yes, I'm going for a Bachelor of Science. Mostly by distance."

Sabrina's smile was more genuine now. "Sorry, I seem to have horrified you with a compliment. I think you definitely *do* need to read Hendrick's book."

Emily rolled her eyes, but with an exaggerated movement grabbed the book. "Debrief and run-through for tomorrow in ten minutes. If Nick okays it, I'll see if Pippi fancies a hot chocolate at the café downstairs until he's done."

"Brace yourself. Another compliment incoming. You're a star."

When Sabrina walked into the conference room, Nick was the only one there. Her steps faltered before she got a grip on herself. Slipping into the chair beside him, she set down her copy of the schedule and fixed her attention on it. There was a short, charged interval in which neither of them spoke, then she said, "We need to sort the plan for the Murder Train on Friday. I thought we could head down with the team and do recce tomorrow afternoon."

She turned her head. Their eyes connected, before her gaze lowered to the hollow of his throat, where his skin gleamed with a bead of moisture. The room was overheated, which was obviously better than sitting here shivering, but she felt sticky herself, under her arms and between her breasts. Which was exactly where his darkening gaze had just momentarily gone, to the undone top buttons of her shirt.

He cleared his throat, and Sabrina had a sudden vivid image of putting her lips to the curve of his Adam's apple. She dug the heel of her hand into her thigh.

"Fine by me." There was the slightest rasp underlying his words. "We need to talk about the situation here, as well. Our helpful little friend." A dry clarification.

The sabotage had been subtle but irritating today, just a stream of minor inconveniences—mostly items misplaced or rearranged—which had collectively made them look disorganised at best, or, to their harsher on-line critics, sloppy and incompetent. Their supposed secret romance had temporarily given them a boost in viewership; but they needed to increase and maintain that, and Sabrina didn't appreciate looking as if she didn't care about her work.

Especially since, despite everything, she was starting to care very much about this job.

"Agreed. And maybe we shouldn't do that here." She coughed. "Let us all learn from example that it's a bad idea to discuss sensitive work-related issues on the premises."

He grimaced.

She hesitated. "I have the engagement drinks tonight with my family." And Akiko, Elise, and Lizzy, Freddy had texted to inform her. Sabrina strongly suspected she was about to be triple-team interrogated about the man beside her, but she was still relieved about an extra buffer in case things swiftly hit the fan with her father. Rupert had always been fond of Akiko, and for a man who'd been too busy chasing the spotlight to focus on his own children until one of them showed promise as the next Ellen Terry, he was surprisingly great with Lizzy.

Not that she was still carrying any childhood baggage at all.

Wryly, she added, "If we meet up after that, it'll inevitably end up online as another secret tryst."

Especially after the interview this morning. Which, despite the additional fuel to the rumour mill, she couldn't seem to regret. She also couldn't take that memory out of hiding without her heart beating harder. His face as he'd called her a catalyst for the pursuit of happiness. That was…maybe the most powerful thing anyone had ever said to her. And his voice as he'd called her by the nickname she was supposed to loathe.

This was Nick Davenport. He was *Nick*. She kept silently repeating that as a sort of protective mantra. But it was starting to— It was starting to mean something different. And that, in turn, was the stirring of fear.

"Should I call you?" With a concentrated effort, she steeled herself and brought her focus back to the conference table and the agenda before them—both the literal paper one and the looming tasks ahead. "Or FaceTime? About eight? Freddy will have to be at the Majestic by seven for tonight's show, so drinks will definitely be over by then." Her brain finally kicking into gear, she gestured in the vague direction of the door and, several floors down, the café. "Or are you still on uncle duty tonight?"

"I strongly hope I'm on uncle duty for life." There was that softening of Nick's chiselled features. "We're going to Claridge's for afternoon tea, because, in news to almost every woman slogging out a living in London today, apparently that's what 'grown-up ladies' do. I'll drop her off at the factory with my mother after."

Sabrina swung her legs sideways in her seat and crossed them. "Did Pippi enjoy the morning?"

"She seemed to. She's now best friends with the sound engineer, and they spent half an hour showing each other photos of their cats." Nick looked amused, but there was a shadow of a frown there.

"What's wrong?" When he tilted his head enquiringly, Sabrina gestured with the pen she was tapping on the tabletop. "I can see it in your face."

He shot her a bit of an odd look then, but he made an

acknowledging sound. "She seems quite down today. It's usually about eight questions or random fact recitations a second. I only got one every few minutes."

"Missing her dad?" Pippi had told Sabrina that her father was working in Paris this week.

Nick shrugged. "I'm sure she is, but she's usually a pretty chill kid about Iain's job. He works from London most of the time, and he FaceTimes her every night when he's away." His eyes went to her pen, and she realised she was now compulsively clicking it.

She set it down. "Do you think it's to do with her mum?" She ventured the suggestion carefully, but he simply nodded.

"Probably." With a candidness that was unexpected, he went on to say, "I'll talk to Iain about it, but I'm at a loss to know what's best to do. I struggled to get my head around a lot of things when my father died, but I was already a grown man, and that was a very different relationship. This is a little girl and her mother." His gaze had gone inward, preoccupied with his own thoughts, but he suddenly focused on her. "Hell. As you know yourself. Sorry."

She shook her head. "It was a very long time ago now."

He had that shrewd, investigative-reporter expression on, which usually raised her hackles something fierce. But it was tempered with what looked like genuine concern. "Does it feel like it?"

A simple question, and one that few people would probably ask. Sabrina didn't know if she'd ever consciously asked it of herself.

"In some ways, it feels so long ago that my memories of her are like a dream," she heard herself say in a low tone. "And sometimes I still miss her so much I feel like she only left yesterday."

She swallowed, and in her turn, her eyes refocused on him. She smiled faintly, then stilled when—very slowly—he reached out and touched one of the rogue curls that had sprung out around her face. He tucked it behind her ear.

She didn't move or even breathe. Then, a swift rush of tension propelling her into motion, she reached up and fleetingly touched his hand, before she pushed to her feet and walked to the window. With her back straight and rigid, she looked blindly out at the view across the river.

He was still sitting at the table, but she could feel his presence so intensely that his body might have been pressed up against hers.

It felt like an endless time later, but was probably only a couple of minutes, before the door opened and the rest of the team exploded inside, chattering voices blending into one general, blessed noise.

Fenella called Nick over to look at the clipboard she was holding, and when he returned to the table, he took a seat at the opposite end of the table from where Sabrina had shakily sat. His profile was like cut glass. Right now *The Nicholas* sculpture didn't seem that inaptly named.

Worry. Anger. Lust. Hard, clashing emotions blurred together inside her, coming out as just…confusion.

They got through the debrief fairly quickly, although Fenella came down hard on the disorganisation in the studio, frowning around at the team heads.

Both Sabrina and Nick, with glances that met and slipped away from each other, like people trying to navigate an icy path, raised qualms about the addition to the schedule for tomorrow.

Frank Gough, one-time MP turned businessman and author, was notoriously controversial, and as far as Sabrina was concerned, uninteresting. She'd been too young when he'd been in office to remember him as a politician, but she disliked the way he blatantly stirred shit just to keep himself in the headlines. He was the sort of person who'd refuse to like anything popular just to be different, regardless of his actual opinion and usually without knowing anything about the subject; and then he'd attack the intelligence of those who disagreed with him.

Basically, he was the token dickhead in every management team-building exercise who would only listen to his own voice and passed the buck when things went wrong.

"Obviously he's outspoken," Fenella said, "but he currently has a top-five release, he's already done *Rise Britain* this week, and a good deal of the book is relevant to the mortgage crisis. As far as I know, he has no personal beef with either of you, and you're extremely adept people-handlers. Things should pass off smoothly. If it were Peter King dealing with him, it'd be fisticuffs over the morning fry-up."

Sabrina did recall a much-publicised feud between King and Gough some time ago. Battle of the egos.

"Gough only narrowly escaped the Halston-Fischer scandal with his job and reputation intact. Are we quite sure the man is coming in with no personal biases?" Nick enquired, tapping his pen on the table. "I can't imagine he was a massive fan of my father." He glanced at Sabrina again; and even in the midst of a conversation like this, his eyes…they did change a bit when he looked at her. She was consciously watching for it now. "Did you interview him on *Sunset Britain*?"

"No, although one of my co-presenters did. And called him 'a surprisingly good bloke.'" As that co-presenter had also been a gobby, obnoxious prat, however, it wasn't the best character reference.

"The man clearly has a well-developed and fragile ego. You're both experienced in that department," Fenella said, somewhat ambiguously. "But he has a book to sell. I doubt if he's going to rank a secondhand connection to a years-old scandal higher than his profit margin. A scandal that he managed to ride out, moreover. Keep a close rein, and I have every confidence."

Nick stayed back after the meeting to speak to Fenella further, and Jess was hovering, waiting to brief him on a personal appearance later in the month, so Sabrina left them to it.

On her way to her dressing room, she passed Nick's. The door was open, and Pippi was sitting in an armchair, an iPad on her lap. Nick was right—there was definitely a downward pull to her mouth and, when she looked up, something not quite right in her eyes. It twanged at memories that Sabrina seemed to carry in her chest rather than her brain.

"Hello, again," Pippi said, very politely. "Good job on the show today."

Sabrina suppressed the smile that threatened. If there was ever an old soul. And she had lovely manners—much improved on her uncle's. Kudos, Nick's grumpy brother.

"Hello, Pippi. Thank you very much," she said,

equally solemnly. "Are you by yourself here? Where's Emily?"

"She got called away to do something, but I'm quite all right to wait until Uncle Nick comes. I'm eight," Pippi informed her, with the kindness and exaggerated enunciation of one explaining something to a very small toddler.

Sabrina couldn't completely hold in the smile that time. "I didn't doubt it for a minute, and your uncle should be along very shortly." She nodded at the glass of orange juice on the table beside her. "Would you like something to eat? If Nick doesn't have anything but gherkins, I'm pretty sure I have some biscuits in my room."

Pippi giggled, transforming her serious face. "Isn't it gross? He just eats them whole, not even in a burger or anything. And if we go to McDonald's, he steals mine."

"Fiend."

"He told me you pinched one from him yesterday, but unfortunately Scotland Yard were too busy to take his call about it. And thank you, but I don't really eat biscuits. They're not very good for you. Which is a bit awkward sometimes," she confided, closing the cover of the iPad, "because my granny owns a factory that makes loads of them. Would you like to sit down?"

Amused, Sabrina went fully into the room, which was moderately untidy and smelled like its owner's cologne, and pulled out the desk chair. "I do know. We're doing a show live at your grandmother's factory next week, for the launch of her new biscuit for the Shining Lights charity. And I'm afraid I *do* eat biscuits. Quite often."

The chair slipped back as she sat, and she came close to another arse-to-ground encounter.

So glad she was consistently living up to that reputation for elegance.

"Ooh, careful," Pippi said, concerned. "You don't want another fall."

Oh, good. Even eight-year-olds had seen this morning's tabloids.

"I saw pictures of you and Uncle Nick today," Nick's niece confirmed, studying Sabrina with great interest.

Shifting into a more stable position, Sabrina cleared her throat. "I don't think—"

"I'm not really supposed to read the online papers. My dad hates them. He says they're a load of rubbish." Pippi set the iPad aside and reached for her glass. "But I look sometimes if Uncle Nick's in them. He's looking at you kind of weird in every photo."

She drank her juice, apparently done with the conversation.

Unfortunately, Sabrina had not sunk so low that she was going to request clarification from a little girl.

However, after swallowing the last of her juice, Pippi went on, in what Sabrina would have found absolutely hilarious in different circumstances, "Sort of the way my dad looks at his cakes. You know, all 'how amazing is this, this is mine, isn't it beautiful.' Dad's all funny about his cakes, and Uncle Nick's all funny about you."

It was a good thing that eight-year-old minds were capable of immediately jumping to a new topic, because Sabrina was currently unable to form one coherent word, even silently in her thoughts.

"Emily took me to the café downstairs," Pippi told

her, putting her glass down. "We saw her dad there, and he got me a free sandwich." She glanced at Sabrina. "Actually, he's her stepdad. She told me. Stepfamilies are very common in the UK, you know."

Sabrina finally recollected that she was a fully-grown woman. "Yes, they are. Very."

"My granny is my step-granny, and Nick is my step-uncle, really, but we don't use the 'step' part. My dad says that if you love people and they love you back, and you're happy for each other when things are good and help each other when things are bad, and you don't even mind too much when people in-ev-it-a-bly—" she sounded out the word "—try to grind your gears, then it's family. He says if you're related to someone and they don't treat you well, they don't deserve to be called family, and you can meet someone as a total stranger and they can become the *best* family."

"Your dad sounds like a very smart man to me."

"Do you think so, too?"

"I absolutely, categorically think so, too."

Pippi nodded. "He's got quite a bad temper, but he never yells at me." Said with a certain complacency, followed by an honest, "He does get cross if I'm running late for school." With a sideways glance between her lashes that put Sabrina instantly on guard, she added, "My friend's mum said he's very handsome. He's quite old." A regretful addendum. "But I think he *is* handsome. It's a pity you're Uncle Nick's cake, or maybe you could be my dad's girlfriend."

Sabrina sincerely hoped nobody was in the corridor outside, listening as she was designated as Nick's cake. Feeling as if she were picking her way tentatively through a potential minefield that was really none of her business, she said, "Would you like your dad to have a girlfriend?"

Pippi pulled hard at the end of her plait. "Or he could get married. My step-granny is the same as a real granny, so I could have a stepmum and maybe she'd be—" She stopped talking, and her hazel eyes were suddenly very wet.

Sabrina stopped caring whether she was intruding on a situation that had nothing to do with her. She reached out her hand, and the little girl immediately took it. Her grip was hard and pinching; Sabrina just held on firmly. "I was nine when my mum died," she said, and Pippi looked up at her, her lips pulled in. "I still miss her very much. I know it's so hard."

"How did she die?"

"In an accident. She was hit by a car."

"My mum was climbing, and she fell. She was meant to come home on Friday, but she didn't. She didn't. She didn't come home."

The backs of Sabrina's own eyes were stinging. She squeezed Pippi's fingers.

Pippi rubbed the back of her other freckled hand across her eyes. "I don't want to forget her."

"Oh, Pippi. You won't. I promise you won't. Do you—" Sabrina hesitated. "Do you talk to your dad about your mother? About how much you miss her?"

"Yes, but..." That air of odd maturity had completely dispelled now. Pippi looked like what she was, a worried, very sad child. "He doesn't like it when I'm sad. It makes him upset, and then he starts stepping from side to side and talking all low and grumbly like a bear."

"Nobody likes it when someone they love is upset,

darling. But they still want the chance to help. If you need to talk, make sure you do tell your dad, or your granny, or your uncle. I expect he's pretty decent at hugs."

"Even if he does like yuck gherkins." A small smile curled on Pippi's wet face, and Sabrina smiled back.

"Even with that terrible character flaw."

"Dad didn't love my mum," Pippi mumbled. "Not like me. We didn't live in the same house. I only used to stay with him on weekends. And I used to wish that I could see him every day, but now...now sometimes I want to go home."

Sabrina had never felt so helpless in her life. She sympathised with Nick's feeling of inadequacy entirely; she just didn't know what to say.

Pippi looked down and swallowed. "All my friends were going to work with their mums today."

There was a sound behind them, and Nick came into the room and closed the door after him. He'd obviously heard at least the last thing Pippi had said. He went down in a crouch, taking Pippi's other small hand into his large one. "Liana would have loved to have you at the lab with her, Pip. And she would completely understand everything you're feeling, and so would your dad. I wish there was something I could say or do that would mean you didn't have to go through this. It's totally unfair." With his free hand, he smoothed his palm over her head. "You'll always love her, and she'll always love you. We all love you very much. I know it doesn't seem like it now, but it won't always hurt so sharply as this."

Another tear ran down Pippi's face, and Nick pulled her into a hug. Small arms went around his neck and held tightly. Pippi's words were muffled, but still audible. "Do you think I'll see her again one day?"

Nick stroked Pippi's plait, as his fact-addicted, grieving niece hit him with one of the biggest questions in existence. The great unanswerable. "I don't know, Pip. Nobody knows that for sure, and everybody is entitled to their own belief about it."

Pippi pushed back to look at him, rubbing at her running nose. "What do you believe?"

Nick's gaze was level. It wasn't an adult pacifying a child, it was one human being talking their own truth to another. "Personally, I believe you will."

His niece studied him, and then sniffed again and looked at Sabrina. "What do you think?"

"I'm not sure," she said, honestly, and her eyes met Nick's. "But I'd like to believe that's true."

"It probably is." Pippi squared her shoulders. "Granny says he has a nasty habit of being right. May I please have a tissue?"

With a tinge of light, welcome laughter uncurling inside as Nick rolled his eyes, Sabrina dug into her pocket for a clean tissue and passed it over.

"It was good I cried again." Pippi scrubbed hard at her already red lids. "Tears are an endorphin, did you know? They can make you feel a bit better, like for real."

"I did not know." Nick stood up. "Where did you pick that one up?"

"Dad bought me a 'Fact of the Day' calendar. Yesterday it said that some people used to keep presents inside the branches of a Christmas tree instead of under it."

"Speaking of Christmas trees, Emily wants to know

For just a second, there was nothing but emptiness and the long-ago echo of desolation and fear.

She jumped a little as Nick's hand touched the back of her head. He didn't stroke her hair, or really…presume in any way; he just let his palm rest there, lightly, until she felt the memories lose their bite, release their grip on her body.

As she took a deep breath and felt herself relax, he said, in the low tones that glided around her bones like warm honey, "She read *The Brambletons* to you. And she must have been beautiful."

She shot him a fleeting smile. "Yes. I remember her voice, still. I used to worry I'd forget, but I never have. And the smell of her perfume. And…her light. She had a personality that just lit up from within. Freddy has our father's hair and eyes, and she was too young to really remember our mother, but she's so much like her. In the ways that matter."

Nick had lowered his hand, but she still felt a prickling sensation on her hair. "You say that like you don't think you have that light."

"I've never felt that I did." She didn't say it as self-pity, just fact. She wouldn't go so melodramatic as to say the thorn to Freddy's rose, but—the Marmite to Freddy's jam, maybe. Sharper and more of an acquired taste.

"You do."

His breathing, deep and even, and hers, too light and shallow in her chest.

"I have to get going," Nick said, at last. "I have a fancy date with some scones and very small sandwiches."

Sabrina stood up, relieved that her legs were rock-steady. "So, tonight…"

"FaceTime me when you're done with drinks."

"Right."

"Sabrina."

She waited.

"They probably won't want to hear it, but congratulate Griff and Freddy for me."

A flash of green suddenly caught her eye, on the messy bench by the door. The knitting needles she'd loaned him in France were sitting on a pile of papers. She'd forgotten all about them. The disastrous grey effort from the cellar was gone, replaced by a dozen rows of a finer wool. Still askew, but not terrible. And a pretty shade of pale mint. He'd found different wool. He'd possibly *bought* wool.

"Why don't you call Griff and congratulate him yourself?"

"Because he's probably blocked my number and rigged some sort of remote explosive if I try to call his?" Nick offered, his mouth a satirical twist.

Sabrina raised her eyebrows. "You've never backed down from a challenge. Despite your dubious tactics in the past, I'll give you this—you fight for what you want. What's important to you. If you know what that is."

His expression flickered; that comment had hit home.

She closed her hand over the doorknob. "Not long ago, I'd have said the *only* thing important to you is your career. At all costs. Personal gain before people."

Nick's jaw worked. He adjusted his stance. It was the reaction of someone who'd been physically hit—not felled, but hurt.

At that moment, she felt as if she could reach out and physically feel a connection vibrating and twanging violently between them. "I wouldn't say that now."

As she left, she thought she saw him take a step forward.

Chapter Ten

As a popular restaurant for performers and crew in the West End, Tragicomedy was packed even at five o'clock, with most of the current occupants likely to be twirling and singing across historic stages in the next few hours. All that pre-show anticipation combined into a buzzing energy, similar to what Sabrina could feel when she visited Freddy backstage. She remembered it from childhood as well, that unique atmosphere in live theatre, the magic—she'd actually thought it *was* magic, during her young years—of watching her father transform into an entirely different person. She saw in her mind Rupert's lean, expressive face as Iago, the night a piece of the set had fallen at the Majestic, ending his acting career in seconds. The Majestic, the same theatre Freddy was performing in tonight. Life, turning in endless circles.

That image of his youthful, bright-eyed face, his quick, darting movements on long thin legs, faded into the version of her father who sat across the table from her now. His head of ringlets had faded almost entirely to grey, and deep creases marked his brow and cheeks, running into each other like lines marking rivers on a map. In the dimness, all the figures around the table were gently aglow under the fairy lights that strung through a Titania's bower of indoor trees. No surprise this was Freddy's favourite restaurant; she always looked right at home here, and was currently fizzing with happiness next to Griff. Across from them, Lizzy was sitting on Rupert's knee, loudly requesting his opinion of the pictures she was drawing on a piece of notebook paper. He pointed at unrecognisable shapes and nodded.

Sabrina turned to Freddy as her sister nudged her arm and held out the bottle a waiter had just opened for them. "Champagne?"

"Thanks, but I think I'll keep you company and stick with sparkling water tonight." She lifted her glass. "I've maxed out the number of hangovers I can handle for one month."

Griff refilled Freddy's own glass with water. Without breaking his conversation with his parents, he handed it to her and lightly kissed her bare shoulder, then tugged up the cashmere wrap that was slipping down into her lap.

Freddy tucked her arm through his, touching her cheek to his shoulder, and reached for another piece of garlic bread. "I probably shouldn't be eating this. I've got to kiss Jeremy Bury at quarter to nine."

Halfway through a caustic-sounding response to something his father had said, Griff picked up the basket of garlic bread and set the entire thing in front of Freddy. She grinned.

Sabrina took a sip from her glass and wiped off the red lipstick mark with her thumb. "So—wedding plans? Quickie vows and rings at the register office or posh country wedding at Highbrook?" She hadn't been

back to Griff's family estate since the night of the plagiarism broadcast and her final break-up with Ferren,
but if anything was going to replace those memories
with a good one, it would be watching Freddy walk
down the aisle. "Or too early to ask?"

Charlie, who was unlike his older brother in every
possible way, put about eight chips in his mouth,
chewed, and swallowed with difficulty. "Griff's gorgeous bride and his even better-looking best man need
a more impressive setting than some tin-pot ceremony
on the King's Road. Full works at the family pile in the
summer. The roses will be out, and it gives me time to
help you ladies plan the hen."

"I think you're meant to do the stag night." Sabrina
stole one of the remaining chips before Charlie could
scoff the lot.

He inclined his scruffy red head at his immaculately
combed blond sibling. "I'll go you a tenner that means
whiskies with a bunch of film-crowd tossers and a grim
chat about the economic downturn. Not a nipple tassel
in sight. Freddy's hen, however—guaranteed to make
Mardi Gras look like an afternoon nap at an old folks'
home. Bet it starts in the Westminster clubs and ends
on a yacht in Mallorca."

Griff also reached for one of the chips his brother
was trying to stockpile behind the salt shaker. The fingers of his other hand entwined in Freddy's loose curls
and he rolled one around his finger. "If Freddy gets
on a yacht, it'll end up at the bottom of the sea within
an hour, and I'll be bailing you out of a Spanish jail."

Freddy twisted to loop her arm around his neck, her
eyes dancing. "Sounds like a decent night out. Ditch
the film-crowd tossers and come with us." She pulled

his head to her and kissed him lightly in the middle of the restaurant.

It was just a short peck and the room was dark enough that people could barely see farther than their own table, but still—James Ford-Griffin, biting critic, despiser of humanity, general soothsayer of doom, engaging in a spot of PDA.

Besotted.

And he wasn't the only one. His parents were holding hands over their shared menu, and Elise was resting her chin on Akiko's shoulder.

Charlie glanced around, rubbing at the scattering of stubble over his jaw. "I'm feeling left out," he announced, and lifted a brow at Sabrina suggestively. "I'd ask if you fancied a quick snog, but I'm man enough to admit it: Nick Davenport could kick the shit out of me. And we know he's a stealthy bastard behind the smooth spiel. My hands," he finished grandly, holding them up, "will remain safely on my pizza and away from his bird."

"Your pizza's going up your nose if you refer to me as anyone's 'bird' again." Sabrina reached for the bottle of sparkling water to refill her glass.

Charlie picked it up and poured for her. "In journalistic speak, I don't think that was an official denial, proxy big sis."

Lizzy clambered off Rupert's knee and went over to see the photos of the new bespoke dollhouse Griff's parents were building. Under cover of all other eyes turning in that direction, Freddy leaned close to Sabrina and spoke in a low tone. "That *was* a fairly interesting show today, Sabs. Or should I say 'Sparks'?"

"I'd rather you didn't."

"Nick wasn't dicking around. What he said about you bringing out the best sides of people. That's dead accurate. And he meant it. The way he looked at you—"

Sabrina could have thrown out any number of flippant comments to brush it off. Banter. Sarcasm.

She bit her lip.

"And for that matter," Freddy said, her gaze sharpening, "the way you looked at him. Not quite the usual mix of loathing and budding murder."

"More like another lap dance was imminent." Apparently, Charlie had very acute hearing. "I feared for the morning censors."

Freddy tugged thoughtfully at a curl by her ear. "I have to say, for a heartless, soulless, back-stabbing bastard? His *smile*. The real smile today, I mean, not that 'I'm a celeb, aren't I pretty, tell me all about yourself' thing that both of you do with your teeth."

Sabrina had just put the rim of her glass to her lips. She lowered it with an emphatic thud. "Jesus. That's it. You're demoted from favourite sibling status. Charlie, you're up."

Charlie raised one arm in a victory gesture.

"I mean, he *is* really fit." Freddy's tone was more worried than flattering to Nick.

"I'm sure Griff will be thrilled to hear you say so," Sabrina said, and Freddy turned to look at her fiancé, who was talking to his dad. Her face immediately went full Barbara Cartland, and Sabrina was surprised the smoke drifting from the candles on the table didn't turn pink and form heart shapes.

"Well, obviously nobody's fitter than Griff."

"Vision that poor, and she can still wiggle and warble through an entire three-hour show," Charlie said, with enormous admiration.

With deadly accuracy, Freddy threw a salted peanut at his nose. "Warble? Fuck off," she said, grinning. "I got enough stick on my solo in your brother's review, thanks. Consider yourself uninvited to my hen. We'll sink the yacht without you."

"To be fair," Elise said suddenly, turning towards them, and evidently *everyone* was listening to this, "if there's an accident-prone Carlton sister, right now I wouldn't point the finger at you, Freddy."

"What, the daily *Wake Me Up London* comedy block?" Charlie looked questioningly at Sabrina. "But it's a put-on, isn't it? Scripted?"

"The segment intros are scripted. The ruined baking, and tripping over forgotten power cords, and seeing how many guests we can insult in one show—not so much." She held back from saying anything further. She had agreed with Nick that their suspicions on that score should remain between the two of them until they had a better idea what—or specifically, who—they were dealing with.

Petty sabotage and secrets. By the time they left the Murder Train on Friday, they might as well just slap on Nancy Drew and Frank Hardy masks and be done with it.

She vaguely remembered when she'd had a borderline dignified, even sophisticated career.

Although nobody could say work these days was dull.

Her father's voice suddenly cut through the general hubbub, the first time they'd really spoken all evening after the initial greetings. "As ratings ploys go," Rupert said, "I'm not sure it's wise. It makes you look unprofessional and as if you don't want to be there, and it's overdone and disingenuous." Exactly the tune Fenella was crossly singing. And if her father had left it at that, it would be difficult to argue. Unfortunately, he added, in his most managerial tone, "Audiences cotton on very quickly to falsity."

"Henrietta's long and glittering career would suggest otherwise." It was out before Sabrina could stop it, more snarky habit than anything else, and she caught Freddy's quick glance.

Returning one of silent apology, she straightened and pushed away her glass, trying to ease out the tension that had shot into her neck and shoulders the moment their father had started speaking.

He'd stiffened as well, as he always did, even now, at criticism of their grandmother. "I think it's better we don't discuss your grandmother," said the man who'd talked about very little *but* Henrietta for the first thirty years of Sabrina's life.

"Yes," Freddy cut in hastily. "What about this new business of yours, Dad? What is it, some sort of investment?"

"Yes," Sabrina echoed. "What *about* this new business of yours?"

She was still apprehensive about that, and it came through clearly in her voice.

Rupert's lips thinned. "It's not a business, as such. I'm still assisting Carolina and James with their marketing," he said, with a tight smile at Griff's parents, who beamed back at him in their perennially vague way.

"Oh, he's working wonders for us," Griff's mother

enthused. "We have commissions booked until next October, and since our *Anathorn* installation went up in the foyer of the Majestic, two other theatres have expressed interest in mechanical displays of their own, to enhance the experience of their shows."

"That's fantastic." Sabrina smiled at her, genuinely delighted about that. The couple deserved to have their considerable talents recognised, and Griff and Freddy deserved to have his parents financially solvent and not constantly chipping away at the estate finances. And she'd never deny that her father was a savvy manager, when he wasn't overly invested and acting on personal biases the way he had with Freddy, or lying through his teeth, à la *The Velvet Room*. Turning back, she said, "But you're working on something else, on the side?"

"Could you not make that sound questionable?" Rupert spoke with a hint of bite. "Since finances are a little tighter these days—" a slightly sour look at Griff, who was now in rightful possession of a whack of money her father had illegally obtained from *The Velvet Room* royalties "—I take on extra work when it comes along."

Completely not answering the question.

Before Sabrina could push it further, forgetting where they were and her resolve to just raise a glass and play fully happy families tonight, her father turned things back on her. "I've been dabbling in a bit of writing again, if that passes your scrutiny, Sabrina. And a more pertinent subject might be your own recent choices."

Freddy shifted at her side, and Sabrina put a hand out to touch hers.

"I'm aware that in the parenting stakes, you usu-

ally rank me somewhere between Lear and Egeus,"
Rupert went on tightly, "but I do care about your happiness and security, and you seem to be sabotaging
both. Again. That never-ending disaster of a relationship with Joe Ferren, a self-absorbed waste of space
with the acting ability of a block of Stilton. And now
you've taken up with yet another mass of conceit. The
man, moreover, entirely responsible for splashing our
name across every headline in the country."

And ruining my career were the words that hung
silently and accusingly—and inaccurately—in the air.

The reference to the Shakespearean characters was
very Rupert. Sabrina had grown up used to a parent
who could turn the most mundane conversation into
an Elizabethan soliloquy—her dad had once just about
reeled off into iambic pentameter because they'd run
out of toothpaste—and she hardly noticed anymore.
Tonight, though—irritating. To put it mildly.

"I think we're all well aware of the amount of sh—"
Sabrina looked at Lizzy, who was bent over her draw-
ings again. "The amount of rubbish the tabloids spin.
But setting that aside and addressing the actual facts—
Nick was a part of what happened last summer." Her
voice was so tight that she felt like a rubber band about
to snap. "He broke a story that already existed. He
didn't seek glory and recognition that wasn't his, and
he didn't live a lie and force other people to unknowingly profit from it with him. He behaved badly, but
he's not some big villain in a melodramatic saga."

She'd been almost unaware of the others at the table
for the past minute or so, but her eyes now connected
with Griff's. His were narrowed, and he was watching her very closely.

"And I am? Is that it?" Rupert asked bitterly, and suddenly, Sabrina just felt tired.

Tired of arguing. Tired of anger and deceit and blame. Tired of feeling as if she'd grasped at a connection with the only parent she had now, again and again throughout her life, and every time she'd thought she had a thread that would hold, it slipped away.

"No," she said, and rubbed her hand over her forehead. "Not you. Not Nick. Not Henrietta. Not even Ferren. There is no villain—"

"Somewhere, Sadie Foster feels disrespected," Charlie muttered under his breath.

"This is life, not a script where everyone can be neatly slotted into protagonist, antagonist, good, bad, whatever. It's all been a mess, but it's over, and it's time to move on." Every word of that came out slowly and speculatively, as if she were examining each syllable for truth as it passed her lips.

And she meant it.

The grand Shakespearean tradition, however, meant hammering in the last word.

"That's all very well," her father said, "but this situation with Davenport looks to me like a repetition of history, likely to end in tears. And I've made terrible mistakes, I acknowledge that, and strongly repent that—but I did always act to protect the family." Even Freddy moved abruptly at that one. "And considering the trouble Davenport caused— Whatever's going on at that studio, your behaviour at the moment smacks of disloyalty."

"I think that's enough." Charlie's baritone, usually amused and teasing, cracked like a whip, then.

Griff had taken on the body language of a large,

dangerous jungle cat, and Akiko and Elise both pushed forward in their seats.

Griff and Charlie's parents clearly had no idea what was going on, but were mildly concerned.

Lizzy was colouring in a picture of a three-legged dog, with her tongue sticking out.

In a script, the outraged daughter would now rise from her seat, hiss something furious and dramatic, and flounce out; with Act Two to bring either retribution or reconciliation.

Their father had pulled this kind of shit on their mother as well, trying to turn every real-life situation into a Rupert Carlton production.

Sabrina looked at Freddy, who'd lost some of the happy glow that had surrounded her for months. Pushing back her sleeve, she glanced at her watch. "There's still about half an hour before you have to leave," she said. "How about chocolate tart all round? And don't even think about picking up the bill for tonight. It's my treat."

"Halfsies," Charlie broke in, in a much more normal tone. "We'll split it. Don't make me look like the cheap in-law."

A slow breath left Freddy and her grip on Sabrina's arm relaxed. Griff leaned forward and kissed her temple, and Freddy turned to rub her cheek against his chin.

"That was quite a defence," she murmured close to Sabrina's ear. "Nick's no longer the one-dimensional comic-book foe, then?"

"No," Sabrina said. "It's very upsetting."

She got up to order the dessert. Her father rose to his feet, reaching for his walking stick as she reached the head of the table. "Sabs," he said, and at the unusual use of her family pet name, she stopped. "I apologise. That was out of line. But I'm still your father, and I have a right to be concerned." He leaned both hands on the carved head of the stick. "Even when your baby girl is a grown woman—still your baby."

Sabrina looked down at where his fingers interlocked. His skin was lined there, too, and just the slightest bit papery in texture. At some point, she was going to blink and he'd metamorphose into an old man, with no greasepaint, no illusions or tricks this time.

When he lifted one hand and touched her arm, she looked up and into his eyes.

Freddy's eyes. Henrietta's eyes. Big and brown and candid.

Deceptively guileless in Henrietta's case. Accurately so, in Freddy's.

And Rupert…

The great tragedy in the life of a natural-born actor—perhaps it wasn't a career cut short.

Perhaps it was that even when you spoke from within and not from a script, professed to care, resonated with sincerity…the people you loved were never—quite—sure.

It was completely dark outside and freezing cold when Sabrina left the restaurant. When she was cuddled up in her flat, a cup of tea in her hand, she enjoyed winter. The clothes were fab, and there were a lot of excuses to knit. Out on the streets, when it was barely dinnertime and might as well be midnight, she was less of a fan. Debating taxi or Tube, she broke free of the throngs of people surging homeward and stopped in a small alcove to stare at the lit-up Christmas tree in a shop window.

And nonsensical, disarming tears threatened.

She didn't even really know why she wanted to cry. Nothing had fundamentally changed over the past hour and a half. *Fundamentally*, nothing had changed in her relationship with her father for a long time.

Inhaling deeply, the cold air a bite in her lungs and the smell of the city making her nose wrinkle, she released the breath, and dug in her bag for her phone.

Nick picked up after three rings. "Hi."

At the sound of his voice, her fingers tightened on the phone. "Hi."

"What's the matter?" The almost lazy note was gone. "Drinks didn't go well?"

The lights on the Christmas tree stretched into glowing lines when she narrowed her stinging eyes. "Pretty much what I expected. I'm heading home now, but I need to stop off at the supermarket first and I'm probably going to have to defrost in the shower, so I might be half an hour late with the FaceTime."

Her phone beeped, and she looked down to see a request flashing. Casting her eyes up, she accepted, turning around to face the street for safety reasons, and taking a step back so she was well out of people's way. A few faces in the passing crowd peered at her with recognition and interest.

"Or apparently we're going to FaceTime right now."

It was not normal that Nick looked like that even on a low-res, slightly jerky screen.

He took one look back at her and said, "You *are* upset. You're— Are you crying?" His voice was sharp.

She scrubbed her hand over her brow. "I'm fine. I'm

just tired. I'm still adjusting to the early mornings, and it's hanging over everything all the time that I might not *have* to get up before dawn next year. It's all just getting to me a bit."

There was a short silence. Nick looked off-screen, apparently debating something. When his gaze returned to hers, it was with a strange sense of resolution. "Did you just leave Tragicomedy?"

"I'm just down the road. Why?" she asked warily.

"You're not that far from me. Do you want to come over?"

"Come over?" she repeated, like an apprehensive parrot. Come over. To his flat. "I—" She wished they hadn't switched to video. She'd prefer he wasn't watching her mouth open and close. "The press speculation isn't going to tone down if I'm photographed entering your flat."

But…she did want to go.

Tears were threatening again, and her current, driving instinct was to head straight for Nick Davenport like a homing pigeon.

Bloody hell.

"You're about three seconds from tears—in all these years I've never known you to cry—and the rock-dwellers at *London Celebrity* can fuck off."

Amen to that last point, all day, any day.

Her heart was beating way too heavily. This wasn't momentous. It was just sensible. They had things to discuss, private things, and even if it was hardly MI6 stuff, it made more sense to do it in person behind closed doors. Ferren's phone had once been hacked, and thanks to that, there was a photo of her in bed online. Clothed, by the grace of God, but it had been a wake-up call to be cautious in general.

Sabrina closed her eyes. "Okay."

"Do you need me to come and get you?"

"No, I'll grab a taxi."

"I'll text you directions. If you come by the back road, there's less likely to be press there. And make sure you do get a taxi. Don't walk."

"I *have* lived in London my entire life. I don't merrily wander backstreets at night."

"Sorry." Nick spoke shortly. "I'm not patronising you. I just—I don't want anything to happen to you."

When they'd hung up, Sabrina wrapped her fingers around her phone, holding it against her chin, wondering what she was doing.

She could still go home.

She gave his address to the taxi driver.

As directed, the taxi dropped her in a quiet backstreet, and she opened the gate that led into Nick's back garden. He lived on the top floor of a tall, narrow, brownstone conversion, with ivy looping around the railings. Someone had threaded fairy lights through the leaves, reminding Sabrina of the bowers at Tragicomedy.

The whole trip over, she'd still felt as if she were heading into something daunting, something that could affect everything. Her heart was thumping, and she expected to feel jumpy and defensive when they met.

But when she saw him standing on the porch waiting for her, the sleeves of his jumper pushed up, a light scattering of stubble on his jaw—everything in her just…relaxed.

She genuinely felt as if she'd just come home after a long journey.

Which was bizarre on multiple levels, including the fact that Nick's building appeared to be very nice, but it wasn't nearly as homely as hers.

Neither of them spoke as they walked up the flights of stairs, through his front door and into a warm and cosy living room. She'd 100 percent pick that a single man lived here, but she loved his paintings and woven rugs and the open fireplace. Carefully, she set her handbag down on his side table and hung her coat on a handy peg, took another quick breath, and turned.

Nick closed the door and they stood looking at each other.

Very slowly, Sabrina lifted her hands, and without hesitation, he took them in his. He tugged, once, gently, and she stepped into the shelter of his chest so fluidly and naturally it was frightening. His back felt hard and muscular against her palms as she laid her cheek against him, and felt his arm wrap around her shoulders, his hand moving over her hair.

"Do you want to talk about it?" His voice was low, his breath stirring the curls at her temple.

"No." Her arms tightened around his waist, and he stopped stroking her hair and cupped his hand around her head, his thumb resting against her earlobe.

He just held her. For a good five minutes, they stood there, and he showed no sign of impatience, of waiting for her to move so he could. It was rare, to her—to feel that she could just hug someone for as long as she needed to be hugged, with no obligation or discomfort or the sense of a ticking clock.

It was the hug of a friend—caring, concerned, and hands in polite places.

However, the relationship between her and Nick was not, and never had been, polite friendship. Sensation started to prickle down Sabrina's neck, and she became very aware of the brush of Nick's cheek against hers. She slid her hand an inch on his back, and felt him tense. When her hair snagged on his jaw, the rhythm of his breathing very subtly altered. Deepening. Quickening.

Gently, he did disengage himself then and nudged her towards the fire.

"Defrost," he said, with a slight smile that didn't match the flicker of heat in his eyes. "I'll make some coffee."

Sabrina's legs felt a bit wobbly at the knees. She sat on the couch and crossed them, and cleared her throat in case her voice came out huskily. Her vocal cords went full Joan Jett when she was aroused. "Frank Gough's bound to be difficult tomorrow. This financial planning book he's written sounds like a hardback sleeping pill. He'll try to generate some headlines by being a prick. Do you think he will bring up your father?"

"Not during the interview." Nick opened a cupboard. "Fenella's right. He has a book to sell, and he's not going to want any public reminders of when he skated on very thin ice. I expect it'll come out more in his attitude." He set out two mugs. "Although he's such a pompous prat most of the time anyway, there may not be any difference."

"I doubt he'll be tolerant of any hiccups. We triple-check everything before we go live. Remind me to look under the dust-jacket to make sure his book hasn't been swapped out for the *Kama Sutra*."

Nick snorted. She listened to the hissing of the espresso machine, and sat back when he came over with the mugs. "We're still on for the stakeout in the morning?" She pitched the question deliberately melo-dramatically, but there was still a telltale throatiness there.

"Just call me Nick Charles. Did you tee up with your driver to do an earlier pickup?"

"All sorted."

He sat at the other end of the couch, and she looked at him through her lashes as she blew on the surface of her coffee, scattering the steam.

"Even with the spectre of Gough as a bucket of cold water, staying on the topic of work would be eas-ier if you didn't look at me like that." He said it with such normal inflection that the words took a second to sink in.

Sabrina was restlessly tracing her fingertips in cir-cles over her knee, and his gaze dropped there. He ran his hand over his head and sat up straighter.

Directing his attention towards the fire, he knocked back a mouthful of coffee. "If we're theorising that this stream of minor disasters is not a coincidence—"

"Which we are." She wrapped the fingers of both hands around her mug, letting the warmth sink into her skin.

"Then it may be someone with an axe to grind against me, you, or both of us. I'll spare you the ef-fort and agree that I'm the most likely target in that scenario."

"Such cheap shots are beneath my abilities." She

sipped her coffee. "After the Wibblet, I think all this is too much trouble to take without an agenda. I mean, something concrete to gain, beyond some petty shit-stirring."

"Agreed. And it's fairly obvious who's standing in that position."

"Peter King."

"The whole thing just reeks of his personality, doesn't it? Childishness and malice, and a streak of ingenuity."

"People would notice if he'd been hanging around the studio."

"He's not exactly a wallflower." Nick set his coffee down on an end table. "Since the merger, several people who used to work with King have come onto the *WMUL* team. Pippi's friend on the sound crew, for one."

"And that's where I hit a sticking point. Because can you honestly imagine anyone who had to work for King being so fond of him that they'd—let's be real here—risk their job as well as ours, doing this. I'd expect them to crack open the Bollinger at getting away from him. One of my friends was a production assistant when he hosted the first season of *Ultimate Cakemaster*. She said it was like working with a spoilt toddler."

"I can't imagine anyone giving him a leg-up to the breakfast contract because they *like* the bloke, no."

She finished her coffee, then leaned back and propped her arm against the back of the couch. She curled her fingers against her jaw. "What? Blackmail?"

Nick shrugged. "Not beyond the realms of possibility. Things get pretty fucked up behind the scenes in this industry."

"Full-on *Dynasty* sometimes." Sabrina groaned. "Oh, God. It's never straightforward, is it? As if it weren't enough to have Sadie Foster flouncing about last summer, whispering threats in people's ears and yanking their strings. I'd really be cool with just the one blackmailer per calendar year."

Nick frowned. "Was she blackmailing people, as well?"

"Oh, yes. Sadie's a multi-faceted irritant."

He grimaced, hard. "In the past, I've written her off as fake and unpleasant, but comparatively harmless. I couldn't be more bloody sorry I had anything to do with her."

"People usually are. I expect Grimes will come to regret his relationship with her, but after the Shining Lights thing, I'm finding sympathy difficult."

The air between them had grown thick again.

"Sabrina." She lifted her gaze. His expression was serious. Emphatic. "I *am* sorry. I really am incredibly sorry."

He didn't need to specify that he was talking about more than Sadie.

She pressed her palm against the cushioned fabric of the couch, feeling the nap of the velvet. Appropriate enough, given the starring role *The Velvet Room* had played in the complete onslaught of hostilities between them.

Then she dropped her hands into her lap and clasped her fingers together. "Okay."

One word, spoken with finality.

Nick's dark eyes studied hers, his body tense. "Okay?"

She nodded slightly. "I believe you're sorry. I accept

your apology." She hesitated. "And if, in the past, I've ever hurt you, I'm sorry." Exhaling, she watched the rise and fall of his chest. "Let's just draw a line now."

The fire crackled.

She didn't know which of them moved first then, but he extended his hand and she put out hers. Their skin brushed, and her breath clicked in a little catch in her throat; their fingers slipped together, interlocking in a light hold.

After a moment, he reached out his free hand and cupped her cheek, his thumb a butterfly-touch along her cheekbone. She shivered.

Nick lowered his head, his thumb sweeping softly across her lips. He looked into her eyes. His were full of heat—and a question.

Her lips parting under his touch, Sabrina drew another unsteady breath, made a decision, and reached for him. Very lightly, she stroked her fingertips over the high arch of his cheekbone and heard his own breath hitch. She slipped her hand around his head, feeling the crispness of his short black hair, and drew his mouth down to hers.

Their lips brushed and came apart. He dusted a soft kiss on her Cupid's bow, then nuzzled his lips to her neck, her cheeks, the tip of her nose—teasing, making her smile despite the warmth pulsing through her. His smiling mouth returned to hers, and the kiss deepened naturally, his tongue pushing against hers, stroking, tingling.

Sabrina let go of his hand to wrap both arms around his neck, and he lifted her, pulling her into his lap. Stroking his ears with her thumbs, she kissed him again and again, tugging playfully at his bottom lip with her teeth. Time drifted into meaninglessness; the whole world compressed to a firelit room and this man's body.

His hands shaped the curves of her back and gripped her hips, pulling her pelvis into him. Squeezing her thighs along his, she ground against him, and he groaned, low and deep in his chest. As she kissed his neck, nibbling at his earlobe, and unfastened a couple more buttons on his shirt, Nick tugged the hem of her shirt from her skirt.

When he stroked up her side and his palm cupped her breast, she leaned her forehead against his shoulder and swallowed. His fingers slipped beneath the lace of her bra, touching her, the pad of his thumb seeking the hardened bead of her nipple. Sabrina clutched his jaw and kissed him fiercely. Her hips rocked in a smooth, rhythmic motion, cradling and rubbing on his erection, dragging another guttural noise from him.

He was kissing her back, hard, his tongue echoing the rhythm of her hips. With the gentlest twist of his fingers, he flicked his nail over her sensitive nipple, and pushed his pelvis up into her, once, twice—and the building pleasure suddenly rippled over Sabrina in one short series of pulses.

She cried out quietly against his mouth and tipped her head against his cheek, blinking rapidly, her breath an asthmatic-sounding squeak.

Oh. Oh, oh, oh my.

As orgasms went, that was more of a fun little surprise than neck-arching, toe-curling oblivion, but still— *Still.* Zero direct clitoral contact. What wizardry was that.

Nick's fingers had dug into her hips and he pulled

his head back to look at her. "Did you just—" His voice was a rasp that dragged over her nerve endings.

Still panting, her hands resting on his chest and her hips moving in little involuntary circles, she found her voice. "Your ego's going to need its own dressing room after this."

His short crack of laughter appeared to be involuntary, but then he was sitting up to wrap both arms fully around her, holding her tight as he kissed her again. Over and over, until Sabrina started making more helpless little sounds and Nick's heartbeat was thumping against the palm of her hand.

With a muttered oath, he lifted his head, breathing harshly. "We have to stop." He was running his palms up and down her back, in a gesture that was probably meant to be soothing.

Closing her eyes, Sabrina rested her cheek on the top of his head and tried to catch her breath. "Do we?"

"You came here tonight upset. I'm not—" Nick broke off with a renewed groan when she tried to shift her weight and accidentally massaged over his cock again. "I'm not taking advantage."

With her arms still around his neck, Sabrina opened her mouth to protest, but something—some tiny instinct inside that her G spot detested right now—kept her silent.

Smoothing back the hair at her temple, Nick nudged her back so he could see her face. His bared chest was still moving too quickly, but there was seriousness behind the arousal that gripped his tense body. "A lot of things have changed. I don't want you to regret this."

She closed her eyes, trying to relax her muscles. She couldn't remember things ever escalating so quickly

before; desire was a throbbing ache. Nick was still caressing her back and playing with loose curls of her
hair, as if he couldn't stop touching her. Which was
kind of sweet, but wasn't making her more inclined to
get off his erection and have a nice cup of tea.

"Okay," she said without opening her eyes, and, with
the last dregs of her self-control, she carefully swung
her leg to the side, easing off his lap. She rested her
cheek against the back of the couch, her body uncomfortable, her mind a chaos of thoughts.

She jumped a little when Nick's weight and warmth
moved close to her, and his lips touched her cheek.
With the lightest of kisses there and on her ear, he
said, his usually smooth voice still a throaty rumble,
"I wasn't expecting—"

That they'd go up in flames?

Likewise.

She'd known there was enough physical awareness
between them that, in some remote parallel universe
where they could stand being around each other long
enough to fall into bed, they'd probably have decent
sex; but she hadn't expected…that.

If she'd ever thought about being in bed with Nick,
she might have imagined the physical sensations—
with those hands and eyes and perfectionist drive, he
was always going to be skilled—but she'd never have
foreseen the feelings driving it.

Still intense and…edgy. Underscored with wariness. But the emotions that were acting on her head
and heartbeat like a jug of tequila were definitely not
born of anger and resentment.

Nick's fingers weren't quite steady as he buttoned
up his shirt over that plane of slightly damp brown skin

and rigid muscle. When she leaned forward to stand up, they bumped one another, and, without thought or intention, she found herself in another kiss, hard and urgent, their hands gripping each other's arms.

"Fuck," she said, dragging in air as they jerked their heads back.

"Ditto." Almost grimly, Nick shoved his hand over his hair, and shaking his head, he stood. "I think I'd better make some more coffee."

"Better make it Irish," Sabrina said, not entirely joking. She crossed her legs and clasped her hands. "Maybe I should get going."

Nick turned in the kitchen and looked at her, one hand resting on the counter. "If you like." Very careful and steady. "I'll run you home if you want to go now."

She didn't want to go now. Despite the usual lure of her beloved flat, she wanted to stay. She wanted to listen to Nick's voice, and watch the movements of his hands and lips when he spoke, and feel that unprecedented mix of lust and security that was ever-growing in his presence.

A lot of things have changed. Something of an understatement.

"I'd like the coffee."

His face was impassive, but something flashed through his eyes.

When he handed her a refilled mug, she sipped it absently, and coughed. Her grin broke through some of the lingering tension. "Did you put a slug of whisky in this?"

"You asked for Irish. I don't have any cream, so you get the lazy version." Nick rested his own cup on his knee. "How are you feeling now?"

She inhaled the delicious scent rising from her cup. "Definitely better than last time. I got a splinter in my knee after the wine barrel."

Calmly, Nick threw a Double Delight at her. He'd set a plate between them on the couch, like a really tasty chaperone.

She caught it and bit in, raising her brows at him. "I feel—" Taking the question seriously now, she swallowed. "He's my dad. I love him." Her lips twisted. "And sometimes it feels like we might as well be strangers. As a child, my life was basically supporting character in the Rupert Carlton stage production. Then I grew up, met Ferren, chased the TV cameras instead of the theatre spotlight, and enacted my own endless melodrama. Just—artificial. All of it." She looked down into the coffee. "As painful as parts of this year have been, life also feels…real now."

There was a short silence, before Nick reached out and touched her brow. He stroked his finger over her eyebrow, and pushed back a lock of hair that was threatening to fall into her mug. "Yes." His voice was low.

Tentatively, she asked, "Were you close to your father?" She'd seen his reaction when she'd brought up his father before, and he'd alluded himself to their having had a complicated relationship.

He looked into the depths of his own cup for a moment, as if they both sought the answers there; then set it down on the end table. "No," he said simply. "I wasn't close to my father. He was the most incredible, dynamic force. A trailblazer. And professionally, a hugely formative influence. But close—no."

"Did he want you to go into broadcasting?"

The set of Nick's mouth was grim for a moment.

"I think the earliest memory I have of him telling me I *would* be a journalist, and preferably either a political or war correspondent, was at eight. He was always about the importance of the press and serious journalism, the—" He stopped, a faint contortion pulling at his handsome features. "The adrenaline buzz of breaking a big story."

She'd been stroking his palm. Her fingers now stilled on his skin. "I see." With her wrist, she nudged back the persistent piece of hair dropping over her eyes. "*The Davenport Report* skewed far more heavily towards serious journalism than *WMUL*. What would your dad have thought of your current gig?"

Nick's hand flexed on hers, before he seemed to realise what he was doing and released her. "He'd have thought it was pointless fluff."

Exactly what Nick's own reaction had been, initially, before his competitive drive had overridden his snottiness about the breakfast show.

Sabrina ran her fingers over her lips.

Touching him, and smelling the scents of his cologne and his warm body, made her stomach flutter deliciously.

But the lust—and the unfurling glow of something she wasn't ready to name—was tempered with disquiet.

Chapter Eleven

A ringing sound was jabbing sharply at Nick's consciousness. He grunted and rolled over to bury his face deeper into warm silkiness. A leg slid against his, and wiggly little fingers pushed up under his shirt, spreading against his ribs.

Breath dusting across his throat. The faint abrasiveness of lace under his hand. A few shades of sleep slipped away, rational thought trying to break through the mists of exhaustion. The ringing stopped, and he stroked the lace approvingly and curled over the body cuddled into his.

A sudden pang from the muscles in his neck brought one eye open a crack. And then the ringing began again, sounding even louder than before.

He came fully awake with a jolt. He was not a morning person, but he was starting to get used to the early starts. For once, he went from zero to sixty, taking in his surroundings with a glance. He was sprawled sideways on his couch, which was not designed for an all-nighter—if that term applied when you got up at this hour—and Sabrina was fast asleep, tucked into his side. Her arm was bent under her head, covered with a rumpled mass of red curls; her other hand was cupping his pec. She breathed quietly and steadily, her lips slightly parted, mascara smudged beneath her lashes. As he looked down at her, the tempo of his heart thudded faster against her palm.

He then simultaneously realised that he had his hand on her breast and his phone was ringing on the coffee table.

Glancing over at the clock on the kitchen wall— "*Shit*." He disentangled himself enough that he could lean forward and snatch up the phone. "Kyle," he said to the studio driver who picked him up every morning, and reached over to run his fingertip down the bridge of Sabrina's freckled nose, rubbing until her eyelashes flickered open. Even in the lamplight, her eyes were shockingly green. "Sorry, mate, we're running late. Be down in five."

"No worries," the cheerful young man responded, and added, with a teasing note, "'We're'?"

Nick winced and ran his hand over his face, feeling the thick rasp of stubble. "You're doing a double today and bringing Sabrina, as well." His brain clicked fully into gear. "Could you do us a favour and give her driver a call? He's probably over at her flat right now."

Her sleepy face starting to morph into horror, Sabrina got up and stumbled over to the table by the door, where she fished out her phone as Nick ended his call.

"Battery's dead," she said, throwing it back in her bag. "Shit. Shit, shit, shit." She looked down at her rumpled clothes. "I'll have to go like this. Oh, God, I don't even have a toothbrush. My breath could prob-

ably fell an elephant right now." She looked up hopefully. "Do you have spares?"

"I hate to discredit the usual tabloid rumours, but my
private life isn't quite active enough to warrant that."

"Well, that's inconvenient," Sabrina said crossly,
rubbing her eyes. She looked tired and fractious, and
he wanted to give her a cuddle.

However, they were already twelve minutes behind
schedule.

"Sorry to disappoint you." He was grabbing his
things together. "I'll have to shower when we get
there." He nodded towards the archway that led into
his short hallway. "Guest bathroom is the second door
on the left. I don't have endless stores of toothbrushes,
but I do have soap and moisturiser." Unzipping his
own bag, he dug into an interior pocket. "And gum."
He threw it over to her.

"You've redeemed yourself." Sabrina unwrapped a
stick and shoved it in her mouth, then dashed off towards the bathroom.

Nick was in and out of his ensuite in less than two
minutes, grabbing his razor on the way out. Sabrina
joined him at the front door shortly after, and they hurried down the stairs, pulling on their coats as they went.

As soon as he pushed open the outside door, a camera flashed in the dimly lit street. One very hardy, probably very cold photographer was waiting by the car,
ignoring Kyle's directives to stand clear.

In no mood to deal with it, Nick kept his body between the pap and Sabrina, and didn't so much as
turn his head, although some of the more suggestive
comments made his teeth snap together. He took Sa-

brina's hand to help her into the car as Kyle held the door open for them.

When they pulled out into the traffic flow, she looked wryly down at herself. "Leaving your flat in the middle of the night looking like something a cat dragged in. I think we've just made our affirmative press statement."

They briefly got stuck in a traffic jam near Somerset House, Sabrina using the time and a hand mirror to change her contact lenses, but overall the roads were clear enough that they still arrived at the network buildings relatively close to plan. The studio was lit up, the walls retina-burning as usual, but not even the earliest crew were on the set yet. Without further discussion, they split up, Nick walking into the kitchen, Sabrina heading for the platform where a "fun science" display was sitting ready and waiting. They were supposed to be making slime and setting off various explosions of foam with the host of a kids' show today; he could just imagine the potential catastrophe lurking if their saboteur had targeted that segment.

Nick began checking ingredients for the cooking demonstration, tasting soy sauce, oil, and spices, looking inside containers and making sure seals hadn't been broken.

Sabrina was also inspecting plastic seals and holding bottles up to the light. "I'm admitting defeat on this one." Her voice carried across the room, which was slightly eerie in its emptiness. "I don't know what half this stuff is. We'll just have to hope that any resultant explosions are intended."

"Kitchen seems clear." Nick joined her at the science table and cast an eye over the array of coloured

bottles and towering glass tubes. "If our mystery foe
has any sense of occasion, they'll go for this one. Standards are slipping since the possessed Wibblet. Pro-
jectile foam would be more interesting than moving a
few props around."

They both heard it, then, a door opening quietly
from the staff corridor, still too early for most of the
crew. As if they'd rehearsed it—on the set of a bad
film—they ducked down behind the video monitors,
and the whole thing suddenly caught at Nick's sense
of humour. A jolt of amusement went through him,
and Sabrina leaned her head against a panel sprouting
wires and tried to muffle a giggle.

"This is serious," he said severely under his breath,
and grinned when she put her hand over her mouth,
her eyes bright with laughter. She made another suppressed sound when he edged over to look around the
bank of monitors.

"Well?" she mouthed, when he'd spotted the intruder.

A vacuum cleaner turned on.

"Are there times," Sabrina asked, her voice just audible over the maintenance staffer's hoovering, "when
you take stock of where you are and what you're doing,
and wonder how the fuck this happened?"

Daily. Never more so than now, as he crouched
on the floor of the ugliest studio in the network, unshaven, in need of a shower and coffee, hiding in wait
for a meddler whose *Scooby-Doo* antics were plausibly
threatening what remained of his job security.

He ought to be fed up to the back teeth, but right
at this moment, he was very aware of the lightness in
his chest.

Without overthinking it, he leaned forward and

brushed his lips over hers. The resigned humour in her expression fading, she looked into his eyes as she bit her lower lip.

"Last night." His voice was slightly raspy. "It was—"

"Good." A flush came into her cheeks, and Nick felt the lines at the corners of his eyes and that warmth around his heart deepen.

"Good?" he teased, and she rolled her eyes, a tiny smile curving as she touched her fingertips to his chest.

Catching him momentarily off guard, she tightened her fist in the fabric of his shirt, pulled him closer, and kissed him hard.

Every time—overwhelming, hot arousal, and blurry sensation. She went straight to his head like whisky. Warmth, and bite, and a golden glow. He loved the shape of her mouth, the feel of her soft lower lip as he caught it between his.

Her breath coming quickly, she drew back and looked down at where her hands held his forearms. With her thumb, she rubbed over the scar winding out under his sleeve. "How did you get hurt?" The words were as husky as his had been.

Diverting into safer territory. She was cautious. An inconvenient, mutual physical attraction was one thing. This was rapidly moving well beyond that, and he could see something in her eyes balk when the walls of her comfort zone rattled.

Considering her past, and particularly considering *their* past, he got it.

Fuck, he *shared* it.

And, so far, she was wary—but she was still moving forward, towards him.

With him.

"It's two scars joined together." Nick pushed his sleeve up farther and turned his arm. "The bigger one is from a school cricket match when I was about fourteen. I was playing in the championship, and I got distracted." He hadn't thought about that incident for a long time. "My father was supposed to be coming." Which would have been a first. He remembered trying to play it cool, and how many times he'd looked over into the family stands. "I thought I saw him arriving. Collided with a teammate. There was a piece of glass in the grass."

Sabrina curled her long legs to one side, resting her hand on her ankle. "Did he turn up?"

"No." He ran his hand over the scar, feeling the ghost of an itch. "It was forever ago. That wasn't meant to be a pathetic Little Boy Lost story."

"It's not pathetic," she said quietly. Reaching over, she touched the second, darker scar that hooked into the old one. "And this?"

It wasn't a wraith of emotion this time; it was a sharp stab. "A falling brick." He met her gaze unflinchingly, but couldn't help the locking of his muscles. "At Highbrook a few years ago. Griff and I spent a weekend doing our best attempt at DIY on one of the outbuildings."

It had been a much-needed break from work. He'd been stressed to the point it had been affecting his health. Funny how much he'd ignored that, blocked that out. His gut twisted. He suspected it wasn't a coincidence that Griff, not one to ask for help in any circumstances, had suddenly required Nick's presence in the country then.

Sabrina's future brother-in-law was a self-sufficient misanthrope most of the time. He was also fiercely protective of people he cared about. Nick had once been privileged to come into that category, before he'd ripped things to shreds in one night.

As the vacuum cleaner clicked off and Nick became vaguely aware of other bustling noises behind their makeshift fort, Sabrina asked, "Have you tried speaking to Griff again?"

He moved his head, a short, negative gesture. It had been like talking to a stranger the last time he'd tried—the stone-faced Griff that most acquaintances saw, not the man with an unexpectedly wicked sense of humour and an acerbic way of managing other people's welfare.

"Ahem."

They both jumped at the dry interjection, and Nick turned. Jess was standing there, looking down at them. Her purple nails drummed on the clipboard she had tucked over her arm. One dark brow arched.

Silence.

She examined them, from dishevelled heads to wrinkled clothes, and shook her head. "I know you're struggling with the early starts. But you don't need to actually sleep in the studio." She cleared her throat pointedly. "Frank Gough's people have been in touch and His Majesty requires an earlier appointment, so we're bumping him up the schedule. When he arrives for the meet-and-greet, should we bring him to the green room as usual, or just tell him to plant his arse on the floor?"

Sabrina stretched. "Incoming wanker."

As Nick stood, he reached down a hand to help her up. "Makes a change it's not me, doesn't it?"

Frank Gough was a tall man who'd kept a relatively muscular build into his sixties, although he was starting to look a bit corpulent about the jaw, and his nose was a telltale red. Too much money and too much drink. Apparently, he had his fingers in all sorts of financial pies these days.

As long as he kept his hands away from anything else. And every*one* else.

Strong lecher vibes, from the get-go.

Gritting her teeth, she extended her hand. "Mr. Gough. Good morning. Thank you for coming in today. We're very much looking forward to discussing your book."

The businessman swept her with a look that started at her hair, lingered at her breasts, and travelled up and down her legs. It only lasted a few seconds, but left her feeling like she could do with another shower.

Gough kept hold of her hand as he smiled at her. It was a spidery sort of smile; the predator sitting in his web, waiting to reel in his lunch. "Rupert Carlton's girl," he said, and she frowned slightly. She wouldn't have picked Gough as one of her father's theatre crowd. "Wonderful to meet you."

His proffered handshake to Nick was less enthusiastic. "And Markus Davenport's son. Taken a bit of a fall from grace lately, I understand." His laugh was not attractive. "Poor old Grimes. Still, you're obviously not afraid to speak your mind, which is a quality I admire—" Nick looked definitely unflattered "—and you clearly have an ear for the truth." Gough's smile was cold now. "Not a chip off the old block in that respect."

Nick's cheek twanged, but his professional composure didn't crack.

Gough turned to Sabrina. "Have you read my book?"

"Yes, I have." She detested the man, and had no interest whatever in his likely dodgy business advice, but she also had professional standards and she did her prep. "Fascinating."

"I'm quite happy to offer a little of my time, if you want to put any of my suggestions into practice." Gough was using his politician's voice, persuasive and polite; but he was still doing the X-ray look, mentally stripping off her clothes with his pupils.

"How kind."

"I hope that your contributions to this interview will encourage other women to read the book. My agent tells me that sales have skewed significantly towards men; but ladies can, of course, also benefit from the course I recommend." He gave another tight chuckle. "Although I must admit the fair sex have devised their own path to wealth admirably. The joys of settlements and alimony!"

What a treat of a human being.

Shocking that he was currently negotiating his fourth divorce.

Gough didn't improve under the scrutiny of the cameras. He cut off questions before they'd finished speaking, tossed in as many endorsements for his personal financial concerns as possible, and bragged about his life achievements for almost ten solid minutes.

"I don't care if the man has the bank vaults of Scrooge McDuck," Fenella said into Sabrina's earpiece. "Ninety percent of our viewers are now in a coma. Wrap this up."

"Your eldest son contributed several chapters to the book," Sabrina cut in smoothly, moving straight to the final talking point on their cue cards. "You must be proud he's following in your footsteps."

Not too closely, she hoped. The world did not need a Gough 2.0.

She'd pegged Gough as the variety of egoist who'd want a bunch of Mini-Me offspring, and his smile gained a bit more smarm wattage. "He's a bright kid," he said patronisingly about a thirty-year-old man. "He's always had ambition. Too many young people these days just sit around, expecting things to come to them. You have to go after what you want. And of course, it's important to set the right example. So many sons follow in the footsteps of unworthy fathers."

That last, with a tiny sneer, and a very direct look at Nick.

Sabrina felt her hackles rise. The surge of protectiveness took her by surprise in its intensity. Fortunately, since she wasn't sure she'd have kept her feelings out of her voice, Nick wound up the interview, completely cool and expressionless.

When Gough had been ushered off the set—and good riddance; it could have kicked off far worse, but the man was a dickhead—Sabrina touched Nick's elbow during the ad break.

"The only thing he's demonstrating to his kids is how to be a complete shit, in one easy step."

Nick finished adjusting the volume on his earpiece. Briefly, he touched his thumb to the line of her jaw. "My feelings about my father have always been conflicted, and used to change weekly, but I'm fully aware of his faults," he said in a low voice. "However, I'd rather have had Darth Vader for a dad than Gough."

On which note, they went over to blow things up at the science table. Fountains of frothing, bubbling pink and green foam almost hit the studio ceiling, but

Sabrina assumed by the expert's manner that every
chemical reaction was intentional. Nothing turned into
a noxious gas and forced a mass evacuation, so their
saboteur had missed a golden opportunity.

Despite how it had begun, she was having fun as
the morning progressed. She watched with amusement
as Nick demonstrated each item in the Christmas gift
guide with the skill of a shopping-channel veteran.

He was working the cameras, purposely lifting the
mood after the slimy snoozefest of Gough. But his
real, from-within grin was out as she tried to twist
away from a hi-tech head massager that did something
she couldn't bear to her nerve endings. Every time it
touched her, she flailed about like a lost octopus.

When she took up the guest's offer of trialling a new
variety of electric skateboard, however, he suddenly
turned into a walking safety manual.

He insisted on checking the board before she used
it, via a very believable series of questions and flat-
tery to the young man who'd brought it in, having him
just about deconstruct the engine on the studio floor.
Fair enough. Given the track record of electronics on
this show malfunctioning, she'd been going to casually manoeuver a look-over herself.

But, having flicked switches and revved things and
peered at the internals, and found nothing to raise suspicion, Nick continued to do a dead impressive imper-
sonation of Molly Weasley.

"You're going to fall." He stood with his hands
slightly raised, as if she were literally about to cata-
pult off and needed Superman over there to swoop in.
She hadn't even stepped onto the thing yet.

"No, I'm not," she said cheerfully, bending to touch

the controls the young man had explained with enthusiasm.

"It doesn't look safe."

"Oh no, it's really easy to use," her new friend assured Nick, who remained unimpressed. "And it's on the lowest setting for an indoors demo. A toddler could play on it." He helped Sabrina stand on the base. "Just, left foot there... Yes, awesome! You're a natural."

"You're going to break your leg," intoned the joy prophet, as she rode in a circle around his towering, glowering figure at the approximate speed of a slow-motion tortoise, and oh my God, had she ever questioned the friendship between Griff and Nick?

Right now—peas in a bloody pod.

"All right, Grandpa." She circled him again. "You can stop twitching now. I'm getting off." She handed it back to its owner, and asked, with great interest, "Are they legal to use on the street? It would be fun on Waterloo Bridge."

Nick's face did not disappoint.

After the show, Jess approached with printouts. "Here's the schedule for the Murder Train broadcast. Are you still heading to King's Cross to final up arrangements?"

Sabrina glanced at Nick, and he nodded.

"Good. Great job today, guys." To a passing tech, she called out, "Hey, Murad, did we find out what happened with the teleprompt?"

Nick's eyes narrowed. "The teleprompt?"

"Yeah, good thing everyone was on tenterhooks about the Gough interview going smoothly. We checked it at the last minute, and a bunch of screens

were lost. You'd have had to improvise half the intro-
duction."

They waited until they were in the corridor outside
their dressing rooms before they spoke.

"Next step," Nick said, "we'd better check back the
CCTV footage."

"I thought about it after the Wibblet, but we'd have
to file an official request to see it. You can't just swing
by and demand to see the security footage for no reason."

"I have a contact. I'll sort it."

"Why am I not surprised?" Sabrina unlocked her
door and pushed it open. "And here I was thinking our
helpful friend was either out sick or having a change
of heart. We're lucky he or she didn't target the foam
explosion or the gift guide. Those ran comparatively
like clockwork." She anticipated his rejoinder before
he said it. "Oh my God. Those skateboards are safe."

"Do you know how many people end up in A & E
because of—"

Her ringing phone cut off the lecture. Unexpected
new irritating side of Nick. A person fell in the Thames
one time and they were marked as a walking hazard,
unsafe to operate moving machinery. Dashing in to
grab her phone before it stopped, she glanced at the
screen and didn't recognise the number. "Sabrina Carlton speaking." She smiled as she recognised the voice
at the other end. "Oh, hi, Arthur, how are you?"

The elderly owner of The Toy Chest in Paddington
spoke in his kind, roundabout way, and after a second
or two, Sabrina gestured quickly at Nick, still standing
in the doorway. He came in, brows lifted, and closed
the door.

"Thank you so much, Arthur," Sabrina said after they'd chatted for a few minutes. "I'll come in tonight and pick it up. You're an absolute wonder."

She ended the call. "The sweetest old man in the world has managed to find me a Wibblet for Lizzy, which I'll collect tonight, *and* he has a friend with a toy store near York, which also still has one, that you can give to your brother for Pippi. The owner is holding it for us, so we can pick it up when we get off the Murder Train. We could just hire a car for an hour or two, then catch a normal afternoon train back to London. Two demonic creatures, two happy little girls, Father Christmas comes through. Sorted."

Nick pushed back his jacket and propped his hands on his waist. "I clearly wasted my time worrying about you on the skateboard. It wouldn't have dared bump you off."

"It's so nice we're finally getting to know each other properly."

Chapter Twelve

11 Days until Christmas Eve

The showgirl lay sprawled across the floor of the carriage, her face pale against the black bob of her hair, her lips as red as the stain creeping across the sequins on her gold dress.

"Half their expenses must go on dry-cleaning" was the loud remark from the one woman on the train who'd persistently refused to get into the spirit of the performance.

They'd carefully avoided filming her during the *WMUL* broadcast.

The rest of the invited celebrities, VIPs, and ticket-winners were enthusiastically embracing the brief.

"Ooh, she's holding something." A reality star from *Babes in the Wood* knelt by the actress's outflung arm and tried to pull the note from her fingers, giggling when the "corpse" refused to let go.

"The clock stopped when it smashed," pointed out an opera tenor who patently fancied himself as the next Poirot, down to the curled moustache—which was genuine, unlike the revolting strip of fake hair glued to Nick's own upper lip like a lost caterpillar.

The Murder Train, a three-course meal and inter-active whodunit, usually did a circuit at night around outer London, but today's charity trip was chugging along from King's Cross to York, and the carriages were packed with people eating salmon bruschetta and poking around with magnifying glasses. The train actors bantered and flirted, answered the guests' questions, claimed them for alibis, and planted weapons under bags and coats.

So far, with the social-media involvement of the *WMUL* viewers at home for the first storyline, the mysterious widow had been implicated for the poisoning of the offensive magistrate; now, with the broadcast over and the journey on its last leg, they were finishing up the second performance of the morning and the show-girl had succumbed in the restaurant carriage.

Sabrina was taking it very personally. Having been cast as the sassy flapper, she'd compared feathered costumes with the showgirl, and that was it. Chatting and laughing all through the first mystery, the two total strangers might have been best mates for twenty years. It was a phenomenon Nick had observed in the past with Tia when she'd suddenly befriend someone in five seconds flat.

"You just *know*," she'd informed him loftily once. "She gets me."

Nick did not just "know." Working a crowd, sooth-ing a guest, networking at an event—child's play. Legitimate friendships, people with whom he truly connected, were far rarer.

Which was why he was going to respect and protect the bonds he had, fiercely, from now on.

"Come on." Sabrina caught at his hand. "I have an idea."

He let himself be towed through the carriage. Despite his atrocious costume, he'd admit that it had been a fun morning, and worthwhile just for the laughter constantly dancing in Sabrina's eyes.

And *her* costume— He let his eyes travel downward. Sequins, feathers, not much fabric, and legs for days.

He'd give up half his salary if this were a sleeper train, and not full of his work colleagues and a bunch of athletes and soap stars.

In the corridor of the next carriage, on impulse, he opened the door of an empty compartment and pulled Sabrina inside.

His mouth cut off her surprised squeak.

"Nick," she said against his lips. "I have *clues* to follow."

Her fingers, however, were sneaking up his sides, and she was smiling as he kissed her again.

As she'd said earlier in the week, life right now was a constant series of surreal moments.

He'd begun this year as a man with a secure job, a moderately sized fan base, and a decent private life, dating at events and good restaurants, and always keeping a cool head. Come December, and he was dressed as a 1920s playboy, unsure if he'd still be employed by Christmas Day, and kissing Sabrina Carlton in a train full of amateur sleuths.

Objectively, bizarre.

Yet even with every road ending in uncertainty, something inside him, some bone-deep restlessness and discontent, was easing.

Although he could happily lose the bow tie and spats.

"Waste of time. It's the butler," he murmured, pushing his hand farther up her thigh under the sequinned dress. He lowered his head and kissed the curve of her neck, breathing in the light scent of patchouli. She wore a perfume that was unapologetically sexy, no frothy blend of a sweet shop and a spring garden for Sabrina. Arousal was a dark, seductive pulse through his body.

With a sudden movement, he linked his fingers through hers, and pulled their arms up over her head. Kissing her hard, his tongue stroking into her mouth, he pushed his hips into hers. She made a sound in her throat, raspy and full of need, and it sent a whipcord of sensation through Nick's spine. Her fingers clutched his tighter as she planted a row of kisses down his cheek towards his ear, and he nuzzled his head against hers. Her chest was rising and falling rapidly, threatening the low neckline of her costume, and pleasure was becoming a dangerously rhythmic beat.

Too dangerously.

Releasing her hands, Nick eased his body back, putting a few inches between them. He closed his eyes, his hold slipping to her waist as his heart pounded hard and fast against his ribs. Sabrina's head came forward and rested against him, and she placed her palms on his chest, taking deep, shaky breaths.

Officially he and Sabrina were off the clock after the broadcast, but he wasn't such an exhibitionist that he wanted to be caught pants-down by the actor who'd been playing a soap-opera patriarch since Nick's school days.

And the very thought of Fenella popping her head in was bloody horrifying.

Sabrina drew in another deep breath. "It definitely is not the butler," she said, her voice still an octave lower than usual. When he touched her, she went all throaty, like an '80s rock star; he fucking loved it. "That is clichéd and generic, and unworthy of the Tommy to my Tuppence. Agatha Christie judges you."

"His alibi was cocked-up." Nick couldn't help nipping the earlobe she put in proximity to his lips, and she shivered. "He couldn't have arrived on the fifth. The time difference between Australia and England would have to work the other way around."

"It's the vicar's wife." Sabrina's fingers traced a tickling circle above the bow tie. "Fifi was obviously boinking Reverend Brown. Her garter was in the pocket of his cassock."

"Let's hope it wasn't the flapper or the gigolo. If one of us was the hand on the pistol, the murderer's done a bunk."

Sabrina ran her index fingers under the straps of the braces that clipped onto his crisp trousers. "I do like the get-up."

The click and clatter of the rails beneath their carriage was starting to slow as they came to another station.

She pulled on the braces, and Nick leaned forward and kissed her once more, a closed-mouth touch that was undeniably affectionate and somehow twanged inside him harder than the driving heat of minutes prior.

The door to their compartment opened, and they both turned, her hands still holding on to him, his arms around the small of her back.

"Oh," said one of the women who stood there, blinking. Nick mentally placed them as the board members of one of the recipient charities. "I'm so sorry. Jean left her bag in here. I'm guessing this isn't part of the plot."

"No. No, this is definitely unscripted." Sabrina released Nick and found a friendly smile. "How's progress?"

"We've solved it," another of the women said enthusiastically, holding up her scorecard. "We just need a photo with the murderer."

"Oh, who is it? The vicar's wife?" Sabrina asked.

"It's the butler," Nick said again, and she cast up her eyes.

"Fifi was blackmailing the baron's ne'er-do-well son after their affair went sour, and he shot her," the woman said.

Hell.

Sabrina cleared her throat and leaned into him. "Is that you?"

That was the official role on his costume card, yes.

The women brightened. "Oh, *is* it you? Fantastic. It's so hard to keep everyone straight, we were going to check the cast list."

"Just screams it, really, doesn't he?" his helpful sidekick piped up cheerfully. "Spats, villain moustache, natty trousers. Obvious philanderer."

Nick's fingers curled into the dip of her waist, and she ducked away, laughing.

He produced his best villainous leer while Sabrina snapped photos of him with the thrilled charity executors, before they returned to the front carriages to watch the presentation of the prizes.

The train chugged into York at close to noon, by which time they'd changed back into their normal clothes and he'd lost the horrific moustache. Their hire car was a relatively new Audi, and Sabrina took one look at it and offered to go rock-paper-scissors for driving rights.

He tossed her the keys. "Knock yourself out," he said, sliding into the passenger seat and stretching with a yawn. "After a morning going homicidal on unsuspecting showgirls, I'm very happy to be chauffeured."

Sabrina loved York, and Nick had always been drawn to the city as well, so they took a roundabout route, enjoying the sight of the Minster rising into the still grey sky. He always felt as if he'd stepped back in time here, as if the drumming footsteps of the Roman troops still echoed on the stones, and the oars of the Vikings were coming through the fog, slicing through the dark water of the River Ouse. The Shambles had been lit up for Christmas and looked like a page out of *Harry Potter*, and when they stopped for a ten-minute wander to pick up some sandwiches and coffee, Sabrina was like an excited kid.

She ran up to a window that glittered with lights and tinsel, and turned back to smile at him. Her cheeks were red in the biting air, and she looked relaxed and happy.

A passing couple stopped and said hello to her, and she posed with one of the young men while his boyfriend snapped a photo. Nick's attention was so focused on her that he didn't notice the elderly woman who'd stopped on the paving stones, pale and wavering, until Sabrina excused herself from her friendly fans and ran to put a hand on the other woman's elbow. She lowered her head to speak to her, and Nick joined them quickly to offer his arm. There were no benches around, so they helped her into the nearest café.

"Goodness. So sorry," the woman gasped, sitting down heavily. She was still clutching Sabrina's hand. "It's this dratted low blood pressure. Catches me un- awares."

Sabrina knelt in front of her. "Can we drive you home?" She put her other hand over the frail fingers. From the painful distortion of the woman's knuckles, she suffered badly with arthritis. "Nick—maybe a cup of tea?" she murmured, looking up at him.

"Oh no. Thank you. That's very kind." The woman seemed flustered. "My daughter and my grandson are coming back to collect me shortly."

Nick went up to the counter and ordered a cup of tea and half a dozen cakes and pastries. "And a couple of the gingerbread men. Cheers."

The elderly woman's name was Jane, and she chat- tered with the air of a person who probably lived alone most of the time, and not by choice. Sabrina asked her questions and made her laugh, and admired the photos that emerged from a battered handbag.

Jane seemed completely overcome by the paper bag of cakes and biscuits. "So kind," she kept repeating, as a concerned-looking woman rushed towards them with a sulky preteen trailing in her wake. Before Jane left with her daughter, she smiled and touched two cold fingertips to Nick's hand and Sabrina's cheek. "You're a lovely couple."

Sabrina chewed on her lip as they watched her walk slowly and painfully away. "I hope her flat is warm. My dad's pain is always worse in winter. Her poor hands. Her daughter seemed nice, though." She pushed back a strand of red hair that was blowing in the breeze. "You bought gingerbread biscuits because she said she had a grandson."

"The staff has a much lighter hand than I did with the decorating. Although to be fair, their boss probably doesn't blindfold them for a laugh."

Sabrina didn't smile. She gazed at him silently for seconds that stretched out long enough to weave tension into the air. Then she reached up and lightly kissed him on the mouth.

It was a strange moment, on a cobbled street in wintery York, outside an old-fashioned café, his ears numb with cold, to finally, properly, acknowledge that he was in love with her.

It had been growing for longer than he'd been able to admit, sweeping him along in its tide—his feelings for her had started as something that had *happened* to him, something inside him reaching out to her, something he'd had no control over. He'd never been good at ceding control. But now it was as if he made a conscious choice. He accepted he loved her. He chose to love her.

He was standing, unmoving, half aware of people moving past him, and Sabrina's face tilting into a question.

She touched his arm. "Hey—you okay?"

The connection between them was constant and deep. Sabrina's hand closed fully over his arm and she rubbed him, instinctively trying to comfort; as the wind picked up, she stepped closer, into the shelter of his body.

Sexual sparks undeniable. The instinct to protect breathtakingly fierce. Arguments between them softer-edged now, no longer ugly, no longer designed to cut deep and hurt. But how *far* it went beyond that, for her—he genuinely didn't know.

She'd spent years chaotically infatuated with Ferren. And she'd despised Nick since the night they'd met.

Things had changed. But—

The underlying uncertainty that gripped him suddenly had teeth.

Sabrina reached up and brushed her fingertips along his brow. "Nick."

He shook his head, once, almost grimly, before he straightened and took her hand, putting it in the hook of his elbow. "Sorry. Just thinking. We'd better get some food for ourselves and make tracks. What's the name of this village we're looking for?"

"Blenheim Morley." Sabrina was still frowning, but she didn't push it further. Another small crowd of people approached at that moment, asking for autographs and selfies, which dispelled at least the surface tension as he scrawled his name over and over, and slipped by rote into his public persona, the version of himself that strangers expected.

He said little in the car, and Sabrina shot him occasional narrowed glances as she drove.

After several wrong turns, since for some reason neither of their phones' GPS apps believed that Blenheim Morley existed, they found the affluent-looking village on the banks of a narrow river. It was like an adult-sized Sylvanian Families village, minus the anthropomorphised woodland creatures. Nick was fairly sure that Pippi owned small plastic versions of the thatched cottages, the early nineteenth-century bakery, and the quaint little church.

"How fucking cute." Sabrina got out of the car and

immediately started taking photos. She reverently stroked the stone wall of what appeared to be an old-fashioned general store.

Apparently there was no age limit on the lure of a Sylvanian Families village.

The toy store, aptly named The Toy Shoppe, was located at the end of a narrow, winding cobblestone path. It was the ground floor of a two-storey cottage that looked so completely fairy tale that Nick was starting to have qualms. "If we end up locked in a cage and turned into life-sized dolls, I will entirely blame you."

"Fair enough."

The bell above the door tinkled as they walked into a small retail space stuffed floor to ceiling with toys. Even though they were here to pick up one of the most technologically advanced and irritating gadgets on the market, he still expected most of the stock to be classic wooden toys and handmade dollhouses. But however twee the exterior, the owner was moving with the times. There were wooden blocks and porcelain dolls, but they were displayed alongside gaming consoles and drones, and eye-watering price tags hung off everything. Not quite a ye olde village shoppe where you could pick up a toy truck for pennies.

He picked up a fire engine that looked exactly like one he remembered from his childhood, and opened the side flap to see if it had an extendable hose.

Sabrina cleared her throat, and he looked up. She was standing there with exaggerated patience, while a bored-looking teen, who ought to be at school, leaned on the counter and played with the lollipop sticking out of her mouth.

"Hi," Sabrina said, flashing a smile at the young

girl. "I think we have a Wibblet on hold to pick up? For Carlton?"

The teenager slowly removed the sweet from her mouth and looked Sabrina up and down. "Cool boots."

"Thank you."

The lollipop went back in, and around it, the girl said, "Sorry. We're sold out of Wibblets. New shipment expected before Christmas." Having seemed totally disinterested in anything but Sabrina's boots, she now showed an unexpected flash of sympathy. "But I've heard there's a major supply problem, and they probs won't be in until January. You've left it pretty late for Wibblets."

"Oh—I spoke to…your father on the phone?" Sabrina ventured.

"My grand-da."

"He said you had two left yesterday, and he'd put one aside."

The girl suddenly swore and pushed the sweet into the side of her cheek. "Grand-da had an early call-out this morning—he used to be the vet and he's still on-call if he's needed—and he did say something when he left, but I was on my phone. I'm really sorry—Mikey Waters came in and I sold the last two Wibblets to him. He's giving one to his kid, and donating the other one for third prize in the competition tonight. First place is an iPad. I'd rather have that," she added, and Nick didn't blame her.

With huge foreboding, he said, "Competition?"

The girl looked at him directly for the first time and suddenly blushed. Removing the lollipop, she hid her hand beneath the counter and tugged at her jumper. "The annual Christmas Stick-It at The Morley Arms."

Brightening, she offered, "You could enter if you like. It's not just for locals. People come from all over. Starts at eight o'clock. It's a tenner to enter, but you get a free bag of crisps."

"'Stick-It'?" Sabrina repeated, warily. "That would be—"

"Darts," the girl said succinctly, and Nick smiled slowly.

"How do you feel about a night in Blenheim Morley, Sparks?"

Nick Davenport. Frequent sarcastic dickhead. Second-best TV presenter in London. Mediocre knitter.

Phenomenal at darts.

Sabrina sat curled in her cosy booth close to the roaring log fire in The Morley Arms, and watched the place go up in cheers and hollers again as Nick flicked his wrist and slammed home another dart.

Raising her fingers to her mouth, she whistled, and through the crowds of people either cheering or jeering him, with equally good nature, he looked over at her and grinned. The lamplights and fairy lights—apparently it was considered better sport to chuck sharp objects about in half-darkness—were casting a glow on his skin, and he looked tall and ruffled and—God— kind of *dear*, standing there.

And sexy as fuck.

A woman about her own age, Jenny, who'd introduced herself earlier as the local medical receptionist and immediately bought Sabrina a glass of wine, leaned close to her ear. Over the general racket, she echoed the sentiment. "Don't take this the wrong way, but your man is *fit*."

Sabrina bit down on her thumbnail. Nick was laughing and joking with a crowd of men, and she'd never seen him so relaxed and dishevelled. In a suit, he was inarguably gorgeous.

Happy, he was…devastating.

Her man?

She found a smile for her new friend. "Yeah," she said, slowly. "He is."

"Come on, city boy," taunted the man who'd dubiously taken Nick's ten-pound entry fee earlier, and had heckled him ever since. He smacked Nick on the back hard enough to send him through the stone wall. "Let's see if you can bring it home, then."

Sabrina glanced over at the bar, where the night's prizes were lined up in a guard of honour. Beyond a sign emblazoned with a number three, the boxed Wibblet was looped with a ribbon. Eyes glared out through the plastic, glowing in the light.

Why did she feel like, if Nick won the thing tonight, she was going to wake up and find it sitting at the end of the bed.

Only her budding affection for Pippi overrode her desire to bump Nick's arm and let someone else take home the furry force of evil.

He was the last to throw, and he sent Sabrina a lightning glance over his shoulder before he flung the dart with one sharp motion. It thudded into the board, just missing the bullseye and landing in the outer ring for twenty-five points.

Dropping him neatly down to finish third.

As Nick accepted the teasing commiserations from his fellow finalists and shouted the pub another round of drinks, Jenny grinned at Sabrina. "Uh-oh," she said.

"He's got the creepy toy. I'd happily take one of your bedfellows off your hands tonight, but you're welcome to the other. It's close quarters at the inn, too."

Nick came over to the booth with a glass of wine in each hand and set them in front of Sabrina and Jenny.

"Get your victory kiss, then," someone called, grinning. "Third place doesn't quite warrant a full snog, but it should get you a peck, I reckon."

Nick looked down at Sabrina, his eyes dancing with laughter and a question. He'd been so preoccupied and silent earlier today—which not so long ago, she'd have considered a blessing; be careful what you wished for—and it was a relief to see the animation back.

So much so that she reached up, grabbed him by the ears, and planted a smacking kiss on his mouth. Caught by surprise, he almost fell forward, catching himself with one hand on the table, the other automatically cupping the back of her head.

He returned her a second kiss, teasingly touching the tip of his tongue to her lower lip before he straightened, to wolf-whistles and laughter.

Sabrina shook her head, smiling.

By eleven o'clock, her eyelids were starting to droop. She'd been up since half past four. Across the pub, where Nick had been dragged into another round of darts, this one just a friendly, he caught her eye and gestured enquiringly with his head towards the door. Stifling a yawn, she nodded, and they made their goodbyes.

Jenny grinned at her as she handed Nick the boxed toy. "Maybe leave the Wibblet on the landing tonight," she joked. "The voice recording function could be a bit awkward."

Outside in the small forecourt, Sabrina pulled her coat tighter under her chin, already shivering—it was *freezing*—and tucked her arm through Nick's as they walked down the street towards the Mulberry Tree Inn.

"Impressive throwing arm you've got there, Davenport." Her teeth were chattering.

"I honed my skills throwing paper aeroplanes into girls' ponytails at school."

"How'd that go for you?"

"Five black eyes before I was twelve, and I didn't have a girlfriend until I was nineteen."

She laughed.

The village might be cold, but it was incredibly pretty. She said so to Nick as she gazed around, and he steered her around a puddle before she ended up calf-deep in sub-zero water.

"Do you want to move to the country some day?"

"No. I'm definitely a city dweller. I wouldn't mind living in York at some point, though. Much farther down the line career-wise." She screwed up her nose. "Although if we don't get the permanent contract for *WMUL*, there won't be any immediate professional ties to London."

Nick was silent for a few moments. The only sounds were the echo of their footsteps in the quiet night and the faint beat of music drifting from the pub. "When this situation was first—not so much dangled as a carrot, but held up as a last-ditch booby prize, I wanted to succeed for the sake of success. Failure goes against the grain. I'd never had any desire to work the breakfast shift, and after headlining my own show, this was a step down."

Sabrina nodded, carefully keeping her eyes fixed on the road ahead.

"I care now." His voice was almost curt. "I'm actually enjoying this. Even with the sabotage shit, I've had more fun with work recently than I have for years. I don't want King taking our show, and it's not only about the competition anymore. It's starting to feel like I was just…treading water for a long time. Stagnating. Not actively unhappy, but…" She sensed him look down at her. "Not happy."

It was on the tip of her tongue to ask if he was happy now, but there would be no ambiguity as to her meaning, and she wasn't quite ready for that conversation yet.

She said nothing, but she reached down and linked her fingers through his.

It was a short walk to the inn, and the pretty thatched building was in sight when, in the stillness of the night, came a distinctive, horrifying Wibblet warble.

"*Sabrina.*"

She almost jumped out of her fucking skin. One nightmare second later, she smacked her fist into Nick's shoulder as he danced back, wheezing.

Giggles escaping as her nerves settled back into place, she gasped out, "Oh my God, you're such a cock."

With a burst of adrenaline, grabbing each other's hand again, they ran the last stretch to the inn, like a couple of kids. Blenheim Morley didn't run to 24/7 reception, so the owner of the inn had given them a key. Nick locked up behind them, and they went upstairs to their room.

When they'd checked in this afternoon, he'd asked

how many rooms to book. She'd glanced at him, blushed—*blushed*—and at last said, "One."

The look in his eyes had made her toes curl in her boots.

They were curling again now, as she sat on the edge of the turned-down bed, and watched him ditch the Wibblet, and close and lock their door. The inn was about four hundred years old and the walls were a good two-feet thick. Highly soundproof.

She merely noted.

Reaching down, she unzipped her boots and kicked them off.

The laughter and puffing breathlessness outside had abruptly turned into tension.

Nick turned, pulling off his coat and tugging open the buttons of his shirt. Her breath coming quicker, she watched his fingers almost helplessly as rows of abs started to appear, rippling under a stretch of smooth skin. She'd been with some pretty ripped guys in the past, but she couldn't remember any of them inspiring such an urge to…bite.

He pulled his shirt off, shoulders flexing, and stood looking at her. His chest was moving with deep, uneven breaths. "We don't have to do anything," he said, and despite the obvious arousal in his body, it was a straightforward statement of fact. No pressure. No obligation.

Sabrina looked at him, then flopped back on the bed. "Come on, Davenport. Get your kit off and get down here."

His spontaneous laugh was deep and rich. He slipped off his shoes and came forward to put a knee on the edge of the mattress. Walking his hands up either side of her body, he propped his weight on his arms, his hips over hers. "What a born romantic," he said, and kissed her.

It was a gentle flirting of lips, but as his tongue played with hers, and Sabrina's hands started drifting over his bare torso, the intensity surged, sweeping over them, and suddenly it was a head rush of sensation. The feel of his skin, little pebbles of goose bumps, the ridges of a scar on his shoulder. His smell, spicy and woody. And his voice, murmuring husky things in her ear.

He wasn't a dirty talker. He was…a beautiful talker. Those gorgeous, warm, honey tones told her she was beautiful, and clever, and caring. As he pulled off her jumper and unhooked her bra, pressing open-mouthed kisses over her throat and along her collarbones, he spoke to her skin, telling her things that, at another time, from a different man, she'd have brushed off as empty compliments, but here, now, the words seemed to sink right into her, warming her from within.

She *felt* beautiful on that bed, under his sheltering body. She felt clever and caring, and funny and dedicated, and all the other things he kissed into her.

They pushed back the covers completely, and Sabrina caught at Nick's throat with her mouth, touching him, tasting him, feeling the shudders ripple down his spine under her caressing hands. Coaxing him over on the mattress, she stripped off her jeans, and lifted up to straddle him.

His eyes were molten as he watched her. She took his hands, kissed them, and pushed them over his head. He lifted his hips obligingly when she pulled his trousers down his legs, and made a deep sound when she stroked her fingers over the hard bulge in the tight boxer-briefs.

Lowering her head, Sabrina circled the tight bead of his nipple with her tongue. He drew in a breath between his teeth with a hiss, and one of his hands came down to tangle in her hair. He stroked her head, then tightened his hold and gently pulled her back up for another hard, wet tangle of a kiss.

Cupping her neck, Nick kissed her cheek and the corner of her mouth, her jaw and her throat, before he caught her earlobe between his teeth and worried at it gently. Her stomach clenched.

Her fingers trailed back down his chest, and breathing hard, she watched his big body quiver as her touch slowly passed over each muscle in his abdomen. When she reached the edge of his briefs, she cupped him, and wrenched another hoarse sound from deep in his chest.

Gently, she massaged with the heel of her hand, and his eyes closed. His jaw was tightly clenched. His whole body went as rigid as iron when she moved to kneel between his hard-muscled thighs and carefully pulled down the briefs.

His erection sprang free, bouncing against his stomach, and she took it in her hand, stroking him from base to head. She bent her head to close her mouth over him, and he grunted and gave an involuntary thrust up before he caught himself.

She swirled her tongue, and sucked hard, hollowing her cheeks. He held still for three pumps of her fist, and then she was up and on her back on the bed, and his shaking hands were buried in her hair as he kissed her.

"Fucking hell," he said against her mouth. His thumb teased her right nipple, circling, stroking, gently flicking, while his lips travelled over the beads of sweat forming on her throat, and he caught her left nipple lightly between his teeth.

It was her turn to hiss, and she gripped his head as he sucked. When she was panting and moving restlessly, he released her with a wet sound, and his fingers nudged between her legs.

Without hesitation, Sabrina parted them, and with an impressively athletic manoeuvre, he hooked his fingers around her calves and slipped his shoulders under her thighs.

As he stroked her, and went straight for her clit with his tongue—no faffing about with Nick—she smacked her head back against the mattress, with a few silent vows of gratitude to whichever higher being in the universe had decided to smile on her.

It wasn't the fast, headlong rush to orgasm of last time; however, the slow build-up was far more intense. One of his fingers was inside her, testing, teasing. When he added a second and hooked them to press unerringly on the right spot, he increased the suction on her clit, and Sabrina pulled in deep, ragged breaths, her stomach compulsively clenching and releasing. With her eyes tightly closed, she pressed the backs of her hands to her forehead.

Finally, with a last flick of his tongue and the press of a wet thumb, the intensity broke into deep, pulsing waves, and she bucked against him, hard, and made a guttural noise.

He kissed the soft freckled skin on the inside of her thigh, and rubbed her knee.

She brought her legs up and lay catching her breath, as he dropped kisses on her mouth and her forehead.

"So gorgeous," he murmured, and nuzzled her nose with his before he stood up to get the condoms they'd bought with other necessities this afternoon.

Slowly, Sabrina sat up on the wrinkled bed and curled her legs to the side. Nick tore the edge of the packet with his teeth, and rolled the condom over his erection with swift movements. She reached out and curled her hand around him again, loving the way his body reacted. He knelt on the bed, cupped her face with warm, slightly shaking hands, and kissed her.

With the covers in a crumpled heap at the foot of the bed, Nick lifted her by the waist. Swinging her leg carefully over him, Sabrina settled into his lap and kissed the tip of his nose, before she put her hand down between their bodies and eased him in.

She bit her lip a few times, frowning, and he held back patiently, his eyes closed and face strained as he nuzzled kisses into her neck. Finally, she slid down on him and he filled her completely, and they moaned against each other's mouths.

Lifting her hips, she cried out under her breath again at the delicious drag of friction, which sent sensation jolting right down her legs. Nick's hands gripped her, moving from her back to her bottom, and he started to rock up into her in small movements.

"Need to stop?" he asked in a low rasp when, clasping his shoulders, she had to adjust her weight after a quick wince, and she shook her head.

"Just—" She found the right angle, and tipped her head back. "God."

They moved together tentatively at first, and then things clicked. *Emphatically.* Rocking her hips at a continuous, sinuous pace, until she was gliding on him,

Sabrina caught his groans in her mouth, but had to bury her face against his shoulder when his thrusts up into her grew hard and fast.

She came again, and their movements eased into a rolling, sensual rhythm. With her arm wrapped around his head, she stroked his damp hair as he kissed her throat, his eyes closed and his face contorted into tense lines of pleasure. Her heart was thumping rapidly, and she could feel his muscles shifting as she traced her fingers over the hard curves of his shoulders, the dips and hollows at the base of his neck and under his arms.

With five short, fast thrusts, he threw his head back and his whole body locked as he let go, abandoned to the intensity of it.

His chest heaving with his breaths, both of them drenched with sweat, Nick collapsed back against the pillows, taking her with him, holding her tightly.

Sabrina lay with her cheek pressed to his shoulder, their skin sticking together, their hands stroking anywhere and everywhere.

As her mind returned and her heartbeat slowed, she closed her eyes and turned her face to kiss his collarbone. "Nick?" Her voice was a husky wreck.

His fingers in her hair, his thumb stroked a line on her damp forehead. "Mmm?" From that one indeterminate grunt, his vocal cords weren't in much better shape. He sounded like she'd broken him.

She started to speak, hesitated. Shook her head. He held still, before he started stroking her hair again.

They dragged themselves into the shower before they got too drowsy. Nick fell asleep within minutes of pulling up the covers, lifting his arm for her to cuddle in, and moving her hair out of his face so he could breathe.

Sabrina was exhausted, but she was still awake an hour later, tucked into his side, her head resting on her curled arm. The sheets rustled in the quiet room as she shifted, and she pushed up on an elbow and looked down at his sleeping face. It was pitch-black outside, but the incredibly bright digital clocks on each bedside table were casting just enough of a glow that she could make out the lines of his profile, and see his parted lips as he breathed very quietly.

With the lightest of touches, she stroked the pad of her thumb over his lower lip and, again butterfly-soft, ran the back of her finger down the bridge of his nose.

"Sparks," he said, in his sleep, a low murmur, and she bit her lip, her mind too busy for the shattered bonelessness of her body.

Slowly, she lay back down and placed her hand over his heart.

Chapter Thirteen

8 Days until Christmas Eve

Monday back at work after a weekend of extremely satisfying, emotionally charged sex was always going to suffer by comparison.

But the *WMUL* advent calendar was delivering a clanger of a prize today.

The interview with Sadie Foster and the other female star of *The Velvet Room* revival had been hovering like an unspoken spectre. Sabrina had, she'd said, drawn a line under Nick's actions in the summer. He believed her when she said she'd forgiven him. Her personality was playful, but she wasn't a game-player. She hadn't raised it as an obstacle between them again, in either word or action.

He wasn't sure where things between them were going, but he didn't want them derailed by a spiteful, borderline sociopathic troublemaker who'd enjoy every moment of it.

"Batten down the hatches, folks," Jess had said when she'd arrived this morning. She also had prior experience of the real Sadie. "The Wicked Witch of the West End is flying this way."

Now, in the green room, she muttered something about a broomstick malfunction.

Nick looked up at the clock from where he stood, adjusting his mic and earpiece. They were going live in ten minutes, and *The Velvet Room* was the first guest segment. The team was expecting high ratings today. Many viewers were aware that Sabrina's relationship with Ferren had ended after her last live interview with Sadie. The public were also fully versed on the situation with the Carlton family and *The Velvet Room*.

Nick had a lot of respect for Fenella as both a producer and a person. But fucking hell, could she stir the pot, if she'd booked this one.

One star of the play was made-up, mic'd up, and ready to go. Lily Lamprey, a former TV actress, was used to live interviews and call times, and unlike her currently very late co-star, respected them. She, too, kept glancing at her wristwatch.

"She'll turn up." Nick moved the collar of his shirt to hide the cord clip. "With your opening night so close, she'll be keen to promote the show as much as possible."

"You would think." Lily raised a hand with a faint smile as Sabrina came into the room.

And made Nick's stomach feel like he'd just knocked back a slug of champagne.

Just from a split second of eye contact. God, he was in trouble.

"Hey, Sabrina." Lily stood to exchange cheek kisses. "I haven't spoken to you since you started the show— congratulations to you, and yay for me. You were the best part of *Sunset Britain* interviews." With a slightly awkward gesture, she tugged on the end of her nose.

"I—um, saw the interview with Sadie a few months ago." Her brown eyes briefly returned to Nick, with a definitely assessing quality. "And obviously the fracas with *The Velvet Room*—so that I have a heads-up, are we addressing that this morning, or do you want me to steer back to our production and keep the focus off the past?"

Nick and Sabrina had discussed that point, both with the production team and in private.

She said now what she'd said then, and he agreed with the inevitability: "The public knows of my connection to the play, and they're going to expect the elephant in the room to be addressed. My family and I already gave an extended statement on *Sunset Britain*, so I think we just acknowledge the facts—that the identity of the true playwright has now been established, the play has been enmeshed in scandal, but it's still the same excellent piece of drama that it was. And then we move on to the current production." Sabrina added without emotion, "Obviously, it's Sadie who's likely to keep pushing the past forward."

"If she shows up at all." Lily cleared her throat and dropped her voice. "I mean, I'm perfectly happy to just do the interview by myself. I wouldn't mind a breather, to be honest. I'm in rehearsals with her all day after this."

Sabrina winced. "You've got a long run ahead of you. I assume you were signed to the project before she was brought in to replace the original leading lady?"

"Yes. Although I didn't initially realise what she's like. I'd only seen her at the odd event before, and she always seemed nice enough."

"The infamous two sides of Sadie Foster," Sabrina

said. "Though, actually, you're married to one of the top directors on the West End. I'd have thought you'd get the full syrup treatment. She usually knows which side her bread is buttered. She's always been vile to Freddy, but around anyone in theatre who can advance her career—sunshine and roses."

"She was extremely polite for about three days," Lily said, "and kept suggesting we meet up for drinks and bring our other halves. And then I saw her go off at a poor woman on the makeup team, and I expressed my opinion about that."

"Instant frost?"

"Stalagmites form as we walk across the stage." Lily touched her earpiece, moving it a fraction. "She may *not* come. Our call time was an hour ago. And she's usually quite punctual. More's the pity. The producers didn't think the understudy was a big enough name to carry the lead full-time, but she's actually brilliant in the role."

"Sadie will know we don't want to do this interview." Sabrina spoke without a fraction of doubt. "She'll be here. She's just prolonging the tension."

Dead on the money.

Three minutes after they'd opened the show with the morning current affairs headlines, Jess clicked into their earpieces and hummed the character tune for the Wicked Witch of the West.

Sabrina exchanged a grim glance with Nick.

Let the game begin.

When the women were shown onto the studio set and took their seats, Sadie immediately started talking, keeping herself in the camera shot. Nick waited to see which tactic she'd choose.

At the most surface level, Sadie and Lily were not physically dissimilar. Both blondes of the Hollywood bombshell prototype, both very camera-practiced. But no matter how convincing a façade people put up—however experienced the mask—in the end, eyes betrayed intentions.

Sadie's eyes were big, apparently candid, and hard as nails.

She addressed most of her comments to Sabrina. Nick had obviously put himself beyond the pale following their confrontation over her spreading the rumours about Sabrina.

To the casual onlooker, the women might have been reunited best friends. Sadie was at her most exuberantly charming and warm. She steered clear of any mention of Ferren. Wise. Her reputation had taken a small hit after that incident, and she wouldn't want to remind viewers of her part in it. As Sabrina had expected, several comments about the plagiarism were woven into places they didn't need to be.

"Of course, I'm afraid that from our perspective, the scandal has been beneficial in some respects." Sadie's manner was apologetic. Her eyes were full-on shark. "It's certainly awoken public interest in the play, which is wonderful—not just for us, although naturally we hope that as many people come to see us as possible—but it's such an important, iconic piece of literature. It's a shame that the true playwright never saw it performed, but we're dedicating opening night to her memory."

"That's a lovely gesture," Sabrina said evenly.

"Yes, it is." Nick changed the subject. "You've had a shorter rehearsal period than usual, having to come in and pick up the reins at short notice, after Mitzi Housken's unfortunate withdrawal. Is that the only setback the cast has suffered?"

Sadie's eyes narrowed a fraction.

With a little laugh, she said, "Are you hinting at the rumours of a poltergeist or two in the theatre? Rehearsals *have* been quite eventful. We're all starting to wonder if the revelation of the plagiarism has set things in motion. A bit of cosmic unrest."

Sabrina crossed her legs and tapped her cue card against her thigh. "I really don't think my grandmother's ghost is haunting the Metronome, turning off lights and hiding scripts."

Sadie touched her fingertips to her throat. The very suggestion. She was *shocked. Bat, bat*, went the eyelashes. "Oh, no, of course not." She brought out her dimples. "The new Metronome hasn't seen many productions yet. A few growing pains is normal."

Lily had been listening with one brow slightly raised. "I didn't come into the production at short notice," she said now. "And the only mishaps I've observed were the props assistant tripping over a lighting cord, and some silly gossiping at the press party."

Calmly, she leaned forward and picked up her glass of water from the table. She sipped, ignoring the no-longer-demure stare boring into her cheek; Nick bit back a grin.

Apart from further icicles forming in the air between the two leading ladies, the interview passed off without major incident. When Lily and Sadie were politely ushered out, and he moved with Sabrina towards the kitchen set, he saw a certain stiffness go out of her shoulders.

"We'll be here with Chef Marco after the break," she said into the new camera. "It's the season for a bit of indulgence and excessive amounts of chocolate. He has a chocolate mousse cheesecake for us that looks—"

"If you try to show me up in public again, you'll have to suck more than just your husband's cock to get your next job." The voice, biting and unmistakable, came through the studio speakers, cutting off Sabrina's scripted intro.

Her lips stayed parted.

"You show yourself up the moment you open your mouth." Lily's cool response also echoed around the set. "And if you can't treat people with respect, your handlers shouldn't let you loose in public."

"People like Sabrina Carlton? Oh, I do respect her." Sadie's voice was equal parts malicious and matter-of-fact. "She's a real grafter, isn't she? Made a *pile* from her dodgy gran and set herself up for life, then fucked Joe Ferren to get herself in front of the paps. As if she'd have got on TV if she hadn't clung to him. She's played it smart her whole career."

Everyone in the studio had frozen. Just total, disbelieving, "Is this actually happening?" stillness. Even Fenella was standing with her mouth partly open and her clipboard drooping. Suddenly there was at least one movement in Nick's peripheral vision. The person in charge of the bleeper going into a panic.

Sabrina's wide eyes locked on Nick's. Inside him was a rising tide of fury on her behalf, but he didn't move.

He didn't keep the disbelief off his face, and Sabrina had tucked her hand against her lips, but neither of them said a word.

Perfect Princess Sadie, who'd never so much as swear in public, unintentionally ripping off her crown for the viewing pleasure of thousands.

Far be it for her humble plebs to interfere.

"I know it's difficult," Lily's voice remarked, "but could you try not to be *completely* vile? We don't all use other people to make our way."

Fenella finally jolted back into action and hissed off a stream of orders, and immediately crew members rushed off-set.

There were certain hazards that came with broadcasting live. It was house procedure for guests' mics to be turned off as soon as they left the set. This was a staggering example why.

However, even if someone had failed to cut the connection to the individual mics, their voices shouldn't be projected right through the studio. They'd been hooked into the main sound server.

"Bit rich, coming from the woman with no stage experience who jumped into bed with the first theatre director she met and conveniently scored a leading role," Sadie drawled. "Hon, your career has the same shelf-life as your face and your tits. And since you obviously have an eye for…should I be nice and call it *networking*? You should know who *not* to piss off. I repeat—get on my wrong side, and you'll be back bed-hopping and lash-fluttering on the soaps."

"You're a terrible person." Lily sounded totally unruffled. "And I think you overestimate your influence. You've been letting your guard down recently. You dropped the act with me in less than a week. People are starting to catch on. If you're counting on your 'other half" to do your bidding, I'd be careful. To achieve his level of success, he must be fairly sharp."

The noise Sadie made caused a burst of static, but her next words were still loud and clear. "Lionel? Cockled. Keep most of his brain on his stumpy dick and the rest is open to suggestion." *And for viewers watching at home, that shattering sound you just heard was someone taking a sledgehammer to their own career.* "Trust me, he's not going anywhere. What—"

There was abrupt silence.

So much silence that when Sabrina shuffled her papers together, tapping them on the counter, it might as well have been a car backfiring. Several people jumped.

His own "other half" straightened her shoulders and looked into the camera. "As I said, the chocolate mousse cheesecake sounds like an absolute dream. Stick with us until after the break, and Chef Marco will share his best tips. Apparently if you want the 'wow' factor this Christmas, you need to beat your egg whites properly, resist the urge to peek in the oven, and forget to turn your mic off."

Yeah, he fucking loved her.

"Ding dong, the nightmare's gone."

Elise's voice was deadpan as Sabrina slipped into the booth at The Prop & Cue, next to Akiko, and passed over the shopping bag containing the Wibblet. Elise peeked in and blew her a kiss; Akiko saw what it was and looked aghast.

Sabrina looked across the table to Freddy, who was texting.

Her sister laid down her phone. "Sadie is *out*,"

Freddy said, her words ringing with disbelief and a slightly guilty thrill. Even the dark curls sticking out of her top-knot were quivering. "Of *The Velvet Room*. Unceremoniously sacked. They're promoting the understudy to permanent billing. I think she's just trashed her entire stage career in about forty-five seconds." She shook her head. "Bad enough to show herself up as an utter cow with what she said about you. And I swear to God, I'd almost feel sorry for her now, but after that final straw, she can fuck right off. But Lionel Grimes has big money in almost every production in the West End. What the hell was she thinking? Even backstage, to say all that aloud."

"Grimes has binned her," Elise said, holding up her own phone. "The whole thing is headline news. Her publicist is going into major damage control, but good luck with that one, mate. And the tide of public opinion has turned massively in your favour, Sabs."

"I'd have thought some of them would agree with her, re: using Ferren to kick-start my career." She'd actually got her first job in TV before Ferren had got his in film, but whatever. It was ancient history. "There've certainly been months of agreement about me filling my bank accounts thanks to my 'dodgy gran.'"

"But people like you, and they also like Lily Lamprey. For the most part, it's thumbs-down Foster, and heart emojis for Carlton and Davenport. I think Nick should send Sadie a thank-you bouquet—she's giving *his* public takedown of Grimes a run for its money."

"Although I think the whole country could have done without the 'stumpy dick' reference." Akiko was rubbing her stomach in slow circles. Her eyes were fixed on Sabrina, who could see full well where the conversation was about to turn. "Speaking of Carlton and Davenport—"

"The comedy act has definitely turned into a love scene, then?" Elise's wicked grin faded into something more enigmatic. "Or is that a bit Hallmark Channel? Are we talking more physical than cerebral?"

Sabrina traced her fingertips in patterns on the tabletop. "It's definitely physical." She suspected half the pub could hear the residual echo of about nine orgasms in those words.

"Davenport's got moves, does he?" Elise said unenthusiastically.

"Mind your own business. And yes. But it's not just sex."

However, after they'd spent most of Saturday and all of Sunday holed up in her flat, she was never going to look at her fireplace rug the same way again.

"Obviously not," Freddy said. "Since you're tracing his name on the table."

Sabrina looked down, her finger stopping halfway through the letter *C.* "God," she said, and reached for the bowl of nuts beside an unlit candle. "I'm sickening."

Freddy propped her hand on her fist. "So, a bit of an understatement to say we no longer despise Nick?"

"He apologised for what happened in the summer. I believe he's sorry. I don't want to hold on to resentment about it." She touched Freddy's arm. "But you and Griff were equally affected by the fallout, and your opinions and rights are your own. If you're still angry with him—I get it."

Freddy grabbed hold of Sabrina's fingers and squeezed. "It takes a lot for me to hold a grudge. They're bad for your sleep, and your mental health, and they give me spots. If you're giving Nick a second chance, then obviously I will, too. Whoever's on your side, I'm on their side."

"Anyone got a spare pound? I'll put Sister Sledge on the jukebox," Elise teased, but she was smiling.

Freddy threw a peanut at her, but didn't move her focus from Sabrina. "There's obviously been *something* sparking between you two for years. And I haven't seen you so… I don't know. The past few weeks, you've been—"

"Zapping," Akiko filled in unexpectedly. "Electric. You're putting out contagious energy. I'm constipated, have feet the size of melons, and got about three hours of sleep last night thanks to Elise's dream-kicking—"

"Sorry." Her wife winced.

"—and I still feel more up just being around you right now," Akiko finished. "Your vibe is positive."

"That was very Zen," Elise remarked, and Akiko made a face and stuck the straw of her lemonade in her mouth.

"I know. The hormones and the birth podcasts are getting to me. I'm feeling very at one with the earth."

Despite Freddy's warm and totally unsurprising show of support, there was a frown in her eyes. Sabrina knew her sister's expressions. "You have doubts," she said in a low voice, as Akiko and Elise started arguing about something to do with vitamins.

Freddy chewed on her lip. "Do you?" she countered, also softly, and Sabrina breathed in slowly.

"Nick's not a cheater. He's not emotionally manipulative."

"Agreed."

"He's not what I thought he was. I think we stopped

each other from really *seeing* us. And I think there's a good chance he's going to end up one of the best friends I've ever had."

"I did always think you two were quite similar, in key ways."

"You never said so."

"It does help, in my line of work, if my head remains attached to my neck."

Sabrina's grin was fleeting. "We both care about our jobs. About doing them well."

They were nearing the sticking point, and Freddy rested her hands on the table. "But?"

"Years of unofficial professional rivalry, followed by direct competition for a position. And then unexpectedly thrown together to work for a common goal. We've very quickly had to realign, mentally, to think and act as a team. On a personal, intimate level—that's happening as well, and so…naturally, it's surreal. Professionally—"

"Nick has acted ruthlessly in the past."

Sabrina considered her words. "When we were told about the *WMUL* trial, Nick didn't hide his feelings about it. A step down. An insult. But he's competitive and his dedication to his work is ironclad, so he was always going to give it a hundred percent."

"But you think he still doesn't really want to be there."

Sabrina was silent for three taps of her fingers on the tabletop. "He says he's enjoying it, and that it's settled something he didn't realise was restless. That it's a path he would never have taken voluntarily, but somehow it's ended up the right one."

"Whatever Nick is, he's not a liar. If he says that, he probably means it."

"No. He's not a liar."

"But you do have doubts?"

"We were both backed into a corner with *WMUL*. I enjoy all TV work, and I've never felt that success is contingent on being only in one branch of it. But until a couple of months ago, Nick had a night show named after him, and he grew up with a father who disapproved of magazine-style shows and constantly pushed him towards hard investigative journalism. I—" Sabrina shook her head. "I don't know."

Freddy opened her mouth, but before she could speak, Sabrina's phone rang.

Glancing down at the screen, Sabrina frowned and took the call, with an apologetic glance at Freddy. "Fenella?"

"I can hear café sounds, so I won't keep you long," her producer said briskly. "But there's something you need a heads-up about."

Nick was met at the door of the Mackintosh flat by a very excited Alan and two people with identical expressions.

"I see it's true that couples grow to look alike," he said as Tia ushered him into the kitchen. She was literally bouncing up and down. He bent to rub Alan's head. "You both look disgustingly smug. This better be about a winning match or a National Lottery sweep."

"Eee." Tia gave up all restraint, made a noise that was frighteningly similar to a Wibblet expressing affection, and dove in to tackle him around the waist.

Pushed back a step, he put an arm around her before

they both fell over, while Tosh looked on disapprov-
ingly. "What was *that*? How many times, babe—proper
technique. Plant your foot as close to the target as possible, lower your shoulder, and drive from the legs. You
don't just fling yourself at someone's gut and shove.
We need to get back out in the park."

Ignoring her husband's three steps to a professional
tackle, Tia squeezed Nick and stepped back. "You and
Sabrina. Oh-my-gawd. You've finally sorted your love
life. I despaired."

Nick picked up Alan and tucked the dog against
his chest. "Yes, I am unofficially dating Sabrina. How
was work?"

"Oh, come *on*," Tia said, tapping her socked foot.
"I am *invested*. I need *details*."

"Not too many details, thanks," Tosh inserted hastily, and Tia rolled her eyes.

"Not those kind of details. Fucking men, seriously,
that's all you think about."

Tosh spluttered. "Excuse me? Who bloody jumped
me when I was trying to take a nice, relaxing shower?
There was I, gathering my thoughts from the day, and—"

"Alan and I are too young to hear this." Nick looked
around for the basket of Alan's stuff—for someone who
was seven inches tall, the dog did not pack lightly—
and spotted it by the couch. He walked over to collect
it, and Tia shot in front of it.

"You're not getting off that lightly, Nicholas. And
my day at work was bloody chaotic thanks to the Sadie
Foster incident that's probably going to get its own
Wikipedia entry. Don't take that as a complaint. I'd
work through lunch all fricking week for the epicness
of that sixty seconds. Long time coming. *Prime* TV

viewing. The *WMUL* ratings have got to be looking good."

"They were already improving. But I imagine catch-up views of the interview today will be off the charts."

"So—things are looking promising that you'll be offered permanent contracts for next year?" Tia's bubbliness had fizzed down a notch, and she looked at him with discomforting intensity.

"We won't find out for sure until Christmas. But if we can keep things on track, and avoid any major disasters courtesy of our mysterious 'friend,' it's within reach."

"If your 'friend' was responsible for the mic incident—"

"Odds on. The audio came through the main studio PA. That doesn't happen by accident."

"Then I have to say, Unknown Foe improved the morning of many folks in London today. But they'd have had no idea what the guests would say, so just another attempt to make your control of the show look slipshod?"

Nick grimaced, and Tia frowned. "You have no idea who it is?"

"Slippery as a fucking eel. And we're not in the dark for lack of trying. We've started checking CCTV footage, and have seen nobody committing any obvious nefarious deeds on the set itself, or in the green room, or any of the monitored areas. We've gone full Sherlock and Watson."

"Which one are you?" Tosh enquired with interest.

"Watson. Obviously." Nick's tone was sardonic but he couldn't help a flicker of a smile.

Tia tilted her head. "Nick. Do you seriously *want*

to stay presenting *WMUL* next year? Just taking your Sherlock out of the equation for a tick."

"I can't take Sabrina out of the equation. On every level. She's part of the experience with *WMUL* and I can't separate that out."

"So, it's not the job as such? It's working with Sabrina?"

More slowly, he said, "Sabrina is a huge part of why I'm enjoying work right now. She has a knack for making things fun. But she's not the only factor. Now that I'm getting used to the early mornings, I prefer the pace of *WMUL*. With the exception of one unknown, the team is second to none; we've met some incredible people—and some…memorable ones, and it's like things are starting to…unknot."

Tia was chewing on her lip. "Well—that's good. Great," she amended as he raised his eyebrows at her hesitancy. "It just seems like such a change—"

The rest of her doubts were lost to the buzzing of his phone. He pulled it out, saw Fenella's name on the screen, and glanced with a frown at the time. It was after six. Their producer was usually fanatical about her work-life boundaries, unless it was a dire emergency. He answered with some apprehension.

Fenella cut to the chase. "Sorry to cut into your evening. Are you with Sabrina?"

"Not yet." They were meeting at his flat shortly.

"Spoken to her?"

"What's this about?" he asked crisply, then more sharply, "Is Sabrina all right?"

Tia and Tosh were watching him with concern.

"She's not thrilled." Fenella's response was dry. "But she's physically in one piece, if that's what you mean. I tried to get hold of you this afternoon, but your phone was off."

"I had the interview and photo shoot for *Gentleman's League*."

"Oh, yes. I hope your publicist has vetted the interview."

"Thanks for the vote of confidence. But yes, she has. What new disaster have I missed?"

"It better not turn out to be a disaster," Fenella said warningly. "I'm relying on everyone's professionalism here." Suitably ominous. "I've just received word that this Friday we're on the circuit for the promo tour of *The Lost Boys of Agincourt*."

"That means exactly nothing to me."

"It's the Stephen Cossack film that was put in the cold-freeze the past couple of years and is finally coming out on Boxing Day."

"Right." A clip of impatience was coming back into Nick's voice, and Fenella cleared her throat.

"Starring Joe Ferren."

Chapter Fourteen

The conveyor belts zipped and zagged all over the production room, rising high into the air like a scene straight from Willy Wonka's factory, squirting neat lines of chocolate over thousands and thousands of Peppermint Pixies. Sabrina was in her element. She'd already eaten three, for the benefit of the viewers at home. The people needed to know the biscuits tasted as good as they looked.

With her hair tucked into a net, she stood with Maria Campbell, Nick's mother, who was the complete driving force behind every facet of Davenport's, a company with an amazing vibe. Her staff clearly adored her.

Concisely, humorously, Maria explained the production line, as the raw dough passed through giant blades, emerging in neat lines of rectangles, systematically punched with holes by descending spikes. Sabrina's favourite part was the end-stage wrapping, the machinery scooping the finished biscuits and flinging them neatly into recycled plastic packaging. As the self-proclaimed number-one Davenport's fan, this was her idea of Father Christmas's workshop.

"And everything started in your parents' kitchen?" Sabrina asked, fascinated, and Maria nodded.

"My parents had a commercial kitchen for their own food business, and they let me experiment there." She laughed. "With one recipe, it took me ages to work out why I couldn't get the flavour balance right, until I realised that the scents of their spices were infusing into my dough." Her smile became warm remembrance and pure love. "My father in particular encouraged me to go after my dreams. He was just…unshakable. Steadfast belief that I could achieve whatever I set out to do. When it's coming from someone you love, their words sink into you. For good or for bad." Just for a moment, her eyes went to Nick, who was on the other side of the huge room, down on his haunches, talking to two of the children from the Shining Lights foundation. Both kids were giggling shyly. Maria's mouth twisted ever so slightly. "I've never forgotten that constant flow of support from my parents. I've carried it with me, like a safety net, knowing that whatever happens, someone was proud of me and will always be proud of me."

She seemed to come back to herself. "Of course, it was quite a jump when I really made the transition to commercial production."

She chatted briefly about the early days of Davenport's, and the ways in which they hoped to keep expanding in the future.

"We try to support as many young start-ups as we can. We're very excited about a new scholarship and apprenticeship programme."

A frail-looking little girl appeared between them, her footsteps so light that Sabrina hadn't heard her approach. She was holding a toy mouse with a knitted jumper, and moved a tiny paw to carefully tap Maria's hand. "Can we have sweets now?" she whispered, holding her friend in front of her face, and Nick's mother bent to address the mouse.

"Absolutely. You didn't come in your best jumper just to watch us talking. Shall we get this party started?"

With a cascading fall of glittering gold confetti in the anterior foyer, Maria welcomed all the Shining Lights foundation families who'd come for the launch, and Sabrina and Nick opened the fundraising lines for the *WMUL* viewers at home.

This was a big day for the charity, and obviously a huge treat for a lot of the children, and Maria had gone to enormous trouble to create a carnival atmosphere. A *happy* atmosphere, despite the circumstances behind these families needing to be part of Shining Lights.

Sabrina and Nick each joined a team captained by an excited child, for a very messy game that involved balloons filled with either sweets or slime. Nick, crouched down with devilry in his eyes, helped a little girl with pink cheeks and wispy hair throw a ball at a lever, which burst a slime balloon right over Sabrina's head.

The little boy with whom she was solemnly discussing strategy retaliated a few seconds later, once Nick had seen their intention and stepped a few feet away from the giggling little girl, and Sabrina high-fived her partner through laughter and dripping slime as another balloon burst and glittery pink goop slid down over Nick's shoulders.

He'd selected a suit from The Closet today that he didn't like.

They had booths outside taking public donations, and roving reporters covering the launch parties taking place at various supermarkets around central London, and the initial fundraising figures coming in on the ground and online were brilliant.

A donation from Lionel Grimes boosted the digital tally by six figures. Sabrina wasn't impressed it had taken this highly publicised event and Sadie's equally public insults to prompt his conscience, but at least the foundation got the much-needed funds.

Nick's actress friend Lainie Graham, the charity's founder, was also dripping with slime and convulsed with laughter. Her husband, the West End star Richard Troy, whom Sabrina had met several times through Freddy and once in a very difficult interview, had rolled up his sleeves and was helping his group of kids with the skill of a trained general. Unlike the rest of them, however, the broodingly handsome actor had so far managed to come through the combat with not so much as a ruffled black curl.

Pippi had the day off school and seemed more cheerful today, Sabrina was happy to see. Despite her disdain for biscuits, she was walking around helping the other kids, and noticeably copying her grandmother's body language, which was just fucking cute. Her father had also turned out in support. Pippi periodically returned to Iain Campbell's side to update him on progress and explain how the filming worked, imparting all the knowledge she'd picked up from her day in the *WMUL* studio. The fierce-looking man, who'd once had his own TV series and would know the mechanics backwards and forwards, tilted his head down to his daughter, listened patiently, asked questions in a low voice, and acted as if he'd never heard of a boom mic in his life.

Father Christmas arrived at the latter end of the broadcast and distributed armloads of toys to the excited children, courtesy, Maria told her in a whisper, of Lainie and Richard. Even Sabrina and Nick got presents, and, expecting a gag gift, she was surprised and quite touched by the skeins of gorgeous wool she unwrapped. Lainie was very thoughtful and she'd done her homework.

Nick scored a bottle of whisky, the same brand that they'd sipped all night in France. He held it on one palm, looking down at it, then at Sabrina. The caramel lights in his eyes deepened.

"Thank you so much for everything you've done today," Lainie said when the event wrapped up. She pulled her fingers through the ends of her long ponytail, trying to scrape out the dried slime. "We couldn't have asked for a more successful launch for the campaign. And we're so grateful for your mother's collaboration, Nick, I can't even tell you."

"I see Grimes had a sudden change of heart and opening of wallet," Richard said in his melodious drawl. Sabrina had grown up around scores of actors, but she'd encountered few people with such a classically Shakespearean voice as Richard Troy. Despite his difficult reputation, he was deservedly lauded as one of the best living theatre actors in the country, and he'd probably still be commanding stages and stealing scenes as an elderly man. Her father wasn't easily impressed, but he'd always held Richard up to Freddy as a career exemplar.

Her sister, however, was one of the few long-time West End performers who didn't find Richard intimidating. She'd once, to the stupefaction of all around her, described him as "sort of like a really disgruntled older brother. Sarky, but he knows what's up."

Lifting a slightly Mephistophelian brow, Richard continued, "Obviously, step one of some serious ego rehabilitation. As Sadie Foster has now ripped off the Disney plaster and aired the scab underneath, he looks like a lecherous prat for putting up with her as long as he did."

Which was a revolting but accurate way of putting it.

"Bar none, she's the worst person I've ever worked with," Lainie said, "and she brought that downfall on herself, but it's not pleasant seeing anyone completely self-destruct. And online hate goes so far these days."

Richard, apparently automatically, reached up to stroke his hand down her ponytail; abruptly, he pulled his fingers away from the crusty slime. "I agree on that point, but I think your sympathy's wasted in this case, my love. Sadie's burned her bridges on the West End, but she's already dashed off to the States, where she has several powerful connections. She'll score at least an independent film role off her notoriety within a month. The woman is a narcissist to her core, and even public pillory is not going to permanently affect her. Her vanity is as close as it gets to bulletproof."

Lainie opened her mouth.

"And to save you the effort of pointing a finger," her husband continued in the same calm tone, "vanity and self-awareness are not interchangeable. People need to acknowledge their own abilities; it just needs to be grounded in hard graft, ethics, and gratitude. Arrogance is unattractive, but false modesty is irritating and a waste of time."

Sabrina slid her glance sideways, and Nick caught her expressive look. His fingers lightly nipped her arm.

Richard continued to stare down his aquiline nose at his wife, whose lips were twitching; then his expression cracked into a grin that transformed him from villain to leading man. He leaned forward and kissed Lainie's forehead, and Sabrina suddenly felt as if she were intruding on a private moment, in an intimate space. The couple left shortly after, fingers entwined, eyes locked, shagging obviously imminent.

Maria and Neil, Nick's stepfather, a grey-haired Scotsman with a weather-beaten face and the kindest eyes, had invited Sabrina to their home for afternoon tea and cakes. It took a horrendously long time to navigate the traffic—the closer it got to Christmas, the more London turned into a gridlock—and when they arrived at the lovely Edwardian house, Sabrina was grateful to sink into a puffy armchair and accept a cup of tea.

Pippi poured it for her and carried it over carefully, before skipping back to fill a plate with cakes.

"After all the biscuits we've eaten this morning, Sabrina may want slightly fewer than nine cakes, Pip," her father remarked from the couch, where he sat with his long legs extended and ankles crossed.

Iain had been polite to her all morning but watchful. He was a big man, packed with muscle through the chest and shoulders, softer around the middle. He was built like a cuddly bear, but his demeanour would not encourage anyone except his daughter to go up for a snuggle. Sabrina remembered him from his days on TV about six years ago, although it had taken a while for her to connect the infamously grouchy chef with

Nick. As far as she could recall, he'd reluctantly agreed to do the show back then to keep his restaurants in the black and his staff employed.

It was a bit of an eye-blinker that he was now most well-known for his spectacular wedding cakes.

She didn't look at him and immediately think closet romantic.

However, his eyes had softened when he'd thanked her for her kindness to Pippi, in his grizzly-growl of a voice with a slight Scottish accent. She'd responded, and meant it, that she thought his daughter was a darling.

That had almost got her a smile.

Neil was apparently an avid gardener, and he excused himself for a few minutes to check on the hydroponic lettuces he and Pippi were growing. His granddaughter raced along at his side.

Nick had been surprisingly quiet for a few minutes, sitting on the couch beside Sabrina, absently running his fingers in circles over her crossed knee. She glanced at him. There had been a bit of constraint between them last night, after the newest addition to their work schedule.

Sabrina hadn't spoken to Ferren for months now. It was not a great prospect, sitting down on a couch with him and Nick, to make small talk in front of five cameras and half the nation.

But she'd woken up this morning, curled on her side, looking into Nick's sleepy eyes as he lay in an identical position opposite, his biceps bulging as she ran her finger over the arm he'd bent under his head—and she'd lost some of that apprehension. She was nervous about seeing Ferren again, but she could handle it.

Right now, and especially after spending the day with so many incredibly brave people who were going through unimaginable hardship, she was feeling pretty damn lucky.

"Nick." Iain stood and inclined his head towards the door. "Could we have a word?"

Nick looked up, lifting his brows. "Yeah. Of course." Turning his head into Sabrina's, he murmured, "All right?"

"Of course."

He squeezed her leg, and stood up to follow his brother out of the room. Sabrina watched him go, unable not to move her gaze down the breadth of his back. Normal new-relationship horniness was one thing; this constant state of edgy physicality around him was enmeshed with a feeling that felt a lot more permanent— and *really* not the time to dwell on this, when she was having tea with his mother.

When she looked up from the pink coconut sugar cake on her plate, Maria was smiling at her. She was a beautiful woman, and such a blend of friendly compassion and extreme capability. If Sabrina were ever stranded on a desert island, she'd rate her survival chances high if Maria Campbell was in her lifeboat.

Regardless of the other woman's emanating warmth, Sabrina would be drawn to her simply because it was like looking into her eyes and seeing Nick.

Almost impossible to believe that, had she met Maria back in the summer, that resemblance would probably have stirred feelings of residual anger.

"I've been very curious to meet you. You've given my son quite a hard time the past few years," Maria said in her frank way, and Sabrina coughed on a shred of coconut that stuck in her throat.

When her eyes were no longer at risk of watering, she wiped a cautionary finger under her lashes in case of mascara smudges. "It was good for his soul. He has enough people around him to puff up his ego. He needs someone to go nose to nose with him."

His mother looked at her for a split second before her dark eyes lit up with laughter. The way her whole face almost danced when she was genuinely amused— totally Nick.

"I couldn't agree more." Maria looked down at her plate to break off a piece of tart. When she raised her head, the lines of her face were still relaxed, but edged with seriousness. "He's given you a difficult time, as well."

"It's probably good for my soul and ego, too," Sabrina said, equally frankly. "I need someone to go nose to nose with me—"

"And to stand hand in hand with you?" Maria asked, unexpectedly, and Sabrina's heart gave a sudden thump.

After a moment, she said, slowly, "Yes."

"I know there were several consequences for you and your family after the story Nick ran." His mother spoke carefully now, and Sabrina kept her internal wince from her expression.

She really didn't want to get into another rehash of this.

"Have you got past that, where he's concerned? Truly."

She looked steadily back at Maria. "Yes. I have."

His mother continued to study her. "When that situation occurred— For years, I'd seen the influence of my first husband's behaviour on Nick. To me, that was the pinnacle of it."

Surprised, Sabrina wasn't sure what to say. She was uncomfortable discussing this subject behind Nick's back.

But Maria went on, "Markus was a demanding father. He set very high standards for Nick, according to his own beliefs and priorities, and made it almost impossible for Nick to reach them. I tried to combat that pressure, and our marriage suffered in consequence. Markus and I went nose to nose frequently; hand in hand, never." She lifted a hand slightly as Sabrina started to speak. "I'm telling you the bare bones of this only because I saw my son's face when he looked at you today. He's protective of my privacy, so I doubt if he's told you himself. It wasn't widely known, but my husband and I separated, and if he hadn't died, we'd have gone on to divorce."

She shook her head. "Markus was a brilliant journalist, but he unapologetically prioritised his profession over his personal relationships. He brought Nick up to follow in his footsteps, but he really knew nothing about his son as a person. He couldn't have told you the names of his friends, or his favourite foods—"

"Stew and gherkins," Sabrina murmured without thinking, and Maria's grin flashed.

"At least he doesn't eat them together." She sobered. "Markus's work brought about real and necessary change in many political arenas. We were all extremely proud of that. And at a macro level, he did fight for the greater good, if you like to put it that way. But he would sacrifice personal friends—*innocent* friends—to his cause with barely a pause. And he bore the consequences of that. When he died, he was honoured, far more than he was mourned. That is not the life I want for Nick." She spoke more rapidly, the discomfort at having to speak so personally to a more-or-less stranger starting to come through. "If you're told enough times what you *have* to be, sometimes it's difficult to learn what you *want* to be."

Those words woke an echo in Sabrina's mind, as she sat without speaking. Of years watching Freddy struggle to live up to Rupert's expectations, and the persistent, hollow feeling of being seen almost as a prop piece, a peripheral part of someone else's story, rather than a person at the centre of their own.

Maria cleared her throat. "Recently, I've seen a lot more of the side of Nick that's always appeared when he's relaxed and happy. The only side of Nick that Pippi knows. As far as I'm concerned, that *is* Nick. He's ambitious and he's competitive, but he's not ruthless. He cares."

She hesitated, and her final comment on that subject fell heavily. "But years of being pushed in one direction—"

In the silence, Sabrina listened to the ticking of the small clock on the mantel.

At last, Maria added wryly, "The vanity, I'm sorry to say, was there from birth. His first words were literally 'I'm cute.'"

Through the tension that gripped her, Sabrina was relieved to be caught up in a spontaneous giggle.

Apparently feeling she'd said what she wanted to say and that it was over and done with, Maria leaned forward and gestured at Sabrina's bag, where her knitting needles were sticking out. "What are you working on?"

Sabrina pulled out the shawl she'd started, and Maria admired it. She was a talented embroiderer and showed Sabrina some of her work. "You do need acute vision for the finer work. So, it was unfortunate that my eyes almost dropped out of my head at Nick's flat the other day when I discovered that my son also has knitting on the go."

Sabrina grinned. "He's actually not bad. He keeps randomly pulling it out during editorial meetings, and you could hear a pin drop every time. And the competitive drive has well and truly clicked in. We've gone from the beginnings of a misshapen basic scarf to him googling tutorials, and he's now attempting wrist warmers. He actually went out and bought new wool."

"Green wool," Maria said. Pointedly.

"Yes." Obliviously.

The other woman gestured at the shirt Sabrina had changed into, after they'd showered off the slime at the factory. The pale mint silk shirt.

"If I recall correctly," Nick's mother murmured, "most days I've tuned in to see the show, you've been wearing some shade of green. I wonder who the wrist warmers could possibly be for?"

Oh.

Oh.

For some reason, Nick had thought Iain was pulling him aside to talk about Sabrina.

Perhaps because what seemed like half of Britain wanted to comment on their relationship, on a daily basis, and he'd had to mute notifications on his phone. Most people were positive. Some people were dickheads.

However, when Iain got typically straight to the

point, resting against the counter of their parents' kitchen, the conversation was a blind-sider. "Do you remember Roderick Speight?"

Nick pulled his focus into the unexpected subject. His mind had been firmly in one place all day, and she was currently sitting alone with his mother, whom he didn't trust not to pull out baby photos.

Fortunately, he'd been an exceptionally attractive infant.

"Executive producer when you worked for AML-TV?"

Iain nodded. "We've kept in touch, and he's working as director of programming for LightStarr."

Nick's eyes narrowed at the mention of the increasingly popular streaming service.

"They're launching a hard-edge current affairs show next year," Iain said. "Single-presenter format. Initial twelve-month contract. From what I understand, considerable opportunity for both travel and executive input. It sounds like big money. Your name is on Speight's shortlist. You're about to be approached to sound out your interest. I thought you'd appreciate a heads-up."

"I do appreciate it," Nick said. The effort to keep his face expressionless, as his brain immediately went into chaos, resulted in his voice coming out flat.

Iain didn't seem to notice. "Right," he said matter-of-factly. "Now we can discuss the more pressing matter. What the hell is that purple thing that's apparently going under my tree on Christmas Eve?"

When people had a busy work schedule and were trying to get to know each other as a couple, they had to snatch opportunities for dates when they arose. Do "normal" activities together. Have fun. Bond.

Activities such as going to the cinema.

However, as cinema dates went, Sabrina wouldn't highly rate a private viewing of her ex-boyfriend's latest film.

Her fingers were linked through Nick's as they headed into the boutique theatre where Fenella had arranged for them to see a preview of *The Lost Boys of Agincourt*, so they would know what they were talking about when they discussed it with Ferren on Friday.

A photographer caught them going in, and Nick tightened his hold on her hand. He'd been weird and tense since they'd left his mother's house this afternoon. She wasn't self-centred enough to think it was solely down to an evening of watching Ferren stomp about in armour, waving his sword.

"Is everything okay with your brother?" she ventured, as they showed their security passes and were directed into a small viewing room.

Possibly trying to make amends, Fenella had secured them their own screening, so they didn't have a room full of press peeking at them.

Nick stiffened. "Why do you ask?"

"Because you've been acting like you're holding on to a hot poker for hours." She unbuttoned her coat but didn't take it off before she sat down. The heating wasn't great.

Nick took a seat beside her. "Iain's fine." There was definitely an odd note in his voice.

She turned in her seat. "Are you going to tell me what's wrong?"

He didn't deny that something was, but uncharacteristically, he hesitated over his words. "It may be nothing. I need to find out— And I…need to get it straight in my head. It's important that I'm sure, that it's—" He made a slight, vague gesture with his hand, as if he were turning a key in a lock.

Sabrina ran her fingers over her lower lip. Who *wouldn't* be apprehensive about a comment like that, but it was important to her that she had her own mental space when she needed it. And it was important that he had his. "Okay."

A faint smile appeared on his mouth, and he touched his knuckles to her chin, lifting her face. His kiss was gentle, catching her lip between his, sucking lightly, nuzzling at her.

Sabrina put her hand on the back of his head and kissed him back as the lights in the room went off and the projector screen turned on.

Three minutes later, she was on Nick's lap.

Three hours later, she could say with confidence that Ferren's film was about a war, there were definitely swords, and she was very fond of Nick Davenport's hands.

And they were going to have to bone up on a detailed plot summary, or the interview on Friday was going to start and end with "Hey, Joe, cool armour."

Chapter Fifteen

4 Days until Christmas Eve

Sabrina's fingers linked through Nick's, her hips rolling against his, her internal muscles catching at his erection every time she lifted and circled, sliding him in and out. Sweat was beading on her forehead, a drop edging towards her lashes; Nick was equally damp and stretched taut with tension. The tendons down his neck stood out as he tilted his head back against the pillow, his low grunts now a deep, guttural noise.

Releasing his hands, Sabrina caught herself with one palm beside his head, and touched herself where their bodies connected most intimately, rubbing and circling her clit hard as the pulsing started. Nick's hands moved to her breasts, stroking her nipples.

When she shut her eyes and arched her neck, he pushed up on one elbow and cupped her head, pressing his lips to hers to catch the last of her helpless, panting cries in his mouth.

As she caught her breath, holding on to him, Sabrina deliberately flexed her contracting muscles, squeezing him hard, and his "Oh, *fuck*," was almost desperate.

She expected him to grip her hips and slam up into

her then, but he took her by surprise, circling her with his arm and smoothly turning her under him. With his body half over hers, he looked down at her. He was very still, only his chest moving with his deep, ragged breaths.

Blinking away the fog of her orgasm, Sabrina stared up into his eyes. Questioningly, she touched her fingers to his cheek. "Nick," she said softly. "*Are* you okay?"

His dark gaze searched hers, intensely, but he didn't reply, just kissed her again deeply; until she couldn't help making a needy sound in her throat. Tucking her leg over his hip so that her foot rested against the small of his back, Nick shifted his full weight onto her and started to move. His lips nuzzled kisses to her throat and murmured in her ear as he thrust. It was a lazily sensual rhythm and gentle orgasms, and would have been a lovely start to any other morning.

In the shower afterwards, blinking in the artificial light, Sabrina cast a side glance at him. His shoulders were locked tight with brooding tension. He rubbed conditioner through his hair and ducked around her in the small stall to grab the shower gel. Seeing her looking at him, he squirted her with the shower gel, then pulled her forward with a hand in her wet hair to kiss her again.

Despite the playfulness, as they dried off and dressed she could still see a frown flickering between his brows.

They were sticking with the earlier pickups and their comprehensive checks of the studio. The whole thing still screamed Peter King, and it really was so ridiculous now that it had taken on a perverse element of humour. She and Nick had made a competition the past two days to see who could spot the sabotage, as if they were playing a twisted game of *Where's Wally?* They were currently one-all.

And, as Nick pointed out, "They're failing." His hair still damp from the shower, he clipped on Alan's lead. They were dropping the Yorkie off at Doggy Daycare on the way to the studio. "We caught on to it quickly, and we're taking measures to head it off." Emphatically, he added, "We're also doing a damn good job. We're both talented presenters, you're daily winning back more of the lost support—and a huge number of people fucking adored you regardless—and the majority share of viewers are enjoying the changes to the format. The show is on the up. A fact of which King is well aware. This is a pathetic bid to get a job he isn't suited for, and the only thing that's really bothering me about that situation is not knowing which member of the crew doesn't want us there."

Nick's phone started to ring. She'd changed his ringtone to a Christmas carol to help them feel a bit festive amidst the stress.

"'Tis the season to be jolly..."

Sabrina shoved on her wool hat, pulling her thick plait over her shoulder. "'Tis the season of people being total twats."

"On which note, let's go talk to your ex-boyfriend in front of a million people."

"Fa la la la la, fa la la la."

Without knowing why he needed it, Sabrina was giving him thinking space, and her attitude towards him remained teasing and increasingly affectionate. But she was obviously worried, and Nick could sense her darting glances at him in the car.

Reaching out, he took her hand.

He'd thought, not so long ago, that given a pen and paper, he'd probably be able to draw her features in minute detail. Even after this short amount of time, the picture he'd draw now would look very different to that hypothetical sketch. When he thought about her, the image in his mind—she was laughter, and acerbity, and deep generosity and kindness, knitting furiously, trying to sneakily steal his gherkins. She was beautiful—she was fucking gorgeous, but he couldn't even objectively see her physical features anymore. He just saw *her*, which was something that only happened with the people he cared about the most.

Something had locked in him so hard where she was concerned that he was feeling quite matter-of-fact about the interview with Ferren. Despite Sabrina's complex history with the actor, and the undeniable chemistry between them that had always grated on him, any sense of unrest was for her sake. Ferren had hurt her badly, and Nick didn't want her hurt further. But she'd done absolutely nothing to make him doubt her, or what was building between them.

It felt as if things had clicked exactly where and when they were meant to. He believed in it, in her, in them and where he hoped things were going. And even though his prior long-term relationship had ended in his wife returning to her ex, which might have been considered an unfortunate precedent, he wasn't threatened by Joe Ferren.

Bloody detested him. Not threatened by him.

Sabrina was growing tenser the closer they got to the

South Bank. He squeezed her fingers. Clearly not the time to broach the subject of the possible job offer from LightStarr. And until Roderick Speight's team actually made contact, there wasn't much point in throwing that particular cat among the pigeons. Things changed quickly in this industry, and more projects disappeared into the wind than came to fruition.

If it did eventuate—

He was currently split down the middle.

The moment the words had left Iain's mouth, Nick's radar had switched on by ingrained instinct, his mind immediately flashing through the prospects. Major breaking stories. Potential production credits. Money.

Theoretically, it sounded like a more logical next step in the career he'd been building for the past few years.

Years in which he couldn't remember *once* feeling as present and motivated as he had in recent weeks.

The car pulled up outside the studio. It was public knowledge that Ferren was appearing today, and the press presence outside was pandemonium.

Sabrina glanced out the window and took an audible breath. She turned to him. "All right?"

Yes. He hoped it would be.

Sabrina was officially territorial about this job. She liked the people, she enjoyed the format, she got to come in every day and have a laugh, often the guests were inspiring, once or twice they'd made her cry a little, and—still astonishingly—she had come to naturally think of Nick as her partner. And it just felt right.

But right now, sitting beside him on one couch, her body still tingling from a close-to-simultaneous orgasm with him in the darkness of the night, while her ex sat opposite and the camera lenses acted as a portal to hundreds of thousands of spectators, she didn't think she was being paid enough.

"We trained in Avignon…" Ferren pushed a hand over his head as he spoke. His hair was currently shaved down to his scalp for a role, and he looked tired. He was also acting very oddly. Nick was taking most of the weight in this interview, asking questions about the film, making up a load of rubbish about how much they'd enjoyed it, and generally saving Sabrina as much awkwardness as he could. Ferren wasn't cooperating well—he wasn't hostile, but nor was he forthcoming. He didn't hold eye contact with either of them for longer than a few seconds and he seemed preoccupied.

He was actually being quite a dull interview, which was so out of character that Sabrina was fighting to keep her frown internal. Ferren had a solid ego. He liked to look good in any public venue, and he could usually be trusted to promote his work with enthusiasm and a boatload of charm.

Obviously, this was not a normal situation—Ferren knew she was dating Nick, the public knew Ferren had cheated on her, and the last time anybody had seen them together, her fist had been smashing into his nose. Anyone could be forgiven for being off their game.

But it wasn't like him.

His eyes met hers again, and something danced fleet-footedly across his expression, before he shifted his gaze over her shoulder and kept talking stiltedly.

Nick tried to redirect the conversation about the film down more interesting channels, with a very slight edge to his voice.

Sabrina suspected their viewing numbers were

through the roof right now, but if people had been hoping things would kick off, they'd be disappointed. This was so decorous and restrained it made Buckingham Palace garden parties look like a boozy night out in Benidorm.

As they watched the short preview clip of the film, Nick put a hand on Sabrina's knee and stroked her with his thumb. His face had clouded into the preoccupation of the past couple of days, and he obviously didn't realise what he was doing, but it pulled Ferren out of his own reverie.

His attention locked on Nick's fingers curled against her leg, the touch not posturing and possessive but simply intimate. Affectionate. Natural. Ferren's jaw jerked.

Just for a second, something hot and angry slipped into his face.

And she felt so little in response that it genuinely shocked her a bit. She was concerned for him; something was clearly causing him considerable strain—something she was quite certain had nothing to do with her—and of course she still cared. He'd been part of her life for so long it was impossible to just switch that off. But sitting here with him, it felt surreal. It was as if she viewed him from a distance, like her intimate memories of him belonged to someone else.

She had changed, since the summer, and not just her relationship and her job.

The person she was now was not the woman she'd been then.

However—hooray for general happiness and confidence, but this particular experience could end at any time. Ferren was still glaring at Nick's hand, and ants of awkwardness were starting to march up and down her spine.

Nick sat forward as the clip ended, his arm falling away, and they wrapped up the most boring interview of the entire month with a few additional banal comments. They were moving straight into the next segment after the ad break, so Jess rushed in to usher Ferren out. She looked both star-struck and disappointed. Fenella had issued a stern warning about appropriate behaviour today, like a harried mother waggling a finger at two toddlers—it had raised Sabrina's hackles and pissed Nick right off—but Sabrina would put good money on it that a lot of the crew had privately hoped fists would fly again.

In the temporary privacy as they went to break, she stood, nervously tucking her blouse tighter into the back of her pencil skirt, and Ferren caught her arm lightly with his fingertips.

"We need to talk." That husky voice and strong Mancunian accent had once had the power to dictate her moods and her actions. Now, she simply shook her head, and spoke in a low tone.

"I think we've said and done everything we were meant to, Joe."

Ferren's jaw moved again, in a sort of flinch, but the slashing gesture of his arm was impatient. "There's something you need to know—"

Nick was looking over at them, frowning now, and Jess politely cleared her throat.

"We're back on in two minutes," Sabrina said, stepping back. "You have to go."

He hesitated, but glancing around at the hovering crew, bit back a curse and followed Jess out. At the door to the back corridor, he turned and shot Sabrina a stare that was loaded with meaning.

"What was that?" Nick asked at her shoulder, and she shrugged.

"I don't know. I'm not sure what *any* of that was."

"He missed an opportunity to play up to his fans. I was expecting shades of the betrayed hero, taking the high ground in the face of our long-time affair," Nick said with a heavy thread of sarcasm. "That was more like background extra worried about missing his bus."

Decent description.

Fenella signalled to them, and Sabrina set the Ferren puzzle aside for now. All in all, she was relieved it had passed off so uneventfully. She'd take ten minutes of boring viewing over another week of scandal-mongering headlines. The press would still put a spin on this morning, but blank faces and polite chit-chat about fifteenth-century swordplay wasn't exactly click-worthy.

Their next feature was a group of guide dogs in training, and Nick perked well up. Holding a wriggling golden retriever puppy against her heart, Sabrina watched him crouch on the ground, playing with three more excited pups. A black Labrador licked his chin, and he laughed, and sweet Jesus. She could see why "hot men with puppies" was a thing.

The final segment of the morning was a performance by a singer who'd just won a talent quest show on YouTube. Sabrina wasn't a huge fan of her voice, and she didn't like the song the woman was going to sing. When they'd gone through the schedule, the puppies had seemed the one shining bright spot in an otherwise trying day.

She expected five minutes of pasting a smile on her face and trying not to wince at the highest notes, which had just about broken her kitchen window when she'd watched the winning performance on her laptop at home.

She didn't expect to wind up in A & E.

It all unfolded in a bit of a blur. The beaming singer strutted out to the staging area, where Sabrina and Nick stood waiting to exchange a few words before they left her to it. She shook hands with them—she might possess the vocal range of an air raid signal, but she seemed like a lovely woman—and raised her arm to meet the mic that was supposed to descend smoothly from the filming platform above, straight into her hand.

It dropped on the poor woman like a dive-bombing pigeon, and she reacted, in Sabrina's opinion, perfectly appropriately to being smacked in the forehead with a microphone. Letting out a surprised exclamation, she stumbled forward, and lost her footing.

Both Sabrina and Nick instinctively shot forward to catch her, and all three of them collided. They ended up in a tangled knot on the studio floor, and unfortunately for Sabrina's left wrist, her arm bore the brunt of the impact and the momentum of their combined weight. There was no dramatic crack, for which her squeamish stomach was profoundly thankful, but she definitely felt something bend in a way it oughtn't. She lay for a few seconds with the collapsed singer across her legs and Nick heavy against her back, the wind knocked out of her, and then pain—sharp, intense, and shocking—rocketed up from her hand to her armpit.

Nick said something close to her ear that would generate several letters of complaint from their most easily offended viewers, and managed to get off her without putting more pressure on her squashed body. Several crew members rushed in to help the speechless singer to her feet.

Nick put his hand on the back of her head. "Sparks." He sounded appalled. "Hell, I'm sorry—*Sabrina*. Are you all right?" The question was sharp and urgent as she turned her head and stared at him blankly. He was crouched at her side, his hand moving from her face to her back, touching her very lightly, as if afraid to hurt her more. "What is it? What hurts?"

Reinflating her lungs was a short, painful, and undignified process. Ignoring sharp commands from Nick and Fenella to keep still, she wheezed her way up to sit on her knees. She held her left arm against her chest, her teeth clenched as she breathed in and out through her nose, until she felt she could speak. Then, "My arm," she said tightly, and looked with a—probably ghoulish—smile to the camera. "Apologies, folks. With footwork like that, it's amazing that *Strictly*'s passed us by, isn't it? I'm so sorry, Hayley," she said to their unfortunate guest star. "Are you hurt?"

The other woman blinked a few times before shaking her head. "Very minor bump. I mostly ducked in time and it really just brushed my hair. But—oh my God, are you—"

Nick said something in a low, rough voice into his mic, and within seconds, Fenella had switched the camera view, and Meg, their back-up presenter, took over. She'd been standing by to read viewer tweets in the final moments of the show; she repeated the apology and assurances, and started shoving in filler material.

Jess's and Emily's shocked faces hovered in the background.

The show medic was by then crouching at Sabrina's side, examining the arm she was still holding protectively, while Nick put a supporting hand low on her back.

She could feel his fingers through the thin silk of her blouse. Warm and unsteady.

"I'm almost certain it's fractured," the medic said calmly. "And, Ms. Grant, you need to have that bump looked at. Nick—?"

"I'm fine," Nick said tautly. "I came out on top in that utter fuck-up. Literally." His voice was vibrating with anger, but his eyes were dark with concern as he stroked her back. "We need to get you to A & E."

She groaned. On the job for less than a month, and they'd wound up at the hospital twice. The first time had been entirely her own fault, but this— Suddenly, Peter King and his little helper didn't seem such a joke after all.

Nick obviously agreed. His expression was tight with fury, although his touch remained gentle. Sabrina started to shiver, then, her body quaking with uncontrollable shakes; shock was creeping in with a vengeance.

Nick swore, and moved his hand to press against her stomach. "Do we have a blanket?" he asked with a snap, and one of the production assistants immediately rushed off.

The young woman almost bumped into Ferren as he suddenly stormed the stage setup. Sabrina, trying to stop her teeth chattering, frowned up at him as he crouched and reached for her. She hadn't even realised he was still in the building.

"Jesus," Ferren said. Usually tanned from filming on location, he was very pale. "Sabrina. What the fuck?"

Her shaking increased, and all of a sudden—she was so done with this morning. Her arm was one throbbing mass of pain, she was jerking about like a jelly, and they only had one more show left before Christmas and Judgment Hour—what a bloody awful penultimate effort.

With a small sound from deep in her chest, she turned and hooked her right arm around Nick and put her face in the curve of his neck.

He held her head to him, shielding her face from all the prying eyes and Ferren's unwanted attention.

In the back of the car on the drive to the hospital, Sabrina let her head rest against his shoulder. "If that was our secret adversary, they got more than they bargained for today," she murmured.

Nick was still infuriated. "I'm going to wring our adversary's fucking neck," he snapped. "And forget his bid for the *WMUL* contract—Peter King better be thrown out of *The Arts Review*, and the entire network, on his arse."

She could feel the tension in his muscles beneath her cheek, and he kept accidentally squeezing the fingers of her right hand too hard, until she had to politely point out that she was going to need at least one functioning arm.

"What? Oh—sorry." He lessened his grip, and then a few minutes later, clamped down on her again.

She gave up and let him steam.

Friday in a London hospital meant hours waiting

about in various cubicles. Sabrina gratefully accepted the painkillers she was offered shortly after they arrived, and suspected that she was taken to a bed sooner than she would have been if the triage doctor hadn't recognised them.

Having progressed that far through the process, they came to a halt. Nick started pacing the cubicle like a caged tiger, while Sabrina sat back against the pillows on her hard bed, with her knees drawn up and her arm resting on a dense cushion. Her attempts at conversation seemed to set him off further, and all she got was intermittent grumps, growls, and threats against Peter, interspersed with stroking on her head. She received a couple of forehead kisses and one measly peck on her mouth. Apparently when she was injured and in pain, she was a fragile little flower and in need of the maiden-aunt treatment.

Akiko and Elise both texted, and Freddy called, asking if she should come in. Sabrina, watching Nick stomp about, assured her sister that she was fine and she'd text her when she got home.

She was grateful for the nurse, who offered them cups of tea and assurances that they were moving through the queue for X-ray as quickly as possible. She was a friendly British-Jamaican woman named Patricia who watched the show on her mornings off, and as she checked and recorded Sabrina's vital signs, she chatted cheerfully about where they'd gone to school, and what they were doing for the holidays, and if they had any traditions with their families.

As always when Nick talked about any member of his family—with the notable exception of his father—his expression softened.

He even laughed at one point, and by the time Patricia flashed a thumbs-up as she went out, his body language had relaxed a good bit.

Sabrina cleared her throat and lifted her good arm. "Do I get a hug now?"

His mouth tipped up, and he came over to very carefully ease onto the bed beside her. Sabrina sat up so he could get his arm around her. In the clinical starkness and cool air of the hospital, Nick felt familiar and comforting. Like a piece of home in an unwelcoming environment.

She closed her eyes, feeling a bit drowsy with the painkiller, and breathed in his scent.

"How's the pain?"

"Muted." With the back of her good hand, she rubbed his chest. "Your grandparents sound like they were amazing."

Nick's fingers traced light, tingling circles on her cheekbone. "They were. Zippy, my grandad, was an absolute gent. He also didn't take shit from anyone. If I talked back or didn't clean up after myself, I got a long anecdote about the sad life of a disrespectful child. My favourite was Sam, the boy who wouldn't take a bath when his grandfather told him to. A circus elephant sat on him."

She smiled as she shifted against him, cuddling closer. "Was Zippy a nickname?"

"Yes, but I have no idea why we called him that," Nick said after a moment. His breathing was lifting her head with the easy rhythm of his chest. "I've never thought about it. I'm not sure why my grandmother was called Lala, either. Her real name was Grace."

Sabrina sensed him glance down at her, but the

soothing motion of his touch didn't falter. He was quiet, then he spoke slowly. "I've never forgotten the feeling of immediacy when I was with them. The present moment mattered. You experienced it, you felt it. It didn't just…vanish into the worry about what might happen in the future. What you had to do next."

Sabrina listened, her own breathing slow and even, her eyes closed, his voice wrapping around her.

"I thought Lala's fingers were like the branches of an oak, gnarled and knotted. She suffered badly with arthritis, like Jane in York, but she was still a blur of energy at work, and then she'd throw herself down and sit talking—gaffing, she called it—with her friends, and laughing for hours, and she was just pure joy."

With his thumb, he followed the curve of Sabrina's lower lip. "She could weave images with words. She'd describe a day out with her parents in New Amsterdam, the feel of her mother's hand, the way her skirt moved in the wind, and you could see it, hear it, coming alive in your mind. A flower falling from a tree into her outstretched hand as she walked up and down a street for hours when her sister was ill. Moonlight shining through a pavilion when she danced with Zippy for the first time."

Sabrina opened her eyes to see him grin briefly.

"One day they rode on opposite sides of a London bus all afternoon because they'd had an argument. They didn't want to talk to each other, but still wanted to be near each other. When they got back to their stop, they walked home without a word, holding hands." Again, he was momentarily silent. "Endless moments threaded together into incredibly vivid lives."

Nick's smile faded. "I remember it so clearly when

she died. People kept bringing food. I can still see a plate with scraps of fried fish and cassava bread. I can't even smell cooking fish in the street without going back to that room for a moment."

Sabrina thought of a plate of ham sandwiches and a white crochet tablecloth, and turned her hand to press her fingertips against him.

"There was a keening sound. My grandad—but I wasn't scared. There was sadness, but no fear. There was never the sense that she was *gone*, just that she'd moved on. Change, but not loss." Nick stopped, and made a slight sound. "Sorry—that took an unfortunate turn in a hospital."

Sabrina lifted her head, propping her chin against him, and looked at him. As he smoothed her hair back from her forehead, he said, "That appreciation of the here and now—not constantly striving for more and never being satisfied, it was difficult to hold on to that when I was with—"

She rubbed the edge of her thumb on his chest. "Your dad?"

Nick looked at where his fingers were tangled in her hair, then his gaze met hers. "Yes. It's…important. And I feel more like I'm finding that again."

Sabrina searched his eyes. Her heart was thumping more quickly. "Yeah," she said quietly.

His hand moved to where hers rested on him, and he flicked at her fingers, coaxing her hand up so that their palms pressed together. He measured his thumb against hers, then their fingers interlocked.

"Sparks." It was a low murmur against her skin.

Sabrina felt the oddest flip-flop in her stomach, then—not lust; she had a probably fractured wrist, she wasn't in the mood for sex.

It was that sense of rightness again…and an anxiety beyond what she'd ever experienced in the past, of losing this. It was still early days, but so deeply hooked—it felt as if they were on a precipice, where it could either get stronger and stronger until it was rock solid. Unbreakable.

Or it could crack under pressure.

When Patricia came in to check on her again, the nurse was carrying a small stack of magazines. She was tailed by a young girl holding a posy of three yellow flowers tied with a ribbon, and a tall man with permanent resting grouch face.

"Reading material." Patricia set the magazines down beside Sabrina's right arm. "X-ray in around thirty minutes, at this stage, and I found some people outside who may belong to you."

Sabrina was still a bit dozy and her arm was starting to hurt again, but she smiled at Pippi, as Patricia left the cubicle and Nick levered up to greet his niece and brother.

"Hi, Pippi. What lovely flowers. Thank you very much." Sabrina took the proffered posy with her good hand and admired it, while Pippi came to stand carefully by her bed.

"Pippi's school is out for Christmas, so we watched the show this morning," Iain said. Still brusque, but he was looking at her with concern. "She was worried and insisted on coming here. Sorry to intrude."

"Is your arm broken, Sabrina?" Pippi asked, staring at Sabrina's cushioned wrist.

"I'm not sure yet, Pippi, but even if it is, it'll heal. And you're not intruding," Sabrina said to Iain. She smiled at Nick's niece again. "The concern is appreciated."

Pippi chewed her lip. "Did you know that bones keep growing until people are in their twenties? And your bone density is at its peak when you're about thirty. After this, you'll start losing bone mass. Maybe one day you'll have hardly any." She looked thoughtful. "Will you just flop around then? Like a doll? Just spongy inside?"

Sabrina blinked.

"On that disturbing thought," Nick said, "how was end-of-term yesterday, Pip?"

Pippi brightened. "I won a certificate in assembly." She started to shrug off her backpack. "Would you like to see it?" she asked Sabrina.

"I'd love to see it."

"Five minutes, Pippi," Iain warned his daughter. "Sabrina will be tired, and she has to have an X-ray of her arm soon."

"Will you get a cast after that?" Pippi pulled out a slightly bent certificate with gold stickers on it. "I'd like a cast. Do you think you could get a purple one? That's my favourite colour."

As Sabrina looked at Pippi's certificate, she heard Iain say to his brother, "Any word yet?"

She glanced up in time to see Nick shake his head slightly. At the look on his face, her eyes narrowed.

Before she could say anything, Pippi opened one of the magazines, turned a page and pointed at a small photo. "Oh, look. It's Emily's stepdad. Is he famous?"

Sabrina glanced down and froze. Nick, too, was staring down at the man in the photo under his niece's glittery lilac fingernail.

Peter King.

Chapter Sixteen

The Christmas tree in the lobby was twinkling, Sabrina could hear people laughing, and the whole building was starting to take on a holiday atmosphere. In the lift, however, things were decidedly tense.

"You ought to be at home in bed," Nick said for the sixteenth time, as he jabbed the button for the *WMUL* floor.

Sabrina entirely agreed. She would very happily be in bed right now, preferably with a good audiobook, and with him. But— "We've been in this together up until now. We'll see it through." With her right hand, she held the immobilised fingers of her left. Her cast— bright purple in honour of Pippi—was tucked carefully into a sling and ached like blazes. "And since we still have zero actual proof of this, we're going to have to tread cautiously."

"And I'm likely to go in with the subtlety of a drunk elephant, is that it?" The nerve in Nick's jaw had been flickering like a faulty lamp for hours now. "Do I need to point out who has the flaming temper in this partnership?"

"I'm not mad right now." Sabrina leaned back against the mirrored wall and closed her eyes. She didn't need to see her ghostly-looking face and the dark rings under her eyes, reflected four times over. She had a slight headache, too, and a heavy, dragging feeling low in her abdomen. That was all she needed, to come on to her period. The day was shit enough. "I'm gutted. I like Emily. And I genuinely thought she liked us."

"She does like us. Or, if she doesn't, she ought to be headlining a major production on the West End."

"Then why—" Sabrina broke off and shook her head as the lift doors dinged and opened. "Oh, *hell*."

In reception they were immediately surrounded by a rush of concerned colleagues, people looking at her cast and making sympathetic noises. As patiently as she could, Sabrina returned the greetings and repeated assurances that she was fine. Minor fracture. No surgery required, it would heal on its own.

Although it was all downhill from here for her bones, apparently. *Thank you, Pippi.*

"Is Emily Warren still here?" Nick asked. It was almost five o'clock, the sky swiftly darkening outside, but Emily was on break from her studies and had picked up extra hours with the admin team for the last few days before Christmas.

"I think she's in the research office," one of the production assistants said. "Fenella put her on to help with travel arrangements for the Monday line-up."

"What do you want to bet the Monday guests would have accidentally ended up in Southampton?" Nick muttered as they headed for the rear offices.

Emily was alone in the research office, her back to them as she stood at the printer, her fingers lightly holding the paper that was coming out.

"Emily," Sabrina said. "We need to have a word."

Their assistant's back stiffened visibly the moment Sabrina spoke. The paper between her fingers crumpled a little.

For a short moment nobody moved, and then Emily's shoulders lifted and fell, and she turned. She was crying, and obviously had been for a while.

With one look at their expressions, she scrubbed her hand under her nose and said thickly, "You know, don't you?"

"That Peter King is your stepfather, he wants to score the contract here by default, and we think you've been giving him a…helping hand?" Given how furious Nick had been earlier, Sabrina hadn't been sure how he'd deal with this. His body was still taut, and his voice was stern—but not unkind.

Emily's face crumpled further as she looked at Sabrina. "I'm *so sorry.* I never meant for you to get hurt."

"You just meant for her to get fired?" Nick asked. A hint of acerbity now, and Emily turned red.

"I didn't— When I started here, I didn't know you. I didn't expect to like—" She didn't seem to know what to do with her hands. "To be honest, I thought you seemed like a bit of a prat—" Sabrina couldn't help a muffled snort, and Nick cast her a speaking look "—and I reckoned Sabrina would be really up herself. I didn't really think about what it would mean for you." She looked miserable. "I just wanted to help my dad. He's worked so hard and he really deserves this job. But I didn't want anyone to get hurt, I swear I didn't."

Sabrina lifted her cast in the sling. "You couldn't have anticipated that the three of us would do an impromptu tango and go down like dominoes, but Hayley could have been hurt by that microphone. Anyone could have been hurt in tumbles and stumbles on other days. Even that bloody Wibblet might have caused an accident. You just didn't know, that's the point. Not only did you betray our trust and let down the entire team—they all work extremely hard, and your behaviour made everybody here look sloppy and disorganised at times—but you could have injured someone else. This is really serious," she said in a low tone, as Emily's tears flowed faster.

"Speaking of that Wibblet," Nick said. "Exactly what field are you studying at uni?"

Emily pressed her lips together. She swiped at her wet cheeks with the back of her hand. "Computer science. And—I'm in a club. For programmers."

Sabrina breathed in deeply, and put her good hand on her hip. She looked at Nick, silently asking a question.

He addressed their tearful assistant firmly. "Did you do this entirely off your own bat, Emily—or did Peter put you up to it?"

"It was me," Emily said quickly—too quickly. "Dad doesn't know anything about it."

Sabrina's eyes met Nick's again. He hadn't missed it, either. There had been a tiny but noticeable pause before that hasty denial.

"You're obviously very loyal to your stepfather—to your father," Sabrina said, and Emily nodded and tried to say something else, but she was crying in earnest again. "Emily, he shouldn't have put you up to this."

"He d-didn't! It was me." Emily coughed and scrabbled fruitlessly in her pocket, and Nick pulled open a cupboard and took down a box of tissues. He passed them over and she took a few with mumbled thanks.

"How did you get this job?" Nick asked quietly, and Emily jerked.

"I applied."

"The current team for *WMUL* came about through internal restructuring." Nick spoke levelly. "Most of the staff were either here already or transferred from other shows. None of the assistant jobs were advertised externally. If this is your first position with the network, somebody wrangled you in—and I'm guessing that it wouldn't take much investigation to trace that back to Peter. A little strange, isn't it, in the circumstances, that he would want his daughter working not only for *WMUL* during our trial, but directly—personally—with us?"

Emily was swallowing a lot, but she repeated stubbornly, "My dad knew nothing about it. I did it to help him, but I didn't mean for it to go this far, and I'm really—I'm really s-sorry—" Her bravado was dissipating again. Croakily, she asked, "What happens now?"

Nick shoved his hand over his head, cupping the back of his neck. There was nothing pleasant about this situation, and no winners here.

"We trusted you, Emily," Sabrina said. She bit her lip. "Nick even entrusted his niece's care to you the day she was here. And we enjoyed working with you. I accept that you didn't intend to cause physical harm, but you could have seriously damaged more than one career."

"Inadvertently, you *did* do that," Nick pointed out. "Although nobody's denying that Sadie Foster did largely bring that spectacular downfall on herself. Most people wouldn't expose themselves quite so dramatically with a rigged mic. However, I wouldn't have put it past her to take legal action against the network." He looked again at the crying girl, and grimaced. "This isn't a school prank. I'm not sure you fully realise the consequences."

Emily was pale. "I'll resign," she said in a rush, and a sudden cough sounded from the door.

"I don't think you'll have the opportunity for that," Hania Aronofsky said grimly. The programming director was standing with a pile of papers in her hand, and by the look on her face, had overheard enough of the encounter that Emily was right to look horrified. "I'd like to see you in my office. Right now." She was already flipping open the cover of her phone and moving her thumb over the screen. Her forbidding gaze moved between the three of them, where they stood immobile. "Melody? Could you contact Peter King, thanks, and request a meeting with him in my office as soon as possible? His presence is not optional. Please emphasise that. Thank you."

She hung up and stepped pointedly to one side. Using her papers to make a sweeping gesture, she said to Nick, "Could you show your assistant where my office is, please."

Emily's unscrupulous loyalty to her stepfather and meddling acts had caused a lot of hassle and stress this month, and the young woman was partly responsible for the pain throbbing up and down Sabrina's arm—but this situation was just awful, and she was furious with Peter King. She'd eat her winter hat, pompom and all, if the man hadn't—at the very least—encouraged this. She'd bet a decent sum that he'd instigated it.

Emily would carry any disciplinary action taken

against her for the rest of her career. What kind of parent put their child's future in jeopardy to promote their own interests?

Nick was silent as he escorted a trembling Emily out, and he looked as disturbed by the whole thing as she felt.

"Unpleasant situation," Hania said crisply, and Sabrina nodded wordlessly. Their boss looked at her purple cast. "I hope you're going straight home? Fenella has arranged for Meg to sub for you on Monday." She spoke over Sabrina's immediate objection. "Lionel wants you and Nick representing the show at the Carols by Candlelight benefit on Christmas Eve as arranged. Take the opportunity to rest." She lifted a brow. "And clearly there's been more to your frequent mishaps this month than met the eye, but you do seem to live an interesting life. I don't recall your assistant forcibly pushing you into the Thames, for instance."

Sabrina screwed up her nose, and Hania's expression lightened with a small smile.

"Avoid any further incidents before the benefit. Nick's fully capable of carrying the show without you for one day. Although, the two of you as a pair has turned out to be ratings magic. To the point that Grimes is prepared to overlook Nick's unfortunate character assessment, and offer you both the permanent contract on the show next year."

Sabrina's heart jolted. "We've got it?"

"As soon as you both sign on the dotted line, consider yourselves the new faces of *Wake Me Up London* going forward. But—" and her voice turned serious "—I did want to broach this with you first, alone. Because I need to make this clear—the offer is contin-

gent on your dual acceptance. Lionel wants you as
a team, not separately. You're either both in, or both
out. Although if the latter, the offer clearly will not be
extended to Peter King in your stead. I'm not having
that sort of behaviour from our headline presenters.
Disgraceful."

She turned a shrewd look on Sabrina. "When we
sat down and initially discussed this trial, I had a pair
of circling, baiting wildcats in my office. You had
every reason to resent being forced to work alongside
Nick. And you've risen to the occasion gracefully."
Sabrina felt her cheeks redden at the look Hania gave
her then. "I realise that the dynamic between you has
warmed. To volcanic levels. I'm assuming you're no
longer averse to this professional partnership, but given
the circumstances in the past, I felt I owed it to you
to speak to you privately, before the offer is also extended to Nick."

"I would have no problem working with Nick on a
permanent basis." Sabrina heard a slightly off-note in
her statement, and Hania hadn't reached her current
position by missing the nuances.

She tilted her head sharply. "But? Do you think he
would have an issue working with you?"

"No. I think he enjoys working together," Sabrina
said honestly, and hesitated. What was she doing here?
Was she actually going to imply to their boss that she
still doubted if Nick would really find this job professionally fulfilling? Way to sow seeds of doubt behind his back, potentially unwarranted. She smoothed
out her expression. "He's happy with our dynamic, as
well."

That, at least, was true.

Hania eyed her narrowly for an uncomfortable few seconds. "Good. A formal offer will be made next week."

Nick reappeared shortly after Hania left the research room. He was still grim-faced. "Emily's in Hania's office. And now you're going home to bed."

They made one brief stop to pick up Alan. In the back of the taxi, as she rubbed the Yorkie's ear, it was constantly on the tip of Sabrina's tongue to relay what Hania had said.

Something kept her silent.

She did raise the subject of Peter King. "What do you think will happen where he's concerned?"

"If I had my way, he'd be sacked. The man's a spiteful, immature troublemaker—and if he coerced Emily into doing this, it's emotional manipulation at best. But if she continues to protect him, there's no actual proof of his involvement. He'll probably get away with it. I'll be damned if he's running away with our contract, though."

Sabrina looked at him quickly, then out the side window.

At home, Nick got her fire going, and Alan immediately hurled himself onto his back on the rug.

Exhaustion and reaction catching up to her, Sabrina sat shakily on the edge of the couch while Nick put the kettle on. He came to kneel in front of her, his hands resting on her knees. "How're you doing?"

Gently, she cupped his cheek, feeling the shape of his cheekbone with her thumb. In reply, she leaned forward and touched her lips to his. The kiss was light and delicate, mutual comfort. Nick held the sides of her head, his thumbs running little circles on her earlobes, and kissed one cheek, then the other, and the tip of her nose, before he stood and went to make the tea.

The dragging sensation in Sabrina's pelvis was suspiciously intense now, and she was getting a few one-two knife jabs to the ovaries. Pushing up from the couch with her functional arm, she went into the bathroom, checked, swore grumpily, and opened her bathroom cabinet.

"Oh, hell." She'd let several things slide this month, including her weekly shopping. Making a quick dash to her handbag in the living room, she checked all the interior pockets. "Please, please."

"What are you looking for?" Nick put two mugs of tea on her coffee table.

"My period's started and I don't think I have anything." She pulled out her iPad and notebooks, and tossed them onto the table. Knitting, lipsticks, tissues, mints. A sweet from the flight home from France. Not a single solitary tampon.

"I'll make a quick trip to the shops." Nick was already reaching for his coat. "You could do with a few things for the fridge, too. Pads or tampons?"

"Probably both, for the first few days. I have heavy periods." Sabrina put her bag down. "Are you sure?"

Nick looked slightly baffled. "Of course I'm sure." Slipping his phone into his pocket, he kissed her again. "If you won't want a bath at the moment, I'll get something we can use to cover your cast in the shower."

She caught his fingers. "Nick—thanks."

He smoothed her hair behind her ear. "Painkillers, tea, and for Christ's sake, would you put your feet up."

Sabrina adhered to that bossy advice because it suited her. She sat down on the couch to turn on Netflix, with a bright purple cast on her arm that she'd only just now realised was the shade of a Wibblet, and a wad of paper towels stuffed in her pants.

Really living that glamourous London life.

She was just about asleep, her head lolling back against the cushions as Jennifer Aniston cracked a joke, when her intercom buzzed.

Drowsily, only half-aware, she got up and went to check the security cam. Nick had her keys, so he would just let himself in, and Freddy would be on her way to the Majestic by now—

She came fully awake when she saw who was standing outside, his head lowered, hands pushed into the pockets of a designer coat.

For a full ten seconds, she just stood there and openly considered pretending she wasn't home. Then, with a muffled "Fuck," she reached for the intercom button.

"Why are you here, Ferren?"

His head came up, and Sabrina was shocked anew at the lines of tension on his face. In a few months, he'd aged five years.

"Can you let me up?" His voice sounded carefully regulated. Not a hint of his usual heavy-dealing charm and banter. "I need a word. It's important."

Her instinct was to refuse. She wasn't in the mood for company of any sort right now, barring Nick and Alan, and she definitely didn't want another argument with Ferren. But his continued uncharacteristic behaviour held back the outright no.

"Can you come back in half an hour?" she said at last. "Nick's gone to the shops, and he should be back by then."

Ferren turned a look of disbelief into the camera. "What the hell would I want to talk to Davenport for? If the bastard's out, all the better. Sabs—come on. Buzz me in."

"Refer to Nick like that again and you can fuck off. And you don't have to talk to him. But if you're going to come in, I'd prefer he was home."

A slight sneer made Ferren at least 60 percent less good-looking. "Do you have to ask his permission before you can invite someone into your own flat? What kind of fucked-up relationship have you walked into?"

"It's not about permission." She leashed her annoyance with an effort. She and Ferren could fire up at each other under the best of circumstances, but throw a snapped bone and paper-towel pants into the mix, and he was seriously veering into the danger zone right now. "It's about respecting your partner and their feelings. I'm aware it's a foreign concept for you."

Ferren shifted his weight. He was starting to look as irritated as she felt, but she could almost see him counting to ten in his head. In a determinedly conciliatory tone, he said, "Look, I don't have long. And I really do need to speak to you. It concerns your father."

Her dad? Sabrina's hands suddenly felt cold, and the tingles of pain breaking through her meds intensified.

Without another word, she buzzed Ferren in.

And guiltily, her first thought was not *Has something happened to my father?*

It was *What the hell has he done now?*

Whatever it was, she couldn't imagine how Ferren could be involved. He'd never got on with Rupert, even in their earliest days of dating, and her father unrepentantly thought Ferren was a complete shit.

When she let him in the front door, he came to stand in the middle of the lounge, looking around. The trace of a smile passed over his face. "I forgot how much I like your flat." He shot her a meaningful look. "We had some good times here."

"Past tense. What about Dad? What's wrong? And how do you know?" Sabrina put her hand under her sling for support.

The movement caught his attention, and he frowned. "Your poor arm. It's broken, then?"

Alan, belatedly realising there was an intruder, came scurrying out of her bedroom, barking. He took one look at Ferren, stopped barking, turned around, and ran straight back in.

Cute as a button. Shit as a guard dog.

"When did you get a dog?"

"Ferren." She was losing patience. "Get to the point. My dad?"

Ferren looked from her arm to her face, his own suddenly twisting into an emotion she couldn't categorise. He sat down, heavily, on the couch. "I—" He swallowed. "I'm not sure how to say this."

Sabrina eased down onto the edge of her armchair, her eyes fixed on his face, apprehension starting to curl sickly in her stomach. "What? What's happened?"

He couldn't seem to meet her eyes now. "I happened," he said, with a short laugh that contained no humour. "I've landed myself in a hole, and I'm trying to dig out of it, but—" A pause, then, succinctly, "Gambling debts."

She closed her eyes briefly. Ferren's gambling habit had been the cause of more than one of their break-ups. He'd always insisted it was "weekend flutters," but the intensity of the gleam in his eyes when he saw a card table or roulette wheel told a different story. "Oh, Joe."

He ran his hand over his shorn head and propped his arm on his knee, and just for an instant, he was the man who'd approached her in a smoky pub, before years, ego, ambition, and loss had changed them both irrevocably.

"How much do you owe?" she asked, and he lifted his head.

"A lot." He spoke grimly. "The residual cheques I'll get for *Agincourt* will cover most of it. That's not the main issue."

Sabrina waited, her heart beating harder.

It came out now, in a clipped rush. "About six months ago, I was brought into a Mayfair club. Men only. You know the sort of thing—"

Unfortunately, she knew exactly the sort of thing. The old boys' den of expensive booze and cigars, blatant classism and snobbery, and in many cases, revolting prejudice and misogyny. Despite everything, it wasn't Ferren at all. "Why the hell would you—"

"Money." His mouth was tight. "They played with very high stakes. And because of my status, I was asked into the inner circle of the club, run by a very well-connected businessman, where the stakes were even higher. And…not entirely legal. Eventually I was made party to what was going on behind the scenes." He ran his hand over his face. Tersely, he said, "Information commerce."

Sabrina looked at him unblinkingly, then sat back. "Please tell me that's not code for insider trading. Jesus Christ, Joe."

Ferren shook his head, but it wasn't a negation.

"Look, I didn't get involved. Not with that. There *are* limits, fuck. But I'm entwined deeply enough with the club that it looks bad. And Gough—"

Her right hand came shooting up, fingers spread in an involuntary *Stop!* gesture. "I'm sorry, what— This 'well-connected businessman'… Are you involved in an insider trading club with fucking *Frank Gough*?"

"Peripherally. Yes." Ferren's jaw was jerking about wildly. "And it's coming out. Not my connection to the club—I bloody well hope. I think I've—"

"Covered your tracks?" she asked with a snap, her mind tumbling in horrified circles, and his cheeks went ruddy.

"Gough is about to be busted. A friend of mine is connected with the investigation, and he gave me a heads-up."

Sabrina was staring at him in disbelief, and his flush deepened.

"I know it sounds…grubby."

"You think?" she burst out. The chill in her body turned icy. "What does this have to do with my dad?"

"Gough has approached your father to 'edit' his next book. Essentially, ghostwrite it. And he's just been invited into the club." Ferren's eyes were level on hers now. "Rupert and I have never been great mates," he said, with another twist of his mouth. "But despite everything that's happened, I care a fuck of a lot about you, Sabrina, and for your sake and for Freddy's sake— he needs to extract himself from this. Right now. Or he's going to be dragged into the net, and your family will take another battering."

Sabrina's mouth was dry. She forced herself to ask. "Does he know? What's going on?"

"I don't know," Ferren said with apparent honesty. "I doubt it. It's kept well down-low until you're fully enmeshed. But—" He shrugged.

There was a moment of silence, in which all Sabrina could feel was the physical pain in her body, and the nausea catching at her throat.

Slowly, she stood up, and Ferren, too, rose. They moved like a pair of centenarians.

"I'm sorry." His right hand had closed into a fist, and more lines appeared around his mouth. Gruffly, he said, "I've brought a lot of unhappiness into your life, haven't I?"

Holding on to her cast, she stared down at the rug beneath their feet. "Not always. I think we were what each other needed…for a time."

"A time that's over?" he asked after a heavy pause.

Sabrina nodded.

Ferren shoved his hands into his pockets. "I miss you."

Even a couple of months ago, she'd have been tempted to retort that perhaps he shouldn't have cheated on her, then. Now, deep inside, the anger was gone. There was no room for it anymore. All she felt was a slight sadness for what had been, natural concern for someone whom she knew so well, and intense frustration. And dread, where her father was concerned.

"Just remember all the times I drove you mad," she said, and Ferren smiled without humour.

"Right now, I'd give a lot to have you back and driving me up the bloody wall." He swallowed. "Nobody ever believed in me like you did."

"Like I *do*," Sabrina said, emphatically, and he lifted his head. "I still believe in you. I think you're going to be great. I think you're going to *do* great. Just—get your act together and stop doing shit like this. Fuck's sake, Joe. Enough is enough. You're *better* than this."

He looked at her, and an unexpected grin broke out. He shook his head. "I always could rely on the Carlton sisters to keep my feet on the ground." With an expression that didn't match the lightness of the words, he said, "What am I going to do in the future?"

"Grow up," Sabrina said, "sort your shit, and be happy."

They stared at one another in silence for long seconds.

At last, Ferren pulled his hands from his pockets and exhaled. "I should go. And you need to call your father."

"Yeah." Her heart felt like a rock in her chest. "That's going to go down a bloody treat, isn't it."

"Rupert's never been the father you deserved," Ferren said abruptly. "If he kicks off... If he still doesn't come through for you now, what was that line from *Agincourt*? 'Draw an amiable line.' You said it yourself, Sabs. Enough is enough. Draw the line."

She gave a faint nod, and Ferren reached out and put his hand on her arm. It had been months since his skin had touched hers—and yeah. Well and truly over. She could still appreciate his looks, she could still recognise how attractive he was. But that strong internal pull was, absolutely and in every way, gone.

So she wasn't expecting him to kiss her.

For a split second as his lips touched hers, she was motionless with surprise. Then—*wrong* slammed into her brain, in capital letters with flashing lights, and she jerked her head back, pushing against his chest and twisting out of his arms. Her cast banged against his outstretched hand, hard, and with a muffled sound, she ended up falling back onto the couch, with Ferren leaning over her.

"Oh, *fuck*," she said between her teeth, clasping her upper arm and digging her fingers in, in a futile attempt to dull the explosion of pain in her wrist.

"Shit, I'm sorry." Ferren looked horrified. "I didn't mean— I wasn't thinking—"

"Obviously not." Sabrina squeezed her eyes shut and leaned forward in a hunch. She couldn't believe how much it hurt. Her body must have protected her in the shock of the initial accident, because there had been some numbness then. Definitely not numb now. And she wasn't due more painkillers for a good couple of hours. "Which part of 'dating someone else'...?"

"I know, I know." Ferren touched her again, and she pushed him away, crossly. "Can I—"

The key sounded in the lock.

Sabrina looked up as Nick came in, holding a bulging canvas bag of shopping and a large paper bag that smelled unbelievably good. Ferren's hand was on her good arm, uselessly patting her. Ominously slowly, Nick closed the door behind him.

She realised that involuntary tears of pain had sprung, and hastily pulled free of Ferren's grip to dab at them with her sleeve. Nick's eyes moved from that telltale wetness to Ferren. For a man who was both a professional actor and an inveterate gambler, Ferren's poker face was absolute shite. He looked guilty as hell. Sabrina suddenly felt exhausted.

At the arrival of food and the return of his father, Alan came tearing back out, barking with excitement and renewed bravery.

Nick walked over to the kitchen bench and set down the shopping and the bag of takeaway. He automatically knelt to stroke the wriggling pup, before he came swiftly to her side. Ignoring Ferren completely, he touched her face, his thumb gently sweeping under her spiky lashes. "What's going on?"

Nick's father had spent years living in Cork as a child, Nick had told her. Markus Davenport had obviously retained shades of an accent from that time and passed it on, because when Nick was at his most angry, out came the hint of Irish. He also got very quiet and watchful.

She, the milk-bottle thrower, couldn't relate at all.

"Ferren was just leaving," she said pointedly.

"Did he hurt you?" Nick asked, and Ferren obviously heard that lilt of danger, as well.

A person with sound self-protective instincts would issue a polite no and backtrack out the door now. Ferren chose to inflate like an overblown balloon.

"As if I'd ever fucking hurt her," he snapped, and, entirely unplanned, Sabrina and Nick turned identical "Seriously?" expressions on him. He flushed. "I meant physically." He glanced at her arm. "On purpose. Oh, fuck!" He threw up his hands in an exasperated gesture. "Look," he said to Nick. "I'm aware you hate my guts, because it's entirely mutual. But I had to speak to Sabrina. I'm sure she'll fill you in on the reason why. And despite the fact that I've completely fucked everything up, as usual, she still tried to keep my head up—because she's a good 'un. The bloody best one. And I'm still not used to not having the right… I tried to kiss her."

Nick stiffened, and Sabrina put her good hand on

his clenched fingers. She brushed over his skin with
her thumb, and he looked at her. His fingers turned
over and slipped through hers.

"She twisted away and I accidentally knocked her
arm." Ferren was breathing too quickly. Briefly, he
closed his eyes. "I'm going now." Lifting his head, he
grimaced. "I've got shit to sort," he said, with meaning.

At the door, he turned back to Nick. "Every so often,
you luck out in life. Recognise it. Appreciate it. Don't
chuck it away like I did."

When the door had clicked behind him, there was a
short silence. Nick's hand had momentarily tightened
on hers, but now he very lightly stroked the fingertips
sticking out of her cast. "How bad does it hurt?"

"It's gone from a blinding nine to a thumping
seven." Sabrina tipped her head back and sighed as
Nick's fingers moved up to rub a comforting circle on
her aching temple. "That's nice."

"So, what exactly has Ferren fucked up this time?
Besides the obvious."

She pushed back her hair and tried to summon the
last reserves of her energy. At the very prospect of the
forthcoming task, every cell in her body was trying to
put up a Do Not Disturb sign and crawl under the covers. What a shit of a day. "It's not Ferren I'm worried
about. It's my father."

Nick's gaze sharpened. "Your father?" Then, as Sabrina tried to sit up and found herself physically drooping, he put a supporting hand on her back. "You're all
done in. Shower first," he said firmly. "And I've picked
up some food. Whatever trouble Rupert's got himself
into now, it can wait."

"I don't think it can." But she stood up with Nick's

help, and went over to the shopping bag he'd brought home, while he went into the bathroom to turn on the light and the heater.

Pulling the bag forward, she lifted out a box of maxi tampons, then slowly sifted through the rest of the contents. He hadn't just grabbed at the first things he saw in the aisle. He'd bought things for someone who'd said she had bad periods. Including— She unearthed a family-sized block of chocolate. And a microwave heat pack. And, in a Waterstones bag, an Agatha Christie paperback. *Partners in Crime.* Tommy and Tuppence.

Nick came out of the bathroom. "Did you find the plastic storage bags? I'll tape one over your arm. At least you don't have a full-length cast." He lifted a brow. "What?"

Sabrina was staring at him. He'd taken off his jumper and rolled up his sleeves, and he looked as tired as she felt.

Her throat felt thick when she swallowed, and tears stung at her eyes again, without the excuse of pain this time.

Christ.

She really was in love with Nick Davenport.

Proper, bone-deep, mad love.

This-man-could-break-my-heart-into-minuscule-pieces love.

She shoved her good hand over her eyes as a tear slipped down the side of her nose.

Nick made a low sound, and a moment later, his arm was around her, carefully pulling her against his chest, his other hand coming up to cup her neck. "Pain?"

"God, I hope not," she said, her fingers spread against his back and her voice muffled in his shirt.

She took a shaky breath. "Bloody meddling universe. No going back now. Fuck."

"How many painkillers did you take?" Nick asked cautiously into her hair, and she made a sort of snorting noise and hugged him tighter.

He was strong and warm against her. He then proceeded to put the takeaway in the oven on the warming setting, and cover her arm in plastic so she could have a shower. Which felt so good after the hours in hospital, she almost spontaneously orgasmed again. When she was out and dressed in leggings and a cosy jumper, and had exhausted herself drying her hair, he sat on the couch and used his uncle skills to French-plait it for her.

So going to be the love of her life.

The self-protective part of her heart wished she were joking.

As he painstakingly plaited, and accidentally pulled out several strands of her hair, Sabrina told him what Ferren had said. With her back to him, she couldn't see his face, and had to measure his reactions by the pauses in motion. When she got to the part about Rupert, Nick stopped plaiting for a good five seconds.

With no inflection, he asked the same question she'd asked of Ferren. "Do you think he knows what he's getting into with Gough?"

Sabrina pulled hard at a loose thread in the cushion she was holding on her lap. "I don't think so."

Her hair was curly enough not to need a tie at the end, and Nick pushed the plait gently over her shoulder as she twisted to face him. "But you're not sure?"

Stupid emotional tears were threatening again. "I'm *almost* sure that my father would never knowingly get involved with something like that for money." She bit down on the side of her cheek, and narrowed her eyes until they stopped burning. "It's not the best, though, is it? That there is a qualifier in that."

"You're not going to be able to sleep until you talk to him."

It wasn't really a question, but she shook her head, and without another word, Nick got up and went to get her phone from her bag. He passed it to her, and Sabrina didn't give herself time to overthink it. Curling her legs up, she called her father's number.

Rupert eventually answered after about seven rings, sounding preoccupied. And surprised. "Sabrina?"

"Dad." She had to clear her throat. "I need to talk to you. Could you come over? Tonight."

Understandably, his tone became more startled. "Why? Are you all right?"

"Did you watch the show today?"

"I'm afraid not. I've been in back-to-back meetings. Did something happen?"

"Slight accident, but that doesn't matter." Sabrina pulled on her plait and realised that her fingers were shaking. Nick's hand was resting on her ankle; he moved his thumb in circles over her skin, then picked up Alan and put the dog where she could pat him.

Her heart twinged.

"We need to talk," she said again, clearing her throat. "It's important."

"All right," Rupert said, the note of wariness loud and clear. "I'll be there shortly."

Ending the call, Sabrina held the phone against her chest. She didn't have a good feeling about this. Right now, she and her father could have a conversation about their favourite type of crisps and it would end in an argument. Asking if he was involved with illegal activities run by one of the biggest knobs in London—

Looking down at Alan, curled up against her lap, she stroked his ear. "This is not going to be pretty."

Nick got up. "One thing at a time. Food first. You need to eat." He touched her head as he passed, resting his palm against her hair for a second.

He'd already asked her if she liked Caribbean food, which she did, and he'd bought a selection, as well as a couple of Guyanese dishes. Sabrina tasted the pepperpot and made a sound of appreciation as the meat flaked and the depth of flavour in the rich gravy hit her tongue. There was a knot in her stomach at the thought of the upcoming confrontation with her father and she hadn't thought she'd be able to eat, but her hunger suddenly returned.

"It's not as good as mine." Nick put a few spoonfuls of rice on his plate. "But we needed quick and comforting, and it needs at least a few hours to cook. You can't make pepperpot in a pressure cooker, it's shit. I'll get some cassareep and make it for you another time."

He was speaking fast and lightly, trying to keep her mind from worrying.

"Oh, I'm going to see these much-vaunted cooking skills, am I?" Sabrina bit into a fried plantain and raised an eyebrow at him. "I don't know. I think you might be all talk."

Nick leaned forward and brushed back a curl at her temple. "Sparks," he said, his fingers sending little tingles of sensation through her scalp and down her spine. There was a wicked and very sexy gleam in his eyes. "I am *never* all talk."

If half a dozen circumstances weren't conspiring against super-hot sex right now, they would have been back on her fireplace rug immediately.

For once, Rupert didn't waste time in coming to see her. The intercom buzzed as Nick was carrying the leftover food into the kitchen. Sabrina looked up from the floor where she was scratching Alan's round tummy.

"Do you want me to get it?" Nick asked, and she shook her head.

"Thanks, but—I need to deal with this." Getting to her feet, slightly awkwardly, the butterflies in her stomach raging, she checked the security cam and let her father in.

"Good God," he said when she opened the door. "What have you done to your arm?"

"On-set incident," she said briefly. "Falling equipment."

Then she stopped, their eyes meeting as she recollected who she was talking to, and that long-ago accident at the Majestic locked into her mind, the loud crack and crash as the set fell, the sound her father had made as it hit him—

She swallowed and saw something cross her father's expression. He still suffered daily from those injuries, but that flash of pain hadn't been physical.

Leaning on his stick, Rupert walked into the living room and stopped when he saw Nick. "Davenport." His eyes went to her slightly accusingly, and she just managed to resist rolling hers.

The months-old scandal about Henrietta and *The Velvet Room* was going to be small fry compared to Gough's insider trading scheme, especially if people as high profile as Ferren were involved.

Rupert's behaviour had already hurt Freddy. If their father had knowingly betrayed her trust and damaged her career for a second time—

Frustration surged, and she couldn't hold back. The words tumbled out. "Dad, Ferren was here earlier."

Rupert frowned, also looking exasperated. "Oh, for God's sake, Sabrina. You're not—"

"No. I'm not," she said unequivocally, briefly looking at Nick as she spoke, before she turned her scrutiny on her father. Rupert had the elastic features of a classical actor and a highly trained voice, but he couldn't entirely control the expressions in his eyes. She would know, if she saw. "But he had several things to say. About you. And Frank Gough."

He blinked, a bit taken aback.

But as yet, nothing more. Tentatively, something deep in her loosened its grip.

As she continued, fast, concise, however, her father's demeanour gradually frosted over.

There was a moment of absolutely chilling silence when she stopped talking.

"Do you seriously think," he bit out, at last, "that I would be involved with something like that?"

Sabrina folded her arm across her ribs. Nick had come to stand a few metres away, leaning against a bookshelf, not interfering but just being there. He looked between them, his jaw tight.

"I was almost certain you wouldn't," she said, and Rupert unconsciously copied her stance, folding his arms.

"*Almost* certain," he repeated.

The back of her throat felt thick and painful. "A year

ago, I would have been completely, indisputably sure that you would never be party to plagiarism."

"So, because you can throw that in my face, you think—"

"I'm not throwing it in your face. I—" Her voice kept cracking. "I said we all need to draw a line and get past that, and I meant it. But—I don't…" Again, she had to stop.

The truth was that—fundamentally, deep down—they didn't know each other well enough to be certain of anything.

She couldn't bring herself to say that.

"Why would you want to be associated with Gough at all?" she asked instead. "Didn't you once call him an attention-seeking prick?"

Rupert's lips thinned. "I wasn't planning to run for office with the man. He approached me with a preliminary discussion about working on a book together. It would have been a business transaction, and it's just one of several proposals I was considering."

"Technically speaking," Sabrina said, "whatever twisty deals this club is making could also be considered 'business transactions.' That doesn't make them either moral or legal. And essentially acting as Gough's voice, the filter transferring his views to paper and posterity—you might as well have gone into office with him."

"I've lost a lot of money recently—"

"That wasn't yours to begin with, and you're not exactly on the poverty line. That doesn't hold a lot of water, Dad. Maybe you should vet the other proposals on your desk a little more carefully."

Things devolved from there.

Finally, when Rupert snapped crossly at her, Nick pushed abruptly away from the bookcase and stepped forward.

Before it got out of hand, Sabrina said tautly, "Just tell me you're not going to jeopardise Freddy's reputation any further and you're cutting ties with Gough and his revolting club."

"I would never knowingly jeopardise either of your careers, and I never *had* ties to Gough," her father retorted. "Nor have I even been to a meeting of his 'revolting' club yet. Christ, you're like your mother sometimes."

Instinctively, both of her hands tried to clench, and pain shot up her forearm. She made an involuntary sound, and Nick came to put his arm around her.

Rupert stared at her cast, then his eyes lifted to her face. For once, the emotions there were stark and real and unguarded. Anger, frustration, pain. Sadness. He ran his hand over his face and scrubbed his fingers through his grey curls.

"You should be in bed," he said, his voice flat. He looked and sounded very tired. "I think it would be best for now if I leave."

Sabrina held on to Nick's wrist and said nothing. Her chest felt heavy.

"I'll sever all connection with Gough as of now." Rupert's jaw worked. Suddenly, he came forward, leaning on his stick. And very fleetingly, he touched her cheek. "I'm sorry, Sabs."

Her lip trembled, and she bit it hard.

"I'll see you soon," her father said, and she nodded.

She didn't move when the door closed behind him. She could feel the gentle movement of Nick's chest and the warmth of his breath against her cheek.

A tear fell and she squeezed her eyes shut, but at her tiny sniff, Nick turned her, looked into her face, and pulled her properly into his arms.

And she cried in earnest. For her father. For her mother. For the way things had turned out with Emily, and with Ferren; all the stress and intense emotion of the year flooding out as she buried her face in his neck.

Careful not to bump her arm, Nick picked her up and took her over to the couch, settling her on his lap. He held her, rocking her slightly, stroking her hair and her back, murmuring little sounds of comfort.

Sabrina pulled in a shaky breath. "When I was little," she said huskily, "I wanted to be a baker. On my twelfth birthday, my dad took Freddy and me to Paris, and arranged for me to spend a day with a famous patisserie chef." More tears fell, and she caught them with her fingers. Nick ran the back of his index finger down her temple. "Freddy reminded me of that last summer, and I said I didn't remember. I do." She swallowed. "There were days like that. Wonderful days and memories. Just—not many. And no matter how hard we try, now, it just—" She shook her head, and Nick's hold tightened on her.

"I understand having a picture in your head of what your relationship with your father should be," he said in a low tone, "that's very different to your actual experience."

She looked up and put her hand on his cheek. "Yeah. I know you do."

Nick kissed her fingers, and she closed her eyes. "I do believe that he loves us," she murmured. "And I know he gets frustrated, too. This isn't the way he wants it to be, either, and God knows, I've made my own mistakes." She released another long, slow breath. There were certain fruitless hopes she needed to let go, a reality she needed to be okay with, because she was lucky enough to live a life full of love, in all forms, and spinning fairy tales in her mind did nothing but hurt. "But we just don't have that foundation from back then. And I don't think anything has ever compensated for the loss of his stage career. The centre of his life, the driving force—it was always theatre."

Professionally, though, there was one glaring difference between Rupert and Freddy. Despite her sister's enormous talent and love for the stage, Freddy acted because she adored it. If she ever stopped enjoying her work, she'd leave and do something else. She was driven only by the pursuit of happiness, and she generally found it.

Their father was always grasping at a goal that would never eventuate.

Sabrina placed her palm over the steady beat of Nick's heart.

She had seen what could happen when a person was forced down a path they didn't want to take. When they never got what they strove for, and were unfulfilled by what they settled for.

Spirit broke down. Love broke down.

Once more, worry stirred.

Chapter Seventeen

3 Days until Christmas Eve

The night was restless and interrupted. Sabrina's arm hurt, and she started to feel sick from the painkillers about three o'clock in the morning. She sat on the edge of the bed, breathing deeply, while Nick, almost swaying with exhaustion, rubbed her back and ignored her mutterings to go back to sleep.

She'd finally drifted off when he got up himself, and she found him in the kitchen taking ibuprofen. He'd pulled a shoulder muscle in the studio accident and said nothing about it. With her good hand, she rubbed the painful knot there, while he tried not to groan, and ignored his bossy commands to go back to bed.

They finally slept, tumbled together, Sabrina's arm propped gingerly on a pillow, and it was almost nine o'clock before her eyes cracked open again. The room was a dull shade of grey, a sliver of weak light coming through the curtains. Hard to believe that they'd be halfway through a show by now on a weekday.

Her eyes felt dry and itchy. Scrunching up her face, she carefully eased Nick's arm off her waist, sat up and reached for her glasses. He was sleeping so deeply behind her that his breaths ended in light snores, which in her experience of sharing a bed with him so far was unusual. Alan was curled around the lump of his feet, and she rubbed the dog's head before she padded to the bathroom.

In the kitchen, face washed and eyes almost fully open, she fetched one of the yoghurts Nick had bought from the supermarket, so she could take her pills. Her phone seemed to have disappeared during the night, and she temporarily pinched his to read the headlines while she ate. Poking at the home button until the thumbprint ID went away and she could tap in the key code he'd told her, she leaned against the counter and spooned a mouthful of yoghurt into her mouth.

His open mailbox appeared on the screen, the most recent email automatically appearing.

She didn't mean to read it. Journalism degree or not, she didn't nose through other people's letters, electronic or otherwise. But it was just *there*—and the first sentence jumped out at her.

Her stomach tightening, she read the handful of sentences and the brisk request that followed.

For a moment, she stood, her mind and body still. Then she laid down the spoon.

A muted ringing made her jump. It was her own ringtone. Her mind kicking back into gear and whirring a hundred miles a minute, she acted on autopilot, tracking the sound until she found her phone down between two couch cushions.

She'd missed the call, but a text message rapidly followed. Ferren.

A little birdy's been singing. Wild guess—Davenport.

That might as well have been a string of emojis for all she understood it. The dots of doom appeared as he kept typing, one-two-three, one-two-three.

Thank the fucker if it was. It's going to be a shit of a week.

Still zero comprehension.

She fired off a quick What?

The response came rapidly: All over the news, babe. Cheers very much.

The last dregs of sleep replaced by foreboding, Sabrina thumbed through to the recent headlines.

Hell. The story about Gough had broken, with a vengeance, and he wasn't the only one in the hot seat. Dozens of names from politicians to professional athletes had been thrown into the ring of fire, accused of insider trading, match fixing, and extortion. Her heart beating frantically, she scanned through two articles, then three, but saw no mention of her father.

There was plenty of speculation—and some outright accusations—against Ferren, though.

The exposé had broken on TrackMedia, the main news outlet for LightStarr, the media corporation that had just emailed a request for a meeting with Nick, regarding a new show.

For a second—for the tiniest second—she wondered, and deep in her stomach, she felt traces of that sinking feeling that had gripped her months ago as she'd stood watching headlines roll past about her grandmother, at Nick's instigation.

Almost as swiftly, and exactly as her mind and body

had reacted to Ferren's aborted kiss yesterday, every-thing inside her went *no*.

Fuck no.

Whether or not Nick had been courting LightStarr, he hadn't dashed off covert emails to them last night. There was no way in hell. If she'd needed a test of her trust in him now on that subject—confirmed.

But he hadn't said a word about LightStarr, and judging by his bloody odd behaviour the past couple of days, this interview was not a bolt out of the blue.

"You're up." His voice, thick and husky with sleep, came from the door, and she turned to see him rub-bing his hand over his face and head, before he slipped his glasses on. His boxer-briefs were slung low on his hips, and he'd brought the throw from her bed, toss-ing it around his shoulders against the morning chill. "How's your arm?"

Obviously barely awake yet, he joined her at the counter and, completely absently, transferred the throw to her own shoulders. He kissed her temple, blinked at her, and finally seemed to register the look on her face.

It was amazing how fast he could shed the vestiges of sleep when he had to. "What's the matter?" Quick and crisp.

She turned her phone so he could see the news head-lines. "Gough's in the shithouse. And probably on his way to prison. Crying shame there. But Ferren's been implicated, as well."

Nick took the phone and thumbed down, his brows rising. "Hmm," he muttered. "Bit more to the story than he told you. Or than he knew himself." He was reading rapidly. "The allegations against him seem thin based on what's reported here. If he's telling the truth that his involvement extends only to the gambling, he'll talk his way out of it. Hell of a reputation blow, though. His career won't survive many more of them. Might be the kick he needs to get his act together."

"I couldn't find my phone when I got up. So I borrowed yours."

"That's fine." Nick was frowning as he read. At either her pause, or some quality in her voice, he looked up.

"Your emails came up automatically," she said. "I didn't mean to read it."

His frown deepened. "Read what? And why does this sound like the first act of a 'hell hath no fury' play? I can categorically state that the only other women who would send me personal emails are Pippi, my mother, and Tia."

"Not personal." Sabrina tucked her hand under her cast. "Very much professional. A request from Light-Starr. Apparently, they want to talk to you on Tuesday afternoon. Getting in right before Christmas with the job offer."

The sound as Nick placed her phone next to his on the kitchen counter was loud in the sudden stillness. His eyes locked on hers. "Iain gave me a heads-up the other day that this new show was being mooted, and that my name had emerged as a possible prospect. Nothing concrete. This is the first I've heard of definite communication."

"You didn't tell me."

"No. Not while it was only nebulous word-of-mouth."

"Something was obviously bothering you. I didn't push, because I think people should have their own

space, mentally and physically, when they need it."
Her arm throbbed, and she lifted it to hold her wrist
lightly against her chest. "But this— This, I think you
should have told me. If you take this job, it affects me.
And if we're…together, then I bloody well care about
major things going on in your life. It feels like you've
gone behind my back."

Nick nodded once. "I didn't intend to make you
feel that way. I didn't want to throw more stress on
the pile, with the uncertainty over *WMUL* still hanging over everything."

Sabrina bit her lip.

There was a rather significant development there,
that she'd kept from him thus far, as well.

Well, hell. Hypocrisy was never fun.

"I'm sorry," Nick said, obviously sincerely. "I didn't
mean to hurt you or make you feel sidelined. I just
wasn't sure if an actual offer would ever eventuate, and
in any case—" He stopped, and ran his hand over his
unshaven cheek. "It may well be irrelevant anyway. I
meant what I said about *WMUL*. It's turned out to be
an experience that feels right, and there's a long way
to go, a lot more goals to meet. We've improved the
ratings, but I want the show to keep growing, to see it
permanently take the top spot, and I emphatically believe that it can."

Sabrina said nothing for a moment. "This other job,
though…from what I read in that email, it sounds more
up your alley."

"It sounds more like the path I've trod by rote for
years," Nick said evenly. "Without reflection and under
the lingering influence of pressure from my father.

Both directly, and through the shadow his own career cast. What I need to be sure of is what *I* actually want."

She nodded. "Yes. I agree. I think—" She hesitated. "Things *have* happened very quickly. Changed, very quickly. And I don't want you to have regrets. About anything."

"I believe in gut instinct," Nick said. "But I haven't always listened to mine. The only thing I regret—would ever regret—where you're concerned is that I shelved every message my body sent about my real feelings for you, for a long time."

Her heart was thumping. She held her cast, feeling the abrasion of the plaster beneath her fingers.

"But where work is concerned, you're right—this does concern both of us." Nick's eyes were still direct on her. "And I need to make a decision with complete confidence that it's the right one."

"If *I* didn't want the *WMUL* contract, just theoretically," Sabrina asked slowly, "would you, still?"

It was Nick's turn to be silent. Seconds ticked into each other, and her skin started to prickle.

"Yes," he said. "It wouldn't be the same, but I would still feel like I'd found something I didn't expect with *WMUL*. However, I'm not denying that a huge part of the appeal is working with you. We click."

They both smiled then, fleetingly, instinctively.

"I'll say." She studied him. "But at least part of you is still drawn towards LightStarr."

Her phone beeped with a text and they both automatically glanced down.

Another message from Ferren had appeared on the screen: It wasn't Davenport. One of the bastards in the club dropped me in it. Owe him money. Sorry.

It took a moment to register the stiffness that had crept into Nick's body, but when he raised his head, she almost took a step back at the look in his eyes.

"Did you think I leaked the story to the press?"

There was no point in adding further secrets and subterfuge to this situation. He'd just given her honesty; she gave it back.

"For about point-five of a second, I wondered. And then *my* gut vigorously rejected the idea. We've come very far in a scarily short time. I know you regret what happened before. I know you wouldn't do it again."

"But you did wonder."

"*Momentarily.*" At the continued look on his face, a thread of temper started to coil through Sabrina's chest. "I'm human, it was a lightning-flash reaction, and frankly, with our history, I think we're doing pretty goddamn well that I rejected the possibility that fast."

"I told you I'd never intentionally do anything to hurt you again."

"Yes. You did. And I heard you."

Their breathing was, by now, mutually loud in the quiet room. Days of built-up stress finding an outlet in jagged inhalations.

Her phone beeped.

"What does he want now?" Nick's voice was impatient; with difficulty, she didn't snap back.

Picking up the phone reluctantly, she read the message and her heart jumped. "Oh, hell."

"What?" Nick asked again, but there was a note of concern beneath his own temper.

"It's Elise. Akiko's in labour." And she was part of the birthing team. She'd been horrified when they'd asked her the first time, with Lizzy, but Akiko had said, simply, that she needed Sabrina there, and that had been that. It had turned out to be one of the most incredible experiences of her life. She looked up, different feelings shredding her. "I have to go."

Nick nodded without hesitation. His own phone buzzed, and tearing his eyes from hers, his expression conflicted, he picked it up. "Damn. I forgot to drop off paperwork for Neil yesterday. I'll have to do it this morning."

She threw some clothes on, and when her taxi arrived ten minutes later, Nick helped her in—so, so gentle of her arm—and they looked at each other for a moment.

"Keep taking your pills," he said, "and don't exhaust yourself."

"I'm not the one who'll be doing the work. Thank God." She tried to infuse a bit of lightness into her tone, but the look lurking in the back of his eyes was making her want to cry. "We'll talk later?"

His jaw moved jerkily, but he nodded. When he shut the door and stepped back, and the taxi pulled out into the light stream of traffic, Sabrina sat back and closed her eyes.

Pursing her lips and blowing out a breath, she tried to shut off her mind to the turmoil and uncertainty. For now, she needed to focus on her friends—but it was impossible to keep her thoughts from winging back to him.

"How's the knitting going?" Maria teased, as she poured out three cups of tea. Nick didn't know why she was bothering making one for Neil. His stepfather had thanked him warmly for delivering the paperwork and was now in his glasshouse, peering at pots of dirt and scribbling things down on a piece of paper. He'd be immersed in botanical problems for hours. "Shall I put in my order for a jumper now?"

He shoved his mind back into the room, and forced a smile. "Up to you, but it may end up with two neck-holes and one arm."

His mother handed him one of the cups and sat down. "What's the matter?"

His smile became slightly more genuine. "Motherly instinct?"

"Your thundercloud face," Maria said. "Although the motherly instinct never switches off. Is it Sabrina?"

A renewed fist clutched Nick's gut. That text message had slammed into him like a knife this morning. He'd thought, in that horrible rush of ice-cold seconds, ticking off as they glared at one another, that she really didn't trust him—and the intensity of that hurt made him realise how deep the bond between them actually was, now.

"I've been asked to come in for a job interview. To headline a current events show on LightStarr."

"Ah." Maria had been lifting her cup to her mouth. She lowered it. "And do you want it?"

He set his own cup aside. "Depends which part of me you're asking."

His mother was quiet, then she asked, "Head or heart?"

Nick's lips twisted. His heart was out of the equation. Gone. Irrevocably attached to a temperamental, annoying redhead. His head— "Not so long ago, I'd have gone after the job without a second thought. And a voice in my head is still pushing me in that direction."

"You know I'll support whatever decision you make."

He could see the irresolution on Maria's face, knew she wanted to say more but wouldn't want to influence him. He weighed his words, then spoke. "I spent years trying to live up to an impossible standard. Following someone else's path. And I've let ambition take over in the past. I've done things I shouldn't have."

"I know." Her response was grim.

"But I also grew up with three of the best people I've ever known. I have a mother who chased her own dreams." She looked up. "Who never gave up, who loved openly and laughed all the time, who fought against injustice and stood up for what's right, and always, always put people first." Very rarely did Maria Campbell cry, but she looked close to it now. "I was raised pretty damn well, Mam. I've learned from my mistakes. I won't repeat them. And whatever happens with my job—I have happiness within grasp right now. I won't let it go."

Chapter Eighteen

She was the most beautiful baby. A solid nine pounds, with a wrinkled red face, perfect little fingers, and a dandelion puff of black hair. Sabrina held her new goddaughter close and breathed in her lovely scent.

"You look pretty good like that." Akiko smiled at her from her mountain of pillows. She looked exhausted and very, very happy. Elise was curled around her on the bed, and Lizzy was fast asleep in the chair by the window. "Sure you don't want one yourself?"

Sabrina kissed a tiny eyebrow. "I'll keep my already limited sleep and my boozy holidays, and just get my cuddles from yours." She adored babies she did not have to give birth to or cohabit with. "And Freddy's guaranteed to produce hordes of little Carlton-Ford-Griffins at some point. I have grand plans to become the eccentric aunt of fiction. I'm thinking cats, a caftan, and gin."

She foresaw no difficulty at all in getting Alan, a terrier, to exist in the same flat as her hypothetical dozen cats.

"Not any time soon, Freddy isn't," Freddy said, touching the baby's hand. The minuscule fingers closed around her thumb, and she made a cooing noise. "Although, God, she's cute." Her voice went a bit dreamy. "Imagine lots of miniature Griffs walking about, being all stroppy."

"Let's not terrify the poor child before she's even an hour old."

Her sister kicked the back of her leg.

Sabrina passed over the baby for a cuddle, and Freddy tickled one chubby cheek with her fingertip. "Have you decided on a name?" she asked Akiko and Elise, and they exchanged glances.

Akiko reached out to Sabrina, who took her hand, squeezing her fingers. "Actually—if it's all right with you two, we'd like to call her Eleanor."

Sabrina had already cried more in the past twenty-four hours than Mary Anne Spier had in every Baby-Sitters Club book combined. For the thousandth time, her vision shimmered.

Akiko added softly, "Your mother was the only one I ever knew, and I'll forever be sorry that she never got to enjoy the amazing women she brought into the world. I'd like to remember her through our daughter, but not if you guys would rather we didn't. I mean that."

Sabrina glanced at Freddy, whose lashes were also wet. Her sister nodded, and Sabrina got up to put her good arm around Akiko. They held each other in a strong hug.

"I think it's a perfect name," she said, and kissed Elise on the cheek. "And now I'll let you guys get some sleep and have some family time." At the door, she stood back to let Freddy go out first, and Akiko called her name.

She turned, and her best friend looked at her seriously. "Just so we're clear, Sabs," Akiko said, "you are our family. Always will be."

Sabrina blinked hard. "Likewise." She blew them a kiss, and quietly closed the door.

In the corridor, Freddy yawned and leaned her head against Sabrina's shoulder. "Oh my God, I'm knackered and all I did was snuggle her. You must be shattered. And with your arm, too. Straight home to bed or do you want a cup of coffee in the café first? I've still got some time before I need to be at the theatre."

For hours, Sabrina had done her best to keep her mind totally on Akiko, and Elise, and what they needed. Now, it was like everything flooded back in at once, and her legs went shaky. She needed caffeine, and she needed to get her head together before she spoke to Nick again. "Café. My shout."

"No." Freddy looped her arm through Sabrina's with a pointed look. "*My* shout."

Over a small corner table in the hospital café, Freddy set a cappuccino in front of her and sat down with her hot chocolate. "It's a lovely gesture, calling the baby Eleanor."

"Yes, it is."

Her sister played with her teaspoon, seeming to debate something. Then she looked up. "You haven't talked about Mum for a long time. To me, at least."

Sabrina lowered her cup. She looked back at Freddy, studying her sister's face. "No, I haven't."

"And—" Freddy hesitated. "You don't really talk to me much about Dad these days, either."

Sabrina shifted, just a fraction, on the hard chair. "Freddy…"

"I know." Freddy's mouth tipped into a small smile.

There was wryness there, but also warmth. And love. "You never want to upset me. You've always tried to look after me. And I appreciate that. You'll never know how much. I grew up with a safety net under me, all the time. I knew I'd never fall, whatever happened, because I had you." A fragment of memory, then, of Nick's mother saying something similar, about that innate feeling of security. Freddy reached across the table and took her hand. "But I'm here for you, too. Always. Forever. And you can tell me anything."

Oh, God. She was going to cry *again*.

She linked her fingers through Freddy's. "I didn't mean to shut you out."

"I know you didn't." Freddy gave her hand a little shake. "But if things are ever bad with Dad, I want you to tell me. And…you remember Mum. I don't. I'd like to know her. Through you." Her own voice went husky. "I wish she *could* see us now. I wish she knew that we're happy."

Sabrina swiped at her cheek, glad that there was a large indoor plant between their table and any other. "Nick thinks you don't ever really lose someone. Maybe she does know." She blew out a shaky breath. "I hope so."

"Me, too." Freddy scrubbed at her eyes with a paper napkin. "God, I hope you don't have any lurking paparazzi." She lifted her head. "Is my mascara smudged?"

"No, you're good."

Taking a large, fortifying gulp of her hot chocolate, Freddy swallowed. "How are things going with Nick?"

Sabrina's stomach knotted. The image of his face

this morning had been pushing at her consciousness all day.

He'd looked so hurt.

"Not well?" Freddy leaned forward, concerned. "What's happened?"

After a large swallow of her own drink, Sabrina started talking. When she eventually trailed off, Freddy's frown had deepened. She cut straight to the chase. "Does Nick know? That if he's offered this contract with LightStarr and he takes it, you're out of a job?"

"No," Sabrina said. "Hania hasn't told him yet, and something held me back. I'm glad, now, that I didn't say anything."

"But don't you—"

"Care? Yes. I do. On all counts. And don't get me wrong, I want this job. I'm good at it, I'll do it well, and if Nick does go to work for LightStarr— It wouldn't be the same without him, but I will fight like hell for my contract regardless." She shrugged. "But I care more about Nick." She felt the truth of it, and heard the resonance of it in her words. "I don't want him to have a job that doesn't fulfil him. I don't want him to be unhappy. And if he made a decision solely for my sake, where would that leave our relationship in the end?"

Freddy's dark eyes were thoughtful. Apparently completely unconsciously, she reached out and lightly hooked her pinkie finger with Sabrina's. It was the gesture of their much younger days, Sabrina's childhood way of comforting tiny Freddy when she was upset or afraid. "I love you, Sabs."

Sabrina squeezed her finger. "I love you, too."

"I just—" Freddy raised her shoulder. "I think you're so great. I know that sounds silly, but I do. You're amazing, and you deserve the job you want, and the man you want, and if you don't get them, I'll—"

With welcome amusement starting to bloom, Sabrina said, "Yes?"

"I'll do something," her sister said ominously, with all the deep theatricality of her profession. "I'm capable of great wrath."

"Oh, I believe it."

"You're off on Monday, right?" Freddy cleared her throat. "Do you know that Griff's doing the show on Monday morning?"

"What? Since when?" The schedule she'd seen for the last show before Christmas definitely hadn't included Griff.

"He got a call from the network this morning, ordering him on to discuss the arts funding scandal that's just broken at the Metronome, although that piece of news was pretty much drowned in a sea of dirty politicians and dodgy-dealing celebs." Being very politic, Freddy didn't mention Ferren beyond a darting, curious glance.

"So, Nick's interviewing Griff?" As far as Sabrina knew, the two of them still hadn't spoken privately.

"Mmm," Freddy murmured. "Without you as a buffer, too. Would it be terrible if I came over on Monday morning with popcorn?"

She insisted on driving Sabrina home, and the whole way back to her flat through the nightmare traffic, watching the lights flash past through the window, Sabrina wondered if Nick would be there or if he'd decided to go back to his tonight. She'd texted him short updates throughout the day, but they hadn't spoken yet. It needed to be in person.

Her body was taut with tension—in her exhaustion, caffeine and the serious need for a hug were the only things propelling her forward right now. When she turned the key in her lock and heard the scurrying of Alan's feet on the wood floor, something hard and painful eased.

She pushed open the door, and Nick was there, glasses on, shoes off, sleeves up, looking equally exhausted and just as on edge.

Without a word, she put down her bag and went into his arms.

His chest moved against her as he released a long breath and pressed his mouth to her neck. She spread her fingers on his back and held him tightly.

"Akiko's all right?" he murmured into her hair. "And the baby?"

"Both happy, healthy, and tired. And beautiful." With a final rub of her cheek against his shoulder, Sabrina stepped back and followed him into the living room, leaning down to greet Alan as they walked. The dog was doing his level best to trip her up.

"You must be knackered, as well," Nick said, as she sat down with a sigh on the edge of the couch.

"About to drop," she agreed frankly, and looked him straight in the eye. "Nick. This morning. I really am sorry. Honestly, it was just a knee-jerk thought, gone literally in a second."

"I know," he said, coming to sit in the closest chair. He leaned forward, forearms resting on his knees, hands linked. The movement made his shoulders look huge. It was a serious moment, not the time to ogle, but she still had eyes. His mouth was wry. "Within three minutes of dropping you off, I'd cooled down enough to acknowledge that was completely understandable, and reasonable. It just hurt, thinking you didn't trust me, after it feels like we've come so far. Like we're—" He hesitated. "Building something important."

"We have." Sabrina reached out and he took her hand. "And we are. I do trust you. I trust that you wouldn't knowingly, deliberately hurt me again. And I trust that you'll make the right decision for you."

"For us," Nick returned, immediately, and she nodded again.

"If it's a choice that's going to make you fulfilled and content, professionally," she said quietly, "then it's the right decision for both of us. Whether that's working together or not." She tilted her head. "You *are* going to go to the meeting?"

"You think I should." It wasn't a question.

"I do. I think you need to know more about the LightStarr job. You need all the facts on the table." Sabrina lifted a shoulder. "If all else fails, it'll be Christmas Eve—you'll probably get a complimentary drink on their expense account."

He gave a half smile, but his eyes were still troubled.

And her stomach was twisting and turning like mad.

1 Day until Christmas Eve

"And from all of us here at *Wake Me Up London*, we'd like to wish you a very happy Christmas," Meg said cheerfully, "and we'll look forward to having you back with us in the new year." The relief presenter smiled into the camera as Nick added his own warm sign-off.

From her position off-set, Fenella raised her hand.

"And we're out." The producer spoke into their ear-pieces. "Happy holidays, team, and bloody well done."

Nick thanked Meg as he unhooked his mic. "That couldn't have gone more smoothly, and you were fantastic with the guests today."

Meg lacked Sabrina's natural charisma in front of the camera—Sabrina exuded an irresistible warmth that drew people to her; she was attractive in the truest meaning of the word, and that wasn't only Nick's bias—but the other woman was competent and friendly, and the final show of the year had gone off without a hitch.

One or two people had commented on Emily's absence, but a few of the other younger staffers had finished on Friday as well—voluntarily—so there had been no gossip.

"I enjoyed it." Meg grinned at him. "But fear not, I'm not coveting Sabrina's role. The two of you are magic."

That sentiment was repeated by a good number of the team. Jess came over to hug him, and gave him a bottle of wine. "And this is for Sabrina," she said, handing him a small gift bag. "How is she?"

Fiery.

Stubborn.

Total pain in the arse.

He loved the fuck out of her.

"Disappointed to miss the last show," he said, "but she's watching from home."

"Last show of the *year*," Jess pointed out, and squeezed his arm before she left the studio. "But the beginning of an awesome era, I reckon." She grinned at him. "And cheers again for the champers."

He and Sabrina had gone in together on champagne
for the crew, and several people had already cracked
open their bottles.

Nick turned and was met with Fenella's quirked
eyebrow.

"Well," the producer said. "We didn't exactly arrive
here without a hiccup, but from frankly dismal beginnings, we've come out gold. It's a pity Sabrina didn't
get to bring down the curtain in person, but I sincerely
hope she'll be here reopening the show in January."

She extended her hand. "Nicely done, Nick."

From Fenella, that was a very high accolade. Nick
shook her hand, and before he left the studio, he stood
looking around the now familiar set.

The beginning of an era.

In the green room, Griff was sitting on the edge of
a couch, casually flicking through his phone. His segment had finished half an hour ago, but as he'd crisply
concluded the interview, his direct look had spoken volumes and Nick had expected to find him here.

He suspected that their respective Carlton sisters
had watched that interview avidly. Griff had been his
usual matter-of-fact self, speaking concisely on an issue
that neither of them really gave a shit about.

He stood now, and they surveyed each other.

"Too early for a drink?" Griff said at last, and Nick
shrugged.

"It is almost Christmas."

They ended up at a wine bar near the river. The
South Bank was absolutely packed, and being so close
to Christmas, naturally every second person was in a
vile mood, stressed, and shivering.

Nick set his glass of wine down on the wooden table

in their booth and glanced out the window. He could see a glimpse of churning grey water, and distinctly remembered both the feel of it closing over his head and Sabrina's icy-cold fingers clutching at him.

He looked up into Griff's cool gaze.

"I got your messages." Griff picked up his glass, but didn't take a drink. "You seriously fucked up this year."

"Yes. I did." Nick had no excuses, and no desire to find any. "My actions hurt somebody you love. And they hurt somebody *I* love." He didn't look away. "Two people I love. I betrayed the trust of one of my best mates, and I'm sorry. I'm very, sincerely sorry."

"You came onto my property and you spilled my family's private history all over the press, a story you knew had to have us reeling. You've been like another brother to me. You gutted me." Simple, painful words from a man who'd never been demonstrative. Nick didn't let himself flinch. He deserved it, and he'd take it. "And you did badly hurt Freddy, and the sister she adores. Whom, against the odds, I'm becoming pretty bloody fond of, myself." Griff put down his glass. "You've clearly come to an understanding with Sabrina, and Freddy's ready to forgive all. She makes Winnie the Pooh look vengeful." Despite the caustic words, the look in his eyes was suddenly warm.

He looked at Nick without speaking for a few moments. "I believe in second chances. And you're family. But where Freddy and Sabrina are concerned, if it ever becomes necessary for a third chance—"

"It won't." Nick spoke with finality.

Griff nodded, a short inclination of his head. "I don't hug," he warned, and Nick grinned.

"Not even Freddy?"

"Freddy's an exception." Griff's mouth lifted, as well. "To most things." He extended his hand.

Nick clasped it, and felt another knot inside him unravel.

Griff sat back. "Someone you love?"

That had slipped out, and Nick had no intention of revisiting it with Griff. He was not the person who should hear it first.

He simply raised his brows, and Griff smiled slightly and lifted his glass again. "Changing the subject, then, I assume you've heard that Peter King has resigned from *The Arts Review* and is leaving the network?"

Nick looked up sharply. "No. I hadn't heard. And I'm bloody amazed. *I* assume you've had the full story through the Carlton grapevine, and I thought King would deny all involvement."

"I've heard whisperings." Griff's many connections were always right on the money. "King is close to his wife, and he raised her children as his own. He's taking ownership of what happened with his daughter, and—I agree, surprisingly—evidently has enough of a conscience that he's resigned. Unfortunately, he'll probably keep his new theatre column. They keep seating me next to the prick on press night." A trace of a grimace. "He's still scheduled to introduce an act at Carols by Candlelight tomorrow night, by the way, and knowing King, he may have done the decent thing but I doubt if he's done it happily. In the interests of peace and goodwill, and steering clear of scandal for five minutes, you might want to avoid a run-in with him."

In bed that night, Nick told Sabrina about Peter King; she was equally surprised.

"I'm so glad you've sorted things with Griff,

though." She tightened her arm across his ribs in a little hug. Her chin was propped on his chest. "What time is your meeting tomorrow?"

"Three o'clock. I'll meet you after at the Royal St. Michael."

They were introducing the French singer Célie Verne to the audience at Carols by Candlelight at just after eight, but the full group of presenters were required to kick off the night with the first song at seven.

Sabrina nodded. "I'm sure it'll go well." Her eyes were enigmatic and unfamiliar tonight, but there was nothing but sincerity in her voice. A small smile curled her lips. "If you need a character reference, just point them towards Nick's Chicks. Who would pass up the opportunity to have the 'fittest, sexiest mountain of man-flesh' on staff?"

His response was brief and to the point, but he couldn't hold back a grin as he watched her laugh.

"Sparks," he said, and she looked at him, the laughter still in her face. "Whatever happens professionally, it won't change this."

Again, he couldn't quite read Sabrina, then. But she shook her head. "No. It won't change anything." After an infinitesimal pause in which he watched several emotions chase through her expression, she asked, with suspicious blandness, "Did you, by the way?"

That look, he knew. And didn't trust. "Did I what?"

"Start Nick's Chicks yourself?"

He encompassed his entire response in a short hand gesture that time, and went to sleep that night with cold feet tucked against him, vast quantities of hair in his face, and the echo of her giggles still in the room.

Chapter Nineteen

Christmas Eve

Christmas Eve in London, even with the crowds, the stress, the increasing commercialisation—around every corner, there were still pockets of magic.

With twenty minutes until he was expected in a top-floor office of the LightStarr building, Nick had come into the biting cold to clear his head. Wandering down a narrow lane, he glanced up at a block of flats behind an iron railing. A row of doors stretched ahead, painted in the colours of the rainbow. In the first flat, above the indigo door, he could see a child systematically eating the chocolate decorations on a Christmas tree. Every third sweet was passed down to a shorter sibling. Smiling slightly, he kept walking, passing windows of people laughing, arguing, kissing—a microcosm of humanity in one tiny, frosty lane.

Outside the red-door flat, he stood for a moment, watching a very elderly couple stop decorating their smaller tree to focus on draping gold tinsel over each other's head. The wife arranged a garland around her husband's hunched shoulders. He held a couple of baubles to her ears like oversized earrings. They were giggling at each other like a couple of mischievous kids.

Still lost in thought, he walked back out into the busy street. A bus stopped in the traffic flow, and he found himself looking at a promotional image of himself and Sabrina. It was from the same photo shoot they'd done for the *Media Times* cover, one of the few shots where they were making eye contact. Sabrina's eyes sparkled a challenge beneath her winged brows. His head was turned towards her, his brows lifted. In a last-ditch attempt to get them interacting, the photographer had introduced props, and they were each holding one end of an oversized Christmas cracker. The whole thing looked flirty as hell.

Nick was fairly sure it had been taken right after she'd called him an arrogant knob.

One of the many heartwarming memories they'd built.

His instinctive grin faded as he continued to look at the promo shot.

The bus pulled away with a roar of exhaust, Sabrina's image slowly disappearing as the rest of the traffic flowed in.

Nick stood there for a minute longer, hardly aware of the strangers stepping around him, a few glances of recognition.

Then he straightened his tie with a jerk, and headed for LightStarr HQ.

An executive assistant who kept glancing at the clock, obviously counting down the seconds until she hit the pub for a holiday drink, showed him into a huge office with a stunning view, where Nick took a seat across the table from Roderick Speight and two stone-faced underlings.

Speight actively and publicly detested Lionel Grimes, so the man was favourably inclined towards Nick from the get-go. This wasn't so much an interview as a hard sell.

They wanted him and were prepared to make the deal as attractive as possible, and he couldn't deny it was ego balm after the last time he'd sat in an executive meeting on the cusp of a new professional path.

And on paper, the role with LightStarr appeared to have been crafted specifically for him.

As Nick listened to Speight's vision for the show, and shared thoughts of his own—enthusiastically received—every word, every rustle of paper, might have been punctuated by the echo of his father's voice.

This is everything you've worked for. This is what you're meant to do. This is who you are.

He could do this job, and he'd do it well. They took him to view the studio, which was modern and streamlined, not a garish yellow wall in sight. Nick stood by the leather chair at the wide black desk and looked out at the crisp set. It was a blank canvas, a piece of marble ready to be sculpted.

And he could see himself here, could see the future playing out very clearly in his head.

When they returned to the upper offices, Speight got down to brass tacks and produced a preliminary salary range. Nick kept his reaction to a slightly raised brow, but they sure as hell weren't messing around.

The discussions went on for a long time; at the end of it, they stood and Speight studied Nick's face closely, before he extended his hand.

Inclining his head, Nick shook the director's hand firmly.

He didn't realise exactly how long the meeting had run until he checked his watch as he left the offices, and swore. Fortunately, he'd factored in the Christmas Eve traffic and brought his tux in the car just in case, because there was absolutely no way he'd have time to go home first. He was going to be pushing it to make it to Kensington on time as it was.

With half the population apparently trying to leave London at once, it was a slow inch across the city. By the time he'd parked his car miles away and managed to get a black cab the remaining distance to the Royal St. Michael, the lit-up façade a glowing golden beacon in the freezing-cold night, he arrived in the pandemonium backstage very definitely late.

Firing off a quick text to Sabrina, Nick flagged down a harried-looking young attendant. Dropping every vestige of stress from his own face and demeanour, he wished her a happy Christmas and asked if there were any free rooms in which to change, and she led the way through the busy stone-floored corridors and pointed him in the right direction.

"The west dressing rooms have been taken over by anyone needing a costume change during the performance," she said over the loud bee-drone of voices, "but quite a lot of presenters had to get ready on-site and we've opened up the dressing rooms in the original wing. Uh, you don't have a lot of time, though."

To put it mildly.

Nick opened the door of the first dressing room he came to, and almost walked straight into Peter King.

The confrontation had been successfully avoided for about three and a half minutes.

King might have admitted some culpability, but as Griff had rightly surmised, there was clearly no personal remorse towards Nick. His lips pinched, and he started to push past with a sneer.

If the final accident hadn't occurred, Nick might have been able to continue to write off the sabotage as petty, pathetic and, in the end, borderline amusing; but he'd sat up in the middle of the night, rubbing Sabrina's back while she almost dry-retched from pain meds. He was still furious.

With an effort, his muscles locked tight, he counted down in his head, and stepped aside.

The other man's own resolve toppled at the last minute; with a half-turn, he said, making no attempt to hide the bitterness, "I suppose congratulations are in order where the contract is concerned."

Holding his tux over his shoulder, one finger hooked in the hanger, Nick shoved his other fist in his pocket. He had to take a few seconds to keep his voice even. "Actually, I think an apology is in order."

"You got what you wanted, didn't you?" King didn't meet Nick's icy stare. "Quite the network golden couple."

"What I've got," Nick said with a hint of bite now, "is a partner who'll be in a cast for weeks and is still in a lot of pain, thanks to you possessing the intellectual maturity of a six-year-old, and your emotional manipulation of a daughter with misplaced loyalty."

King took a step forward, his cheeks turning a shade of red that was so close to purple the man ought to have his blood pressure checked.

"I wouldn't." Nick didn't move, but King obviously heard the note of danger.

The air between them was sparking.

With a movement best described as a flounce, the other man left the room, and Nick shook his head and stepped inside.

The door slammed after him and he heard the distinct snick of a lock.

Turning in disbelief, he tossed his tux over the back of a dusty-looking brocade couch and turned to tug futilely at the handle. Un-fucking-believable. King had really just locked him in. Had he said maturity level of a six-year-old? Regress that to two-year-old.

"Pain in the arse until the very end, Peter," he muttered, and pulled his phone out of his pocket.

And realised there was, apparently, no service in the basement level of the RSM.

His text to Sabrina that he was running a few minutes late had been flagged with a non-delivery alert. She was upstairs waiting for him, with absolutely no idea where he was.

For God's sake. He was actually going to have to resort to banging on the door and shouting. Fingers crossed for a resumption of dignity and a bit more game in the new year, because this one was a bloody joke.

Although it had also brought the best thing that had ever happened to him; a decent trade-off, he supposed, for frequently looking like a public twat.

There was a small crack in the panelling of the door, not wide enough to see through, but had anyone been in vicinity of the dressing room, they'd definitely have heard him.

Several minutes later, he left off banging on the

heavy wood and leaned his fist against the door. The show was starting in less than thirty minutes. The audience would be filing in by now, and he strongly suspected that the entire backstage company was now up on the ground level.

It was Christmas Eve, several thousand people were currently milling about over his head, Sabrina had memorised her half of a script for two people, and he was locked in a freezing-cold dressing room.

Fuck.

If Nick was trying to be fashionably late, he was being a little overzealous.

Sabrina tugged nervously at the bodice of her tight-fitting black gown. Her hair was perfectly smooth and glossy, woven into an intricate knot at the base of her neck, she was having a good makeup night thanks to the network glam squad, and she was wearing her mother's emerald earrings. Despite the purple cast, she felt pretty and sexy, it was Christmas, and she quite fancied the prospect of candlelight carols with a handsome man by her side.

However, the handsome man seemed to have disappeared into the ether.

A familiar figure pushed through the milling crowds backstage, and Sabrina forced a smile to her face.

Hania was wearing a suit with a gorgeous off-the-shoulder velvet blazer and very high heels. She had the air of someone who was not on painkillers and didn't have to turn down the complimentary champagne. "Hello, Sabrina. Happy Christmas. I'm just checking in with all our team presenting tonight, before I head back up to the box." Their usually no-nonsense boss was buzzing; evidently, it was getting very festive in the network VIP section.

With an expectant smile, Hania looked around. "Where's Nick?"

Good question.

Before Sabrina could formulate a response that was neither a blatant lie nor "He went to interview for a job with the competition this afternoon and hasn't been seen or heard from since," the other woman spotted someone through the crowd.

"Back in a tick," she said, patting Sabrina's arm. "You look wonderful, by the way."

She disappeared into a group of chattering, glittering bodies, and Sabrina put her hand to her forehead. *Nick, come on.* She went up on her tiptoes, trying to see above heads, but gave it up. Between the celebrity performers and presenters, and the choir, there were well over a hundred people in a relatively small space. And thousands more out front.

She checked her phone again. Coverage was very patchy in this building, she'd noticed. Nonexistent in the basement levels and flickering in and out upstairs. Holding her skirt out of the way of her high heels, she started to squeeze her way to the back doors. She'd already called Nick four times and his phone was diverting straight to voicemail, but if the service was dodgy—

Standing just inside the doors, she checked her screen, and tried again.

"Hi, this is Nick. I'm sorry, I can't—"

She made a muffled sound of frustration, just as her phone buzzed with a text. Her heart jumped, but the message was from Freddy. As she focused on the

words, however, it was another rush of stomach flutters, for a different reason.

Is it true? Nick's taken the LightStarr job? Or just the
usual fact-less shite from London Celebrity?

Biting down on her lower lip, Sabrina thumbed
through to her web browser. She didn't usually give
London Celebrity any additional clicks, but—

It was there, in their gossip sidebar. Nick Davenport
leaving *WMUL* in the new year to headline a much-
hyped new night show for LightStarr. They even had
a photo of him in a studio setup, and it had been taken
today. She'd been holding on to that blue tie a few hours
ago as she kissed him.

She tried his number once more, and when it still
went to voicemail, she scrolled to another contact.
Freddy picked up after a few rings. She was on break
for two days from *Anathorn*, and was spending Christmas Eve with Griff's family at Highbrook, his estate
in Surrey.

For once, her bubbly, voluble sister cut straight to
the point. "Well? Did he take the job?"

"It's *London Celebrity*. The masters of bullshit.
When have they ever reported straight facts? But that
photo—" Sabrina took a deep breath and lifted her
chin. She didn't know what decision Nick had made,
she'd meant it that she'd be happy for him whichever
way he moved, if it was right for him, and she would
continue to ruthlessly shut her mind to it in the mean-
time. "I don't know what his plans are for next year.
I'm more concerned about where he is right now."

"What?" Freddy asked, startled. "He hasn't turned up? Aren't you guys due onstage in like ten minutes?"

"Yes." She worried at her left earring, tugging the back fastening, and forced herself to stop before she lost it. "I can't leave it much longer before I have to alert someone."

"What time was his meeting with LightStarr?"

"Three o'clock. He should have been here by now."

"Do you think that means he probably *has* taken the job?" Freddy asked bluntly, and Sabrina didn't hesitate in her response.

"Even if he has decided to go to LightStarr, he wouldn't skip out on a commitment, and he for damned sure wouldn't just leave me hanging. His phone is going straight to voicemail." She chewed on her lip. "I'm starting to get worried. I'm going to do one more sweep of the place."

"Okay, good. Call back if you can't find him, but I'm sure he'll turn up, Sabs. And—it'll be okay."

Freddy was always a reassuring presence in a crisis; she genuinely did believe things usually turned out for the best.

Sabrina slipped her phone back into her clutch and ducked back into the crowd. She did a wide circle past Hania, who was chatting with the woman who'd just been announced as the presenter of their new evening show. Funny how long ago the battle for that contract seemed.

It was chaotic backstage, with the choir getting ready to go onstage for the opening number. Sabrina checked her watch. Hell. Hell, hell, hell.

An attendant passed her, did a double-take, and stopped, hovering in a distinctly bashful way. Sabrina managed a preoccupied smile, and the young woman, thus encouraged, approached her.

"I'm sorry to bother you," she said shyly, "but I just wanted to say that I'm a huge fan of your sister. I've loved theatre since I was little, and she's my favourite performer on the West End. I'm saving up to see *Anathorn*." Hastily, she tacked on, "And I really enjoy your TV show, too."

A bubble of welcome amusement rose in Sabrina's chest. "Thank you, that's nice to hear. I'm a big fan of Freddy, as well."

The girl rhapsodised about Freddy for a bit longer, which would usually be music to Sabrina's proud ears, but right now, other matters were pressing. As she was about to extricate herself politely, her sister's admirer said, "I hope Mr. Davenport found everything he needed?"

Sabrina looked up sharply. "I'm sorry?"

The attendant looked slightly startled at her reaction. "He was looking for somewhere to change earlier."

"You've seen Nick? Where was he?"

"I pointed him towards the dressing rooms in the original wing," the girl said, worried. "Is there a problem?"

"No." Sabrina remembered her manners. With a fervent word of thanks, she opened her clutch and pulled out one of her cards and a pen. Propping the card awkwardly against her knee, she scrawled on the back of it and handed it over. "That's my personal email. Shoot me a message and I'll arrange for front-row seats to *Anathorn* for you, and I'm sure Freddy would be happy to meet you backstage if you'd like."

She left the young attendant stammering and actually trembling with excitement.

She ducked through the hot press of people, and as soon as she was in the maze of corridors backstage, she picked up speed and just about ran, her heels clicking on the stone. Down the stairs, and into the colder basement level where everyone had passed through security.

Tonight was the first time she'd been backstage in the RSM since her father had performed here over twenty years ago, but she still remembered where the original dressing rooms were. As soon as she rounded the hallway and saw the line of closed doors, she called, warily, "Nick?"

"Sparks?"

At the sound of his voice, she released a short breath and a lot of tension. "What the hell are you doing?" she asked the empty corridor. "We're due onstage in less than ten minutes. Where are you?"

A thumping noise came from the closest door. "I sent you a text." Nick's disembodied voice floated out again. "I didn't realise there was no service down here. I was running late and had to change here, and unfortunately this dressing room had a prior occupant, and Peter King is an irredeemable dickhead."

Sabrina took half a second to assimilate that. "Peter King locked you in?"

"Yes." Tightly.

"Wine cellars. Dressing rooms. I hope this isn't going to become a habit."

"Yeah, I don't want to rush you here, Sparks, but if you could find someone who can get this door open, I'd appreciate it."

She reached for the handle. "I could. Or I could just unlock it."

An even tauter instant of silence.

"Did he leave the bloody key in the lock?" Nick sounded personally offended by the incompetence. "Jesus Christ. The man's useless. He's not even a satisfactory villain."

Sabrina turned the key, and Nick immediately pulled the door open. He looked cold and annoyed, and sharp as hell in his tux.

"Handsome," she said, and felt her smile right down to her heart.

The irritation draining from his face, his eyes turned molten as he scanned her slowly from head to toe. "Stunning," he returned with emphasis, and reached for her. His mouth diverted to her throat at the last minute to avoid smudging her makeup, and she shivered in a hard jolt.

"Come on," she said, and slipped her hand into his. "Three and a half minutes and counting until curtain."

They had to flat-out run, their footsteps so loud in the echoing space she was sure people would be able to hear them in the busy stands above, and when they joined the group of people about to head onstage, with seconds to spare, Sabrina was totally out of breath.

Halfway through an energetic rendition of "Deck the Halls," which was a lot more impressive when swelled to the domed roof of the Royal St. Michael by over two thousand voices than it was emerging tinnily from Nick's ringtone, she managed to drop her heart rate back to normal.

Although it fluttered again every time she looked away from the rows of flickering candles and up into the eyes of the man standing next to her. Their fingers were still linked, hidden by the row of stand-up comedians in front of them, and Nick rubbed his thumb over her knuckles. Holding her cast against her ribs, she leaned against his shoulder, and he squeezed her hand.

When they returned backstage, one of the first people Sabrina saw in the throngs was Peter King. He looked at them with a small, irksome smile, and she felt Nick stiffen.

"Ignore him," she said, turning her back and doing just that. "He's not worth it."

Very lightly, Nick touched her cast. "He's indirectly responsible for this."

"To be fair, in the chain of blame for that incident, there's also Emily and our spectacularly ungraceful footwork." She shook her head. "Just forget him. It's Christmas, he's accepted some responsibility, and—" Nick looked down at her, and she spread her fingers against his chest "—things are good," she finished simply.

He touched the backs of his fingers to her cheek in a gesture that made her eyes sting.

At eight o'clock, they introduced Célie Verne to the stage, amidst a few scripted and not fantastically written festive jokes; and Sabrina stood for a moment in the wings, listening to the Frenchwoman's rather haunting rendition of "Coventry Carol" and feeling the rise and fall of Nick's chest.

It was time.

"How did the meeting go?" she asked quietly, without turning around, and his cheek brushed hers.

The evenness of his breath didn't falter. "They offered me the job."

Sabrina nodded. "I thought they would." She did turn, then, and looked up at him. "Congratulations."

"Thank you," Nick said. "I turned it down."

Célie's voice wrapped around them, clear and sweet and heady like wine.

Sabrina didn't move. "Are you sure?"

"It's a good job. It was a tempting job." He made no attempt to touch her, either. "I sat there and I could very clearly imagine signing that contract, and the next year unfolding, and the year after that. I'd have ended up in a slightly stronger financial position, with solid footing on the path my father's life took. That *was* my father's life, in the end. And I'd probably have burned out by forty. There would be endless pressure. Constant flights." His eyes held hers. "Waking up alone in hotel rooms. Becoming harder all the time. More alone. That's not who I want to be. That's not who I am."

Sabrina felt as if she were barely breathing as she stood there, very still, very quiet.

"I also thought about taking on the *WMUL* contract." Just fractionally, the rhythm of Nick's voice started to lift. It was a subtle tell, and something deep within Sabrina's body started to relax. "There's so much more that can be done with that show." He tilted his head, and she recognised that expression. Nick Davenport, bound and determined to get what he wanted. She started to smile. "From just a few days in, and against the odds, that's been our studio. Our team. Our show."

Slowly, Sabrina lifted a brow. "So, we're doing this, then?"

Nick's eyes crinkled at the corners and his lips

curved. He extended his hand. She looked down, her smile growing, and clasped his palm.

So suddenly that it startled a laugh from her, he pulled her forward, against his chest, and managed to get an arm around her without bumping her cast.

Smoothing her fingers over his chest, she mused, "Christmas carols. Candlelight. Future looking good. This is very romantic. Wanna split this joint, go home, and bang under the tree?"

"Practically Tennyson," Nick teased, his mouth coming down on hers.

Having done their contractual bit, they collected his other suit from the makeshift dungeon downstairs and sneaked away.

Outside, on the historic stone steps, Sabrina reached into her clutch and pulled out her phone. "How did Roderick Speight take your refusal?"

Nick shrugged. "He wasn't happy, but he took it well enough. Shook my hand and wished me the best."

The *London Celebrity* report of his career change was still up on her browser. She turned the screen to face him, and he took the phone, frowning.

Unlike the so-called journalists at the tabloid, Nick required few words to express himself. "Fuck."

"Where did they get the photo?"

"Speight gave me a tour of the new studio. Someone must have snapped a shot and shared it online." With a few impatient flicks of his thumb, he scanned the rest of the article before he handed her back the phone. Frowning, he studied her expression intently. "You must have thought—"

"What I've always thought. *London Celebrity* is the

very dregs of the gutter press and I wouldn't accept even their weather report without fact-checking it."

A voice called their names then, and Sabrina turned to see Hania excuse herself from a small group of companions and come towards them.

"Didn't fancy sticking around for the final hurrah, either?" their boss asked pointedly, before she directed a laser stare at Nick. "I've just been alerted to an interesting news report. Are congratulations in order?"

Her tone made it clear they wouldn't be offered.

Nick's response was totally unruffled. "That depends whether you have an offer to make."

Hania's eyes narrowed. "If you're expecting more money—"

He started to speak, then paused, subjecting her to a thoughtful look in return. "I am, actually. You wanted a significant increase in *WMUL*'s ratings. We've delivered. Next year, we'll double that." He placed a warm palm against the small of Sabrina's back. "An extra 10 percent on the current salary. For both of us."

With a lot of difficulty, Sabrina kept her face blank.

The silence stretched out tensely as Hania glared at Nick.

At last— "Seven percent," she snapped.

He smiled. "Deal."

A bubble of totally inappropriate laughter was trying to rise in Sabrina's chest.

Looking thoroughly peeved now, Hania said, "I'll see you both in my office on the third. Don't be late. And if I catch wind of you sniffing around the competition again, all deals are off the table." She turned to Sabrina. "Is the other half of Team Carlton-Davenport still on board?" Heavily sarcastic. "Or do you want to push your luck, as well?"

Sabrina stopped trying to suppress her smile. "Both on board."

Nick's fingers stroked a shivery line up her spine. "Although we can discuss the order of surnames later."

"Alphabetical seniority," she murmured, and he grinned.

"And moral. I remember."

"There may be room for compromise. I've since decided you're not half bad."

"Careful, Sparks. That was dangerously close to another compliment."

A thread of reluctant amusement broke through Hania's professional annoyance. "You can count your lucky stars the public finds you less irritating than I do, and that Lionel cares about his profit margins. He's dead set on your commercial appeal as a pair, and I'm clearly going to go grey before the first year is out." She sighed, then seemed to take heart. "Could have been worse. He actually mooted the possibility of bringing back Tara Whitlow if one or both of you refused to sign, and I'll be damned if I'll have that woman on my staff again. People threw salt over their shoulders at her farewell do, in case the demon returned."

She lifted a hand at her group. "Go home," she said to Sabrina and Nick. "Before we all freeze to the steps. And I'll see you in the new year."

Sabrina watched Hania walk briskly back to her friends. She carefully didn't look at Nick, who had gone very still beside her.

"If one or both of us refused." His voice was low and level.

She remained silent.

"The contract was completely dependent on both of us signing."

Her breath misted into the night. "Yes."

"You knew that."

"Yes."

Nick's hand on her arm turned her to face him. His eyes—lit by the floodlights on the steps, and unreadable—searched hers. "You didn't say anything."

She made a tiny, dismissive motion with her head. "How could I say anything? If you'd known that my current job security was tied that inextricably to your decision, you wouldn't have even gone to the interview today." He didn't deny that, but a muscle in his jaw flexed. "It seems that I genuinely want you to be happy. Who'd have thought it?"

It was Nick who wasn't saying anything now, and it was making her feel twitchy.

"I would have stood my ground where the contract was concerned," she said, "and I think I'd have stood a chance of talking Grimes around. I'm not the one who called him a ballsack. He's got to like me more than he likes you." She lifted a shoulder. "But, when it comes down to it, I care more about you than I do about the contract. And would you please stop *looking* at me like that—"

Any further words she'd have babbled were cut off by his lips as he kissed her so hard that she stumbled back a step. He caught her with his arm around the small of her back, hauling her up on her tiptoes.

Lifting his head, he murmured, with a casualness offset by the look in his eyes, "Do you know, Sparks— I really fucking love you."

Her breath was already coming short and fast; it hitched now. Unconsciously, her fingers curled around his lapel. "Yeah," she said faintly. "Me, too."

His body language had been slightly guarded; now, she saw incredible warmth suffuse in. The creases fanning out from his lashes deepened. His head was ducked down close to hers. "You, too?"

"I love you, too." She twisted in his hold and pressed her forehead to his shoulder. "Oh, God. Shut up. I've gone all shy."

She felt the laughter in Nick's chest. "As I've said. Born romantic."

Then his hands were in her hair, and her right hand was sliding up his back, and they danced forward a few slippery steps under a Victorian lamppost, in a pool of golden light and glittering diamonds of ice.

This time, when the paparazzi shot appeared in the press, Sabrina framed it.

Epilogue

Summer

The sky above Windsor was a beautiful, brilliant blue, the trees moved gently in the breeze, and the stones of the castle glowed warm in the sunshine.

The perfect day for a wedding.

Sabrina stood doing her mic test, one hand to her earpiece. Her dress swished around her legs as she moved to the cameraman's directions, blocking out the best angle. A few steps away in the press pavilion, Nick was also doing a sound check. He caught her looking at him and raised a supercilious eyebrow.

She really oughtn't find that so sexy.

When she got the thumbs-up from the cameraman, she walked over and Nick looked at her enquiringly.

"You look very pensive."

"Just admiring the pomp and circumstance."

Nick glanced at the crowds and pageantry around them. "There's definitely a unique atmosphere at a royal wedding. There must be a good thirty thousand more people than expected." He frowned. "Security must be costing a bomb."

"And you say *I'm* unromantic." Sabrina touched a

fingertip to his chest. "And actually, I was referring to your tie. Very swish."

Nick automatically straightened the expensive silk.

"It's a shame Xander Grimshaw's wearing the exact same thing," she added sympathetically, and Nick's head jerked up.

He stepped up on a raised platform to see over to the *Rise Britain* team, then turned to look down at her.

Sabrina pressed her lips together.

"I'm reopening salary negotiations," Nick said. "I don't get paid enough to put up with you."

Before she had time to move, he was off the platform and diving at her, sweeping her up off her feet. Sabrina wrapped her arms around his neck, laughing, as their workmates looked at them with amusement.

Nick dropped his forehead to hers. His eyes were smiling. "Sabrina Carlton, you're a pain in the arse."

She cupped his cheek; and with a casual jerk of his head towards the wedding festivities around them, he asked, "What do you reckon? Doesn't look so difficult. Want to tie the knot?"

The words were laced with teasing, with laughter, with happiness. He'd proposed to her properly last night, with shaking hands and hard kisses and love whispered into her ear. Sabrina touched her thumb to her engagement ring, turning it around. The emerald was a deep, rich green in the sunlight. She looked up at him and delicately lifted one shoulder. "Might as well. I quite like you most of the time now."

His grin met hers, and Fenella interrupted with a cough.

"I realise it's the day for happy-ever-afters," she

said, shaking her head at them, "but we do have work to do."

Nick set her feet back on the ground, and Sabrina straightened her dress.

When Fenella raised her hand and the cameras went live, she stood at Nick's side as he kicked off the coverage. "Good morning, Britain." His voice was easy and relaxed, and his fingers brushed hers. "We're live from Windsor."

The sun was warm on Sabrina's face as their eyes briefly locked, before she looked down the lens with a smile. "And it's going to be a beautiful day."

* * * * *

Reviews are an invaluable tool when it comes to spreading the word about great reads. Please consider leaving an honest review for this or any of Carina Press's other titles that you've read on your favorite retailer or review site.

To find out about other books by Lucy Parker, and to sign up for her newsletter to be alerted to new releases, please visit Lucy's website at www.lucyparkerfiction.com.

Acknowledgments

As always, there are a lot of people who made the experience of writing this book infinitely better, and who make my life in general infinitely better!

To my editor, Deborah Nemeth, who's always supportive and encouraging, constantly helping me to improve and grow as a writer, and who never fails to make me see what more the story could be.

To my agent, Elaine Spencer, for your constant support for me and my writing, always cheering me along and helping me believe in myself.

To Angela James, whose vision, encouragement, and kindness since the beginning of my publishing experience have been so very much appreciated.

To the entire team at Carina Press, forever working so hard, and with such care and passion for what you do.

To my talented, compassionate, funny, beautiful friends—the world is a better place for having each and every one of you in it.

To my family—you're my world and I literally couldn't do any of this without you. You give unconditional love and you have it right back.

And to every person who reads my books—I can never say enough how much I appreciate it.

Thank you all so much.

About the Author

Lucy Parker lives in New Zealand, where she feels lucky every day to look out at mountains, lakes, and vineyards.

Her interest in romantic fiction began with a preteen viewing of Jane Austen's *Pride and Prejudice* (Firth-style), which prompted her to read the book, as well. A family friend introduced her to Georgette Heyer, and the rest was history.

When she's not writing, working, or sleeping, she happily tackles the towering pile of to-be-read books that never gets any smaller. Thankfully, there's always another story waiting.

She loves to talk to other readers and writers, and you can find her on Twitter: Twitter.com/_lucyparker, on Facebook: www.Facebook.com/lucyparkerauthor, on Instagram: www.Instagram.com/lucyparkerauthor, or on her website: www.lucyparkerfiction.com.

Chapter One

Almost every night, between nine and ten past, Lainie Graham passionately kissed her ex-boyfriend. She was then gruesomely dead by ten o'clock, stabbed through the neck by a jealous rival. If she was scheduled to perform in the weekend matinee, that was a minimum of six uncomfortable kisses a week. More, if the director called an extra rehearsal or the alternate actor was ill. Or if Will was being a prat backstage and she was slow to duck.

It was an odd situation, being paid to publicly snog the man who, offstage, had discarded her like a stray sock. From the perspective of a broken relationship, the theatre came up trumps in the awkward stakes. A television or film actor might have to make stage love to someone they despised, but they didn't have to play the same scene on repeat for an eight-month run.

From her position in the wings, Lainie watched Will and Chloe Wayne run through the penultimate scene.

Chloe was practically vibrating with sexual tension, which wasn't so much in character as it was her default setting. Will was breathing in the wrong places during his monologue; it was throwing off his pacing. She waited, and—

"*Farmer!*" boomed the director from his seat in the front row. Alexander Bennett's balding head was gleaming with sweat under the houselights. He'd been lounging in his chair but now dropped any pretence of indifference, jerking forward to glare at the stage. "You're blocking a scene, not swimming the bloody breaststroke. Stop bobbing your head about and breathe through your damn nose."

A familiar sulky expression transformed Will's even features. He looked like a spoilt, genetically blessed schoolboy. He was professional enough to smooth out the instinctive scowl and resume his speech, but with an air of resentment that didn't improve his performance. This was the moment of triumph for his character and right now the conquering knight sounded as if he would rather put down his sword and go for a pint.

Will had been off his game since the previous night, when he'd flubbed a line in the opening act. He was a gifted actor. An unfaithful toerag, but a talented actor. He rarely made mistakes—and could cover them better than most—but from the moment he'd stumbled over his cue, the additional rehearsal had been inevitable. Bennett sought perfection in every arena of his life, which was why he was on to his fifth marriage and all the principals had been dragged out of bed on their morning off.

Most of the principals, Lainie amended silently. Their brooding Byron had, as usual, done as he pleased. Bennett had looked almost apoplectic when Richard Troy had sauntered in twenty minutes late, so that explosion was still coming. If possible, he preferred to roar in his private office, where his Tony Award was prominently displayed on the desk. It was a sort of visual aid on the journey from stripped ego to abject apology.

Although a repentant Richard Troy was about as likely as a winged pig, and he could match Bennett's prized trophy and raise him two more.

Onstage, Chloe collapsed into a graceful swoon, which was Richard's cue for the final act. He pushed off the wall on the opposite side of the wings and flicked an invisible speck from his spotless shirt. Then he entered from stage left and whisked the spotlight from Will and Chloe with insulting ease, taking control of the scene with barely a twitch of his eyelid.

Four months into the run of *The Cavalier's Tribute*, it was still an undeniable privilege to watch him act.

Unfortunately, Richard's stage charisma was comparable to the interior of the historic Metronome Theatre. At night, under the houselights, the Metronome was pure magic, a charged atmosphere of class and old-world glamour. In the unforgiving light of day, it looked tired and a bit sordid, like an aging diva caught without her war paint and glitter.

And when the curtain came down and the skin of the character was shed, Richard Troy was an intolerable prick.

Will was halfway through the most long-winded of his speeches. It was Lainie's least favourite moment in an otherwise excellent play. Will's character, theoretically the protagonist, became momentarily far less sympathetic than Richard's undeniable villain. She still couldn't tell if it was an intentional ambiguity on the part of the playwright, perhaps a reflection that humanity is never cast in shades of black and white, or if it was just poor writing. The critic in the *Guardian* had thought the latter.

Richard was taunting Will now, baiting him with both words and snide glances, and looking as if he was enjoying himself a little too much. Will drew himself up, and his face took on an expression of intense self-righteousness.

Lainie winced. It was, down to the half sneer, the exact same face he made in bed.

She really wished she didn't know that.

"Ever worry it's going to create some sort of cosmic imbalance?" asked a voice at her elbow, and she turned to smile at Meghan Hanley, her dresser. "Having both of them in one building? If you toss in most of the management, I think we may be exceeding the recommended bastard quota." Meghan raised a silvery eyebrow as she watched the denouement of the play. "They both have swords, and neither of them takes the opportunity for a quick jab. What a waste."

"Please. A pair of blind, arthritic nuns would do better in a swordfight. Richard has probably never charged anything heavier than a credit card, and Will has the hand-eye coordination of an earthworm."

She was admittedly still a little bitter. Although not in the least heartbroken. Only a very silly schoolgirl would consider Will Farmer to be the love of her life, and that delusion would only last until she'd actually met him. But Lainie had not relished being dumped by the trashiest section of *London Celebrity*. The tabloid had taken great pleasure in informing her, and the rest of the rag-reading world, that Will was now seeing the estranged wife of a footballer—who in turn had been cheated on by her husband with a former *Big Brother* contestant. It was an endless sordid cycle.

The article had helpfully included a paparazzi shot of her from about three months ago, when she'd left the theatre and been caught midsneeze. *Farmer's costar and ousted lover Elaine Graham dissolves into angry tears outside the Metronome.*

Brilliant.

The journo, to use the term loosely, had also complimented her on retaining her appetite in the face of such humiliation—insert shot of her eating chips at Glastonbury—with a cunning little system of arrows to indicate a possible baby bump.

Her dad had phoned her, offering to deliver Will's balls on a platter.

Margaret Ward, the assistant stage manager, paused to join the unofficial critics' circle. She pushed back her ponytail with a paint-splattered hand and watched Richard. His voice was pure, plummy Eton and Oxford—not so much as a stumbled syllable in his case. Will looked sour.

Richard drew his sword, striding forward to stand under the false proscenium. Margaret glanced up at the wooden arch. "Do you ever wish it would just accidentally drop on his head?"

Yes.

"He hasn't *quite* driven me to homicidal impulses yet." Lainie recalled the Tuesday night performance, when she'd bumped into Richard outside his dressing room. She had apologised. He had made a misogynistic remark at a volume totally out of proportion to a minor elbow jostle.

The media constantly speculated as to why he was still single. Mind-boggling.

"*Yet*," she repeated grimly.

"By the way," Margaret said, as she glanced at her clipboard and flagged a lighting change, "Bob wants to see you in his office in about ten minutes."

Lainie turned in surprise. "Bob does? Why?"

Her mind instantly went into panic mode, flicking back over the past week. With the exception of touching His Majesty's sacred arm for about two seconds—and she wouldn't put it past Richard to lay a complaint about that—she couldn't think of any reason for a summons to the stage manager's office. As a rule, Robert Carson viewed his actors as so many figureheads. They were useful for pulling out at cocktail parties and generating social media buzz, but operated beneath his general notice unless they did something wrong. Bob preferred to concentrate on the bottom line, and the bottom line in question was located at the end of his bank statement.

Margaret shrugged. "He didn't say. He's been in a bad mood all day, though," she warned, and Lainie sighed.

"I could have been in bed right now," she mused wistfully. "With a cream cheese bagel and a completely trashy book. Bloody Will."

On the flip side, she could also still have been in bed *with* Will, enjoying the taste of his morning breath and a lecture on her questionable tastes in literature. From the man who still thought *To Kill a Mocking-*

bird was a nonfiction guide for the huntin', shootin' and fishin' set.

Life could really only improve.

On that cheering thought, she made her way out of the wings and backstage into the rabbit's warren of tunnelling hallways that led to the staff offices. The floors and walls creaked as she went, as if the theatre were quietly grumbling under its breath. Despite the occasional sticking door handle and an insidious smell of damp, she liked the decrepit old lady. The Metronome was one of the oldest theatres in the West End. They might not have decent seating and fancy automated loos, but they had history. Legendary actors had walked these halls.

"And Edmund Kean probably thought the place was an absolute dump as well," had been Meghan's opinion on that subject.

Historical opinion was divided on the original seventeenth-century use of the Metronome. Debate raged in textbooks as to whether it had been a parliamentary annex or a high-class brothel. Lainie couldn't see that it really mattered. It would likely have been frequented by the same men in either instance.

Personally, she voted for the brothel. It would add a bit of spice to the inevitable haunting rumours. Much more interesting to have a randy ghost who had succumbed midcoitus than an overworked civil servant who had died of boredom midpaperwork.

Aware that Bob's idea of "in ten minutes" could be loosely translated as "right now," she headed straight for his office, which was one of the few rooms at the front of the theatre and had a view looking out over the busy road. Her memories of the room were associated with foot shuffling, mild sweating and a fervent wish to be outside amid an anonymous throng of shoppers and tourists heading for Oxford Street.

"Enter," called a voice at her knock, and she took the opportunity to roll her eyes before she opened the door.

Her most convincing fake smile was firmly in place by the time she walked inside, but it faltered when she saw the two women standing with Bob.

"Good. Elaine," Bob said briskly. He was wearing his usual incorrectly buttoned shirt. Every day it was a different button. Same shirt, apparently, but different button. He *had* to be doing it on purpose. "You remember Lynette Stern and Patricia Bligh."

Naturally, Lainie remembered Lynette and Pat. She saw them every week, usually from a safe distance. An uneasy prickling sensation was beginning to uncurl at the base of her neck. She greeted Pat with a mild unconcern she didn't feel, and returned Lynette's nod. She couldn't imagine why the tall sharp-nosed blonde was here for this obviously less-than-impromptu meeting. She would have thought her more likely to be passed out in a mental health spa. Or just sobbing in a remote corner. Lynette Stern was Richard Troy's agent, and she had Lainie's sincere sympathies. Every time she saw the woman, there was a new line on her forehead.

It was Pat Bligh's presence that gave Lainie serious pause. Pat was the Metronome's PR manager. She ruled over their collective public image with an iron hand and very little sense of humour. And woe betide anyone who was trending for unfortunate reasons on Twitter.

What the hell had she done?

She was biting on her thumbnail. It was a habit she had successfully kicked at school, and she forced herself to stop now, clasping her hands tightly together. She had been in a running panic this morning to get to the Tube on time, and now she wished she'd taken time to check her Google alerts.

Nude photos? Not unless someone had wired her shower. Even as an infant, she had disliked being naked. She usually broke speed records in changing her clothes.

She blanched. *Unless Will had taken...*

In which case she was going to hit the stage and make short work of borrowing Richard's sword, and Will was going to find himself minus two of his favourite accessories.

"Sit down, Elaine," Bob said, his expression unreadable. Reluctantly, she obeyed the order—Bob didn't do invitations—and chose the most uncomfortable chair in the room, as if in a preemptive admittance of guilt.

Get a grip.

"I'll come right to the point." Bob sat on the edge of the wide mahogany desk and gestured the other women to sit down with an impatient wiggle of his index finger. Reaching for the iPad on his blotter, he flipped it open and keyed in the password. "I presume you've seen this."

He held the iPad in front of Lainie's face and she blinked, trying to bring the screen into focus. She could feel the heavy pulse of her heartbeat, but dread dwindled into confusion when she saw the news item. *London Celebrity* had struck again, but she wasn't the latest offering for the sacrificial pit after all.

It appeared that Richard had dined out last night. The fact that he'd entered into a shouting match with a notable chef and decided to launch a full-scale offensive on the tableware seemed about right. She took a closer look at the lead photograph. Of *course* his paparazzi shots were that flattering. No piggy-looking eyes and double chins for Richard Troy. He probably didn't *have* a bad angle.

God, he was irritating.

She shrugged, and three sets of pursed lips tightened. "Well," she said hastily, trying to recover her ground, "it's unfortunate, but…"

"But Richard does this kind of shit all the time," was probably not the answer they were looking for.

And what exactly did this have to do with her? Surely they weren't expecting her to cough up for his damages bill. The spoon in baby Richard Troy's mouth had been diamond-encrusted platinum. He was old family money, a millionaire multiple times over. He could pay for his own damn broken Meissen. If he had a propensity for throwing public temper tantrums and hurling objects about the room, his management team should have restricted him to eating at McDonald's. There was only so much damage he could do with paper wrappers and plastic forks.

"It's getting to be more than *unfortunate*," Lynette said, in such an ominous tone that Lainie decided to keep her opinions to herself on that score.

Pat at last broke her simmering silence. "There have been eight separate incidents in this month alone." Three strands of blond hair had come loose from her exquisitely arranged chignon. For most women, that would be a barely noticeable dishevelment. Lainie's own hair tended to collapse with a resigned sigh the moment she turned away from the mirror. For Pat, three unpinned locks was a shocking state of disarray. "It's only the second week of October."

Lainie thought that even Richard should fear that particular tone of voice from this woman. She flinched on his behalf.

"Any publicity is good publicity. Isn't that the idea?" She glanced warily from one mutinous face to the next. It was an identical expression, replicated thrice over. A sort of incredulous outrage, as if the whole class were being punished for the sins of one naughty child.

Apt, really. If one considered the personalities involved.

"To a point." Bob's nostrils flared. She couldn't help noticing that a trim wouldn't go astray there. "Which Troy has now exceeded." He gave her a filthy look that suggested she was personally responsible for Richard's behaviour. God forbid.

"Men in particular," he went on, stating the loathsome truth, "are given a fair amount of leeway in the public eye. A certain reputation for devilry, a habit of thumbing one's nose at the establishment, sowing one's wild oats…" He paused, looking hard at her, and Lainie hoped that her facial expression read "listening." As opposed to "nauseated." He sounded like a 1950s summary of the ideal man's man. Which had been despicably sexist sixty years ago and had not improved since.

"However," Bob continued, and the word came down like a sledgehammer, "there is a line at which a likable bad boy becomes a nasty entitled bastard whom the public would rather see hung out to dry in the street than pay to watch prance about a stage in his bloomers. And when somebody starts abusing their fans, making an absolute arse of themselves in public places, and alienating the people who paid for their bloody Ferrari, they may consider that line *crossed*."

Lainie wondered if an actual "Hallelujah" chorus had appeared in the doorway, or if it was just the sound of her own glee.

She still had no idea why she was the privileged audience to this character assassination, but she warmly appreciated it. Surely, though, they weren't...

"Are you *firing* him?" Her voice squeaked as if she had uttered the most outrageous profanity. Voiced the great unspoken. The mere suggestion of firing Richard Troy was the theatrical equivalent of hollering "Voldemort!" in the halls of Hogwarts. He-Who-Shall-Not-Be-Missed.

Still...

She wondered if it would be mean-spirited to cross her fingers.

Bob's return look was disappointingly exasperated. "Of course we're not firing him. It would cost an absolute bloody fortune to break his contract."

"And I suggest you don't attempt it." Lynette sounded steely.

"Besides," Bob said grudgingly, "nobody is denying that he's a decent actor, when he confines his histrionics to the script."

That was a typical Bob-ism. Pure understatement. Richard Troy had made the cover of *Time* magazine the previous year. The extravagantly handsome headshot had been accompanied by an article lauding him as a talent surpassing Olivier, and only two critics had been appalled.

"And if he conducted his outbursts with a bit of discretion," Bob said, as if they were discussing a string of irregular liaisons, "then we wouldn't be having this discussion. But Troy's deplorable public image is beginning to affect ticket sales. The management is not pleased."

Lainie couldn't match his awe of a bunch of walking wallets in suits, but she echoed the general feeling of dismay. If the management weren't pleased, Bob would make everyone else's life an utter misery until their mood improved.

"I'm not sure what this has to do with me," she said warily.

"If ticket sales are down, it's everybody's problem," Lynette said pompously, and Pat looked at her impatiently.

"We need some good publicity for Richard." She folded her arms and subjected Lainie to an intense scrutiny, which wavered into scepticism. "The general consensus is so overwhelmingly negative that he's in danger of falling victim to a hate campaign in the press. People might flock to see a subject of scandal, but they won't fork over hard-earned cash to watch someone they wholeheartedly despise. Not in this competitive market. At least not since it became socially unacceptable to heave rotten vegetables at the stage," she added with a brief, taut smile.

Lainie allowed herself three seconds to fantasize about that.

"How badly have sales dropped?" she asked, wondering if she ought to be contacting her agent. She had a third audition lined up for a period drama that was due to begin shooting early next year, but if there was a chance the play might actually fold...

An internationally acclaimed West End production,

brought down by Richard Troy's foot-stamping sulks. Unbelievable.

"We're down fourteen percent on last month," Bob said, and she bit her lip. "We're not going bust." He sounded a bit put out at having to lessen his grievance. "It would take a pipe bomb as well as Richard's presence onstage before there was any real threat of that. But we've had to paper the house four nights running this month, and we opened to a six-week waiting list. This play has another four months to run, and we want to end on a high. Not in a damp fizzle of insulted fans and critics."

Lainie was silent for a moment. It was news to her that management were giving out free tickets in order to fill empty seats. "Well, excuse the stupidity, but I'm still not sure what you expect me to do about it. Ask him nicely to be a good boy and pull up his socks? Three guesses as to the outcome."

The tension zapped back into her spine when Bob and Pat exchanged a glance.

Pat seemed to be debating her approach. Eventually, she commented almost casually, "Ticket sales at the Palladium have gone up ten percent in the last three months."

Lainie snorted. "I know. Since Jack Trenton lost his last remaining brain cell after rehab and hooked up with Sadie Foster."

Or, as she was affectionately known in the world of musical theatre, the She-Devil of Soho. Lainie had known Sadie since they were in their late teens. They had been at drama school together. She had been short-listed against her for a role in a community theatre production of *42nd Street,* and had found shards of broken glass in the toes of her tap shoes. Fortunately before she'd put them on.

She was so preoccupied with a short-lived trip down a murky memory lane that she missed the implication.

"Quite." Pat's left eyebrow rose behind the lens of her glasses. She was now leaning on the edge of Bob's desk, her blunt, fuchsia-painted nails tapping a jaunty little medley on the surface. "And the only genuine buzz of excitement Richard has generated in the past month was when *London Celebrity* printed photos of the two of you attending the Bollinger party together." She again stared at Lainie, as if she was examining her limb by limb in an attempt to discover her appeal, and was coming up short.

The penny had dropped. With the clattering, appalling clamour of an anvil.

Don't miss
Act Like It *by Lucy Parker,*
available now wherever
Carina Press e-books are sold.

www.CarinaPress.com